I0676026

TALES FROM THE VAULT

VOLUME III

A STORY SANCTUM ANTHOLOGY

TALES FROM THE VAULT

VOLUME III

A STORY SANCTUM ANTHOLOGY

Story Sanctum
PUBLISHING

Copyright © 2025 by Story Sanctum Publishing.

All rights reserved. No part of this book may be used or reproduced in any form whatsoever without written permission except in the case of brief quotations in critical articles or reviews.

Cover image by AI via Freepik.

Cover design and interior formatting by Casselberry Creative Design.

Story Sanctum Publishing.
First Edition.
ISBN: 979-8-9928559-6-8

Table of Contents

Introduction

You have entered into the Story Sanctum vault! Welcome!

Inside these pages, you will find a rich anthology of stories designed to speak to your heart, mind, and soul.

Story Sanctum is a shrine for sacred storytelling. We curate compelling fiction and nonfiction stories with a clear point of view that captures the truth and beauty, sacredness and strangeness, heartbreak, horror, and hope of the human condition.

For us, sacredness transcends any one religion and does not have to be religious at all. Our stories honor the sacredness of life found in the human experience. The viewpoints of the writers are their own, but they give us unique insights into their lives and our shared human experience.

These tales were taken from our vault of fiction and nonfiction stories. They represent some of our favorite stories from the past year. We hope you will enjoy reading them as much as we did.

Enjoy!

Story Sanctum Editors

Jen & Shawn Casselberry
Joel Klepac
Soter Lucio
Krin Van Tatenhove
Kelly Wright

NONFICTION

Scarlet

Matias F. Travieso-Diaz

O, we don't give a damn for the whole state of Michigan
The whole state of Michigan, the whole state of Michigan
We don't give a damn for the whole state of Michigan,
we're from Ohio!
- Chant often heard at Ohio Stadium

I was born into a poor family in La Habana, Cuba. I was always an accomplished student, and was able to receive a solid primary and secondary school education thanks to getting a scholarship to attend, tuition-free, one of the best private schools in Cuba. As I negotiated high school, the questions that my parents and I faced regarding life after graduation included whether I should attend college and, if so, what course of studies should I pursue.

I graduated from high school in 1960, at the time when Fidel Castro was turning Cuba into a totalitarian state. The worsening political situation in the island affected, among other things, my professional plans. I could have entered the free University of Havana and pursued there an engineering course, but incoming university students were required to join the Communist Party, which I was loath to do.

I was rescued from my predicament by a friend of the family, who suggested I should apply for a scholarship at the Universidad de Villanueva, a private university run by the Augustinian Priests, like Villanova University in Pennsylvania. There was an opening for a scholarship to study engineering at Villanueva sponsored by Bacardi, the rum manufacturer. I applied, went through tests and interviews, and was awarded the scholarship, the last one that was ever granted by Bacardi in Cuba. It was the autumn of 1960.

I planned on majoring in Chemical Engineering, and Villanueva had a great program in that discipline; it even had built a small sugar mill in one of the school buildings so students could get hands-on experience in industrial chemical processes.

I attended Villanueva through the first one and a half semesters of the 1960-61 academic year, did well and was enjoying myself. Then Fate intervened and forced me to make a drastic career change.

The doomed "Bay of Pigs" invasion of Cuba took place on April 17, 1961, whereupon my university was closed by the government; I was later told it was turned into a warehouse, and all the facilities of the institution went to waste.

That was the end of my education in Cuba. Had matters been otherwise, perhaps I would have become a chemical engineer, and maybe would have stayed in Cuba and enjoyed my professional life there. It was not meant to be.

My parents and I left Cuba and came to the United States in 1963, among thousands of Cubans reaching these shores to escape the oppression of a tyrannical government. Shortly after arrival, I began to look for a way to continue my education. I had a constraint: I could not go away from Miami, for I did not want to leave my family alone so soon after coming to a foreign country. I enrolled at the University of Miami, but Chemical Engineering, my preferred choice, was not one the programs they offered. I had to settle for switching to Electrical Engineering, a discipline that I had never considered before and did not interest me.

I was able to attend school in Miami through a generous loan program developed by the Kennedy Administration for Cuban refugees. Cuban Loan Program funds paid for the four years it took me to get a Bachelor's and later a Master's Degree in Electrical Engineering at the University of Miami. After receiving my Bachelor's Degree, I went to work for an electric utility in its planning department. While that was probably the most interesting job I could get at a utility, the work bored me to tears.

It was out of boredom that I decided to apply for a program at Ohio State University that would allow me to work at an engineering laboratory while taking courses part-time towards a PhD. Thus, in early September, 1967 I made a sharp transition from Cuba (via the four-year stay in Miami, Florida) to the U.S. Midwest.

As I arrived in Columbus to start studies at Ohio State, I realized that the move entailed a complete change in my personal circumstances. I went from living in a Latin ghetto that was a coarse replica of my homeland to a wholly American environment; traded my family home for a small room in a school dorm; ended my employment as an engineer for a power company to become a lowly research assistant at an Engineering lab; and left behind my relatives, friends, and colleagues to become a stranger in a truly strange land.

Everything was different in Ohio from the things I used to know. I had my first taste of midwestern food: chili, beer brats, meat loaf, shredded chicken sandwich. It was tasty, but heavier and plainer than I was used to in Cuba or Miami; the food was pleasant, but lacking in the flavor and zest to which I was accustomed.

The living environment was also unlike what I regarded as normal. Unlike the exuberant Latins, people were polite, low-keyed, and reticent about expressing their emotions. Traffic in Columbus was slower and more orderly than in Florida, and the weather soon turned colder than anything I had ever experienced. I watched the first snowfall of my life in early October, and as fall led to winter it got much colder than I had known. Unlike sunny Florida (and Cuba), Ohio became dark and gloomy after the summer, and the sun disappeared, not to return until mid-April.

I was lodged in a room in a dorm next door to the law school, and discovered that my roommate and many of my other neighbors were law students who spent an inordinate amount of time playing cards and drinking cheap beer, neither of which had been a previous activity of mine. My school courses and work at the lab were difficult and tedious, and gave me no joy.

By Christmas, when I was able to catch a flight to Miami, I was seriously wondering if I had made a big mistake, but decided to persevere, at least until the end of the 1967-68 academic year. Upon returning to Columbus, I made a couple of friends among the residents of my dorm, and was lucky to run, almost by accident, into a Cuban kid I used to know in Miami. Carlos and I became, and remained, close friends, and he introduced me to other members of the miniscule Cuban population of Columbus, so my social circle expanded somewhat. As I got used to the various work and school routines, life became more tolerable, and by the time I returned to my folks in Miami for the summer I had decided to try to stick it out for the next few years until I got my degree.

14

There were marked improvements in my situation when I returned to Columbus for the 1968-69 academic year. Carlos, another Cuban student, and I rented an apartment off campus, within walking distance of school and the shuttle to the laboratory. I met two more young Cubans – Eloy and Jake – who were to remain my close friends in the years to come. I started auditing a Latin American literature graduate course, a pastime that would eventually steer me towards trying my hand as a writer. And I started following the games of the school's varsity football team, the Ohio State Buckeyes.

In the five years since my arrival in the United States I had totally ignored football. The only sport I cared for was baseball – Cuba's national pastime – and I was a devoted fan of the St. Louis Cardinals. Football was unknown to me and held no interest, for it seemed a game of brute force and little sophistication. My disinterest in football continued during my first year in Columbus, since the 1967 season had been a disappointment for Ohio State fans because the Buckeyes had a mediocre team that finished fourth in the Big Ten conference and went unranked in the postseason polls.

Things changed the following year. In 1968, the team became filled with talented sophomores, and began winning one game after another. As excitement grew around the Ohio State campus and the entire Columbus population, I started paying attention to the team's season, without really getting involved in what I still regarded as a local amusement that did not concern me.

Then came the last game of the season, on Saturday, November 23, 1968. I was not planning on attending the game, but a friend insisted that he and I should take advantage of the ability, as students, to get reasonably good seats for what could be a historical event: Ohio State's scarlet and gray Buckeyes would play their archrivals, the maize and blue Wolverines of the University of Michigan. Ohio State was 8-0, ranked second nationally, and was one victory away from a Rose Bowl invitation and a potential national collegiate championship. Michigan, ranked fourth nationally, was also vying for the same opportunity.

I had walked near Ohio Stadium, a gigantic oval that sat over eighty thousand spectators, but never gone in. That afternoon people were streaming into the facility from all directions, many wearing winter coats although the weather was warm for a Thanksgiving weekend in Ohio. I had on just a light jacket, and as the game progressed, I got increasingly chilled. Around me, men were extracting hidden flasks from their coat pockets and taking swigs of whiskey or other contraband. I had nothing to keep me warm.

During the first half of the game, I became increasingly uncomfortable and began formulating plans to leave at halftime. The two teams battled it out on the ground (there was little passing in that game; Ohio State's quarterback was a mediocre passer but a gifted runner, and so was his Michigan counterpart) and, shortly before the halftime mark, the teams were tied 14-14. I was getting my jacket on in preparation for departure when an Ohio State running back took the ball in from the six-yard line to break the tie. I then made a momentous decision: I would stick it out for the rest of the game, even at the risk of catching a cold.

I never learned what Coach Woody Hayes told his players at halftime, but the team that returned to the playing field after the break was energized and proceeded to completely dominate its opponents. Every time Ohio State scored, the crowd (which was the largest ever to attend a game at Ohio Stadium) erupted in ecstatic cheers, whose volume and frenzy only increased as the lead widened. I found myself cheering as loud as everyone else, and by the time the Buckeyes scored the fourth touchdown of the second half and took a final lead of 50-14 I was shaking with emotion, as perhaps were many other spectators.

When I drifted out of the stadium, I was a changed man. I had become one with the crowd that surrounded me, in a manner I had never experienced before. I realized that what separated me from the inhabitants of this northern city were matters of culture and detail, not substance; my basic values were the same as those of an Ohioan, and I could fit, perhaps not perfectly but sufficiently well, with my fellow citizens.

I no longer felt like an outsider, a foreign piece that did not belong in the American crossword puzzle. I remained a Cuban at heart, but also felt like I belonged in this country as much as the blond, husky Midwesterners that walked by my side. It had taken me five years to really start integrating into the land that had welcomed me, but after that moment I started to feel that I belonged.

For the next fifty-odd years I have followed the fortunes and misfortunes of the scarlet and gray Buckeyes, watching virtually every game they played. I have enjoyed their frequent victories and lamented their occasional losses; but, more importantly, I have felt they are *my team*, and this country is *my* second home, where I was fortunate to land after I had to abandon my birthplace.

Dog Park Dharma

Judith Frankel

After I rescued Louis, friends said I'd find a new social life at the dog park. My puppy and I would be welcomed into a community of dog owners, they said, and I loved this idea. My friend Lynn told me her widowed brother-in-law met his next wife at a dog park, which made me love the idea even more. I'd been single for a long time. My armor was starting to melt. I fantasized about joining the pack of San Francisco dog owners every morning at Ocean Beach, a short drive down the hill from my apartment in the Outer Richmond. My little wiener dog and I would gather at dawn with the band of Doodle-owners and Corgiphiles on the sand below the Cliff House. Upswell at high tide, we'd herd our dogs to the roar of waves and barking pinnipeds offshore. All of this satisfied my dream of connecting with a cool San Francisco subculture. After this bracing start to our day, I imagined, we'd go home and suit-up for our day jobs.

As it turned out, I only got Louis out to Ocean Beach

once. That foggy afternoon, my shivering black puppy was no match for the walls of water barreling in on us. If any other dogs were available for play, waves demolished their voices and gusts wrecked any plan to fetch balls.

At the start of the pandemic, my rescue dog and I relocated to the Central Valley. We traded surfers' swells for a patchwork of almond orchards and sheep pastures and raptors big as dogs hanging out on the power lines. This time of year, the sky is shockingly blue and fields are smeared orange with wild poppies. For the most part, walking my dog is sheer delight. But now that Louis is a 20-pound adult, I've abandoned the idea of socializing at the dog park, much less finding my future mate there. Because here's the thing about dachshunds: they are nervous, protective leash-lungers, with a bark fierce enough to slice an eardrum if any other dog is fool enough to approach. My cuddly blanket-burrower, my adorable black worm romping around the house with his floppy alligator toy, transforms into pure menace at the dog park. Marika, owner of Karuna Canine, trainer of the incorrigibles, assured me that it's perfectly OK for a dog to opt out of the social scene at the dog park. *"All those scary rowdy strangers horsing around,"* Marika said. *"Put yourself in Louis' shoes."* And I do, in a forever search for a beautiful place to stretch his stubbly legs, leashless and free.

One place we love is a big regional park re-wilding itself with native grasses. Pulling into the park's fenced-in dog area today, I delighted to see just two vehicles in the lot. Maybe we'd have the grasslands mostly to ourselves! I could sequester Louis away from the social pack in a remote corner where he could let down his guard and scurry around the gopher holes. But once we entered the gate, it was obvious why we were almost alone. The whole place was overrun with knee-high bunches of foxtail, scourge of dog owners everywhere. After a rainy winter, our spring is offering an abundance of blooms and buzzing things both indoors and out. Just the other day I noticed a harvest of dandelions sprouting from my rooftop gutters. While foxtail is common here in springtime, knee-high bunches of the stuff are unheard of. The dog owners we usually encounter would be freaking out at the thought of the vet tweezing a spikelet from an ear canal, or worse, a lung.

To Louis, none of this matters. He was barely off-leash before plunging his tubular body through clusters of purple vetch and feathery rush twice his height. One of the dachshund's few design assets is the ear flap, whose length and floppiness will curtain the canal from foxtail hooks. I always inspect Louis vigilantly before we leave the park. What matters more is the marvel of this nervous, genetically overwrought and awkwardly designed dog busting through his hindrances to run free in the infinite grass. On a clear day like today, to the east we saw with our bare eyes snow-capped Sierra peaks a four-hour drive away. To the north, a flow of yellow mustard grass spilling all the way to the freeway. Roller-coastering in the breeze above us, white-tailed kites and harriers ignored the foxtails, as did several noisy sheep wandering near the fence to get a good look at Louis. Who needs to socialize with other dogs or, for that matter, with dog owners? Maybe our grassland is community enough. Whose idea was it anyway, to find my sweetheart at the dog park? Love affairs end but dogs are yours forever, just as the mountains live forever, and even after years of drought that feels never-ending, the magnificent stands of wild grass return.

Writing and the Forest

Julie Mariouw

The forest seems intent on healing me. Take today, for instance. I was walking on the trail, taking notes on Shakespeare. My latest writing project is about Shakespeare, and I was looking for inspiration. I carried a small notebook and, for the first half of the walk, I wrote down what came to me. Then, when I reached the entrance to the mini-forest, I saw what looked like a hip bone lying on the ground. It was a thick piece of wood shaped exactly like a hip joint. I was a little shocked when I saw it, it looked so much like actual bone. I stared at it a moment, then immediately realized that my writing subject had changed. I was to write about hips, not about Shakespeare.

I've been writing daily for quite a while now—sixteen years—and in this time, I have learned that writing is in charge. When I first started writing, I thought I was in control. I had been taught this in school, and it's how I functioned. But, as I've continued to write in this new way—letting writing take the lead—writing has begun to change me. I never know how writing and the forest will accomplish this. Today it was through a piece of wood shaped like a bone.

I'm pretty sure the forest brought me this gift to help me heal from childhood trauma. I was born with congenital hip dysplasia, which means that my hip joint was not formed correctly in my mother's womb. Some of the risk factors for this disorder include: Being firstborn—*that would be me.* Female sex—*check.* Breech birth—*yep.* Positive family history—*yes.* Joint laxity—*I'm learning I have this.* I was a prime candidate for developing hip dysplasia.

My parents did not catch the problem until I was about one year old. By then, I was already starting to stand and walk. To be honest, my parents weren't paying much attention, or they would have noticed something was wrong. Regardless, the doctors had to do something if I were going to be able to walk. So they put me in traction, then plastered me into a body cast. They try not to do this to babies anymore.

This was too much for my mother. She simply collapsed under its weight. She had trauma of her own, and this triggered it, like one domino knocking down a row of others. This had catastrophic results for me, the most important being the dissolution of my relationship with my mother. Dissolution is a harsh word, but it's accurate in this case. Dissolution: A dissolving or being dissolved; a breaking into parts; disintegration.

Of course, I don't remember precisely all that happened to me as a child. But I can guess, from the way things turned out, that at the point of the body cast, my mother simply disappeared emotionally. Through writing, I have remembered many occasions in which I reached out to my mother. My mother rarely reached back. I don't know how I made it through childhood with a mother who was not only absent, but at times seemed bent on my destruction. For my mother did actively try to hurt me. She was jealous of my relationship with my father. But these are stories for another day.

When my hip failed, my life took a completely different turn—both at the age of one, and again at the age of fifty. I don't remember much about one, but I do remember fifty. Basically, my hip began to fail. I would be walking and suddenly the hip would lock up. I was in extreme pain and totally unable to move. My super-shallow hip joint was now disintegrating. It couldn't hold me up anymore.

I was aware of the trauma I had been through as a child, but I had never been fully able to process it. Now that trauma was breaking through and I was being asked to deal with the emotional roots. But first I would have to fix the physical problem.

I scheduled a hip replacement. I was, of course, unconscious when they performed the surgery, but I can only imagine how this new medical trauma must have triggered the old. I remember the first steps I took with my new hip. I felt like I was falling into the Grand Canyon. It took an impressive amount of willpower for me just to initiate the movement. When my foot touched the floor, a bolt of electricity jumped into my leg, then raced through the rest of my body. Of course, this was not only physical, but also emotional. I understand now that my body was letting go of the tight control that had been wrapped around me as an infant. The body cast was being dismantled.

Sixteen years of daily writing has taught me more about this trauma, and healed me in many other ways. Now nature is adding to the work. Today, as I walked on the trail, my lesson from nature was unmistakable. I suddenly felt as if someone had their hands on my hips and was leading me forward. This was an actual, physical feeling, but, of course, there was no one there. I have had this sensation a few times before—always when I'm walking on the trail. Gradually, I have come to understand that nature is trying to heal me. This might sound strange, but it is true. This sensation has been repeated three or four times.

The pressure on my hips began to rearrange the position of my knees and ankles and, in so doing, changed the way I walked. I'm not saying these physical changes are entirely permanent, as the effects start to fade when I leave nature. But each time the sensation occurs, I'm convinced a small part of me does get permanently healed. Over the long term, my body feels different.

By the time I reached the Frog Crossing sign near the end of the trail, the forest had full control of my hips. It steered me to the entrance, and led me under a tree canopy, and I suddenly found myself in the middle of a vivid childhood memory.

I am visiting my aunt for the summer, playing in the large ravine behind her house. I love this ravine. My favorite thing to do here is to look for salamanders. I don't think salamanders are slimy or ugly, and I'm not afraid of them. I think they understand me. I'm pretty good at knowing which rock to turn over to find the salamanders. I also intuitively understand why they would want to hang out under rocks.

I make up stories with the salamanders. This summer, we are in the middle of World War III. They are soldiers in my army, and I am depending on them to protect me. Together we have to face the enemy and win our secret battles.

I think WWIII might have originally started when I ate a green potato chip. A group of us were sharing a bag of potato chips, and I got one with green on its edge. I was sure I shouldn't eat it, but I was so hungry I ate it anyway. For the rest of that summer I was totally convinced I was going to die. I never told anyone about this, except for the salamanders. They understood and helped me to fight for my life.

I recognize, now, that this was a part of myself who felt she was contaminated. She directed me to eat that green potato chip so I would become aware of her. She came into existence because of what was happening with my father back home. He was violating my boundaries and I was certain it was all my fault.

The salamanders knew that WWIII could help me. They showed me how to get angry. They showed me how to fight for myself. And they showed me how to win. The only problem was, I couldn't take any of these skills back home, as it would have been way too dangerous. But for this short, two-month period, I was as free as any salamander. Nature had come to my rescue.

These days, nature is coming to my rescue again, along with the practice of writing. The two work together to heal the trauma inside me. I never know what I will receive when I walk out in nature, nor how the writing will lead me through it. But I do know that the combination of nature and writing is unbeatable—better than WWIII. Nature kept me alive back then, through unspeakable childhood trauma. It's my turn, now, to pay nature back.

Memory Gaps

Jun A. Alindogan

It is unclear whether memory gaps or lapses are primarily genetic. According to web sources, deteriorating memory conditions such as dementia and Alzheimer's can be linked to a gene called apolipoprotein. Individuals who inherit one or more copies of this gene are at a higher risk, but not everyone is predisposed to developing these conditions even if there is a genetic component. Lifestyle changes, including meditation, reading, diet, and exercise, are recommended to slow down the progression of memory loss. As individuals age, experiencing occasional memory lapses in terms of short-term memory is common, but in some cases, these lapses may become more frequent.

I do not remember if any of my mom's siblings had memory issues in old age until they passed away, except for my mom. One assumption that medical professionals refute is the use of sedation in surgery that causes some memory loss.

My mom had painless childbirth and had her ovaries removed in her younger years. A good friend claimed that after his knee surgery, his memory was also affected and he has become intermittently forgetful.

We suspect that aside from mom's past sedation, her memory loss became more noticeable when she moved overseas to take care of her granddaughter. She was often left at home on weekdays, so she didn't have many opportunities for prolonged social interaction to keep her mind active. To occupy herself, she took up embroidery and completed a beautiful peacock design, which she framed to exercise her psychomotor skills.

Her memory loss worsened when she moved with my sibling to a region where her local language wasn't spoken. By this time, she was well into her senior years. In her new environment, she was often alone as her grandkids went to school and my sibling was busy with farming, fishing, and church activities. There were times when she felt useless, though she never explicitly expressed this as her memory continued to decline.

Mom started repeating the same statements, testing the patience of those around her. Despite this, she remained cheerful and was able to take care of her personal hygiene independently. She also enjoyed going to church when encouraged to do so.

As Mom's memory failed, preventing her from consuming food for two days, she only uttered the Lord's Prayer before passing on.

Now, a year after my senior year, I find myself repeating the same statements to a close friend when we eat together at a fast food joint or restaurant. It wasn't until my friend pointed it out that I realized I had become forgetful. When my friend and I went for a brief holiday in the province, I was also repetitive about him being the nephew of my colleague in church, according to my sister-in-law. I'm grateful that my friend is there to remind me of this. My short-term memory isn't as sharp as it used to be when I was younger. This repetition might be a result of my work as a teacher, where lessons often need to be reiterated for students to grasp how to apply concepts in practice. This is similar to when I deliver sermons at my church. The main reason I continue to read and write is to remember significant episodes in my life and understand how they are connected to other people I have not met or seen. To me, this is a major accomplishment.

We never know when our memory will fail, whether due to aging or a medical condition. I had a colleague at a seminary where I taught who began showing signs of dementia in his early 50s. Initially, he was still able to function, but eventually became disoriented over minor things. I would occasionally visit his wife at home, who was the chair of our English department, for meetings about remedial English in grammar and writing. Once, he joined us for lunch but struggled to use utensils. As time went on, his memory deteriorated, and he passed on. His wife questioned his faith in the Lord, wondering how someone with no memory could connect with God through prayer. I had no answer, except to acknowledge that our memory is not always within our control but under God's sovereignty.

Time and again, our episodic memory may be sharp or faint, depending on our circumstances. However, even our memory loss can be seen as a gift of grace.

The Quiet Dance of Words

Fendy Satria Tulodo

It was a quiet afternoon in Malang, the kind that seemed to stretch forever, like time was in no rush. The sun dipped just below the horizon, casting long shadows across the small garden behind the house. I could hear the rustle of leaves and the distant hum of the city, but inside the house, there was only silence. The air was thick with the kind of tension that comes from not saying what needs to be said, but there it was, lingering between us.

Hera, my wife, stood in the kitchen, chopping vegetables for dinner. I could hear the steady rhythm of the knife against the cutting board, each slice a sharp, deliberate sound. But I couldn't focus on it. My thoughts kept wandering back to our conversation earlier that day. It wasn't a fight, not really, but it felt like something was missing. Like we were both speaking, but not really listening to each other. I had wanted to talk about Chan, our two-year-old, and how he seemed to be growing up so fast. But the words, they never quite came out right.

"You're quiet tonight," Hera said, her voice soft but cutting through the tension. She didn't look up from her work. It wasn't an accusation; it was just a statement, a simple observation. And yet, it felt like she had reached inside my chest and pulled out the truth I had been hiding.

I didn't answer right away. What could I say? I wanted to explain everything—the frustration, the exhaustion, the fear that I might not be enough for them, for our family—but the words wouldn't come. Instead, I did the one thing that felt easier: I nodded.

"I'm fine," I said, though even I could hear the lie in my voice.

Hera paused, the knife hovering just above the cutting board, and for a moment, the silence between us grew even deeper. The sound of the knife against the board started up again, but it wasn't the same now. It felt... hollow, like it was missing something. Like it needed the rhythm of conversation to make it whole.

I stepped forward, wanting to break the silence, but unsure of how to do it. Words are so tricky, aren't they? So often, we speak without truly listening, or we listen without understanding. It's easy to get lost in the noise of everyday life, to forget the importance of saying what really matters. And that's where we were, stuck in a loop of unspoken words.

"Do you remember," I began, my voice almost a whisper, "the first time we talked about having Chan? We were sitting on the roof of that little café in Batu, the one near the waterfall. You told me that you wanted to have a family, to have a child, but that it wasn't just about the baby. It was about us, about creating something together."

Hera didn't stop chopping, but her shoulders relaxed, just a little. She didn't need to say anything. Her silence spoke volumes, and I knew it meant she was listening. Really listening.

"I still want that," I continued, feeling the weight of my own words. "But sometimes, I forget. I forget to listen to you. To listen to what you need. And I... I don't want to lose that."

Hera finally turned to face me, her expression soft but thoughtful. "I need you to be present," she said simply. "Not just physically, but with your words, with your heart. I don't want to feel like I'm always the one carrying the weight of everything we don't say."

I felt a lump form in my throat. She was right, of course. I had been so caught up in my own head, in my own fears, that I had forgotten the most important part of being a partner, a father, a husband—being there, truly there, for the people who matter most.

"I hear you," I said, finally meaning it.

There was a long pause, and for a moment, the only sound was the soft, rhythmic chop of the knife on the board. But then, slowly, Hera set the knife down and came over to where I stood. Without a word, she took my hand, and together, we stood in the quiet of the room. And for the first time in a long while, I realized that the silence wasn't something to be afraid of. It was just the space where we could listen, where we could find each other again.

The dance of words, I thought, wasn't just about speaking. It was about listening too. And in that moment, I understood that communication wasn't just the exchange of words. It was the shared understanding, the unspoken connection that held us together.

And as we stood there, hand in hand, I knew that, despite all the noise of life, we would always find our way back to each other. Not just with words, but with the quiet moments in between.

I could feel the weight of that silence even as I walked

down the familiar street to work the next day. Malang had always been a place of contrasts, from the bustling markets to the peaceful rice fields just outside the city. The old city center was full of history—colonial buildings and shops that had been passed down from generation to generation—but there was always a sense of quiet there, too. I liked to think it was a reflection of the people who lived here: steady, rooted in tradition, yet always moving forward in their own way. That kind of duality was something that had always spoken to me, and I had always appreciated it, especially on mornings like this one.

As I walked, I thought back to that evening in the kitchen with Hera. How easy it had been to let the little things slip— things that should have been addressed, things that could have been said. But silence, in the end, had forced us to confront the truth. Maybe that was the beauty of it—the way it could expose everything without a single word.

I thought of Chan, his laughter ringing in the air like music. He was so young, so full of life, and I couldn't help but feel guilty. How many moments had I missed? How many times had I let my own worries steal my attention? I needed to change. I wanted to change. Not just for me, but for him, for Hera. For us.

I pulled out my phone, tapping a few quick words into a message for Hera. "I love you. I promise to be better. We'll get through this, together." I hit send and slipped the phone back into my pocket, feeling a small, hopeful weight lift off my chest. It wasn't much, but it was a start. Communication wasn't always perfect, but it was a step forward.

At work, I was surrounded by the usual noise of the showroom—motorcycles being revved, the chatter of customers, the rhythmic clanking of tools. It wasn't exactly peaceful, but it was a kind of noise that had always comforted me. There was a routine to it, a rhythm I could follow. But today, everything seemed a little louder than usual, almost like the world itself was reminding me of all the things I had been avoiding. Maybe it was the way the fluorescent lights flickered overhead, or the fact that my mind kept drifting back to the conversation from last night. Or maybe it was just that I had been carrying around too much unspoken weight, and now it was starting to show.

"You okay, Fendy?" my colleague, Rudi, asked, looking up from his desk. He was always one for small talk, the kind that seemed meaningless but had a way of breaking through the noise when you least expected it.

"Yeah," I said, forcing a smile. "Just thinking about... stuff."

Rudi raised an eyebrow, his expression softening. "Everything alright at home?"

I paused. Should I talk to him about it? About Hera, about Chan, about all the things I was trying to figure out? But no, that wasn't the kind of conversation you have in a showroom full of customers. Not yet, anyway.

"Yeah," I said again, this time with a bit more certainty. "Just... working through things. You know how it is."

Rudi nodded, but didn't press further. Sometimes, people just know when to let silence fill the space. And in that moment, I appreciated it. It gave me time to think, to reflect on what I needed to do.

By the end of the day, I was exhausted—mentally, physically, emotionally. The work had been busy, the noise relentless, but as I stepped out into the cool evening air, I felt a sense of relief. It was the kind of relief that comes from realizing you're on the right path, even if it's just the first step.

When I got home, Hera was already in the living room, sitting on the couch with Chan curled up in her lap. She looked up as I walked in, her face softening, and for a moment, I wondered if she could see the shift in me. Could she tell I was trying? Trying to listen. Trying to be there.

I sat down next to her, placing my hand gently on hers. "How's he doing?" I asked, nodding toward Chan, who was already fast asleep.

"Good," Hera said, smiling. "He's growing up so fast, it's hard to keep up sometimes."

"I know what you mean," I replied. "He's... he's amazing."

And then, for the first time in what felt like forever, I truly listened. Not just to her words, but to the quiet in between them. To the rhythm of her breathing, to the soft sound of her fingers brushing Chan's hair. It was a dance of words, unspoken but deeply felt. The kind of dance that doesn't need steps to be understood.

And in that quiet, I found my way back to her.

Speaking Symbols with Gorgons

Laura Lewis-Barr

In March of 2024 my husband and I took a trip of a lifetime—a 14-day tour of Greece. We made our reservations early and gleefully imagined the trip for almost a year. We read and reread the fantastic itinerary which took us to Athens, Delphi, Olympia, and other rural Greek wonders and ancient healing sites. We imagined exploring the Acropolis, and walking around the Mani Peninsula. I practiced basic Greek phrases with YouTube videos. This is how Rick and I love to travel. A joyful year of anticipation, then the trip, and then years of grateful remembering. I couldn't foresee that this trip was going to be different for us. It was going to change my life forever.

I had asked to go to Greece. It was the birthplace of all my passions—my work in the theatre, my studies of psychology and mythology. After many decades, these passions were finally coming together for me. In my twenties I debated between becoming a therapist or pursuing work in the theatre. Madam

Theatre won but I couldn't give up psychology. I continued to study, formally and informally, for the next three decades. I read books of lectures meant for psychoanalysts (including all the books by Jung's colleague Marie Louise Von Franz—Jung himself was too difficult). For many years I only understood about half of what I read, but I was dreaming more and new insights kept popping into my mind. I would suddenly recognize the source of old struggles between Rick and me. Or I would suddenly see an area of aggression in myself. Then Von Franz' discussion of "the Shadow" started to make more sense. One dream showed me, a "dancing wolf." Working on it I realized, with a shock, that this was how I might be perceived at work. This disturbing insight gave me empathy for my coworkers and led me toward changes in behavior.

Studying Jung's work brought me healing. In gratitude I began to spend most of my time making short stop-motion films in homage to Von Franz. Von Franz had shown how fairy tales offered genuine guidance and stories as medicine for the psyche. Now, for vacation, we were going to the place where many of these stories began. I was thrilled to go to the source of the language of symbols.

Even though I had studied symbolic language for many years, I was hardly fluent. Still, I studied daily: in mythology Twitter groups, through journaling about my nighttime dreams, in reading psychological interpretations, and in living with a fairy tale for many months while I made a stop-motion film. Often, it was only after many months (or years) that I would understand deeper meanings of a film I had made. But my fluency in the language of symbols was improving. On our last overseas trip, I not only recognized much more when we visited museums, but also, while walking the streets of Naples, I gasped, realizing that I was reading the symbols in street graffiti and storefront windows. I recognized Pulcinella emerging from a giant popover, in front of a bakery. I saw him everywhere, with his lucky red horn. I knew that this 17th century commedia del arte character could be traced to even older tricksters. Like all good symbols, he was complex– fierce and funny, scheming and generous.

So, Greece was the perfect destination. On the airplane, as I said a prayer for our flight and trip, I decided to pick a tarot card. I opened my tarot app on my phone and uncovered... The Tower. The Tower?! One of the scariest images of the Tarot—a flaming tower collapses as two poor souls dive from the top. Uh... OK. I'd picked the Tower card before. It didn't have to be a big deal. I would probably learn some inner lessons during this trip. Of course I would.

After great sleep on the plane, we arrived in glorious Greece. It was early March but the weather was unseasonably warm and sunny. Miraculously, we had no jet lag. Instead of 60-year-olds celebrating our 25th anniversary, Rick and I felt like teenagers in love. We scampered around the ancient sites and used the Rick Steves' guide to locate hidden gastronomic wonders.

At the Acropolis Museum, I gravitated toward the ancient female gorgons. There was something beautiful in their fierceness. They challenged me, with their gaping mouths, outstretched tongues, and wide, bulging eyes. Historically, these bronze and marble images were meant to be a warning. Of what? Female power? And protection against the evil eye. Of all the photos I took that day, most were of this Gorgon figure, also known as Medusa.

These first few days in Athens were glorious. Now we readied ourselves to join our 14-day tour. We had loved our previous two tours with RS. At breakfast we met a few of our tour mates. They were interesting and friendly. That evening we met our guide. I'll call her Vivi.

Vivi was scary. She smiled broadly but it was a brittle smile. She wanted us to be a "nice" group, not like other groups she had "hated." She quickly set to grooming our very polite collection of Americans. She warned us that she didn't like getting up early and we wouldn't see her at breakfasts. While she said we could "ask her anything," she disappeared as often as she could. She gave us her many directions at a pace too rapid to decipher. We felt so much passive aggression in Vivi that Rick and I were dumbfounded. But no one else seemed to notice or care. Or was it because the tour had a "no grumps" philosophy and our group was abiding by this edict?

We knew the RS touring style. We knew of the early morning packing and departures. These had felt grueling but they had allowed us to see so many spectacular sites. It was with a heavy heart that we noticed that Vivi set our departure time to Delphi at 8:30am. The day before another RS group had left for Delphi at 7:45am.

After a lovely ride through the Greek countryside, we arrived at Delphi. Our local guide, Penny was brilliant. She helped us understand the world of this ancient oracle site. She was funny and kept composure even though Vivi had gotten us there so late. Immediately, as Penny finished our formal tour of the grounds and museum, we were told that the museum was closing. (It seemed that they had stayed open for us.) We did not have a moment to linger. We also didn't have time for anything except a rushed and frantic lunch. As a group we were determined not to grump but several of us quietly voiced our disappointment at missing the chance to explore the museum.

The trip continued. I had to admit that our growing anger toward Vivi seemed bigger than her selfishness. There was something symbolic, something mythic in the way she triggered Rick and me. On the fourth evening of the tour, as we wandered in an old Greek cemetery, we realized that Vivi reminded us, in deep ways, of our mothers. We both had controlling mothers who smiled and were "nice." It had taken us decades to become free of our childhood struggles. Apparently, we were not yet free.

But I was tired of holding the anger against Vivi. I had written a few notes in my phone, preparing for the review I would give the Rick Steves folks. I had hoped that writing it down would allow me to let it all go. But that wasn't working. I realized that I needed to say something.

That night at dinner Vivi began her announcements while waiters passed dishes. The room was loud and it was hard to follow her words. But she wasn't going to stay with us at dinner and there was no way to get further clarification because, yet again, she had a "sudden Zoom meeting" and couldn't stay with us. She asked if there were any questions. Like Oliver in the movie, asking for more gruel, I slowly raised my hand.

"Could we leave earlier in the morning?" I asked. I wasn't angry or even upset. I didn't expect her to change her plans. I just knew that asking the question would help me let go of my frustration.

The room was silent. Vivi handled it well, simply asking, "Why?"

"So we could spend more time at the ancient sites," I replied simply.

Vivi smoothly told an obvious lie about not having the tickets we needed to get in earlier. (She had them with her the following day). I knew it was a lie but it didn't matter. I hadn't wanted to speak in front of the group but Vivi had set it up that way. Now at least it was on the record. At least one of the guests wanted to spend less time in bed and more time at the sites.

Dinner resumed. I tried not to feel like a pariah in the group. Maybe some of the others wanted to sleep in? Not everyone was as crazy about mythology as I was. I tried to let the whole thing go. The room was loud and my table-mate, Veronica, and I began an exciting discussion of her work in education and my work with teachers and films. And then suddenly I felt very strange. I couldn't seem to form my words correctly. Was it the wine? The party swirled around me but I got quiet. Something was wrong with me.

Back in our hotel room I saw that I couldn't smile. The right side of my face had collapsed. My eye wouldn't close all the way. That side of my mouth couldn't move. We were in a remote, mountainous town in Greece, five hours from any large city. It was 9 pm. It would be impossible to leave, even if I could get a hold of Vivi. Rick and I looked at each other. Was I having a stroke? Was this how I was going to die? But then we researched my symptoms and remembered my father. I wasn't having a stroke; I was having an attack of the same ailment that had paralyzed my father's face early in his life: Bell's Palsy.

I didn't sleep well that night. My brain circled around the past 48 hours. This illness felt especially symbolic and I was determined to decode what was happening. First, there was my father. He had been gone since 2017 and his birthday was in two days. I had been thinking about him throughout the trip, and felt his presence. An hour before the attack, as Rick and I walked through the tiny cemetery, we talked about my dad. How he'd been dominated by my mother all his life. How, in the past year, I had struggled to stand up to my mom. We wondered, if I worked on this issue in my family system, could it also help him—wherever he was? Now I was struck with the same illness as my dad. His face had become paralyzed with Bell's Palsy a month before his wedding to my mom.

Then there was Vivi as a symbol of our mothers. We were in a foreign country, in the middle of nowhere, where we didn't speak the language. We were "dependent" on her. Hours before the attack, I had prayed that I would "learn what I needed to learn here." Was this the answer to my prayer??

Vivi had talked about cursing one of her previous groups, she certainly seemed capable of cursing me. (Literally!) But I didn't like the arc of that story—painting myself as a victim. It also didn't jibe with my studies in psychology. I decided to think of the events as if they were a dream and then it was clear! Gorgon/Medusa, my fascination on the trip—the creature that was known to paralyze those who looked at her—she had paid me a visit. I had looked directly at Vivi/my mother and a part of me had been turned to stone. In the middle of the night, I googled and found an amazing article by the Jungian analyst, Marion Woodman. Woodman wrote about our inner Death Mother. Had that part been triggered in me? Had that unleashed the palsy?

Woodman described the Death Mother archetype through the story of Medusa. Woodman wrote that, for some of us, our early childhood experiences of ambivalent or hostile mothering stay, like a virus, inside of us, ready to erupt in physical or psychological symptoms. (Modern medicine's current hypothesis is that Bell's is caused by a latent virus.)

Getting struck with Bell's Palsy felt like seeing the hand of God in a tornado. (And like a tornado, the aftermath of this initial paralysis would take far longer to "clean up" than I imagined that night.) That night I was in awe of a power beyond me and within me. And an illness that felt full of symbolic meanings.

The trip continued. In photos I could only look very angry. Was I being asked to embrace what was monstrous in myself? On the one hand the Gorgon could be a symbol of the dangerous energy in me (the Death Mother). On the other hand, I sensed that I needed some of that fierce energy. I often collapsed inside when family members attacked me. I needed to have some Medusa strength in me. Now her face was my face.

(In the myth of Medusa, the warrior Goddess Athena eventually places Medusa's head on her shield, as protection. I had taken many photos of this, too.)

Aside from self-consciousness and struggles with my eye, I fully participated in the trip. But the first day home was very hard. In Greece my palsy had felt like part of the mythic nature of the place. Now I would see neighbors and friends. I sank into a new level of despair. I felt disorientated. My old smiling persona didn't work anymore. My identity had dissolved and I was living without it. I prayed for recovery, took Chinese herbs, and relentless researched the internet. I had a fear that the ailment would leave me before I learned it's lessons. I needn't have worried! As each month passed, I hoped it would be my last.

After three months, while still praying for my facial nerves to work again, Rick and I took a trip to help some family members. Three times during that trip I rescued a caterpillar. The first was walking on a sidewalk, the second was in the street, and the third was on a hotel balcony. In all three cases I moved the creature to a small area of greenery within the concrete world. I worked on this symbol as if it was a dream. In this family trip I would take myself out of harm's way. And like the caterpillar, I was entering a dormant phase. I would need to stay in a chrysalis state for a while, allowing my old self to dissolve while the new one was formed. This metaphor has helped me stay patient in this process and give myself permission to rest more. Marion Woodman also speaks about the chrysalis state as a vital phase of healing.

These days, I work at getting my face "back" every day. I spend time slowly practicing a tiny pucker and work to keep my eye relaxed so that it won't build a bad habit. So much "wasted time." But these many months of rest and facial exercises have pulled me off my perfectionist treadmill. I was the project manager of so many plans! But now I've surrendered. In the tug of war between my Ego and my Higher Self, my Ego has given up. For now.

I've always been willful, even as a child. My parents tried to break me of my willfulness but they only accomplished this part way, and left me with a psyche filled with fear and guilt. In the rebuilding of the Tower of my Self, I'm starting from scratch. The old me knew how to organize, synthesize, progress. The new me waits for instructions – from my dreams and hunches. I don't expect as much of myself. I realize that I cannot make all my dream projects come true. I'm only one person. I live in a body. I can only do what I can do.

I am surprisingly grateful. I look at my face in the mirror and I smile at myself with love. My face is doing the best it can.

In many of the fairy tales that I study and animate, the hero is put under a spell. Von Franz interprets these spells as symbols of neurosis. Bell's Palsy is helping me begin to break the spells I've been under – my perpetual drives for achievement and perfection.

"Suffering that is not understood is hard to bear, while on the other hand, it is often astounding to see how much a person can endure when he understands the why and wherefore."
- Carl Jung, CW 18, Para 1578

After 8 months my smile has come back 50%, and my eye finally closes. Still, after months of physical therapy and continual facial massage, much of my right side still hardly moves. This is a master class in learning patience. As I struggle to recover well from the complications of long-term Bell's (an eye that seems to shrink, an eye that wants to close when I smile), I am grateful for the lessons I'm learning. And I'm grateful to practice the language of symbols. It is such a difficult language!

And most people in our culture don't seem to recognize or value it. But to me, it is the most vital language to learn. To discover a possible "Death Mother" within me is sobering but also empowering. The story of Medusa can give me guidance in my soul's work. And if my suffering isn't random, but part of my soul's growth and transformation, I can more easily bear it, work with it, and even appreciate it. I can rest in the knowledge that Higher purposes may be at work.

—

Feral cats roam everywhere throughout Greece. One night, as I walked to dinner wearing an eye patch, a one-eyed cat came up to me and stood before me. Same eye. Later at dinner another cat sat near us and I observed him. Then the image cracked open, like a helpful dream. Could I become more like a cat from this event? More free, independent, and less anxious? I am grateful for this image and the symbolic medicine it offers.

Whimsical Underdog

Leah Mueller

I learned to play viola because I felt sorry for the instrument.

In 1969, Chicago-area public schools offered free music instruction. At the beginning of fall term, we shuffled into the auditorium and threaded our bodies into rows of stained, plush seats. It was time for fourth graders to absorb some much-needed culture. On stage stood an array of musical instruments, ranging from somber-looking cellos to slim, chic woodwinds. They gleamed on the platform like jewels.

Our host was an overly excited city employee, burdened with the task of explaining musical dynamics to a group of squirming children. The harried woman dashed about onstage, pointing at instruments. Occasionally, she plucked a violin string or blew into a clarinet.

It finally dawned on our group that she was encouraging us to become prodigies. We were instructed to choose our own instrument from the stage. Free lessons for all, but our parents would need to shoulder the rental costs.

Like everything else, musical selection became a popularity contest. Everyone wanted to play the violin, to the point where its category needed to be shut down. Several girls gravitated towards the flute. There was a short run on the trumpet. A couple of kids whined about the lack of a piano option but were told that pianos didn't fit inside on-site rehearsal rooms.

As each category filled, its display instrument was removed from the stage. Finally, only a viola remained, perched on its stand like a puppy awaiting adoption.

"Doesn't ANYBODY want to learn to play the viola?' the host pleaded.

I glanced around the auditorium. My classmates all stared straight ahead. The room was utterly silent.

"I will," I said.

The entire auditorium erupted in derisive laughter. I had selected an instrument that nobody else wanted to touch. My classmates already intuited that I was a freak. My choice had confirmed their suspicions.

At first, my parents seemed thrilled about my musical future. When they discovered they were on the hook for viola rental, however, their demeanor became more guarded.

"How badly do you want to play the viola?" my mother demanded. "I don't want to shell out a bunch of cash and then have you quit after a month or two."

"Oh, I really want to do it." I tried to make my voice sound emphatic. "I promise not to quit. Just give me a chance."

A few days later, I gazed into the interior of my new viola case and regarded the beautiful, terrifying instrument. Slightly larger than a violin, it rested within a snug, velvet nest. Taut metal strings stretched along the neck. I lifted the viola from its enclosure and peered inside one of its S-shaped apertures. The polished wood smelled exotic. My instrument came from

Europe but somehow found its way into an Oak Park bedroom.

Mr. Schmidt, an elderly man who reeked of cigarettes, served as my viola instructor. His teeth were dark yellow, stained by years of heavy tobacco use. Affable and encouraging, he grinned as I plucked at the strings. Mr. Schmidt felt that I should learn how the viola sounded before attempting to use the bow.

After a week of diligent plucking, I finally held the bow in my trembling fingers. The key was to be gentle but firm. My instrument squawked at first. Two weeks later, I could draw the bow across its strings without producing a godawful noise. I was on my way to becoming a prodigy.

"You're catching on fast." Mr. Schmidt paused, covered his mouth, and had a brief coughing fit. "I think you might be a natural."

I didn't understand what a natural was, but I felt certain that I wasn't one. In the school hallway, peers strutted around with instrument cases, looking like rock stars. Some of them ridiculed my dorkiness, calling me names like "wild cow." A few weeks beforehand, a pupil had discovered via Webster's Dictionary that my first name arose from a bovine origin. Now, classmates mooed loudly every time they saw me.

It was a melancholy existence for both of us—me and my solitary viola. Lacking an extracurricular social life, I spent hours in my bedroom, learning the notes to "Hot Cross Buns." I propped a songbook on my desk and labored my way through the varied offerings. "Danny Boy." "Frere Jacques." And finally, "Ode to Joy."

Once I realized that Beethoven fell within my musical wheelhouse, I felt my own surge of joy. I could play everything; even lessons I hadn't been assigned yet. I'd mastered the book's contents in less than three months. Perhaps I had a knack for the viola, after all.

Mr. Schmidt seemed impressed with my rapid progress. "I think you're ready for the school orchestra. Our Christmas performance is coming up in a few weeks. Would you like to be part of it?"

Dizzy with excitement, I nodded. Then a thought struck me. "Aren't there rehearsals, though? Do I need to stay after school? I have a lot of homework and chores."

"You can do your own rehearsing. I'll give you copies of all the scores. On the day of the performance, play those songs like you would at home. Just follow along. You'll be fine."

For the next five weeks, I practiced as though my life depended on it. I'd show my venomous classmates how gifted I was. They wouldn't dare pick on me again.

When the performance day arrived, I was suddenly seized by terror. I'd spent weeks practicing chords to "Rudolph the Red-Nosed Reindeer," but did I really possess any talent? What if I forgot everything I had struggled so hard to learn?

The auditorium overflowed with bodies—parents, siblings, curious townspeople. Every seat looked full. Meanwhile, the orchestra pit swelled with students, all dressed in high-necked, white polyester shirts. The boys sported creased pants, and the girls wore long, flowing skirts with maroon sashes.

We were the embodiment of elegance. Sweating profusely, I settled my bulk into a folding chair. In front of me sat the violinists—an alpha, confident group, clutching their violins like they'd been born to play concertos. Behind me, a group of cellists squatted in their seats, hugging bulky instruments between their legs.

To my right sat a girl about my age. She was tall, with messy blonde hair and round glasses. In one, outstretched hand, she held a viola.

I felt an overwhelming spasm of jealousy, but then

the girl turned in my direction. "Oh, hi." Her voice sounded friendly. "I heard there was another viola player. My name's Megan. I'm in fifth grade. Glad to meet you."

Why had nobody bothered to tell me? I tried my hardest to glare at Megan, but she was so cordial that I couldn't hate her. Finally, I smiled. "How long have you been playing?" My voice seemed to emanate from the other side of the auditorium.

"Oh, just a couple of months. There aren't many viola players in school, as I'm sure you've noticed. If you're any good, they kind of fast-track you."

Megan was an entire year older. I hadn't even known of her existence. Fifth graders were a rarefied group, kept separate from younger kids. Obviously, she didn't realize what a nerd I was, or she would've been less amiable.

Once the performance began, I realized that I was in big trouble. As the music swelled to its first crescendo, I started to fall behind. The other musicians surged forward with confidence, producing notes that meshed perfectly. I stared at my songbook and struggled to make sense of the squiggly characters. Just a day beforehand, they'd given me no trouble. Why couldn't I decipher them now?

I could play music with ease, alone in my bedroom. When faced with a group, however, I fell apart. Just like every other aspect of my life. I resorted to pulling my bow willy-nilly across the strings, hoping other musicians would drown out my noise. People didn't pay much attention to violas, anyway. If anyone expected me to break into a solo, I'd never be able to return to school again.

Meanwhile, Megan thrust her chin against her viola, giving the instrument everything she had. Her flimsy folding chair rocked with the momentum of her bow thrusts. Both eyes closed, face contorted into a half-smile, the girl appeared to be in another world.

When the performance finally ended, I staggered to my feet. Thunderous applause filled the auditorium, but none of it was for me. Even my viola seemed to regard me with contempt. I placed the instrument carefully into its case and prepared to leave the stage. Was it too early for me to go home? I wanted to crawl underneath my bed and stay there until June.

"Hey, nice to meet you," Megan said. "You sounded really good. I look forward to playing with you again."

After Christmas break ended, I resumed my music lessons. My enthusiasm had vanished, but Mr. Schmidt didn't seem to notice. I went to a couple of orchestra rehearsals and sat next to Megan. She was even weirder than I was, but at least she knew how to play her instrument. Megan seemed excited about the upcoming spring performance, a charade I felt determined to avoid. But how could I get out of it?

In mid-March, I fell hopelessly behind on my homework. The hallway mooing had intensified, despite my mother's insistence that it would go away if I ignored it. One afternoon, in the classroom, I burst into tears and couldn't stop. My life had become a calamitous joke.

My mother realized that I required drastic intervention. She'd heard of a private school on the other end of town—a Montessori-inspired outfit, run by a group of earnest hippies. Students were free to choose individual curriculums. They even called teachers by their first names.

"If you want to switch schools, we can do it next week," my mother said. "There's just one thing, though. That place costs a lot of money. We can't afford both viola rental and the cost of tuition. You'll need to pick one or the other."

I gave the conundrum a moment of thought. The viola had been my companion during a difficult year. I'd worked hard to master its tonal intricacies, and had promised my mother that I wouldn't quit. On the other hand, my instrument served as a substitute for a social life. Now I could start my existence anew, in a fresh environment where nobody hated me. Yet.

"I want to go to that school. Sorry about the viola. I tried my best."

My new school was even better than I'd imagined. Teachers hovered around the edges of the classroom, smiling. They never tried to intervene in our activities. I spent entire mornings inside the onsite library, lounging on overstuffed, paisley pillows.

Even more amazingly, I now had a best friend—Teresa, daughter of the school director. This status afforded me special privileges. Teresa was an aspiring artist. The two of us painted flowers and peace symbols on a flight of cement steps. "How lovely," our teachers said. "So much prettier than that dull gray color."

My bedroom seemed larger without a viola. Occasionally, I snuck a guilty peek at the corner where the instrument case had once rested. I didn't have much trouble beating my remorse into submission. Perhaps the viola had found someone who could give it the dedication it deserved. My own trade-off had been more than worthwhile.

One May afternoon, I encountered Megan on the street, a few blocks from my house. She spotted me and ran in my direction, flailing her arms. When she finally caught up, she was out of breath. A pair of green knee socks had bunched around her ankles, and one of her barrettes hung at a disjointed angle.

"I haven't seen you around school," she said. "Where have you been? Are you still playing viola?"

"Oh, I changed schools. I couldn't deal with that other place anymore." I did my best to make my voice sound breezy, as if I could switch venues whenever I felt like it. "My new school is great, but we don't have music lessons. So, I gave up playing. How are you?"

Megan grinned. "I joined the Oak Park Symphony Orchestra a few weeks ago. Youngest member they've ever had. A challenge, but I like it."

Despite myself, I felt a surge of envy. The local orchestra was renowned for its excellence. Acceptance into such an exclusive club pretty much guaranteed a lifelong musical career. At age twelve, Megan knew exactly where she fit. Polite society had embraced her, but I just winged each day as it came along.

Try as I might, I couldn't resent her. The girl was one with her instrument, in a way I had never been. Besides, she was so darned nice.

"You got accepted fast," I said. "Congratulations. That's great."

"You know how it is with the viola. They don't have many. It's not hard to be accepted into the orchestra. If you were still playing, I'm sure they'd ask you to join, as well."

I peered into Megan's face, searching for a hint of derision. Her expression looked genial, like it had when I first met her. She was the only person in public school who showed me any kindness, even though she could've easily viewed me as a competitor. Or, worse yet, she might have figured out that I possessed even less panache than she did.

Megan brushed a clump of hair from her eyes. "Well, I'd better go. Time for practice." She wheeled around and dashed across the street, finally disappearing into an alleyway.

I was in no hurry to return home. The school year had almost ended, and for the first time in my life, I felt sorry to see it go. A long, Midwestern summer stretched ahead. I hoped that Teresa and I could spend time together, fending off the taunts of my old classmates. They liked to roam the streets on humid afternoons, tyrannizing people they didn't like. But now I had a sidekick who could help me laugh right back at them.

Miss Lilly

John Wenderlein

Working as a Hospice Chaplain, there's never a dull moment. This is true for every patient who comes to our service. You pray, you say, and you do the right thing to give them peace at the end of their lives. My patients have been told they have limited time left; for some, they are more than ready to go. For others, not so much. I want to tell Lilly's story.

Sometimes, patients or family members opt out of having a chaplain visit when coming to hospice care. There are various reasons why. Much of the time, they misunderstand the role of a chaplain. I'll leave it at that.

My responsibility as a Hospice Chaplain is to visit patients in nursing homes—those who, again, have been told they do not have long. My days are never dull; they are filled with the various personalities I meet doing my job. One overwhelming fact about my work is that I will meet a variety of personalities. And for that, I'm thankful.

On Fridays, like most days, I visit a particular list of nursing homes based on their proximity to each other. I remember meeting Miss Lilly on one of these Fridays. On any given day, I will visit six or seven patients, and countless others who are not always my patients. Walking through the door of any nursing home, all that live within those walls are precious to me even if they are not hospice patients. I have also worked with fifty to seventy-five nurses in the nursing homes I visit. When I first meet a nurse, and after introducing myself, I always leave them with one thing: if you think someone needs a visit from a chaplain, even if they are not on my service, you must let me know. I've had several handfuls of people (not my patients) the nurses have asked me to visit. Without question, I find time for them. This is how I met Miss Lilly.

I was called to one of my nursing homes to visit a patient who was not doing well, as she was coming to the end of a life well lived. As I entered the long hallway, I was greeted by one of my favorite nurses—thirty years in that same nursing home. Kathy loved every patient she had, which showed as they responded well to each other. Kathy was slow to talk, which was never a problem for me. I talk enough for three people. Yet this time, she beat me to the draw, saying, "Oh, Chaplain. I 'm so glad you are here. I need you to see one of my patients." Never refusing anyone she wanted me to visit, I asked which one. The nurse replied, "The one thing I thought about all day today, Chaplain, is that she is doing OK, yet I can't get her out of my mind." Over the years, I have grown to know precisely what that means. This patient needs to be loved up. Her family is on their way, but they live out of state.

"Chaplain, I do not think she is going anywhere any time soon, but I was hoping you could work your magic on her." Kathy did not wait for me to ask what room or say yes. When she blurted out the room number, I said, "Kathy, let me

58

see my patient, and then I will go sit with Miss Lilly."

As always, I spent a reasonable amount of time with my patient, saying my goodbyes and promising to return. Then I went to the room number Kathy had given me. As I approached the door, I noticed it was closed, which was unusual. Most nursing homes keep the room doors open to better care for the patient. Knocking is always the protocol for closed doors in these situations. So, knocking on the door, I heard a faint voice say, "Come in." As quietly as possible, slowly opening the door, I entered the room.

The first thing I noticed was that the room was dark. No lights were on, and even the TV was off. My eyes took a moment to focus as very little light was in the room. The room slowly became focused, and Miss Lilly was lying neatly in bed. The edges of her covers were tucked on both sides and pulled up under her arms. Miss Lilly looked so tiny in that bed, as she was a small, petite person.

"Hello, sweet Lilly," I said. "How are you?"

"OK," she said very softly. "I am just so tired. I can hardly keep my eyes open." She said that several times during my visit, which I always followed up, saying, "I won't stay long."

Miss Lilly asked me, "How are you?"

"Fantastic," I said. Can I be anything other than great in the presence of such a sweetheart? A big smile came over Lilly's face, and it made my heart happy to see that smile. I asked, "Any pain?"

"No pain," she answered, "just tired." All the time we were conversing, I looked around the walls surrounding her bed. The walls were covered with photos. Looking at the pictures, I figured at least three generations of family photos were on the walls. I remember commenting on the pictures, saying someone in this room is loved. She replied almost instantly, "Yes, I am."

Finding a chair to put beside her bed, I sat down. Lilly asked me why I was visiting her. "Kathy, the nurse, sent you, didn't she?" Yes, she did. Lilly confirmed what I always knew about Kathy: she is a sweetheart of a person.

I positioned myself as close to the head of her bed as possible and then sat down. "Yes, Mrs. Lilly, I'm a chaplain, and I just wanted to stop by and see how you were doing." Again, she had fallen asleep when I got situated and would many more times before I would leave her. When asked about all the photos around her, she once again got a big smile and, one by one, told me who everyone was in the images. This gave her a boost of energy, and the possibility of telling me about those she loved gave her a bit of temporary strength. During this time, she reached for my hand, and, trying her best to hold it lightly, she finally gave up and just placed her tiny hand in mine. If I had not already said so, Lilly was a petite little lady whose hands were smaller than I imagined. She never took her hand out of mine during my visit. It was beautiful for her to speak of the lives of those she had helped create. I found out later that those photos were of her four boys, three daughters, their daughters, and sons, and some of them had children. So, imagine, from the love of this seventy-pound, four-foot-nine-inch lady came three generations of a legacy that would live on long after she was gone.

In our conversation, she talked about her only love. His photo was on her bedside table. She still blushed slightly when she spoke of him. "There was only one man in my life," she would tell me. "He was all I needed, and when he got sick, all he could do was tell me he was all right and would focus on me. After his passing, my children said to me that he spoke to them individually, explaining that they would need to care for their momma after he was gone. Even with all his suffering, Chaplain, he never let me know until almost the end. And even then, he worried about me. I couldn't have found a better man."

I must admit that at this point in my story that I was at a loss for words. Those who know me would find that hard to believe. But it was true. Lilly was downloading a lifetime in the fifteen or twenty minutes we would spend together.

After finishing her story about her husband Paul, she began going in and out of sleep—at least, that's what I thought it was. Meetings like this with Mrs. Lilly were why I got up every morning and headed out, excited about possibly meeting another Miss Lilly. I'm a firm believer that everyone, without exception, has a story to tell. Lilly's life was just more proof of that fact.

She was asleep again. In our conversation, she had told me she was a woman of faith and believed she would be with all those who had passed before her. Before I went, I whispered that I would leave her with prayer. She smiled, closing her eyes again, and I began to pray. Remember, I never let go of her. Or should I say she never took her hand out of mine? When I was done, I said my goodbyes quietly, not to wake her, and laid her hand back on her chest.

In my profession, I have spent much of my time carefully watching my patients breathe. Miss. Lilly was no exception. That is a habit I have had for years, after standing up and looking down at this sweet lady and pausing to look more carefully. It seemed like minutes, but it was just a few seconds. Then, something came over me. She was gone. No longer here with me. Of course, I thought I could be wrong. I am certainly no medical doctor or nurse. I slipped out of her room and went to find Kathy; she then asked me what was wrong. She could sense by my expression I had something to say.

"Kathy, I think Miss Lilly is gone." Of course, I said all those things like, I'm not a doctor so I could be wrong. I followed Kathy back to Miss Lilly's room, and when Kathy looked at her, even before she checked her vitals, she said she was gone. Kathy said, "Her family will come in the morning to be with her as they do every week, but I am thankful you could visit with her." I told Kathy what we talked about and how she kept falling asleep. Then silence filled the room, and Kathy started to shed tears. Thirty years of caring for older people, and she still cries when they pass. Before I left Kathy to call Miss Lilly's family, I sat back in the chair next to her bed, and Kathy left the room to make those calls. I sat silent, looking at Miss Lilly and all those photos on the wall. I left her room with no sadness, no sorrow. Miss Lilly was with the ones she loved so much. I was thankful and honored to have had my time with her.

Blessings, Miss Lilly.
Chaplain John

P.S. I received several calls from Miss Lilly's family. They all wanted to hear their mother's last words. When I explained to them how she focused on her family and loved them all, that gave them peace. I was blessed to spend time with a lovely person. And from our visit came peace for the family that loved her so.

Bonding

Matias F. Travieso-Diaz

We'll be Friends Forever, won't we, Pooh?" asked Piglet.
"Even longer," Pooh answered.
A. A. Milne

My childhood and adolescence were largely spent in self-imposed solitude. Due to my solitary character, I made very few friends as I grew up; indeed, by the time I graduated from high school, I had only a couple of real friends, though those were true and devoted.

Coming to the United States from Cuba at the age of twenty forced me to leave behind my childhood friends, for none were fortunate enough to escape the hellhole that my country of birth had become under the Castro regime. I lived in Miami for four years, during which time I made a reasonable number of school and work acquaintances, but no real friends, for the strain of life as a penniless immigrant combined with my aloofness to allow me no time or disposition to develop a social network. My departure from Florida in the fall of 1967 for Columbus, Ohio to pursue a PhD in Electrical Engineering at Ohio State went largely unnoticed and unlamented by anyone outside my immediate family.

Moving to Ohio was a drastic change in my personal circumstances. Part of the reason I had avoided feeling lonely during my years in Havana and Miami was the enveloping cocoon of love from my family and the familiarity of the Cuban-like environment in which I operated. The people with whom I dealt were largely my peers and interacting with them was an unconscious source of comfort that was not appreciated until it was taken away by the move.

When I arrived at Ohio State I was assigned a room in a graduate student dormitory. My roommate and most other dorm residents were from other Ohio cities and, as a lot, were friendly and polite, but far more reserved and low-keyed than the boisterous Latins with whom I was familiar. I did not make a friend during my first year in Columbus except for Carlos, a fellow Cuban who was starting school at Ohio State at the same time, and who I had known vaguely in Miami. Carlos and I became (and to this day remain) close friends; he and I moved to a rental apartment, together with another Cuban, the following year.

Through Carlos I became acquainted with members of the few dozen Cuban families that lived in the greater Columbus area – an insignificant minority in an area of nearly one million people. I made no real friends among the Columbus Cubans, but attended social activities and other events held by them, and my contacts with them made my time in the city a bit more bearable.

The number of my Columbus friends expanded the following year. One Saturday afternoon in the fall of 1968, someone knocked at the door of my apartment. It was another Cuban, Jake, an engineer who had just taken a job at Western Electric's Columbus manufacturing facility and moved to the city. He had contacted the Ohio State Student Services Office seeking referrals to Cubans who attended the university and had been given my name and address. Jake, who was an outgoing and expansive fellow, quickly became my friend and remained close to me until his death a few years ago.

One more person was added later that year to the roster of my friends in Columbus. Jake had met at work with Paul, a recently graduated physicist who had been hired by the Bell Labs (a sister company to Western Electric) to clerk for them in Columbus and then proceed to Boston to get a Masters Degree at MIT. Paul was from North Dakota, and in some ways he probably felt as out of place in Ohio as I. Thus, he quickly added himself to the small band of funny-talking Cubans and became one of my closest friends; two and a half years later Paul, Jake and I would rent an apartment in the Columbus outskirts and live together until I left the city in 1972.

There was one final addition to the number of friends I made in Columbus. Eloy, his young wife, and her family moved to Columbus so that he could do the academic work necessary for a PhD in Romance Languages. Eloy also became a very close friend of mine and, in recent years, has been (together with Paul) a crucial supporter of the literary career on which I embarked late in life.

—

My Columbus friends and I engaged in many activities together that tightened the ties between us. The most notable of those was perhaps the hearts game that we ran every Friday night at Eloy's house. Paul and I would show up bringing one or two six-packs of beer; we would be joined by Antonio, a Spaniard who was a friend of Eloy's. Eloy's wife or her mother would prepare some snacks for our nourishment and there would be more beer in reserve in case the game went beyond the supply we had brought. The four players (Eloy, Antonio, Paul and I) would sit around the dinner table, with Eloy's family either watching the proceedings or trying their best to ignore us, an effort that became more difficult as the night went on and the beer made us more boisterous.

Hearts is a trick-taking game. Its objective is to collect the fewest number of negative points while foisting points on other players. Each of the thirteen cards in the hearts suit counts a negative point; the queen of spades counts for thirteen.

The game proceeds in a series of rounds. At the start of each round, all fifty-two cards in the deck are dealt to the players. Before playing, each player selects from his hand three cards he wants to get rid of, passing them to the player sitting on his left in the first round, the player on his right on the second round, the player sitting across on the third round, and not passing at all on the fourth.

The game starts by the player holding the two of clubs laying it on the table. All other players must follow suit if they can, or play anything else if they cannot, except that neither hearts nor the queen of spades can be played on the first trick. Aces are high, twos are low, and the person who plays the highest card of the suit being led takes the trick. The winner of the trick leads a card to start the next trick, and so on until the entire hand is played. Hearts cannot be led unless they have been played in a previous trick. At the end of each round, points are counted. The game continues round after round until one player has accumulated 100 negative points, at which time the player left with the smallest number of negative points wins.

It is possible that a player will take all the hearts and the queen of spades in a round. That is called "shooting the moon" and, instead of his being penalized with 26 negative points, 26 negative points are added to the scores of all other players.

The game is simple to play but allows for a fair number of strategic considerations. For example, the choice of which three cards to pass depends, among other things, on the need to get rid of hearts or the queen of spades, the status of the scoring, and a passing player's perception of the dangerousness of the recipient. Likewise, the choice of what suit to lead or whether to drop a heart on a given trick depends on a player's perception of what is most advantageous for him to do.

All participants in the hearts games at Eloy's house were cutthroat players, eager to win and have fun at the other players' expense. A player giving a particularly wicked pass to another would smirk and declare something like "here is a present for you, buddy;" the recipient might react with fake indignation at the pass by replying "you bastard!" Dropping the queen of spades on a trick would often be done by dramatically slamming the card on the table, and gleefully exclaiming: "take the bitch!" As the night progressed and more beer was consumed, the commentary became more biting. On one occasion, Antonio realized that he could win the game by shooting the moon on the last round, but would otherwise lose. Soon, it became evident that he was trying to collect all the hearts, and everyone tried to prevent him. On the last trick, someone managed to take the last heart remaining, saddling Antonio with 25 negative points and making him lose the game. Someone, probably Eloy, commented: "You went down like the Spanish Armada!" Antonio turned red with wounded pride, but ultimately laughed with the rest of us.

The games of hearts provided entertainment for the players and a chance to vent steam after a hard week at school. For me, they also afforded an opportunity to get to know my new friends and bond with them in ways I had seldom experienced before.

Spiritual Remembering

Ellen Gerneaux Woods

I received the information by postcard: *Sacred Journey to Greece and Turkey, April 20th to May 8, 2009. Join this mystical journey of spiritual remembering.* Printed over a photograph of some twenty columns of unknown ruins, surrounded by trees with vibrant pink blossoms, it continued: *Embody the energies of gods and goddesses living within these sacred sites. Listen to your own oracle. Be embraced by the friendliness and depth of wisdom from the people of these great lands.* It was led by a spiritual teacher who was known for her transformative retreats.

I was in at *Listen to your own oracle.* I had recently left a ten-year meditation practice after my Buddhist teacher, the only woman priest at the Berkeley Zen Center, had died. After feeling ungrounded, floating in my grief, I began to follow a religious practice based in mysticism.

I had never been outside the United States, and at sixty-five I had a feeling it was time. Though I was happily single, I continued to search for a kind of security beyond myself that I could count on. Mysticism reminded me that the Absolute is within the human psyche and my practice had become trusting in my spiritual core to lead me and provide for me as my life unfolded. I did, however, often forget.

Within days of receiving the postcard, I arranged my flight, and six weeks later met up with twenty strangers in Athens where we began the journey of visiting the ancient sacred sites of Greece. It was a whirlwind of bus trips and climbs and endless lines to visit the Acropolis, the Parthenon, the Oracle at Delphi, and other ruins and monasteries. I couldn't get quiet enough inside to meditate or pray. I was stuck in a left-brain torture chamber of guidebooks, informational talks, and the personalities and opinions of my fellow travelers. Was this the spiritual remembering that I'd come for? Though we were given much historical information and a chance to explore and experience places I had only seen in pictures, I became weary and over-stimulated with the facts and travel details. At times it seemed like I was more occupied with remembering what time and where the next bus was leaving and remembering to pee before I boarded.

Midway through the trip we reached Turkey, arriving in Istanbul at the height of the tulip season, where the city pathways were lined with stunning gardens of tulips in red, yellow, purple, pink, and white. The horizon was graced by minarets, narrow cylindrical towers projected into the sky, from which, we were told, a call to prayer was amplified at dawn, midday, mid-afternoon, sunset and nightfall. We arrived in time to hear the mid-afternoon call. It was a haunting melodic chant that rumbled in my body, stopping me and creating an internal response of deep spiritual connection. My thoughts disappeared, and every part of my body came alive. I felt as if I was breathing in sync with humanity. Feeling that way five times a day seemed like an impossible luxury.

I felt excited anticipating the next call to prayer, which would be at sunset.

Along with my fellow travelers, I checked into the hotel. Once we deposited our suitcases in our rooms, our trip guide, Cassie, immediately gathered us together and made plans for an impromptu walk through the neighborhood. Pappo, the oldest member of the group, immediately disappeared into the hotel's bar. A husky red-faced man with a white beard and ponytail, he was a philosophy professor from Philadelphia, and not one for small talk. I wanted to be alone, so I returned to my room to take a nap. There were many ways to absorb a new city, I told myself.

After awakening a few hours later, I walked to the lobby, a spacious entry way with floor to ceiling windows overlooking tulip gardens. I looked around but saw no one familiar so I decided to explore the neighborhood on my own.

As I walked through the narrow-curved streets, shop owners greeted me in the local language, of which I was ignorant, and I smiled, nodded and said the only word I knew, *merhaba*, hello. I entered a small store to look at the wares of colorful pottery, copper pots, and exotic carpets. I was particularly drawn to the round glass pendants which hung in the window catching the light. They were deep blue embedded with a white circle centered by a blue dot. Though I rarely bought souvenirs, I knew I had to have this. I slipped some lira from my money belt and offered it in exchange. The shopkeeper took the bills, gave me change and helped me put the pendant around my neck. Placing my palms together, I bowed my head in gratitude.

As I walked to the next shop I realized dusk was approaching and I needed to get back to the hotel. I tried to retrace my steps but there was no hotel in sight, nor any response to my frantic efforts to communicate with passers-by.

Even if I had met someone who spoke English, I didn't know the name of the hotel, the address, or the phone number. I had left the hotel's card in my room, as well as my cell phone.

The streets were winding and all the shops looked alike. There were no recognizable landmarks.

I was lost.

My thoughts circled back on themselves as I panicked at my inability to ask for help. I feared that I was permanently separated from my group. Alone in a foreign country, I was unable to visualize a solution. I felt increasingly helpless as it got darker.

My heart was pounding so fast I wondered if I was having a heart attack. As I placed my hand on my chest my fingers brushed against the necklace I had bought earlier. I covered the pendant with my hand and in a few minutes my heart stopped hammering. I focused on my breath.

At that moment the sunset call for prayer began. The sounds echoed soothingly inside my head. I sat on a rock under a tree covered with pink blossoms and tried to center myself as I listened to the deep chant-like mantra filling the air as the sun began to set. I felt embraced by the sound, as if a warm light had enveloped me. I looked down and saw a plaque at the base of the tree, written in English as well as Turkish. *Erguvan Tree, commonly called the Judas Tree.*

Suddenly I remembered the name of the hotel.

The Erguvan Hotel.

I jumped up and began walking, turning right, turning left, with a clarity of intention that seemed to come automatically. I arrived back at the hotel just as it got dark.

Over dinner, when I told my compatriots my story of getting lost, Pappo squinted, taking in my words.

"I see you are wearing an Evil Eye amulet," he said. "That's what led you back."

"An amulet? For what?" I asked, touching the necklace I had bought earlier.

I had no idea what it represented. I had simply wanted to own it, to wear it.

"Protection," he said.

It all made sense. My spiritual remembering was not what I had learned or experienced at the historical sites. It was what I learned from trusting my intuition, my spiritual core, to lead me home.

Hi Bill

Kirk Boys

My cousin Bill never learned to ride a bike or throw a rock or drive a car or drop a cannon ball into a lake. Instead he was strapped in a wheelchair with cerebral palsy. We were about the same age, he and I. That's how it was for Bill, an existence dependent on someone else to care for him. In battle with a body that fought him at every turn. Absolutely nothing was wrong with Bill's mind, though.

This is about my regret and how I didn't have the courage to see through Bill's disability to the person locked inside.

Every year on the second Sunday in July I'd see Bill at the family picnic. Always parked in the shade close to the picnic tables, his father or mother in a folding chair nearby. Everyone said, "Hi, Bill," but no one really tried to talk with him that I observed. And usually, Bill would garble out a "Hi," back and fight to smile. There is no easy answer to why none of us, besides Bill's family, made the effort to give Bill more than a few seconds of our time. I think it was fear. Fear of saying or doing the wrong thing, fear of becoming entangled in what we perceived as his sad condition. No we looked away from frustration and pain. Easier to just say, "Hi, Bill." I do not say this as a judgment of anyone; I was no better at finding that courage and that's where my regret lives all these years later.

Bill was thin as a wisp, fighting his body's constant spasms. His mom would push his wheelchair into a circle of conversation, ask him questions and treat him with the respect he deserved, the rest of us tried to act as if he weren't really there struggling to be a part of it.

I had sixteen aunts and uncles and 51 cousins along with their assorted spouses or partners, although attendance thinned dramatically with time. Borst Park sits a hundred yards from a freeway on-ramp and a stone's throw from an outlet mall promising factory pricing. There is a muddy little lake and a pioneer log structure and some baseball fields nearby and most every year it was hot. Relatives swapped stories about a salmon fishing trip, berry jam, and golf scores. Recent surgeries or heart attacks, who was having a baby and who wasn't getting along. What great gas mileage their car was getting. There was horseshoes and pinochle and arguments and hurt feelings, slaps on the back, hearty handshakes and lots of laughter and booze.

I don't know what anyone could have done differently. Outside of talking to him, being physically present, letting him know we saw him and wanted to try and understand what he would have wanted to say to us. Easier to just say, "Hi, Bill." I know for certain everyone felt bad for him and his parents and family who shouldered his care. They didn't want our pity or worthless prayers. They would, I'm guessing just have wanted us to treat him like, well, one of us.

And if any of the aunts and uncles or cousins or their

spouses at Borst Park were being honest, they would say it was easier not to look. Easier to disengage than to engage with Bill. "Hi Bill," was all we could muster. That we could live with. After all it wasn't our brother or son and they felt bad, sure, but what could we possibly do that wasn't already being done? Bill was a sad fact of life.

Cerebral palsy (CP) is an incurable condition. There are some treatments now that didn't exist for Bill. Imagine being a prisoner in your own body, capable of thinking and feeling, but incapable of even the most basic functions. Bill couldn't wipe himself or walk to the mailbox, go to school or make love. You can't catch CP from the air or from drinking the same drink by mistake, but witnessing it will surely break your heart.

When Bill was in his late 30's and he'd lost his mother to brain cancer, his sister Margaret took on his care. Bill was lucky that he had someone who showed amazing commitment and love while managing to raise her own small children. And then a group home was found for Bill. My cousin Johnny told me he used to pick up Bill from the group home, stuff his wheelchair in the trunk of his car and take him to concerts and spend time with him. I wish I had hung out with Bill and Johnny, helped with his wheelchair, took the time to show him I didn't think of him as sad. Johnny took the time to see Bill's humanity underneath all his struggle. "Bill was really great," Johnny told me. "It was a hassle, but well worth the effort it took to get him out and about." That says everything anyone needs to know about Johnny, too.

The family picnics faded off into the sunset along with video stores and disposable cameras, the last of my aunts and uncles not long after that. Cousin Bill passed away when he was 37. I hope there is a special place in Heaven for people like Bill. So I regret I didn't have the courage to get to know him all those years ago. I'd be better for it. That, well, that I know for sure.

Looking back there are a lot of things I would have done differently. I got busy helping raise our family, trying to navigate life's up and downs as best I could, but I could have taken a little time for Bill and I would have been so much the better for it.

Discarded Dog Day Afternoon

Debra J. White

Early in 1989, I faced a mid-life crisis. I surrendered my lease to a rent-stabilized Manhattan studio apartment and moved to Boston with my two rescued dogs, Scottie and Maxine. Was I off my rocker? I lived in a wonderful neighborhood, but my apartment had cockroaches who waited in line to enter my roach motel. A crooked ceiling worried me. Would I wake up covered in soot, dust, and the neighbor above me? Nearby Boston seemed like a good place to resettle. Once I found another social work position and an apartment that accepted pets, I called the MSPCA (Massachusetts Society for the Prevention of Cruelty to Animals) to ask about volunteering. That began my shelter career.

I preferred working with unwanted dogs and cats. Jean, the manager, urged me to learn front desk operations anyway. To start off on the right foot, I agreed. I didn't want to come across as testy or unduly picky. On my first day, a woman arrived to surrender her cat. The clerk asked why, a question posed to everyone surrendering animals. Details like the animal's age, temperament, medical history, etc. assisted in placing them into new homes. The woman signed the relinquishment papers citing the reason as her cat meowed. Dumbfounded, I asked what were you expecting, a Gregorian chant? From the corner of my eye, Jean frantically waved at me as if I should have shut up. I grew up in NYC and am often opinionated. Later, the manager encouraged me not to challenge pet owners surrendering cats or dog, no matter how trivial the reason. Owners got into snits and walked across the street to a park to abandon their pets. I never worked at the front desk during my two years at the MSPCA.

In addition to unwanted animals entering the shelter daily, there were disturbing abuse cases. Employed as a social worker, I experienced more child abuse cases than I cared to remember, but that's for another sobering discussion. The MSPCA introduced me to animal maltreatment. The shelter investigated abuse in and around Boston. Pets seized from abusive owners often lived at the shelter for weeks or months because they were needed in court cases. Removed from his abusive owner, Buster, a young lab mix, lived at the shelter for months while his owner's case worked its way through the justice system. To give Buster a break from confinement, staff members let the dog spend time among the various departments. Buster greeted customers at the animal hospital's front desk. He was quite the receptionist, barking out greetings and soaking up affection from customers, staff, and other volunteers. A judge finally freed Buster for adoption and he landed in a good home. Sadly, a year later Buster became sick and died. At least he escaped further abuse in his last days, and he died in a loving environment.

Each week, I checked out the residents. Unlucky ones lingered; others were new, either strays or owner surrenders.

To shield my heart from shattering, I stopped asking staff about pets I liked. If they burned in the crematory, I didn't want to know. I caved in now and then. Once I took interest in Barney, a senior mix of who knows what, brought in by Boston Police. The dog's aging owner, a single man, suffered a massive heart attack and was rushed to a hospital. Rather than strand Barney, EMTs called the police who escorted him to the MSPCA. The shelter searched for the owner's family, but no one turned up. Every few days, management checked with the hospital, but the owner remained in serious condition. Family never came forward. I took Barney for an extra walk and rewarded him with special treats and a fluffy blanket. We all feared the owner might not recover. By this time, my heart belonged to Barney.

Nearly two months later, the owner showed up saying he felt much better. I missed the wonderful reunion, but the manager said he was so thankful we took care of his dog. In fact, he left a generous donation of $200. Barney wagged his tail as he left with his owner. Hearing the story made my day.

In the summer of 1991, I left Boston for an adventure in Colorado. I enjoyed my time at the shelter, learning about pet overpopulation, animal care, and community support. I had a wonderful time attending shelter fundraisers with my dogs, especially one called Mutts and Stuff Day. My dog Maxine and I won a prize for owner/dog look alike. We were quite a team.

How I traveled across the country with three dogs scrunched in a Subaru wagon loaded with my stuff was a miracle. Finding a motel to accept my canine trio wasn't an issue although I once was given a smoker's room. Rest stops on interstate highways set aside fenced-in areas to exercise dogs. My canine companions traveled well, adjusting to the tight quarters. None got carsick but me. Now and then, I indulged my dogs with French fries and burgers. Maxine preferred hers without pickles.

Once I settled in Boulder, CO with a job and an apartment, I called the local shelter, then known as Boulder County Humane Society, and signed up to volunteer.

Early bird Ron almost always arrived before the starting hour of 7:00 a.m. and loaded a large plastic bucket with donated dog food to serve our occupants their daily meal. Whoever arrived next fed the cats. The third person vacuumed the hallways and front office. Staff then collected the uneaten dog food and headed outside to recycle the food to a motley collection of unwanted farm animals. We had two horses, Patches and Joey, who was blind, three goats (Carmelita, Gandhi and Sassy), a giant pig named Remus, and a flock of chickens. Ducks and geese swarmed around the tiny pond, especially at feeding time.

Remus, with his large girth and noisy snorts, amazed me. A prank at a campus fraternity party, police brought the pig to us. Pigs were usually slaughtered for meat when they were around six months of age or sooner. Remus grew and grew until he weighed probably over seven hundred pounds.

"He leads a good life," Leslie, the assistant manager said.

I glanced at the slumbering swine as he snoozed on a large pile of straw in the barn. "What's to complain about?" I asked.

A social worker monitored a mentally ill client living independently, checking on him daily to make sure he took his medication. The patient owned a black lab mix named Baby. Off his medication, the client lost self-control and beat up on Baby. The social worker felt sorry for Baby and pressed the client to surrender him. He always refused. With a lot of persuasion, the social worker finally convinced the client to relinquish Baby. She brought him to us. The pathetic dog cowered in his cage, fearful of everyone. He whined and whimpered. I treated him to a nice blanket and snacks but that barely calmed his fears. I wondered how many times his former owner had whacked him. Clients refusing medication and therapy often hurt people and animals.

Weeks passed and Baby wasn't adopted. I feared that he'd end up on the dreaded euthanasia list. Baby deserved a second chance, but didn't they all?

To place him into a loving home, the shelter made him pet of the week. The *Boulder Camera* newspaper offered free weekly space to feature one special pet. Baby's story appeared and magic ensued. A kind family showed up and gave Baby the great home he deserved. My eyes watered when I heard the story. Baby owed his life to the brave social worker who saw he was in trouble and to the family who adopted him.

Euthanasia duty rattled nearly everyone. Volunteers didn't participate but I watched the supervisors when they compiled the 'E' list. Supervisors scrawled a yellow 'x' across the cards of the doomed. Sometimes the choice was obvious due to illness, injury, age, or bad temperament. On days when not enough strays were not reclaimed, too many pet owners surrendered animals and few people adopted, gut wrenching choices were made. Life was unfair but the shelter had neither the space nor the resources to keep every unwanted animal alive. Euthanasia tore me apart every time I saw a kennel worker lead a tail wagging dog or carry a purring cat to the back room. I knew what awaited them.

After each euthanasia session, Leslie, the assistant manager, barged through the back door to puff away. I once followed her.

"I thought you were trying to quit," I said.

"I only smoke at work," Leslie said, sucking hard on a cigarette and exhaling slowly.

"It's the stress," I said, acting the role of social worker.

"I hate putting animals down, especially when there's

nothing wrong with them."

"Not for me," I said.

"I didn't think I could either, but it's better to be put down by someone like me than starve, get hit by a car, or live with a sadistic owner."

I totally agreed.

A delivery man worked for a local pet food supplier. A "sell by" date didn't mean the food was rancid or stale. Legally, it couldn't be sold after that date just like food for human consumption. The driver's cheapskate employer tossed the outdated food into the dumpster rather than donate it. I was at the shelter when the delivery man showed up with yet another load of pet food.

"If he knew I brought the food here, he'd fire me," the driver said. "With all the animals you have, I can't see that food wasted."

"Have you talked to him about it?" Leslie asked.

"He said he paid for the food and if he can't sell it, no one will get it."

"I appreciate what you're doing, but please watch yourself," Leslie said.

"He has no idea what I do. I intend to keep it that way," the driver said.

"Thank you again for your kindness," Leslie said.

Of note, the driver never had pets. He was simply thoughtful.

On January 6, 1994, a car ran me over as I walked my dogs, leaving me with a serious brain injury. I spent two months in a hospital/rehab center. Thankfully, my dogs weren't hurt and my neighbors cared for them in my long absence. I'd have been heartbroken without them.

Due to memory loss and mobility problems. I never worked again. To escape the freezing weather and snow, I moved to Phoenix in 1997. I returned to animal shelter work as well as other volunteer jobs. Sitting home all day, watching TV, and snacking on crumb cake wasn't my idea of living. I got a second chance, and I tried to make the best of it. My essay concludes with a few snippets from my experiences in Phoenix. There are too many to include them all.

By mid-October, the extreme heat tapered off and Barb, the volunteer coordinator, sprang into action. The off-site adoption season began. Barb organized adoption events at public parks, libraries, animal boarding kennels, and more. Everything had to be transported, including office supplies, pet food, water, bowls, animal crates, folding tables, chairs as well as the dogs and cats available for adoption. Pulling off these events took massive planning. Barb was a master coordinator.

"Darling," she called me one day. "I need you this weekend for a big event at Cave Creek Park. Can you be there?"

Cave Creek is in the northeast part of Phoenix.

"What time and how to I get there?"

Barb offered a vague set of driving instructions. The brain injury distorted what little sense of direction I had and naturally I botched my way to the event. About an hour later, I finally showed up at a gorgeous public park nestled in the sprawling desert.

"I'm sorry I'm late," I said as I rolled up in my scooter.

"Don't worry," Barb said. "Ride to the parking lot and look for the county truck. Pick up the stack of towels in the back. Dogs and cats need something soft inside the cages."

Barb treated me like a valued employee. "How's your selling skills?"

"I guess OK," I said.

"Good enough," she said. "Got an important job for you."

Barb's dedication to the shelter extended beyond her

paid employment. In her spare time, she assembled gift baskets to benefit shelter dogs and cats. At off-site events, volunteers like me hawked raffle tickets. She plowed the proceeds into the foster care program so that tiny puppies and kittens born to moms that either died prematurely or had to be put down would find a second chance.

Within a short time, I earned a place as one of Barb's top sales agents. I peddled raffle tickets at adoption events and raked in at least $200 at each one. I loved it. The special part was the sight of dogs and cats on their way home with responsible loving owners.

Even Barb's family chipped into her mission. At off-site adoptions, her husband Kenny helped in whatever ways he was needed, mostly hauling supplies, or buying her a hot dog. Her mom brought her organ and played music. Sometimes her niece sold raffle tickets. It was like a family affair.

I was deeply sorry when Barb passed away in February 2001. Not only was she my friend, but she was friend to the homeless animals of Maricopa County.

At Christmas time, PetSmart stores partnered with shelters and rescue groups for a fundraiser called Pet Photos with Santa. PetSmart provided the camera, film and frames then split the proceeds with the rescue groups. I jumped at the chance to volunteer for Pet Photos with Santa to be among people whose pets were cherished parts of the family. Because of poor mobility, a seated position worked best for me. I dressed in a Santa suit to pose with animals. Years of playing Santa still warm my heart, even if a scared little dog tinkled on my leg and a cranky cat clawed at my fake beard. I even posed with a horse outside the store. Now the pet photos with Santa are done digitally.

Around Thanksgiving one year, I met a man who came to search for his lost dog.

"Chickie's been missing for months," he said. "I always hope he'll be here."

"Don't give up. Sometimes dogs and cats show up a long time after they become lost," I said.

"My whole family has been heartbroken over his loss."

"How'd Chickie get out?" I asked.

"The pool guy inadvertently left the gate open."

I heard that story dozens of times. Repair men and women left gates open and curious dogs escaped. Those with tags, if caught, usually went home. Those without had a less certain fate.

If a pet owner found his dog or cat, they had to pay the fine. If the dog didn't have a rabies vaccination, they paid an additional fee. No such law applied to cats.

A little later, the man blew through the door to the receiving area and ran up to me.

"He's here," he said. "I can't believe it."

"I'm so happy for you."

"Wait till I get home. My family will be so pleased. We'll have a happy Thanksgiving this year. And Chickie will get a plate of turkey."

This was a good day at the shelter.

Over the years, I witnessed dogs and cats that were surrendered for frivolous reasons. Dogs and cats came arrived with hideous wounds inflicted by cruel owners. Some didn't make it despite our attempts to save them. One poor dog was given up on Christmas Eve because the family said they didn't have time for him anymore. He whined and whined. I sat there and cried. On the other hand, I also witnessed selfless acts of kindness. A boy perhaps ten years old brought in a carload full of pet supplies. At his birthday party, he asked guests to bring presents for the shelter. I was so proud of this boy's humanity. Seeing dogs and cats leave for good homes was so worthwhile.

Chaining dogs always bothered me. I thought it was cruel and heartless. Dogs are social creatures. Why have a dog if only to chain it outdoors in the brutal cold or blistering heat? Around 2005 or so, I had read of a woman then named Tammy Grimes who started an organization called Dogs Deserve Better (DDB). DDB's mission was to end dog chaining. Inspired by Grimes, I created a children's creative writing/art contest called Breaking the Chain. The Phoenix Animal Care Coalition (PACC) sponsored the contest. Third grade children in the public schools read a short story that I wrote about a chained dog named Joey saved by the neighbor's cat, the Great Harriet. For the next ten years, we at PACC judged the most thoughtful caring and clever stories/artwork then awarded small prizes to the top three finishers in each category. It was my pleasure to visit each school and talk to the children about kindness to animals and hand out the prizes. I felt like a rock star.

The Macerich Corporation, owner of dozens of shopping malls across the nation, stunned the animal rescue community in 2011 by not renewing pet store leases. That surprise announcement was the slow death of at least some mall pet stores. One by one, mall pet stores folded. More emphasis was directed towards rescued pets through dogged determination. There's a long way to go. Millions of dogs and cats enter shelters every year and not all of them are adopted.

The former pet store in Chandler became an adoption center, an extension of the Arizona Animal Welfare League, a private shelter where I've volunteered since 2008. In 2014, I moved closer to the mall and started volunteering there. Each week, I checked out new arrivals. Sometimes there's a dozen puppies and kittens needing attention and a few sad looking older dogs and cats bewildered by life in a cage. Sometimes I wonder how an eleven-year-old dog or cat suddenly became disposable. For the older dogs and cats, both staff and volunteers comfort them with cozy beds and snacks to make their stay as pleasant as possible.

Volunteer duties are routine. I load a machine with soiled rags, towels, or blankets, I check to see what cages need cleaning. There's always another dog or cat ready to occupy the space. There's also feeding time. Most dogs, especially puppies, wag their tails and yip with delight when I dish out kibble. They can't wait and dig their little heads into the bowls.

I check cat cages to make sure their food and water bowls are full. I once heard a desperate meow. I followed the source until I noticed a cat with an empty bowl. I filled her bowl. That satisfied the pretty puss.

After feeding, I take adult dogs in the yard, a small fenced-in area outside the back entrance. I sit while dogs take care of business or wander around. Some play fetch. In summer, it's smothering hot outside despite a covering for shade and sprinklers to keep cool. I fill our little pool with water for the dogs to splash around. I later sniff for poop. We don't take the puppies outside because they aren't fully inoculated yet so they eliminate in their cage. Sometimes, we place puppies in an open enclosure inside the store called the "pit." Visitors adore puppies.

Over the years, I have absorbed much about mall operations. The loading dock hums with activity every day, except Sunday, with deliveries. Workers enter and exit through the back. I've seen workers hang out to smoke or talk on cell phones. Loud noises from the trucks frighten timid dogs. So does the racket from the cardboard recycler. The machine grinds and grunts as it compresses the cardboard. Later, it's picked up by a recycling company to turn into more cardboard.

I've become familiar with regular delivery drivers. A dog escaped from a volunteer one day. Employees and volunteers mounted a valiant search for the runaway. I asked a

UPS driver with a local route to check for our wayward woofer. Thankfully, a Good Samaritan found the dog and returned it to our shelter.

COVID-19 turned the world upside down. Few people, if any, saw the encroaching invisible enemy that would cause havoc around the world. The mall changed too because of COVID. By early March 2020, crowds at the mall slowly thinned then nearly disappeared. One by one, stores closed. Soon, the governor ordered the closure of all non-essential businesses. The mall along with our adoption store shut down for over two months. I missed my routine of snacking on bread samples at Wildflower Café in the lobby and reading the newspapers before my shift. I longed to hang out with the staff, volunteers, and unwanted pets. Since I no longer held a job, volunteering at the pet adoption center was as helpful for them as it was for me. We re-opened in mid-June to many changes. Initially, we kept the front gate down and only opened it to customers with adoption appointments. Everyone -- including staff, volunteers, and customers -- were required to wear masks. Only one volunteer per shift was allowed to limit the number of people in the store. In the early days, the store was quiet without shoppers parading through mostly gazing at the animals. Several months later, we raised the gate and permitted a small number of masked people in at a time. We relaxed our rules and let in more people. More than one volunteer could work a shift, but the mask mandate stood until April 2023 after new guidelines went into effect. During the time we imposed a mask mandate, it created a not so surprising pushback. Let me give you examples. Social media and the press were full of stories about the rabid anti-maskers and anti-vaxxers. Some of those dandies shopped at the Chandler mall. As a rule, a staff member or volunteer like me manned the store entrance for mask patrol. In the beginning, we charged $2.00 for a disposable mask then we lowered the price to $1.00. Then we gave them away for free. We asked visitors if they had their own masks to save money. Some did; some didn't. Not surprisingly, guests were often insulted by the question. I personally heard people say "It's just cats and dogs" to which I responded that masks protected everyone's health. One man claimed my request was just plain stupid. He stormed away then returned to remind me how idiotic I was. I didn't take it personally. Another woman with a snarky attitude said she wouldn't come in our store if I gave her a free mask. I said thank you and have a nice day. Also, I heard people spit out curses as they walked by our store that they'll never adopt from us because you had to wear a mask. Good, keep going. I wouldn't want to send one of our dogs or cats home with such belligerent people like them anyway. Another man cursed and said he'd never buy anything in our crummy store. I said to myself you probably weren't going to buy anything anyway. I remain aghast at some people's hostility and level of anger. Thankfully, no one was injured.

The Chandler mall is an exciting, interesting, and mostly fun place to visit, work, shop, and volunteer. At Christmas time, how can anyone not smile seeing children perched on Santa's lap? Each week a special adoptable dog sits with Santa. Why no cats? Most cats are skittish around crowds, and we don't want a cat to escape inside the huge mall. Security guards patrol the mall for everyone's safety. They keep order and dissuade anyone from causing trouble. I regret that many malls face extinction from on-line shopping and the giant behemoth that sells everything. How can America be America without department stores and shopping malls? It's our tradition; it's in our blood. Online can never replace a day of shopping with your friends or plopping down in the food court for a sandwich or a cup of coffee. I never want to see that day happen. I hope Dillard's, Macy's and the few remaining department stores don't meet the fate of Sears, Nordstrom's, Brooks Brothers, Century 21, and other retailers that bombed because of COVID and on-line competition. I'd miss the store and its employees. I'd also be sad that another piece of America died and was buried. If the Chandler mall goes, so shall our store. How can we let that happen?

I'm older now, in my early seventies, and dealing with issues from aging and the lingering effects from the accident. I'll continue as a shelter volunteer as long as I'm able to. Going to the mall store is as helpful to me as it is for the animals. There were days over the past years when I wanted to give up. The cruelty, the endless euthanasia of healthy pets and the appalling indifference to their suffering sometimes overwhelmed me and I swore I'd never go back. I always did. I'm so glad the accident on 1/6/94 didn't end it all because look what I've have missed out on. My pocketbook became poorer, but my heart became richer because of unwanted dogs and cats and the people who care for them.

Whatever It Takes

Deborah Blenkhorn

It's Thanksgiving at Auntie and Uncle's house. Let's all go around the table and say what we're thankful for. I'm on the periphery of a family group—the poor relation in more ways than one. "The wine," I say when it's my turn, and I mean it. I'm thinking, when and where and how can I get some more of this here Balm of Gilead. I'm thinking, whatever it takes.

Friday nights it's all the same, week in week out. Get depressed and fed up at home. Might as well be a piece of furniture. Well, not even. I meet my friend Dirk for our usual ritual: we fight, we make up, we have dinner. Is the fight over yet, I ask? Can we skip the making up and go straight to dinner? You know I'm on a budget here. Not just money, man—time. Teaching tomorrow morning—Saturday morning—ain't that a crime? Shake me out of this malaise, I'm drowning.

Took the depression quiz on the internet the other day—scored 61. If you score over 54, it's bad. See a doctor, they say.

Well, I've done that. Five years of therapy, what do I have to show for it? Well, heck, let's not pursue that line of questioning: Six years of so-called higher education—what do I have to show for it?

Oh, we're in such dangerous territory now, a Congo of the mind. I swore I'd never write about my present life. It only serves as a harbinger of the past. But I think I may be able to save myself this way, and man do I need saving. I can't see through the forest now, I just look at my feet in front of me, dimly aware that there may be a path down there somewhere. I think of all the first-year students I'm trying to help write their way out of a wet paper bag. I think of myself as disconnected from all but them, and this is dangerous.

Especially at Auntie and Uncle's (well really they are cousins once removed, once removed, infinitely removed)... I am grateful to be here, yet unable to stop myself from being jealous of their circle. I tell my students that the essence of tragedy is this: it's over. Life cannot give forth to life; there are no future generations.

And no baby for me. Everybody else in this world has a child. Well no, I know that's not true.

But imagine living in Auntie's world, where each of your three sons, raised expertly by you and your loving and competent provider-spouse, marries a lovely girl, settles close by, and—miracle of miracles—reproduces yet another generation of kids for your family. I cannot imagine it—I cannot imagine what it takes to carn this, to have this. I have only a vague sense of why I will never be a daughter or a mother in such a family.

I'm happy only in isolated moments—walking with my sad and dear and recently separated friend Ailsa through the woods of the University Endowment Lands, running along the seawall with the vibrant Julia and my personal Madonna, my muse, my Emily. The rest of the time I think, what is the goddamn point? Oh no, we definitely do not want to head down this path. We will end up not in the present but in the past; I will be that strange little person to whom my Nana Hamm pronounces those fateful words: "I think you're a very selfish little girl."

Yes, I am, I think: Nana was right. Even now, as we speak, I'm writing all this crap for a very selfish reason: I pray it may save my soul. I don't really even know the source of my current pain; it would be so easy to blame it on someone else. The truth is I feel I'm a lonely, depressed and pathetic person (as I try to type that word, "apathetic" and "atheist" sprout from my word processor). Really, the present time sucks. Maybe it would do me good to return to a moment in the past.

I'm thinking, Music Camp, Mount Allison University— I'm maybe 13 years old. Young. Feelings I remember: singing the Hallelujah chorus with a hundred other kids, tears of joy and wonder in my eyes; running up a hill en route to a guitar class I was late for—the incredible feeling of physical exaltation I wish I'd ever felt since; swans in the pond; chatty meals with my cousin Callie in the cafeteria, where a jolly chef presided over Mount A's summer suppers.

Gone, all gone. Why bother remembering? Why bother doing anything? Earlier today, resting my head on the top of the coffee pot (of all places), I had this conscious thought: "I wish I were…"

Subjunctive mood.

Well, that was before going over to Auntie's. I think this Thanksgiving dinner with its numerous glasses of wine enabled me to envision a future (albeit a fictitious one) in which I could renew some ancient ties. I can go back as far as I need to, to find those links, the ties that bind me to a family in which I may or may not truly belong. I now realize the true reason for my not going back East this summer: no one invited me. Well, maybe they shouldn't have to. But honestly, how am I to know where and if I'm welcome? I don't just know it—I can't just announce, I'm coming on x date for y amount of time. I just cannot bring myself to do it.

The only place in the world that I know for a fact is mine—pretty ironic, since technically I guess it belongs to the bank—is this condo. Well, really, what is a condo except an apartment that you own? The unbaby unspirit in my barren womb is saying, "That's no kind of place for a baby! A baby needs a house!"

Sorry, baby. I can't even afford this dump, such as it is—I can't seem to keep afloat financially, emotionally, physically, spiritually. It's all sinking, washing inevitably, inexorably down the toilet—leaving skid marks on the bowl.

I think of the cozy house where my paternal grandparents lived in Sackville, New Brunswick; my maternal Nana's pleasant home; the family cottages on the Northumberland shore. Never to be seen again! Oh, I feel that so strongly; I feel it in my bones, like a deep, dark, ache of loneliness and despair. I feel something rotting inside of me—a pungent mass of unexcreted venom.

I see myself as I believe others must see me: straggly hair, pock-marked skin, clothes that never go together, some vague and vain attempt to make up my parched and excoriated face. I look in the mirror and see a shadow of the sunny girl pictured in old photographs, when I knew no better than to venture off to Morton Cove, New Brunswick, confident of my welcome from whoever might be there.

I know the vicious cycle of depression: I can't open up to anyone to heal these wounds; I can only try to placate myself as I struggle through each day. Anything that happens from now on will be too little, too late. I see the bottom of the world—I see the tortured creatures writhing in pain down here—I see my own pallid reflection. I see the apparition of one hand reaching down to drag me up, and baby, you know it's yours.

Laughing in a restaurant the night before with a friend, in the dim light, I make little of my pain; sitting around that festive family table, I hardly know what to think or how to act. It is the blessing of the wine that releases me—I'm suddenly OK with all this, suddenly able to make conversation with all and sundry. What a cute baby! Now how many months old is he now? And his habits? And his daily routine? And where is last summer's photo album? Now who are these people here? And how are they related to whom? How very interesting!

More brandy.

The screensaver on my husband's computer looks like little helmets of little baby space invaders.

Oh, do we not have anything to DRINK in this house? It's a metaphor of course—there's nothing here to sustain me, nothing here I want or need. Or maybe just the opposite—I don't really want what I think I want, don't really need what I think I need. That damn booze would just make me sick, eventually, wouldn't it?

What would it take?

But this is a day on which we are supposed to be grateful for what we have. Here's a list:

Bad hair.

1 and 2/3 jobs.

3.

Oh fuck it!

At what point—if ever—do people finally say: "Enough!" ?

Will I ever get to that point? Am I already there? Yes, you know, I think I am. From now on, I am just surviving. I see that no help is forthcoming. I see that I was foolish to expect it.

My mother called today to tell us how she was doing.

My father asked me if I had bought a ticket back east for him yet.

Well, whatever.

The Next Day.

I wake up at 11:00—unheard of for me. Could have been the wine...My husband brings me coffee in bed—OK, I must be sicker than I realize. He must, finally, be worried. I flash back to the Thanksgiving dinner table yesterday: each of us going around the table saying what we're thankful for. He says he's grateful to me for the opportunity of going back to school. Hallelujah, I think.

Every Thanksgiving is a milestone, every family dinner a moment in time that brooks no argument. This is what it is, as is my life. After dinner, we went across the street to the park; while the children (none of them mine, as I am the barren one who makes all the other women at the table grateful for their children) play on the swings, in the sand, in the jungle gym in the deepening childhood. My cousin-in-law Syl and I sit on a bench, talking about the hermeneutic process of writing down our lives. Let's form a writing group, I suggest: I'm trying to create some part of this family in which I'm not on the periphery. She's surprised, tentative, but basically in agreement that this might be a good idea.

Does Syl understand me? She sees me as a survivor of a strange childhood—a bleak era in which not one but both of my parents decided they weren't up to or into raising me. Oh what a self-pitying comment, Nana Hamm would say. But Syl understands. She looks at her two little boys; she knows she'd never leave them to another's care.

What do you write about, Syl?

Well, back to today. I guess I want to recapture that feeling of yesterday, and to imprint my own pattern on this festive (ha!) weekend. Is it too late to begin thawing the small turkey I bought last week, I ask? We look up the instructions in Nana's old *Good Housekeeeping* cookbook—it's just within the realm of possibility that my harebrained scheme may work out. Into cold water in the sink goes the "Young Turkey," a sacrifice to my needs and mood.

It's thawing as we speak.

But that's not all—I make mashed potatoes to heat and serve later, bread (in the bread machine) for the stuffing, fruited cranberry sauce, rice pudding for dessert, muffins for mid-afternoon tea. I do three loads of laundry, take the dog for a walk, and do the dishes.

My dear friend Emily has invited me to the gym, but I've declined. You can't fight a cold and build up your abs (and whatever) at the same time. "Do you have a good book to read?" she asks. She knows me so well.

I've left a message for my best frenemy Dirk, who's at his parents' home in Tsawassen, having a turkey dinner, his own Waterloo. Is his car fixed? Are we having lunch tomorrow (no pre-fighting necessary on Tuesdays)? Does he want to run after school with me and the girls? Really all of those questions are just excuses to reach out to a lifeline. I know I have to learn to save myself, as he never tires of telling me.

On the walk with the dog—a longer one than usual: it's a ritual to go for a Thanksgiving walk, after all—I satisfy my curiosity to see the house where Ernie (formerly[?] of Ernie and Ailsa) is staying during their trial separation. Ailsa took me out for dinner on Saturday night, to a Mexican restaurant within easy walking distance for us both.

This has been her first week of life as a single mom— she tells me about the day he moved out. He's got the kids for part of the weekend, so she's free to go out to dinner with a friend, unencumbered for a change. I remember another friend telling me how hard her first weekend alone was, when the girls (my cousins) had gone to see their father. When Ailsa called me to ask me out for dinner, I knew it was important to say yes.

Why not? Actually, there was a reason: such a pathetic one, really. My husband and I had planned a "marital harmony" evening, a date, whatever you want to call it. But he was more than willing to change the plans, so I guess I should be grateful for such flexibility.

As far as I could tell, Saturday was ovulation day (maybe—or maybe I missed it as usual, or maybe that's not the problem). I didn't tell him this, of course. He does not want to be complicit in the planning of something that he feels it would be better to wait for. Until we're more financially secure, etc. etc. I tell you, my biological clock is running down and out right now, man. So I seduced him on Saturday afternoon, a miracle of sorts in its own way—we'll see if anything comes of it. I have my doubts. It's not much of a chance, believe me, and it seems less likely every month as I confront the dark red stain of my moral, physical failure at the one human task that supersedes all others in importance.

I hate being the one who doesn't belong. Not really part of the family, just a distant cousin; not really a woman, just a barren failure, a hollow shell. The more time that goes by, the less I feel entitled to anything, anyway. The more I care.

And meanwhile, I pour out this vitriol on paper (my new resolution)—so I won't have to let it poison my interactions with others. It's a Dorian Gray kind of thing. I'll still be reasonably pleasant in the self I present to the world, while this hideous misshapen manuscript festers and grows to its deadly fruition in the blood-darkened womb of my mind.

It's what I can do to survive each week—a project for the Sundays and Mondays that depress rather than relax me. It's better and cheaper than becoming an alcoholic.

I just need something to keep me from drowning right

now.

I must stay afloat on this ocean and pay the ferryman his due.

I must stay afloat. Whatever it takes.

Listening to Schubert in the Spring

Matias Travieso-Diaz

*To pass through this brief life as nature demands. To give it up
without complaint.
Like an olive that ripens and falls. Praising its mother,
thanking the tree it grew on.*
Marcus Aurelius, Meditations, 4.48.

I sat at my favorite spot on the porch one spring morning,
watching the sun paint golden stripes on the trees and amusing
myself with the chattering of the wild birds as they fought for
seeds from the feeder. Suddenly, I was assaulted by a disquieting
thought: how many more spring days like this remained for me?

I was not feeling particularly sickly—nothing beyond
the usual creaks and pains of an eighty-year-plus body—but
nonetheless I was seized by a growing sense of doom. Not too
many spring days in store for me, I told myself.

I retired upstairs, sat at my desk, and turned on the

music of Franz Schubert, which appeared most appropriate to my state of mind. Schubert wrote several profound works in the last year of his short life, presaging his premature death. I directed my attention to my favorite among Schubert's late compositions, the Quintet in C for Strings (D. 956).

The Quintet contains a slow second movement that describes, more accurately than any writings can depict, the coming to terms with the end of life: the painful realization that death is near, the fruitless agony of rebelling against fate, the struggle to cope with the inevitable, the regret of abandoning the world of the living, and the ultimate reconciliation with one's forthcoming departure. Throughout the movement, the first violin and the cello engage in a dialogue that is at times an argument, others a joint outcry of anguish and pain, but is always filled with deep emotion.

I was listening to that Quintet and my mind turned again to the realization that it was almost time for me to let go. The joys and passions, the tears, the disappointments of living would soon recede as I approached the portal that can only be crossed once. I needed to prepare for that moment. But how?

The first order of business was balancing my books. Were there any outstanding wrongs that I needed to remedy? Had I failed to give enough attention to the needs of my friends and relatives, to the country that had welcomed me and was going through a difficult time? I made a couple of mental notes of things I could and perhaps should do, but none were too difficult or extraordinary. If I did not get any of them done, the world would not be much worse for the failure.

How about pleasurable activities that I should undertake while there was still time? "Bucket list" items that remained undone? I could think of a few, like taking a Mediterranean cruise or seeing the Pyramids. However, the death of my wife a few years earlier had left a void that could not be filled with sensory experiences, particularly solitary ones. I would have to leave riding on a camel to others, and perhaps would not regret too much missing it.

As for personal accomplishments, I had worked hard throughout my life and written a few stories and a novel or two, but all my deeds would be forgotten soon after I was gone, if not before. I would probably achieve the complete obscurity that rewards almost every human being since our species began walking on two feet. I would soon cease to exist in the memories of all but perhaps my daughter and a couple of others, and again the world would not be much worse for it.

Near the end of the second movement of Schubert's Quintet, the musical struggle comes to an end and there is a momentary stillness, as if the composer was making up his mind. The quiet is followed by a song of acceptance, neither happy nor sad. The violin's dialogue with the cello now reveals a sense of giving in, consenting to proceed to where one must go. There should be serenity in the face of death, the composer tells us.

And, listening to Schubert's final statement, I realized that I needed not fear death. Instead, I should be grateful for the opportunity of experiencing the miracle of life and, if it turned out that I had made even a minimal contribution to the betterment of the world, that would have been just fine.

FICTION

A Cat Sanctuary Story

Emecheta Christian

I never expected enlightenment in a cat sanctuary, but that's exactly where I met Aufgabe. We often say funny things behind his back, though nobody dared say them to his face. Not that it would have ruffled him—nothing ever did.

I remember the first time I saw him. His head looked glossy under the LED lights of our industrial-chic lobby, and a few strands of silver-dyed hair artfully gelled at his nape. He was pushing a mop across our polished concrete floors with the focus of a Zen master painting calligraphy.

"Hey there! I'm Sage Unix," I called out, my platform Doc Martens clicking against the floor as I approached. "I'm the Development Director. Are you one of our new volunteers?"

He flicked his wrist, sending a shower of cat hair dancing in the morning light; they streamed through the floor to the ceiling and windows. "I am Aufgabe Hank. A fresh start, a fresh day. Nice meeting you, Sage." His voice carried the kind of gravelly wisdom you'd expect from someone who'd seen every corner of the world.

I launched into my usual spiel—the one I could recite in my sleep after five years at Purrs & Purpose, Portland's premier cage-free cat sanctuary. "We're stoked to have you join our family!"

Aufgabe winked at me, but not in that creepy way older men sometimes do. It was more like a Buddhist monk acknowledging a fellow seeker. "I love being here already, it's all vibes," he said—turning back to his mop.

A calico cat with an attitude problem—we called her Queen Victoria—watched him from her perch on our vintage reception desk, her tail twitching with calculated indifference.

"Found any favorites yet?" I gestured toward Her Majesty.

"Today is my favorite," he replied, his back already turned. I'd been filed away in whatever minimalist mental storage system he operated on.

Later, I cornered Lora, our Volunteer Coordinator, in the break room. She was heating some vegan ramen while winding through TikTok. "What's the tea on the new guy?"

"Aufgabe?" She looked up, her purple hair catching the bright light. "Word is he was some big tech executive. Maybe Google or Meta? But like, he just ghosted corporate life one day. Total main character energy."

"He's giving wise sage NPC vibes," I said, watching through the window as he hauled industrial-sized litter boxes like they were made of cardboard. "But make it philosophical."

Lora snorted. "Zara's probably going to think he's either totally Zen or completely unhinged."

Zara, our founder, had built this sanctuary from crypto gains and pure determination after a single rescue cat changed her whole perspective on life. She'd cashed out her Bitcoin at just the right moment, turning her meme coin fortune into a haven for cats that other shelters had given up on.

Our setup was like a luxury cat hotel meets bohemian coffee shop, complete with "cat suites" featuring custom cat trees and LED mood lighting. Every day was a hustle to keep it running—me chasing donations through Instagram and TikTok, Lora recruiting an army of cat-obsessed volunteers through her viral social media posts.

And now we had Aufgabe.

When tornado warnings lit up our phones, Aufgabe mopped. When half our volunteer team called out with the latest COVID variant, Aufgabe continued to mop. While you tried to decode his existence, Aufgabe just... mopped.

"Morning, Aufgabe!" I called out one day, my vintage golden necklace reflecting the light.

"Radiant Sage, good morning." He didn't need to look up anymore; he'd become part of the sanctuary's DNA.

"How's your Thursday energy?"

"Phenomenal."

The answer never changed, but somehow it felt like a different revelation every time.

"Everything in alignment?"

"There are no bad days," he said, his mop moving in perfect rhythm, "only moments that haven't revealed their purpose yet." Left, right, left, right. I could never decide if his mopping was more like tai chi or experimental dance—each stroke was either perfectly calculated or completely improvised.

The cats treated him like their guru. Even as they wrinkled their noses at his industrial-strength cleaning solution (he believed in maximum sanitation), they followed him around like disciples. I kept asking him questions, even when I knew his answers would be more like cosmic riddles than actual information.

"So, what was your life before becoming our resident mystic?"

"Radiant Sage, I'm just a guy with a mop. Had my time in the matrix until I took the red pill." Left, right, left, right. A three-legged tabby named Trinity rolled over at his feet like she was receiving an anointing. "The universe called. I answered."

Aufgabe asked fewer questions than in your average influencer's comment section, but when my attempts to decipher his outlook made me ramble, he listened with the intensity of someone decoding ancient texts. He didn't do the active listening head-tilt thing they teach in corporate workshops. He just absorbed everything while continuing his eternal routine with the mop.

"Morning, Aufgabe! Friday serving the right aesthetic?"

"Phenomenal."

"Your vibe check always makes my day better."

"You've got good energy, Radiant Sage." His mop never stopped moving.

"Not everyone appreciates the positive wavelength." I fidgeted with my crystal bracelet, feeling suddenly exposed.

"No?" Left, right, left, right.

"The world's kind of toxic toward genuinely optimistic people." I adjusted my oversized vintage denim jacket. "Main character syndrome, they call it."

"That so?"

"You know—people who care too much. Animal people. Plant parents. Crystal girlies. But we move forward anyway, right?"

"I just channel my authentic self." Left, right, left, right, paying no mind to the tuxedo cat doing yoga poses before him. "Other people's algorithms aren't my concern. Never were."

Lora and I gave Aufgabe space when his replies drifted into cryptic territory, but Zara was determined to crack his code.

She'd share her findings during our weekly team meetings, like someone piecing together an ARG.

"Aufgabe claims he's been everywhere except South Sudan and mainland China," Zara announced, her green tea kombucha forgotten. "Sounds cap, but he's the most genuine person I've ever met. I need to know more."

Zara questioned everyone. During my interview last year, she'd gone full detective mode about my background. "A degree in Consciousness Studies from Naroda University? Is that even real, or did you manifest it through TikTok manifestation techniques?"

"It's legit," I'd said, cradling a one-eyed kitten named Blinken.

"And why should I trust a burnt-out spiritual influencer to raise money for traumatized cats?"

I was twenty-five and running on pure audacity, powered by the presence of Blinken purring in my arms. "Well, the universe has a way of connecting kindred spirits. Also, I have 50K followers on Instagram."

My official welcome email was addressed to "Sage, Digital Priestess of the Feline Faith."

Aufgabe's daily "phenomenal" was rewiring my spiritual operating system. Like a cat carefully kneading a favorite blanket, his Zen koans slowly transformed my relationship with reality.

Finally, I had to dig deeper.

"Morning, Aufgabe! How's Mercury retrograde treating you?"

"Phenomenal."

"You showed up despite the black ice warning."

"Nature's putting on a light show out there. Sacred geometry in every icicle. What's the worst that could happen?" Left, right, left, right.

"Could be a rough day if you hit a patch wrong."

"There are no rough days, only moments asking for a perspective shift." Classic Aufgabe.

I watched his mop head, looking like some kind of working-class performance art. "Aufgabe, I need to ask you something."

"Mm?"

"Your energy... it's like a daily reset button for my soul. Are you on a spiritual path?"

For once, he paused. He retreated to a corner where Queen Victoria held court, paying no mind to our collective coughing fit from his industrial-strength cleaning solution.

"Everyone's on a spiritual path," he finally said. Left, right, left, right. "But I don't do labels or organized disco fiascos."

"I can't picture you doing group meditation sessions."

"These hands stay busy. But word is you've got some history with the metaphysical realm."

How did he know about my past life as a crystal shop owner? "History and mystery," I channeled his energy. "Pretty deconstructed these days, but... yeah, it's part of why I'm here."

"You're exactly where you need to be." Aufgabe never broke his rhythm. "Radiant. Authentic."

I didn't tell my partner Morgan much about Aufgabe. Years of being called "woo-woo" had taught me to protect the mystics and misfits in my life from skeptical energy.

But for some reason, I mentioned that Aufgabe called me authentic.

"Who is this guy anyway?" Morgan's fingers never left their retro keyboard, the click-clack of their gaming session creating a wall between us.

"He maintains the sanctuary's immaculate vibes. We exchange morning blessings."

"Authentic Sage." Morgan's avatar died on screen. "Well, at least there's another stellar person at your cat commune. It's giving cult energy though."

Morgan had never vibed with my work or my friends— "all those crystal-hoarding plant moms with their emotional support cats." They warned me about getting canceled as a spiritual nerd. They regularly reminded me that "when we need to level up our income, you'll have to touch grass and join the corporate NPCs."

I kept my spiritual awakening journal hidden under a stack of tarot cards.

"Happy Monday, bestie!" I called out, my rose quartz pendant catching the morning light.

"Every Monday's a gift." He stopped mopping—an unprecedented event that made Queen Victoria sit up straight. "Got a sec for this elderly millennial?"

"Only if you're about to drop some life-changing wisdom."

Aufgabe met my eyes for the first time. They were jade green, like ancient Chinese carvings. "Give me a minute."

He propped his mop against the wall (Queen Victoria immediately began inspecting it) and disappeared into Zara's office, leaving me standing there like a glitching game character.

"I curated these for your journey." He returned with an armful of worn books; their spines cracked with experience.

"What are..." he cut me off.

"Ever heard of the Camino?"

"That viral hiking challenge on TikTok?"

"OG version. Ancient pilgrimage through Spain and France. I've walked it six times." He extended the stack. "It's calling you."

"I don't think I can just..."

"You're being called to level up. You'll meet your

115

soul tribe. You'll download wisdom you didn't know you needed." He retrieved his mop, breaking our longest-ever eye conversation. "The cats will evolve, too. Trust the process."

I stashed the books in my thrifted Fjällräven backpack and scrolled through Camino hashtags on TikTok. Later, I floated the idea of a six-week sabbatical to Zara.

"You could run our socials from Mars—I'm not stressed. Just don't come back with a lifestyle brand called 'Wanderlust Witch' or something."

"Zero risk of that."

The sanctuary's TikTok was popping off that fall, and Zara thought the time was right for a major crowdfunding campaign.

Morgan barely looked up from their Discord chat when I mentioned it. "Going viral?"

"Zara thinks we can manifest this." I didn't mention my growing playlist of Camino vlogs.

"Don't let your anxiety write checks your bandwidth can't cash."

"I won't." I kept my Pinterest board of hiking gear private.

The rumor mill said Aufgabe had serious crypto gains— "probably an early Bitcoin adopter," Lora had revealed over oat milk lattes; "a low-key billionaire." I felt strangely aligned asking him to support our campaign. I shouldn't have mentioned it to Morgan.

"The mysterious janitor is secretly Satoshi Nakamoto?" Their Discord friends laughed through the headset.

"Based on my research and social listening."

"Careful, dear. You might scare off your only work friend. Are you trying to get your spiritual advisor to tell you his most cherished secret?"

I scanned Morgan's friend count; mostly gaming

buddies they'd never met in real life and the real world they called "toxic." Their social circle was giving empty lobby energy. The person warning me about losing connections had none.

I guess Morgan has turned out to be a major red flag.

He jumped up and started fake-mopping energetically in my presence, complete with TikTok dance moves. His cyber friends joined in on the drama, their voices went full cringe as they mimicked me:

"Good morning, bestie! What's the tea?"

"Morning, Aufgabe! How are you?"

I tried to maintain my peace, but the mock convo continued.

"Living my best life, queen! What can I do for you today?"

Morgan's performance was very embarrassing and funny to watch.

"I wanted to discuss our crowdfunding campaign..."

Morgan's face twisted into something between a YouTuber thumbnail and a cursed emoji. "Sorry bestie, I have already donated my funds to this place. Take that main character energy somewhere else."

I was annoyed because the actual conversation with Aufgabe usually went differently. Very differently.

The next morning, I found Aufgabe in his usual spot, but something was different. Queen Victoria wasn't just watching—she was walking beside him, matching his rhythm perfectly.

"Phenomenal morning," I said, trying to channel his energy.

He smiled, actually smiled. "Ready for your quest?"

I took a deep breath. "I ended things with my boyfriend last night. He called my work here a 'cat cult' one too many times. Said I was living in a spiritual fantasy world."

"Letting go creates space for growth." Left, right, left, right. He continued mopping "Like these floors—got to sweep away the old to welcome the new."

"About the fundraising campaign—" I started.

"Already done." He reached into his pocket and pulled out a worn leather wallet. Instead of cash or cards, he extracted a small piece of paper. "Your plane ticket to Spain. The Camino awaits."

I stared at the ticket, my hands trembling. "Aufgabe, I can't—"

"The sanctuary's covered for the next year." He never stopped mopping. "Made some calls to my old tech friends. Turns out they love cats, too. Funny how the universe works."

"But why?"

"Because you're ready." He gestured toward Queen Victoria, who was now curled up in a patch of sunlight. "Even Her Majesty knows it. Sometimes the greatest act of service is letting yourself be transformed."

Zara burst through the doors, her eyes wild with excitement. "Sage! The donations—they're insane! Some anonymous donor just matched our entire yearly goal!"

I looked at Aufgabe, but he was focused on his mopping, humming softly to himself.

—

Three months later, I stood on a hill overlooking Santiago de Compostela, my hiking boots worn and my spirit soaring. My TikTok series "Camino Cats" had gone viral—turns out people love watching pilgrims rescue strays along lonely dirt paths. Each episode ended with an affirmation, followed by a short clip of different cats I met along the way.

My last video call with Zara had been full of news. The sanctuary had expanded, adding a "Zen Garden" where visitors could meditate with the cats. Queen Victoria had appointed herself head meditation guide. Funny, right?

"And Aufgabe?" I'd asked.

"Real thing," Zara said, adjusting her camera. "The day after you left, he handed me his mop and said his work here was done. But he left something for you."

Back home, I found a small package waiting. Inside was a single cat toy—a miniature mop—and a note written in perfect calligraphy:

"The greatest enlightenment comes not from seeking wisdom, but from being exactly who you are. Keep mopping, Radiant Sage. - A.H."

I hung the toy mop in my office at the sanctuary, where I now serve as Director of Spiritual Wellness. Every morning, I exchange knowing looks with Queen Victoria as she conducts her meditation circles. Sometimes, when the light hits just right, I swear I can see Aufgabe's reflection in the polished concrete floors, still moving in that perfect rhythm—left, right, left, right—reminding me that every day is, indeed, phenomenal.

And somewhere in my feelings, I know he's still mopping, still teaching, still appearing exactly when and where he's needed most. Isn't that what spiritual guides do? They might come disguised as janitors with a mastery of cleaning while dispersing cryptic wisdom.

Aufgabe taught me something powerful about enlightenment—it doesn't have to always arrive in the package we expect. Sometimes it comes with a mop, cryptic responses, a one-way ticket to Spain, and a cat named Queen Victoria who knew the truth all along.

Phenomenal, isn't it?

The Shaman

Krin Van Tatenhove

Those who do not want to lose their blindfolds for fear of the light, deserve the dark.
– Quechan proverb

Cusco, Peru

Not far now!" shouted my daughter, Jessie, from the front of the line.

Eight of us, a motley crew, were hiking along a train track. It took us 20 hours by bus to get there from Lima, leaning back and forth through endless switchbacks into the Andes. Now, just before sunset, the rails glinted in the fading light. The guy in front of me, a nomad from Australia, was merrily humming a tune I'd never heard, matching its cadence to his feet crunching the gravel. Further up the line, a couple from

Arizona lit a joint, the funky sweetness wafting over our heads.

I inhaled the crisp mountain air and chuckled. Whenever I traveled with Jessie, it was bound to stretch my comfort zone. She's the freest spirit I've ever known, a world citizen, at home in whatever exotic locale she chooses. She had successfully monetized her escapades through YouTube and a podcast, calling them *Wander and Wonder*, so now she was unfettered, roaming at will, needing only her iPhone, laptop, and a Wi-Fi connection. And how can I describe the companions she draws to these treks? Bohemians? Naturalists? Alternative outliers? Take your pick, but I always find them enjoyable.

On that night, she was guiding us to the home of a modern-day shaman, a man named Jorge Vega she had discovered through her network. He had agreed to let her feature him for one of her online episodes.

Vega's story intrigued me, especially since I'm a professor at a liberal arts college. Educated at Harvard, he returned to his homeland of Peru to teach economics at the University of Lima. He had always aligned himself with leftist politics, but the crucible of the Peruvian Teacher's Strike in 2017 radicalized him further. He vehemently voiced his opposition to President Pedro Pablo Kuczynski's right-wing government and began to encourage activism among his students. The school's administration objected, then attempted to censor him, so he made a dramatic decision, resigning from academia to live among the poor in Cusco. There, he married a local woman, a community organizer in her own right, and the two of them worked tirelessly to strengthen farmers' collectives.

That portion of his life's arc was remarkable enough, but Vega had another incarnation. He had studied shamanic practices with a Quechan elder and now, alongside his organizing efforts, he offered spiritual guidance. From what Jessie had told me, it was an odd departure, something Vega's family and friends never expected.

Jessie planned to dig into all of it, and was thrilled that he would participate. She had been generating online buzz for a month. I asked to accompany her because I was curious to meet Vega, but also because a visit to Machu Picchu was on my bucket list.

I heard Jessie say "this way" as she led us onto a side street that ascended one of the hills surrounding the city. Cusco's economy thrives on tourism, but the money only spreads so far. A third of its residents live in poverty, and this *colonia* was visible proof. The dirt street was lined on both sides with humble adobe homes, most of them covered with chipped whitewash. The dwellings seemed half-finished, their roofs studded with rebar, as if this was a temporary settlement. Twilight grew deeper and I could hear chickens clucking from backyards as they prepared to roost.

Jessie paused at a red wooden door, barely visible, then turned to the rest of us. "Stay back a bit and let me speak to him. I wasn't sure how many of us there would be and I don't want to impose."

She knocked and the door opened promptly, interior light spilling onto the street. A thin man of medium height emerged. He had dark hair, a lean face, and was wearing simple slacks, shoes, and a black shirt. Wrapped around his shoulders was a colorful shawl, which I knew was called a *manta*. Woven into its rich alpaca fabric were totemic images of animals and geometric forms.

Jessie is fluent in Spanish, and I could hear them conversing. Vega turned and let his gaze sweep over our crew, his face lighting up with a smile.

"Bienvenidos," he called, gesturing for us to come inside. Then, in flawless English, "You are always welcome here."

—

Vega's home had two rooms. The larger one contained a kitchen, sleeping area, and a dining table. The other was bare and unfurnished, with traditional blankets and sleeping pads piled along the walls. Overhead was a skylight, a break in the thatch and tile that covered the roof, and I could stars beginning to poke through the darkness. Vega told us we could use as much of the bedding as we wished for padding or extra warmth.

Dinner was delicious, and somehow, we were all able to fit around the table. Vega's wife, Killa—Quechan for moon—was short, thin, dressed in traditional garb, with bright eyes and a quick smile. She was also a skilled chef. Our fare was *pachamanca*, a traditional Andean dish of meat, vegetables, and local herbs, cooked underground in an earth oven. Its heady aroma filled the room, sluicing my salivary glands. Killa served it with a choice of strong Yerba Mate tea or *chicha de jora*, the fermented corn drink of Quechan culture.

For most of the meal, we engaged in small talk, but near the end, Vega asked for our attention.

"I understand that Jessie has given you the highlights of my story. If it is agreeable with all of you, will you take turns giving some background on who you are and where you come from? I would like to hear *your* stories."

Again, I was struck by his impeccable mastery of English, not surprising for a Harvard grad. He had an ease and charisma, holding court the way I imagined he had done countless times in his classrooms. His presence wrapped its arms around all of us. We readily nodded and began.

Noah, the young man from Australia, was taking a gap year to travel before medical school. After Peru, he planned to spend time in Patagonia.

The couple from Arizona—Michelle and Kevin—ran a

string of successful Airbnbs in Sedona and Scottsdale, spending much of their time trekking the globe. They were ardent fans of Jessie's YouTube channel and podcasts.

Jen and Emily, two friends from Scotland, had hooked up with Jessie online. They were in their mid-20s, bubbly and gregarious, also on extended travels before the next chapters of their lives.

C.J. was more of an enigma. A man in his mid-40s, he had a dark beard, long curly hair, and the physique of a wrestler. During our entire trip, he had been preternaturally silent. When we attempted conversation, he was polite but left such huge gaps in responding that it was clear he preferred quietude. Now, he surprised us, telling how he had left his home in Massachusetts after his wife died prematurely, intent on traveling to some of the places they had always discussed. Machu Pichu was one of them.

Finally, it was my turn, so I gave the condensed version of my teaching career, my love for Jessie's mother, Ellen, and the ways that both of us stayed connected to the daughter that gave us such pride.

When I was finished, Vega asked, "Are you a Christian?"

The question was so out-of-the-blue, so abrupt, that I was taken aback, even a bit defensive.

"Why do you ask?"

Vega caught my tone and body language. "I don't mean to be rude. It's just that I did a little research before this visit and saw that the college where you teach has a Christian heritage."

I paused, trying to get in sync with his intent. "No," I finally said, "I'm not a Christian. The institution's roots are barely visible today. It's not required to profess any faith to teach there. If it had been, I would have gone elsewhere."

Vega nodded. "Again, I don't mean be too bold. And I will not go into what Killa calls one of my tirades about how

Christianity in the Americas has so often colluded with power structures and worsened oppression."

Killa cleared her throat and rolled her eyes. It made Vega laugh.

"My wife keeps me in check. What I'm more interested in is a passage from the Christian New Testament. Perhaps you know it. It's when Jesus says that he comes to us in the disguise of the hungry, the thirsty, the naked, the sick, and the imprisoned."

"I'm familiar with it," I said. "Why does it interest you?"

"Because I'm a student of not only the spiritual traditions of my own people, but of those around the world. I know that many revered Catholic saints had their conversion experiences because they believed they had encountered Christ in disguise. I think of St. Martin of Tours, who had a vision of Jesus coming to him as a naked beggar. Martin cleaved his cloak with a sword and gave half to the poor man. Later, in another dream, he saw Jesus wearing the half he had given away."

"That's true," I said, warming to our unexpected discourse, something I craved with my colleagues. "Do those stories speak to you?"

"They do, but not because I'm Christian. It has to do with my own tradition. Have you ever heard of *apus*?

"No."

"In Incan mythology, they are the spirits that live in these mountains. It's believed they have the power to shapeshift and appear in many forms—coyotes, pumas, condors, even as humans. Their intent is usually to teach a lesson."

I nodded and said nothing. I looked around the table, expecting that we were boring the others to tears, but they were listening intently.

"In 2016, I had the most lucid dream of my life," Vega

continued. "A beggar came to me with an outstretched cup, asking for alms. His face was grizzled and he was dressed in rags. I reached into my pocket, withdrew a few coins, and gave them to him. He turned and started to walk away. Then he suddenly looked back at me, his face more youthful. He said in a very clear voice, 'What will you tell your students?'"

The memory was obviously emotional for Vega. He took a deep breath and settled back in his chair.

"That's trippy," said Noah. "Do you believe that was an *apu* visiting you?"

"I do," said Vegas, "and it changed me. Profoundly. People have always felt that what caused my departure from academia was my organizing and protesting for the teacher's strike. That was certainly part of it. But the seed planted in that dream by that *apu* is what ultimately drove me to be where I am this moment."

He looked down, as if the memory was still too powerful to fully absorb. His upper lip began to tremble. There was an awkward silence as we entered into his vulnerability.

"Kevin and I are firm believers that spirits communicate with us," said Michelle, as if to break the discomfort. "In the red rocks of Sedona, there are petroglyphs from the tribes that inhabited that area, and many of the images speak of the spirit world."

"In Scotland," said Jen, "there's the myth of the selkies who can shape shift from seals to women."

"And they often appear," added Emily, "to lead people on a spiritual quest to Tír na nÓg, the other world."

Jorge lifted his face, looked around the circle, then lowered his head again. The intensity of his emotion was palpable in the room. Killa suddenly stood from her place at the table and walked behind her husband. She placed her hands gently on his shoulders and kissed the top of his head. I could hear her whispering something to him in Quechan. He gathered her arms around his shoulders like a comforting blanket.

—

C.J. may have been quiet during the day, but he was a world-class snorer at night. Even with earplugs, I could hear him rumbling. I couldn't understand why it didn't awaken the others.

I was restless for other reasons. Vega's story had moved me in unexpected ways. He didn't seem to have an agenda, but was simply sharing a life-changing epiphany, one that had forever altered the course of his life.

I thought about my teaching and the tenure I'd recently received. I thought about my students, most of them from middle to upper middle-class families that could afford the steep tuition. They were usually good pupils from solid families, but they were clearly sheltered from the harsher realities of our world. While other college campuses experienced protests for various causes, ours might see a random sign or two.

Sometimes I felt iconoclastic, with an urge to puncture all that complacency and status quo, but frankly, I feared the administration would label me a radical. The ethos at the university was to guide learners into their own conclusions, not to use our lecterns as pulpits. I mostly agreed with that philosophy, and I calmed my rebellious urges by downplaying my influence. *I'm just a middle-aged professor*, I said to myself. *Who will really listen to me?*

But I couldn't quell my concerns about what was happening in America. The rise of Christian Nationalism. A demagogue as a president, arrogantly crashing through guardrails that protect democracy. The widening gap between the haves and have nots. Brazen oligarchy. The growing intolerance for immigrants. Rising prejudice towards those with various gender identities. And, as Jessie always pointed out, the unsustainable consumption that fueled global warming.

It was enough to cause despair, but again, what could I really do? I thought of some verses from T.S. Eliot's "The Love Song of J. Alfred Prufrock."

I am no prophet—and here's no great matter;
I have seen the moment of my greatness flicker,
And I have seen the eternal Footman hold my coat and snicker,
And in short, I was afraid.

Vega wouldn't hear that snickering. His conviction to follow his own star made me feel an unexpected twinge of shame. It spoke of a passion and drive I hadn't known for years.

As I tossed and turned with these thoughts, breathing in the earthy smell of the room, I heard a flapping of powerful wings and saw a shape pass over the skylight. I looked up to see a huge bird perched on the roof, its head a fleshy pink, its beak curved like a talon. It peered down at me for a moment, then took off, dissolving into the night sky like disappearing ink. The noise had awakened others.

"Dad," whispered Jesse from her sleeping mat. "Was that a condor?"

"It sure looked like it."

"But what the hell would it be doing here at this hour?" said C.J. "Condors aren't nocturnal."

"Sort of creepy," whispered Kevin.

"Especially after what Vega shared at dinner," said Michelle.

Even under two warm blankets, I felt goosebumps rise on my skin.

—

In the morning, Jessie spent two hours with Vega recording his journey. When we left, thanking them profusely for their hospitality, both Killa and Jorge hugged us. When Jorge embraced me, he held me longer than I expected.

"*Tupananchiskama*," he whispered into my ear. "It means 'until next time,' because I sense we will meet again."

Then he released me and held my eyes for a few seconds with his intense gaze and smile.

"The pleasure was all mine," I whispered, my voice a bit hoarse.

We left and made our way to Poroy Train Station for our trip to Aguas Calientes, the city known as the portal to Machu Picchu. We had booked tickets to the site for the next day as well as hotel rooms that overlooked the Urubamba River, only a 20-minute walk to the entrance of the sacred ruins. Our plan was to get up before dawn and hike there to experience the sunrise.

We spent the afternoon in the city, taking photos for each other in front of the statue of Pachacuti, the Incan emperor who oversaw the building of Machu Picchu. We went from there to the bustling Mercado de Aguas Calientes with its maze of stalls selling native foods and handcrafts. Since we all had different shopping agendas, we set a time to rendezvous back at the entrance, then went our separate ways.

The color and bustle of the market was intoxicating, especially the bright and intricate costumes of the women selling their wares. The air smelled of food dishes, fresh flowers, and the loamy aroma of potatoes, the staple of the Incan diet. I had never seen such a display of spuds—purple, green, yellow, red, orange, in a variety of shapes. I bought some dried coca leaves, chewing them the way locals do, letting the mild stimulant enhance my enjoyment of the scene. I sampled a couple empanadas and a tamale, washing them down with *chicha de jora.*

I was intent on finding a gift for Ellen, so when I saw a particular shawl, I knew it was perfect. I approached the older woman tending the stall. She was dressed in a *pollera* and *manta*, the traditional costume. My Spanish isn't great, but it's passable.

"Cuanto por esta manta?" I asked, pointing toward the prize I desired.

She looked up slowly with an amazing face bronzed by the sun and her lineage, her wrinkles speaking of vast experience. Her eyes were dark and penetrating, and they seemed to glint with an inner sense of humor. She gave me a price, we dickered a bit, and I handed her the money. She wrapped the *manta* in plain brown paper and presented it to me. I thanked her and began to walk away.

Then her voice called out to me from behind, "Señor!"

I turned around, wondering if I had shortchanged her. Her eyes were now dead serious.

"What will you tell your students?" she asked, speaking crisp English, her voice completely different from how it had sounded moments before.

A shiver ran up my spine. "What?" I exclaimed.

She just nodded, looked down, and began arranging some of her wares.

I was still tingling when I joined the others at the entrance.

—

The next morning, we hiked to the entrance of Machu Picchu. I hadn't told anyone about my surreal experience in the *mercado*, not even Jessie. I was wondering if I had imagined it, a byproduct of chewing coca leaves and drinking corn beer. All I knew was that the moment—fictitious or real—was an extension of how Vega's story had affected me. I was clearly out of my depth, both emotionally and psychologically.

Let me tell you something. No matter how many travel videos you see about Machu Picchu, there is nothing like visiting in person. When we walked through the portal and I saw those iconic remnants against a backdrop of clouds and Andean peaks, it took my breath away. I felt like we were entering a mystical city in a mythical realm, the impression heightened by the gradual light of dawn spreading over the landscape—a slow, dramatic reveal.

Jessie reached over and took my hand. "Amazing, isn't it?"

"Even more beautiful than I imagined."

Then she took her hand, gently gripped my chin, and turned my face towards her. "Are you all right, Dad? You've been unusually quiet since our visit to the *mercado* yesterday."

She had a raging intuition. I shifted my eyes, a dead giveaway.

"Something happened that I don't even know how to explain. Just give me some space and I'll get there. In fact, I'd like to just walk around on my own, if that's okay."

She searched my eyes again—my delightful, intuitive daughter, an old soul if there ever was one. "Of course, Dad. Let me know if you want to talk."

She kissed me on the cheek, let go of my hand, and we separated to absorb the wonders of that place.

I wandered among the ruins, savoring the mountain air. I climbed to the Guardian House and asked another traveler to snap the classic postcard picture, something I had promised Ellen. Then I hiked back down and continued to walk aimlessly, enjoying the many llamas that graze unmolested among the stone structures.

Some of my friends speak of thin places where the supposed veil between this world and the next is more permeable. I had always scoffed at the notion, but I felt it now with an edge of vertigo.

I found a low wall and sat in the sunlight, surveying the vista as cloud shadows shifted over the landscape. My eyes were drawn to a family walking by. They had a girl with them adorned in traditional garb. A severe cleft palate twisted the lower part of her face. They were almost out of sight when the girl turned and locked her eyes on mine intentionally. She lifted her right hand and pointed at me, nodding her head.

I suddenly heard a powerful flapping of wings as a huge condor landed on the stone wall near me. Like the girl, it turned its flesh-covered head and stared right into me. I rubbed my eyes and called out to another group of tourists passing by.

"Do you see that?" I exclaimed.

"See what?" they asked with tolerant smiles.

I turned back, but the great bird was gone. In my ears, I heard Vega whisper, "*Tupananchiskama*." I heard the Quechan woman ask, "What will you tell your students?"

I knew I would never be the same again, not in my perception of reality, or in how I would communicate to those in my classes. And at that moment, surrounded by the ruins of that timeless place, the thought filled me only with excitement.

The Great Chemistry Test Heist

John F. Miglio

All this happened back in 1965 when the Vietnam War was raging, and my high school pals and I were reading *MAD Magazine* and *The Catcher in the Rye* and rebelling against authority figures like our parents and teachers—especially our teachers. And one in particular, our chemistry teacher named Murray McSwain. Behind his back, everyone called him "Mary McSwine" because he was a classic momma's boy, complete with round shoulders, spare tire around the middle, and no girlfriend or wife. He was also kind of a personal slob who wore cheap suits with ridiculous looking ties that had food stains on them—not to mention the fact that he often had crumbs on his lips after lunch and a bad case of dandruff that stood out on the shoulders of his navy-blue sport jacket like a fresh snowfall on a black tarmac.

Unfortunately, his dorky and unkempt appearance did not prevent him from being a real task master in class and an all-around prick when it came to giving impossible tests that no one could pass—except for the smart kids who really cared about their grades and who actually paid attention to him and studied.

I wasn't one of those kids. Neither were my pals Tommy A. and Howie T., who sat next to me in chemistry class. We weren't dumb—I don't want to give you that impression. In fact, we were all kind of smart in our own ways, but we were just more interested in telling jokes and making each other laugh than listening to McSwine drone on about chemical formulas or the scientific importance of heating liquids on Bunsen burners.

The problem was, all three of us were flunking chemistry and the only way we could salvage our grades was by doing really well on the upcoming midterm, which we knew was impossible, even with crib notes. So, we had to figure something out, some way to do well on the test without actually studying for it. The time for that had long passed and the test was only two days away. What's more, all three of us were on the academic track and our parents were forever pressuring us to get good grades so that we could get into college. Our high school was this small suburban school outside Philadelphia that had a good reputation for academic rigor, but it was pretty clear none of us was going to Harvard or Yale; we were just hoping to do well enough to get admitted to Temple or Penn State.

I think it was Tommy A. who came up with the idea of stealing the test. Tommy A. was a very popular and enterprising guy who knew practically everybody. He was even friends with the school janitor who he would hang out with sometimes in the stock room, and they would do favors for each other. This is how Tommy A. knew the janitor was in possession of the keys to all the locks on the doors and cabinets in the classrooms, and he knew McSwine made up the tests in advance and locked them in a file cabinet that sat behind his desk next to the blackboard. The plan was to wait until everyone had left school for the day; Tommy A. would borrow the keys from the janitor, unlock McSwine's classroom door and file cabinet and remove one of the tests while Howie T. and I stood guard at the ends of the hallways. McSwine used the same test for several different classes, and he always made extras, so we figured he wouldn't notice one missing test.

The next day we put our plan into action, and it worked like a charm. And as soon as Tommy A. returned the keys to the janitor, we left school and went to Tommy A.'s house to look up the correct answers to the test. Even with the three of us pouring over our textbooks and notes, it took us a couple of hours to come up with all the right answers. Then we wrote down all the correct answers on small sheets of paper we called "cheat sheets,' and we were all set.

"You know it's going to look a little suspicious if everyone else in the class blows this test and the three of us get A's," I told the boys when we had finalized our cheat sheets.

"Yeah," Howie T. agreed. "McSwine's dumb, but he's not that dumb. He'll know something's up. And if we get caught, my parents'll kill me!" Poor Howie T. His parents were always going to kill him for something.

"Maybe we should just give the answers to everyone," I offered. "If everyone does well our high scores won't stand out."

A sly smile suddenly swept over Tommy A.'s face. "I got a better idea—we'll sell the cheat sheets. That'll kill two birds with one stone. Our high test scores won't look suspicious, and we'll make some money for our effort."

We all agreed it was a great plan. And since we were the ones who came up with the idea and took all the risks, why shouldn't we profit from it?

This was the question I posed to Peggy D., the girl I was

going out with at the time. I went to her house after I had left the boys and filled her in on our little caper. When I finished explaining it, she rolled her eyes and said, "Oh, brother! This is the dumbest idea I ever heard."

"C'mon, it's a good idea," I said. "And don't worry; I'll give you a cheat sheet for free."

"I don't want your stupid cheat sheet! I can get a good grade on my own."

She was right. She was one of the smart kids in our class who actually paid attention to McSwine and got straight A's on all his tests. In fact, she got straight A's in all her subjects, even Latin and geometry, two subjects I had zero interest in.

"This isn't going to work, you know," she continued to caution me. "You guys are going to get caught."

"How? How are we going to get caught?"

"I don't know, but you will. Besides, it's unethical."

"Is it ethical for McSwine to make his tests so hard that hardly anyone can pass them? He gets a kick out of it too, the bastard. I've seen him smirk when he hands out our bad grades."

She just shook her head.

It made me more than a little uneasy that she took such a dim view of our caper, because she was usually right about this kind of thing. But it was too late to turn back now. The funny thing was, despite being so bright in school, she was actually kind of dumb when it came to guys. She always let guys have their way with her, which was unusual for smart girls when I was in high school. In those days, smart girls tended to be fairly strait-laced and moral, especially when it came to sex. But not Peggy D. She put out for every guy she dated. That's why I was going out with her in the first place. That and the fact that she had the biggest knockers in our class.

Unfortunately, she was also kind of on the chubby side,

which is why I think she was so promiscuous. Chubby girls, it seemed, felt the need to want to please guys more and they used sex as a way to do it. You take the great looking cheer leader types—they're more selective about who they'll sleep with. I realize I'm oversimplifying this because there are other psychological factors involved—like a girl hating her father, for example. And I know for a fact that Peggy D. hated her old man because he was a hot-tempered tyrannical bastard who thought he was right about everything. He wasn't too fond of me either and had made that clear on more than one occasion.

Of course, he was a veteran of World War II and a lot of the men from that era were like that, including my own father, who had been a captain in the army and had won a bronze star for valor. But that experience sure didn't help him with his parenting skills, and my family life was the furthest thing from the happy and well-adjusted family life portrayed on popular TV shows like *Leave It to Beaver*. And get this—one time my father, in a fit of rage, yelled at me: "I created you; I can destroy you!" I don't think he meant it literally, but it was a pretty shitty thing to say. Old Ward Cleaver, the Beaver's father, certainly would have never said something like that. Of course, my pals and I were a pretty cynical bunch, the antithesis, in fact, of a Beaver or Wally Cleaver. What's more, we were smart enough to figure out that the picture-perfect suburban family as depicted on television was just a con, a bourgeois ideal promoted by corporate America to sell their products to the masses—in essence, the epitome of "phoniness," as our idol Holden Caulfield would say.

The day before the test, Tommy A., Howie T., and I started selling the cheat sheets. Word spread like wildfire at our school and before long each of us had sold dozens of them, not only to the students in our class but in other classes as well. We charged a buck a piece for each cheat sheet, and by the end of the day we had amassed a tidy sum. As an added precaution we told everyone not to bring the cheat sheets to class and use them as crib notes, but to memorize all the answers. That way no one could get caught cheating on the test and implicate us.

"You know I was thinking. Maybe we should do this for all the tests," Tommy A. suggested as the three of us walked down the hallway and headed for chemistry class the day of the midterm.

"We could do it for tests in other subjects, too," Howie T. added. "We'll make a fortune."

We walked into McSwine's class and took our seats. McSwine opened his filing cabinet with a key and removed a bundle of tests. Everything seemed completely normal. As McSwine passed out the tests, Tommy A., brimming with confidence, said to him, "I want you to know that I really studied hard for this midterm, Mr. McSwain. I mean I *really* studied."

Jesus Christ, I thought. Leave it to Tommy A. to lay it on so thick.

"I certainly hope so, my boy," McSwine said to Tommy A with a sneer, "because so far you're flunking this course— with a capital F."

The other students who had bought our cheat sheets looked our way and chortled. McSwine was such a moron, he thought they were responding to his clever ad lib.

As we started taking the midterm, I scanned the class and didn't see anyone using crib notes, so I breathed a sigh of relief. Once again everything went according to plan, and by the time the test was over, we realized we had put one over on old Mary McSwine.

Everyone was in a celebratory mood at lunch time. It was pizza day at school and each of us bought an extra slice of pizza in the lunchroom. We could certainly afford it. As we chomped away on the pizza and congratulated ourselves for a job well done, Peggy D. walked up to our table and whispered in my ear: "You've got a problem. McSwine caught a student in another class with one of your cheat sheets."

"What?!!" I nearly gagged on my pizza. "But we told everyone not to bring them to class."

"Well, apparently someone did."

"Who was it?"

"I don't know," she replied and walked away nonchalantly. She didn't say "I told you so," but she may as well have. The implication was writ pretty goddamn large.

I looked at Tommy A. and Howie T. Both of them were staring at me with their mouths agape and their pizza slices drooping in their hands like limp dicks. All I could say was: "We're screwed."

Later we found out who got caught with the cheat sheet. It was this idiot kid in another class named Mickey O. Tommy A. had sold him the cheat sheet and distinctly told him not to bring it to class, but the dumb ass was too lazy to memorize the answers so he brought it with him anyway and got clumsy. He actually dropped the cheat sheet on the floor during the test and McSwine saw it. When McSwine retrieved the cheat sheet and observed that all the correct answers to the test were written on it, he was dumbfounded and immediately asked Mickey O. where he got the cheat sheet. Fortunately, Mickey O. played dumb and didn't snitch on us. He told McSwine he had found it in the hallway. McSwine didn't believe him and gave him a tongue lashing, then let him go.

The next day the boys and I dreaded walking into chemistry class, but we had to do it. If we hadn't shown up it would have looked suspicious. Word was out about what had happened, and everyone was unusually quiet and apprehensive. McSwine stood in front of the class and remained silent for several seconds after all the students took their seats, milking everyone's trepidation like he was a detective in a bad murder mystery. Then he finally spoke.

"As some of you probably have heard, yesterday I found the answers to the midterm written on a sheet of paper that was in possession of one of your fellow students. These weren't just crib notes, mind you; they were the exact answers to all the questions. This means that someone must have gotten hold of the test beforehand."

Then he looked in our direction. "And I think I have a pretty good idea of who it was." He paused and stared directly at Tommy A. and then at me and Howie T. All three of us just sat there stone-faced and didn't move a muscle for what seemed like minutes, although it was probably just seconds. Finally, McSwine made an about face and walked behind his desk. You could have heard a pin drop in the classroom. Then he gave the three of us another penetrating stare, hoping one of us would crack, but we continued to sit there like Mount Rushmore.

"Yes, I have a pretty good idea all right," he repeated slowly and deliberately, "but I just can't figure out how they did it." McSwine suddenly picked up a ruler from his desktop and slapped it on the open palm of his hand. "In any case, because of what has transpired, the midterm will be invalidated for everyone, and I will make up another test in the next few days. And I can tell you this—it will be harder, much harder. So those of you who took the test honestly can thank the culprits for creating more work for you." Then he let it drop and started his daily lesson.

After school I walked Peggy D. home and asked her if she would help me study for the retest. She agreed and was nice enough not to revisit the conversation we had regarding her warning about the probable failure of our little caper. Instead, we just hit the books and studied our asses off. When the retest came up later in the week, Peggy got an A on it, of course, and

I was able to eke out a C. But after that, my relationship with Peggy D. changed. I wasn't sure whether the chemistry test heist had anything to do with it or whether our relationship had just run its course, but soon after, Peggy D. and I began to drift apart. And then she started dating some other guy. I was a little jealous at first, but I didn't exactly lose any sleep over it because I was never really serious about her from the beginning. I mean I never expected to go steady with her or marry her or anything, and I guess she knew that.

Ironically, after we all graduated from high school, Tommy A., Howie T., and I went on to college whereas Peggy D. got knocked up, got married, and never continued her education, even though she had a few scholarships. It seemed like a total waste; she was such a bright girl. But the truth is, just because you're smart in school doesn't necessarily mean you make smart decisions in life. And you know another thing—life isn't very fair. I can tell you that.

Song of the River

Urmi Chakravorty

Which is the more difficult thing to do—love your immediate surroundings for the way they nurture you? Or hate them for all that they've taken away from you?

Such fleeting questions do crisscross our minds occasionally. Sometimes they just peek in and sidle out; at other times, they linger for a while. Pretty much like the ebb and flow of the river flowing nearby. But ruminating on them is a luxury we can ill afford. There are more compelling things we need to attend to. Like, examining the safeness of our mud huts. As one more evening descends, we shut the rickety wooden doors tight and pray for an uneventful night. It's not that we have anything special to look forward to. Or fear. There is nothing alluring about us. We are a motley mix of women—old and young, tall and short, rounded and petite. Ones with an ebony tinge and sculpted faces, or those with sallow skin and jaded looks. But there's one common thread that binds us together. We are all condemned to a life of routine and sameness, so much so that we have consciously started seeking it out, instead of looking for alternatives.

This banality has a strange comfort and solace to it. It keeps us cocooned within its layers of predictability. We have already faced enough surprises, coped with innumerable changes, and seen complete turnarounds in our destiny. Now we crave stability. Like the monotonous meal we consume every night - steamed rice and runny lentils tempered with turmeric, salt, and green chili. If we get lucky, we throw in some diced vegetables which swim in the pools of lentil. Lunch, of course, is better. We have fish, shrimp, crab—whatever we manage to haul from the periphery of the saline river. Venturing out too far into the waters is a strict no-no for the uninitiated like us. Can we ever forget how some of our most experienced ones never returned?

The walls of the huts are regularly smeared with fresh clay that we fetch from the riverbanks. That, and the thatched roofs made of dried *pili* grass and *golpata* (palm leaves), help keep the huts marginally cool at night. We gently twist the knob of the kerosene lantern and lower the flame until only a tiny speck of fire remains, bobbing and flickering in the sparse air inside the hut. We never keep our homes in complete darkness. We need a fire burning right through the night to ward off our dreaded predators—the striped, ochre Royal Bengal tiger. And sometimes, their biped human counterparts, too.

During the day, things look different. Much safer. The numerous tributaries of the mighty Ganga, Brahmaputra, and Meghna snaking through these saline regions of south Bengal are dotted with dense mangrove forests. An environmentalist's delight… a veritable gold mine for the tourism sector. To the unsuspecting, casual tourists, it is just another cluster of huts in a nondescript island which they sight through their designer sunshades and fancy binoculars, while cruising through the riverine delta. But for anyone who cares to scratch the surface and peek underneath, we are the unwitting players thrust into this sinister zone of intense human-animal conflict.

We have been gifted several monikers—evil, unholy, witch, bad omen, *swami khejo* (husband eater). We lap them up as freebies... badges of honor to add a spark to our otherwise bleak lives. In fact, there's another name that almost makes us laugh. The name coined by the genteel townspeople to address us, almost with a hint of respect and sympathy. They call us the *Bagh Bidhobas*—the Tiger Widows of the Sunderbans—cursed women who have lost their husbands to deadly tiger attacks. And this is a special village earmarked for us. An ostracised community of widows—condemned by fate, shunned by their kin.

But we were not always in such dire straits. All of us had happy, wholesome families with husbands and children. Some of us also had aged in-laws or parents living under the same roof—families that bore the stamp of normalcy and honour. Families which worked hard, prayed harder, celebrated births, and mourned deaths. We had always been victims of abject poverty, but we didn't seem to mind that. As long as we had our husbands and family around us. Husbands who occasionally hit us when they were drunk, and later made love to us. Husbands who would venture deep into the forests to collect honey because the denser the forests, the better the honey. And greater are the chances of being mauled. Husbands who would set off on their rowing boats with fishing nets, cooking paraphernalia, and daily essentials in tow, to last at least a fortnight. Around sundown, they would wade in knee-deep water to spread their nets. Or balance themselves on the slushy banks to secure the stumps of the fishing nets, in the hope of hauling up a rich harvest of big and small fish and orange crabs through the night.

In the evening, when we lit a lamp before the goddess at home, we would visualise our men relaxing on their boats, cooking on a slow woodfire, humming a soulful *bhatiali* ditty about home and hearth. But beyond this lyrical, imaginary vision lurked a harsh prosaic reality. The rising winds would carry the tune far and wide. To the lovelorn hearts of fellow fishermen who had left their women behind and were braving the forests, rivers and tides. And also, to those who lay in wait amidst the Sundari and Gewa trees until they found the right moment to strike. Suddenly, the earthy, full-throated singing voice would be drowned under a deafening roar… and replaced by a bloodcurdling cry for help! Followed by a scrrrunch of bones being broken, a neck being wrung, and several pairs of panicky feet bolting across the mudflats and sandbars to higher ground, before an eerie silence descended on the river.

Like everything else in this region, religion, too, has its fair share of peculiarities. All of us living in the throes of danger unanimously bow our heads to our reigning deity, Maa Bonbibi. Hindus and Muslims alike. But more so, the menfolk who forage the forests every day for sustenance. Every time our husbands are out, the onus to placate the goddess invariably falls on us, the women. We are expected to lead a pure, austere life, praying for the well-being and safe return of the men. And God forbid, if a couple of them fail to return, the wives are promptly branded 'impure' and 'sullied.' We are banished from our homes and the village. The slur of immorality is so potent that we lose the right to cultivate our family land. Or even use our family boat—the *kaajer nouko*—for sailing and fishing, lest we taint it.

We try to fight for our marital homes, our children, our family fishing ponds, and tracts of land. We try to argue with the village honchos and family elders.

Parul's husband died of snake bite amidst the lush

mangroves. Sakina lost her man to a deadly crocodile attack while sailing down the creek. But they continue to live in the comfort of their homes, with the rest of their family. They have not been labeled ominous or unchaste. How is a tiger attack any different? Why single us out and punish us for something we have no control over?

It is an exercise in futility. We already know the answer. The tag of dishonor has been ingrained deep in our collective psyche. The lack of rationale makes us laugh, even in such grim circumstances.

The last nail in the coffin of our woes is the absence of financial support from the government. Our husbands, like most of our community members, had ventured into the forests and used the resources without a licensed permit. How could we afford these expensive documents when providing two square meals to the family every day was a burden by itself? In the absence of legitimate papers, we are too scared to seek help from the police or approach the babus for compensation. What if we get booked for illegal entry and use of forest resources? And sometimes, when the tiger leaves no trace of the body, we are forced to treat it as a "missing person" case. Poor Jamila still wails and mourns for her husband who was pulled off the edge of the boat by the beast in the middle of the river. His companions could only shriek in helplessness and horror. Two months down, Jamila still hopes that her husband will return some day. We don't have the heart to tell her otherwise!

Recently, the Nurse Didi visiting the primary health centre in the adjoining village had mentioned something about the world becoming hotter, about the seas rising. That, apparently, made the rivers more saline. When we asked her how, she was not able to tell us. But we did not mind. The fragile ecosystem around us is like our birthing cradle. We know it like the back of our hands. We can feel the imbalance in our pulse. We can see how our tiny patches of land are gradually becoming uncultivable. There is a deep rot that is threatening to swallow us whole. Is it threatening the tiger, too? Are these animals losing their habitat, their prey, and hence, sneaking inland in search of food?

The summer months here are very hot and humid. The sun beats down on us mercilessly. We sweat in buckets. There is a silent heaviness in the air, as if a disaster is going to strike. Our arms ache as we vigorously swing the hand-held palm leaf fan. We still shudder when we remember Nolok, the little girl who was dragged away by the tiger from outside her hut. The ten-year-old was playing *ludo* with her kid brother, enjoying the cool evening breeze. The beast apparated out of the darkness and pounced on Nolok from behind. The stub of the burning candle did little to deter him, so desperate was he! The poor child did not stand a fighting chance of escape. Her body was never found. Her brother continues to have nightmares and screams pitifully in his sleep.

Most of us do not talk much among ourselves. We don't need to. Our eloquent silence speaks volumes. Our hollow eyes mirror the agony of unshed tears. Our shared losses echo aeons of collective rankling. On the surface, each of us is like a port of calm, offering solace and refuge to the other battling a storm. But deep inside our hearts, each one is a simmering cauldron of discontent and angst, trying hard not to explode. We remember the joyful moments of our past and our eyes well up. The imprints of our challenging times brace us for future hardships. The river is our lifeline—it provides us with everything we need. And in one cruel stroke, it takes it all back... often, with compound interest. It is our raison d'etre as well as our nemesis, reminding us of the fragility we live through.

To supplement our peripheral existence, some of us had taken loans from the bank to dig ponds and start cultivating fish. It required backbreaking work and a fair amount of luck. Finally, our resilience and hard work won. We would sell the fish at the *haat*, the bi-weekly village market, and bring home some cash. This continued for a couple of years. Our children started dreaming again—dreaming of buying a new dress for Durga Puja or a pair of slippers for using outdoors. Moving barefoot along the mud tracks had calloused their tender skin. Or of visiting the *Sharadiya Mela* in the nearby town, the autumnal fair heralding the annual visit of Maa Durga. We felt happy for our children… happy to see them harbouring dreams, thinking of the future. What is a life without dreams, goals, and hope, after all?

And just when we were audacious enough to believe that our fortunes had turned, a deadly cyclone struck. For us, it was like a tsunami—all-pervading, cataclysmic, almost diabolical in nature. Is it our imagination, or was the Widow Village actually the worst hit in the whole of the Sunderbans? It battered our lands, flattened our huts and sheds, and flooded our farmlands and fish ponds. And most importantly, it washed away all our dreams and our enterprise in its swirl of murky waters. When the cyclone calmed and the waters receded, we were greeted by dead farm animals, rotten fish washed ashore, and broken mud embankments. Our limited cultivable patches were submerged under a residue of salt. Once again, we found ourselves on ground zero.

It has been a year since. Fate has its quirky way of testing us—the most vulnerable lot, the easiest target. And it is Fate, again, which resurrects us from the nadir of despair. Most of us have picked up the frayed threads of our tattered existence and slowly stitched them back into the fabric of life. But not everyone has been so resilient, so persevering, so mulish, to be treading the same torturous path time and again. Not everyone can handle a litmus test with equanimity. And the losses have truly been irrevocable. It is as if we were born to be destiny's favorite play things—toyed with, tossed around, and broken at whim. And as is the case with damaged toys, some of us were beyond repair or revival. Some of us had reached the end of our tether. Hence predictably, some of us snapped.

As always, it is easy to strike a nasty blow when one is down on one's creaky knees. For us, this blow has come in the form of fairy tale illusions and promises of respite and riches. Subtly proffered by unholy money-lenders, and city-based pimps disguised as recruitment agents. It is not that we're unaccustomed to being leered at. Earlier it was the village men with their furtive glances measuring us up and down. And now, by these middle-aged, paunchy money-lenders and agents— their beady eyes following us, gazing unabashedly at our saree-clad frames, boring into our curves. Our sarees are hitched up to our calves to avoid the wetland slush, exposing our lower limbs. They ogle at those few inches of bare skin, libido writ large on their lined faces.

The surreptitious movements of strangers, the unfamiliar lusting faces, the clandestine meetings at the fringes of the woods, an unprecedented busyness evident in some of the women—it's not that we did not notice these tell-tale signs. Dark clouds brewing a tempest. Those unmistakable bleeps presaging a desperate act of survival. But what could we possibly do? Wait infinitely for better days to dawn on us? Hope for a life free of tigers, crocodiles, snakes, and cyclones? Or act like those three widows who chose to throw themselves at the far end and swim their way up. Unapologetic about their decision. Confident of their action.

One of them was a new bride—her husband wanted her to sample the best honey from the interiors of the jungles. She only received his mangled remains. Very soon, she wanted to break free of this tedium. She wanted to breathe... to live. Not just inhale and exhale, like the rest of us. One had two young children who blamed her for pulling them out of the school in the neighboring village. Children who were too naïve to understand the dictates of a stratified community, or the constraints of poverty. She entrusted them with the rest of us and left, hoping to provide her children with a better, secure future. And then there was a third, who was finding it impossible to sustain her ailing, infirm parents who depended solely on her for succour. Faith and prayer can probably move mountains, but they cannot ensure healthy aging. That requires nutrition and therapy. And both, in turn, need hard cash.

Many of us are caught in the throes of a dilemma—should we give in to temptation and run away? Should we refuse to be typecast in this shared template of pain and penury? Or, should we continue to lead our woebegone lives where we merely exist, only because we do not know what else to do. This dilemma is no longer an elephant in the room. It has taken the proportions of a mammoth, bulldozing its way into our hearts, our conscience, till we can no longer afford to ignore it. More so, when we receive news of our friends who left these sinking marshlands in search of terra firma. And instead, lost their way in the city's labyrinthine alleys where women ply their trade at night. Where our young bride's rose-tinted dreams are dashed every minute by the garish reality of the world's oldest profession. Where the mother silently suffers scars every night so she can pluck the stars for her children at dawn. Where the daughter of our village withers and wastes her fragile self in the hope of buying a panacea for her hoary parents.

Back home, we represent the meek, unambitious women, cowering and grovelling before our destiny, seeking pardon for crimes we have not committed. We are the permanent outliers—accused of infidelity, sundered and cast away like we never existed. We have learned to lead such a life with stoical acceptance. We prefer to remain nameless, faceless statistics in moth-eaten registers gathering dust in *panchayat* offices. We enjoy the anonymity it offers. We till our tracts, visit the river to get fish or crab, and venerate the aura of Maa Bonbibi. At sunset, we dutifully return to the confines of our homes, like birds returning to their nests at dusk. Occasionally... just sometimes... some of us don't. Like those rare birds who lose their way and drift away, never to return to their familiar folds and to their chicks again. Frankly, no one bothers. No one keeps count of those birds lost in flight. Or of the women who do not return from the marshes.

For once, they are not preyed upon by the tiger. This time the hunger is in their belly. It is an irresistible urge, a strong voice of dissent—to march away from the beaten path of submission and instead, tread the irreverent route of comfort and pleasure. It is as if they are under a hypnotic spell, following the mesmeric twinkle of a firefly, only to find themselves trapped in a bog, chasing the ungodly gleam of an ignis fatuus. But by the time they realize it, it is way too late.

Such incidents follow a routine trajectory. They jolt the urban moral police out of their ennui. This is followed by newspaper headlines demanding an enquiry into the deaths and the cases of people gone missing. They seek justice and compensation for the rest of us. And after this byte has been played out on loop, they return to their timetabled life and wait for the next sensational news to crop up.

We continue to walk on thin ice day after day, waiting for the disturbing ripples to ease out. We yearn to return to our lives where the tiger and the river rule the roost. But in our hearts we already know, that's not how it's meant to be. We keep hoping there won't be any more spicy newspaper snippets on our runaway widows. We keep praying that the outsiders stop invading our lives by day, and our homes at night. We keep wishing that the old abandoned parents live on for a few more years. And that the bright young children pick up their satchels and head to school so there are no more generations of Bagh Bidhobas.

Brimfield

Robert Moore

The white GM box truck with '*J Corduroy, Antiques –
Collectibles*' on the side in scraped brown paint bounced us as
the big tires rolled slowly over potholes along the state road,
ours one in a long line of trucks and vans and ancient station
wagons packed full.

"They're pulling 'em in from all over," said my sister
Angie, nineteen, remembering our late father's stock comment
for Brimfield.

She gripped the steering wheel with both hands as
the bumpy pavement torqued it left and right. The engine
needed revving or it threatened to stall. When had it last been
serviced? She pointed out to me a tent advertising tattoos and
piercings.

"Karen, see him? He's new. I'm going to check him
out later. I want a stud in my right nostril." She grinned
mischievously. "Dad swore if I did it, he wouldn't let me in the

house." Her grin faded with the memory. "No longer an issue."

The kid with the official looking baton guided us into the vendor rows.

"Where are we?" Angie asked.

"3-G. We're on 3," I said, dismayed, leaning forward from the bench seat to peer through the vast windshield, checking the hand-lettered signs on pine sticks. "There's A. Crap. I guess we're in the back." I knew Angie was thinking, like Dad, *we're stuck in back with the dumpsters!*

———

The call from Angie, her voice ragged with tears, caught me at work. I was en route to Human Resources—my team had missed its quota two quarters in a row so I already had my personal items in a box.

"Dad's dead," she had said.

"Are you sure?" I asked my sister, a truly stupid question but had I heard correctly? "What happened?" She got the story out as I loitered by a window and ended up ten minutes late to my firing.

That morning Dad was upending a commode-turned-planter in the garage, explaining to Angie the value of plumbing fixtures, when he groaned and fell, taken by a heart attack.

"I was doing what I remember," said Angie, "from First Aid, until the EMT pulled me away. She said he was gone when he hit the ground."

I heard a voice. "I asked if you had any questions?" Judy Bishop, the HR rep, was looking at me, indicating a letter she'd set before me.

I read the first sentence, then the second. 'Disappointing performance...' I could hear the blood rushing in my head. I couldn't focus. It was paragraph two before I saw that my severance was three months' salary, and they threw in a fraction of the bonus I would have collected next month.

"We're sorry it ended like this," said Judy in her corporate voice.

I remembered to breathe, and tried to read the entire letter, but they were hollow words and my brain wandered. I signed the bottom. Judy smiled pleasantly and retrieved an envelope from her desk drawer. I glanced at the typed check, saw five figures, nodded to her and said goodbye.

I had a row to myself on the flight and I cried a little, then again when Angie picked me up at the Riverside station where we both cried. Since my Christmas visit, my little sister had gone Goth: black t-shirt and denim, her hair dyed to match.

"I got things started, thought I'd help," she said, handing me a checklist from a funeral director. She had made some lavish choices. Dad had made me his executor and I confirmed my suspicions about the family finances and canceled all but the state-mandated essentials.

I called the funeral director when we got home. "Hi, yeah, thank you. I'm the executor for Mr. Corduroy. My sister just showed me the order. I'm going to have to cancel most of that." Out with the weatherproofed, polished bronze casket, no limo for us, no wake catered by Legal Seafoods. Pouting, Angie spoke to me as little as possible the rest of the day.

The funeral was four days away, and cleaning up the estate of Joseph Corduroy would require more paper towels and garbage cans than notarized paperwork. Other than a quick shopping trip to get Angie some mourning clothes, we spent most of our time emptying a garage too full of "collectibles" to accommodate a car.

It was closed and smelled moldy and I started sneezing; we had to move piles just to move around. Stacks of old newspapers and magazines that Dad was planning to recycle but the "profit margin was too thin." Tools, old windows, plumbing fixtures, stacked boxes, bike parts, record albums, doorknobs and hinges, old signs, mantels, and behind a rack of moldy clothes, a collection of erotic wood sculptures neither of us knew about, and many, many lawn gnomes. Junk.

I found a long pole filled with old clothing and discovered a scout uniform spotted with mold. "This is Mrs. Sitka's stuff. From twelve years ago. Why is it still here?"

Angie appraised the mess. "He probably forgot about it. I did. We can sell some of this on Amazon." She said it in the confident voice she'd inherited from Dad, and like him, it held more attitude than fact.

"Doubt it," I said tersely, pulling open a box and finding *Reader's Digest*s. "You have to sell volume and make money on the shipping. I have a coworker who used to do it on the side." I saw a signed baseball card in a protective plastic sleeve, but I'd never heard of the player. "We might be able to move some of this on eBay."

"I showed him eBay." She grinned. "I meant to sell our stuff. Then he started bidding with my account."

Late in the day we jammed all five garbage cans over full.

—

"He's our father!" Angie erupted the morning of the spartan funeral, wearing a new plaid skirt, not exactly mourning clothes but good for job interviews, tears blurring her black makeup.

I had become tired of my own voice on the subject. "We can't afford it. He would've wanted it to be simple." My severance check was in my purse, but my father had raised us to be parsimonious.

She scowled until we reached the funeral parlor and saw

Dad, then she crumbled in tears. I let her cry on my shoulder, my own eyes dry.

—

Everyone knew Joe Corduroy. After the well-attended funeral and the brunch of homemade casseroles, after enjoying tales of our father's childhood in Worcester, as recalled by elderly second cousin Wilma from Groton, whom we'd never met, after everyone was gone, we exchanged skirts and blouses for jeans and a couple of Dad's old shirts and returned to the garage.

"I've been looking for a glass vase I got him to buy years ago," I announced. "Maybe he sold it?"

"Dad was more a buyer—"Angie started.

"Than a seller," we said in unison, one of Mom's expressions, and shared a grin. After her death three years ago, the house's upkeep suffered. She had also been the one who'd somehow kept the business in the black and the garage orderly.

Though we'd reduced the rampant piles to more manageable islands, I couldn't find the vase. After dinner, I collected Dad's bills and found his checkbook, little used. Angie did the dishes and wrote an elegy for him on Facebook, her friends pinging back with crying emoticons. She stopped when she heard me sigh. "You look like Mom, when she was paying the bills. Angry."

"I'm sorry I had to be a cheapskate," I apologized. "I asked Dad a couple times if he'd put anything aside. He told me he had a nest egg." I sat cross-legged on a kitchen chair. "As best I can tell, Dad was in the hole."

Angie nodded glumly. "I thought so."

"Even keeping the burial to basics, we owe the funeral ghouls a thousand and change. Normally a life insurance policy would pay for that, but he cashed his in last November to pay taxes."

Angie frowned; she hadn't known that.

"There's less than a hundred dollars in this account." I couldn't believe my father had utterly ignored the future. He didn't have to concern himself with me, I'd told him once on the phone, but Angie needed support, and guidance. He'd stumbled on both, in my opinion.

She grimaced, then said, "Dad didn't like banks."

"I know. I haven't ruled out finding money buried somewhere, but it's more likely to be a roll of quarters than twenties." My pessimism was started to sound tired, even to me.

She looked at me, embarrassed. "Don't you, like, make a lot of money?"

I'd bragged at Christmas about the pending bonus and a promotion I was slaving for, and now my embarrassment was a bottomless pit. Dad had looked amazed a child of his wore a suit to work.

I looked at Angie. "Up until Monday, I earned eighty-two thousand, which isn't bad for twenty-six. But I lost my job the day you called, so it was a bad day all around."

"Shit. Really?" She hesitantly offered me a hug; we'd never been close and now suddenly we were all we had.

—

The house reeked of Dad's cheap cigars, which Angie was savoring. "I can still smell him," she said wistfully, curling fetal on the sagging couch.

"Mom would have killed him for smoking inside," I said, mostly to myself. "So, after Mom died, did he sell *anything*?"

"I think so," said Angie, looking thoughtful, but she said nothing.

I finished skimming the mail for bills. "We need to liquidate the collection, and it would help to get at least six thou for it, which seems unlikely." Looking at her, in a parental voice, I asked, "Did you get the acceptance from Bowdoin?"

"Yessss." After my persistent text messages, she applied to my alma mater. She had the grades, she just hadn't wanted to go to college. And at the time she had a boyfriend she didn't have anymore.

"What do you want to study?" I asked, finally having the sort of discussion with her I'd wanted.

Angie tended to frown when asked to think. "I was thinking of creative writing, but Dad laughed at it. '*Learn the business*, he said, *make a real living.*' It's interesting stuff, but," she looked at me, "we're broke now?" She looked beaten, shaking her head. "So, maybe creative writing is too flaky. I wanted to get a job at Market Basket just to have money for clothes. He kept telling me, don't worry, he'd take me shopping, which he kept putting off."

And just like that we were back in the red. "It would be good to get some tuition money, too." I had gone to the cellar which Dad had always promised to remodel, but there were no surprises. Same tiny bathroom. No updates.

"We can sell the house," I said. "That and a few grants should cover tuition. I know it won't sell fast, and," I looked at the tired paint, the worn floors, "it won't sell for much, but it's all equity."

Water whistled through pipes in the wall. "The toilet leaks," Angie recalled. "Dad was looking for the parts."

"You can buy them for ten bucks," I said, exasperated. "Probably why the damn water bill is so high." Why this reminded me of boyfriends I didn't know, probably the aggravation. In a calmer tone I asked, "Didn't you have a boyfriend? Darryl something?" I recalled a stocky guy with a buzz cut and a lobe stretcher in each ear that made me flinch when I saw him on Facebook.

"Dar-*ren*, Darren Whitley. He joined the Army," she said, sounding tired but not heartbroken. "We aren't *officially* broken-up, I check his Facebook page, but I told him he was a dick for enlisting and he hasn't called for a month, since he went off to basic. Dad didn't like him," she recalled, smiling, a hint of the rebel I'd been.

"I loved Dad, but I think losing Mom hurt me more," I said.

She smiled sadly. "Well, you *were* her favorite. I liked going collecting with Dad."

"I was *not* Mom's favorite," I said, steeped in memories of my departure. "I wasn't anybody's favorite. Do you remember the argument I started, telling Mom and Dad to computerize their inventory?"

Angie frowned. "A little."

I wished I'd been nicer to him. "I told Dad he was a junk dealer. Not 'collectibles,'" I used my fingers to mime quotes. "I'd just bought an Apple and there were all these business applications. I said we could make more money and live in a *nice* house." I blushed at the memory; it stung. "Mom was defending Dad, even though she liked the idea. I wanted them to think I was bright. After that, I finished school and decided to live somewhere else. Especially after Mom died."

"Dad never understood why you went to Chicago. He was always seeing jobs in the paper and saying, 'Here's one your sister could do'. One was bookkeeper for a strip club."

"Is it still available?" We took in the view from the front door, the unmowed yard in the setting sun. "I do have to go back, at least to clean out my apartment."

Angie looked at me skeptically. "You want to sell the house *and* give up your apartment. Where are we going to live?"

That was an epiphany; I now had a housemate. "Good point. First, we need to sell the junk."

"Collectibles," she corrected me, and picked up a framed photo of all of us, taken just before Mom died, when she realized there was no family photo. She looked tired from the cancer, Dad at his most elegant in a disgusting bolo tie, still wearing jeans. I looked bored, Angie was smiling. The frame was aluminum, meant to glisten with hundreds of rhinestones, but only three remained, scattered among empty gray sockets. Dad found it when Mom asked for a picture frame. Not for the first time, I wondered why our only family photo didn't merit a nicer frame in Dad's eyes? He'd taken too much pride from using discards. *There we go, woulda cost us ten bucks in the store.*

—

The next morning, determined, I attacked the collection, moving piles of boxes I'd previously avoided, and I found the vase, shrouded in webbing and dirt. Amid the junk, even in shadow, the stained glass had light and color. "I forgot how beautiful you are," I said in a hushed tone, as though others might discover me and rob my treasure. I'd picked it out at an estate sale in Weston and urged Dad to pay the stickered eighty bucks for it.

He'd been pleased at my interest but not the price. "Honey, I'll offer 'em twenty. Then I'll go up a little. We'll get it for forty, how much you wanna bet?" They stuck at fifty, and I pretended to pray, so he paid, which rankled him. I'd urged him to get it appraised, and then Mom died, and a few months later I was in Chicago.

With the vase resting in the crook of my arm, I discovered, with my big toe, a lawn gnome in overgrown grass outside the garage door. "Ouuww. Motherfu-!" Falling forward, the vase bobbled in my arms and I lunged after it; we both landed softly in the tall grass. "Jesus, that was close." Flip-flops kicked aside, I sat down on the concrete stoop, nursing my big toe, cursing my father.

Angie had begun mowing and stopped to comfort me. "These little fuckers," she said, grinning. Pointing with her thumb, "There's one around back exposing himself." She picked up the gnome. "Dad got to be a pawn shop," she said. "He'd given you ten bucks for these, even broken. I never had the backbone to argue with his sense of charity. I think he really liked them."

"And that's why you have no college fund."

Angie set down the gnome and fired up the mower again, no doubt to shut down my latest rant. She finished, put the mower away, and came up to me, still nursing my toe. "Y'know what we could do? Brimfield."

"That's a great idea," I told her, and it was. Instead of posting pictures on eBay and waiting for someone to bid, we could attend what I'd called the biggest yard sale in New England and unload the stuff for the highest bidder in one day. I called in a one-day registration and Angie went online to price our collectibles.

An hour later, she rested her forehead in her palm. "The gnomes almost aren't worth the cost of the gas to haul them," she said. "There are valuable gnomes, but we don't have any of them." Looking up, "Dad, what were you thinking?"

Stained glass was harder to gauge. I looked more closely and found a name in script—Galle. In a few keystrokes we discovered the value of the French artist. "Holy shit. I *knew* this was worth something." Beginning prices were around six thou, it could be worth up to fifty. "Ha! Dad, I found your investment. But I get partial credit. Maybe we just leave it out and see what people think." Angie shrugged her shoulders neutrally. I wanted to ignite a bidding war. Brimfield attracted savvy buyers with real money. That night I grinned in my sleep, at long last the heroine.

We set out at seven a.m. I offered to drive, but Angie insisted. "She's a handful on a bumpy road."

—

"He brought me here a couple times," I said. I remembered it mostly as a gathering of losers selling junk. "Got to be ten years ago. You and Mom, you had a softball tournament. Dad priced his stuff higher than anyone else. I don't think we made back the gas money. He kept saying 'our stuff is premium.' He spent the day talking to other sellers."

"He liked to talk. Especially about his stuff," said Angie. "I forgot about the softball team. I was a good hitter." She smiled at her refreshed memories.

It felt odd to be part of a mile-long yard sale at nine in the morning. I still expected to be at work, in my office, studying my monitor, manipulating numbers on a spreadsheet. That morning I pulled on gloves and piled tools on folding tables, hammers and old drills clunking into each other, and then the old windows. Already sweating, I collected one under each arm, my little-used muscles trembling.

Angie was lost in thought, holding a gnome. "Honey, could you hurry up?" I said. "As soon as you've got them all out, look around and see what our competition is." I glanced at the erotic sculptures. "See if anyone else has sculptures with woodies. Maybe they'll buy these. I do *not* want to take them back. They creep me out."

"I was remembering something Dad told me," Angie said, resenting my *hurry up*, but leaving nonetheless.

167

I set the vase on the knickknacks table, slightly apart, no price. The truck was finally empty. I leaned against it, my back aching from unexpected exercise, wiped my sweaty forehead, and reminded myself to breathe.

Angie returned ten minutes later with coffee. We gathered at the cashbox under the tarp. "Two sugars, two creams."

I smiled. "Thanks, I didn't even think to ask." I nodded proudly at the vase. "There's my baby."

She glanced at it. "It's okay."

I touched it protectively. "It's beautiful. It's the only thing here I like. I'm hoping we clean up on it."

Angie's inherited optimism was keeping her both happy and sad. "I was thinking about how Dad always had faith that the next twenty bucks he needed was already on its way to his pocket."

"He should have prayed for fifties, not twenties."

She gave me a labored look. "I *understand* we need money. We're on the right track. I saw some old windows, they're getting fifty for them, and the tub we should get a hundred for. The tools go between twenty and fifty." She glanced at ours. "Probably nearer twenty. And there's a guy in 'J' with African wood sculptures. Mostly big tits, between twenty and a hundred bucks. I," she blushed, "didn't talk to him."

"Okay, we price everything a few bucks less and add 'R.O.' Our goal is a roll of cash and an empty truck."

Angie sipped hot chocolate. "Before? I *was* thinking about college. Dad wasn't big on it. He kept saying 'You learn this business hands-on.'"

"I know," I said, sipping my coffee and wishing it was a Starbucks. "If Mom was here, she would want you in college. You need to learn something besides the business. Writing, whatever." I knew how often freshmen changed majors. The

168

good news, I felt, was that Angie was thinking again. She had a lot to think about.

An elderly woman with horribly swollen legs came by, walking laboriously with a cane. Her jacket was old and had many pockets, her cargo shorts stained, and she walked in orthotic sneakers. Her long gray hair was pulled back with children's barrettes. When she spoke she had the smile of a carved pumpkin. "Hello. I'm Elma Sweeney," she said with a deep Downeast accent. "Where's Dick?" Dad's old friends called him Dick for reasons mysterious to us. "Are you his daughters?" *Dottahs*?

"We are. He died last Monday," said Angie with a sad frown. "We're trying to clean out his inventory."

Elma looked stricken. "I'm so sorry. I hadn't heard. I've known him for thirty years. I looked forward to seeing him here. I'm so sorry. How'd he die?" *Hawdee-die?*

"Heart attack. He didn't have any history. It just struck."

Elma shook her head, as though any death was unfair. "Well, you gotta die of something. Dick and I go back a long time. I'm very sorry to hear it. You girls take care."

—

It seemed every dealer had known Dad as Dick, and I let Angie accept condolences, choosing to pretend I was working on a spreadsheet. My job gone, I tried searching job boards but my mind wandered. Right now I didn't want another job. I didn't want someone else to have the power to take that away from me. *Well, you have to do something. That severance won't last forever.* Oddly, it was Dad's voice, someone I thought I'd stopped listening to years ago.

I went for a walk, roaming, pretending I was in a bazaar in another hemisphere. I felt guilty leaving Angie alone, but she kept insisting she could run the show, so I let her. I returned half an hour later to find she had sold all the tools. "How?"

"Another collector," she said smugly. "I offered him a fifteen percent cut to take them all. I know Dad got most of them for a buck or less. See? I can sell stuff."

"Yes, you can," I smiled, hugging her. "Now think about what you really want. And if you aren't sure, trust me, you should at least try college. I think you'll blossom there." Looking around with a jaundiced look, "Not much blossoming going on around here."

Angie rolled her eyes. "Just 'cuz they aren't wearing suits doesn't mean they aren't working."

—

A man in clean denim and a golf shirt picked up a brass doorknocker, set it down, left and came back and asked, "How much for the faucets?"

"Make an offer," I asked.

"Give you eight?"

Angie piped up. "Make it ten?"

"'Kay."

A middle-aged man dressed in painters' whites, who looked like he'd just finished turning a barn red, stopped to smile at the lawn gnomes. "My wife loves 'em." He knelt by one, picked it up, smiled at it, then stood, turned away, and looked over the windows. Then he asked, "How much for the tub?"

"Hundred," I said first, smiling at Angie, a competition suddenly between us. "I'll consider an offer."

"Seventy-five?"

Angie shook her head slightly. I said, "Can you go eighty?"

He looked at the tub again. "Eighty."

"That'll work."

"How much for the windows?"

Without looking at her I said, "Forty-five apiece. There're ten of them."

"How's three-fifty cash for all of 'em?"

"That'll work, too."

I knew Dad had collected the windows on garbage day two towns over. If only he had sold as well as he'd collected, maybe we wouldn't have lived off discards, maybe he'd have seen a doctor more regularly, maybe he'd still be alive. A lot of maybes.

—

I sent Angie back to the tarp of James Hickory, Collector of Curiosities, as engraved on a wooden shingle hung from a tent pole. Behind the Jeep she saw the tent Mr. Hickory had slept in, a sleeping bag rolled up snugly. It was a little chilly for sleeping under the stars.

Beside the Jeep, on the grass, were the mahogany figures of absurdly well-endowed women. Angie glanced for a long moment at his wares, then approached Mr. Hickory. "Help you?" he asked in an accent she couldn't place.

"Hi, I'm Angie Corduroy."

"Jim Hickory. Pleased to meet you, Angie." He smiled. "What can I do for you?"

"Your wooden figures? How much are you asking for them?"

"Twenty apiece. I have sixteen and I can do a deal for all of them."

She nodded politely. "Are you interested in acquiring some different ones?"

His smile changed direction, from genial greeter to lopsided. "What d'you have?"

She tried to describe them without blushing or using her hands.

"Appears your late father—very sorry to hear it, I knew Dick—was collecting the males." Hickory nodded knowledgeably. "If they're genuine they're usually African."

"What do they go for?" she asked shyly.

"If you want to fetch one of yours, I'll take a look at it."

She returned with a smaller one in a paper bag. He rose from his seat and put his glasses on. His brown pants were deeply creased, as though he'd slept in them, and he smelled of his breakfast, a bag of Cheetos. Setting his hat on the table, exposing a shiny bald pate, he turned the male figurine around in his thick hands, one fingernail blackened, looking closer here and there, and then set it down, sighing. He smiled a kindly smile, a little foolish looking, as though confessing to a mistake. "I'm sorry, dear, but I'm ninety-nine percent sure this is a fake." He began explaining and pointing out details.

She smiled politely, her spirits crashing. As soon as he finished, she said quickly, "Thank you, thanks for your help."

She returned and I saw that she'd cried again. "Junk, junk, junk!" she said for my benefit.

—

The man buying windows was peeling bills off a roll when he saw the stained-glass vase. He knelt to see the light shine through it. "Look at you," he said reverently. "Galle?"

"Yes, it is." I felt the adrenaline rush.

He retrieved a soft rag from his back pocket and dabbed at a spot. "Very nice," he smiled. "How much?"

I loved the vase, it was a good memory of a day with my

Dad, a rarity. "Make me an offer?"

He reached for it, then looked at me. "Do you mind? I'd like to see it with more light." He took a step back, raised it over his head to capture the sun. "I'll go a hundred," he said, and dug out his wallet.

"No, that one's worth more," I said, hoping I was right.

He looked at it again. "One-twenty-five?"

Not even close to a thousand. I concentrated on keeping a poker-face. "Let me think about it. You going to be around? I won't sell it to anyone else for a half hour."

He nodded. "Okay. I need to pack up what I've already got. I'll be back."

A slim woman, dressed in elegant, spotless linen, had been idling across the way. She paused before the stained glass and studied it. "How much for this?" she asked in a strong Long Island voice.

"I'm considering offers. The bidding starts at," I felt a bit breathless, "a thousand."

She frowned, bent and looked closely at it, rubbed at imaginary dirt, got up and walked away.

"A thousand?" Angie asked, also breathless. "Dad had *anything* worth a thousand?"

My heart was pounding. "Maybe. We paid fifty bucks for it six years ago. It would be nice to make a huge profit."

Angie dropped the fertility doll on the tarp, by the others, like it was old paper. "By the way—these things? Friggin' firewood."

I mouthed 'oh' and hugged her with one arm. "It's okay, we'll be okay." Then I smiled brightly, "and tonight we have a bonfire!"

The Long Island woman returned with an equally well-dressed man with styled gray hair. He leaned over the glass carefully, dug out reading glasses and got close enough for a nose print, then picked it up, upending it, turned to her and shook his head. She frowned and looked at me as though I'd misled them. "My friend says this is not a Galle. It's a knock-off."

My heart sank. "Are you sure?"

The man, rail-thin, spoke in a British accent. He had oddly long fingers. "He signed Galle, as you have here. The plant is his preferred motif. But underneath?" and he upended it and touched two dimpled spots on the bottom. "See here? This is where the injection mold broke off. This was *mass produced*." He enunciated the words with contempt. "The seam, it's almost invisible." Well, I'd missed it. "It's a very nice piece, for decorating purposes. A beautiful fake," he said, apparently his version of condolences, as I must have looked awful. They walked off and I felt foolish.

"I didn't want to say anything," said Angie, frowning sympathetically. "Dad did get it appraised. They said it wasn't original. I just wasn't sure *they* could tell."

What rattled me more? That I was wrong? That I hadn't learned the business? Or that I'd called my father a junk dealer, and I'd also bought junk, or how did the man put it? A beautiful fake. Dad probably knew it wasn't original himself. My burgeoning self-confidence faded. "I feel so stupid."

"Hey, we've got nine hundred and sixteen dollars. That's more than we ever cleared." She smiled at me, hopeful. "We're most of the way to paying for Dad." Her voice dropped at the end. "I wonder if he thought those wooden idols were legit. I hate to think he paid full price for them." We both grinned and shook our heads in unison—Dad never paid full price for anything. "Hey, is this your guy coming back?"

I picked up the vase, which I still loved, but it was worth a hundred and twenty-five dollars to this man. Unenthusiastically, I said, "If you still want it, you can have it."

He nodded and counted twenties onto the table. I remembered holding the vase up that day, begging Dad to buy it. *"Fifty is top buck. If I pay top buck for it, how do I make a profit?"* he asked, teaching me the business. To my embarrassment, my eyes welled up and I felt tears on my cheeks. He couldn't help noticing. "Are you okay?" He paused, a bill pinched in mid-air.

I'd laughed telling Mom how irritated Dad was when he paid fifty dollars for it. I was blinking away tears, and then my nose started running. I picked the vase up again. "I'd like to keep this, after all. It's a family heirloom."

He was a good sport. Scooping up his cash, "Okay, I can respect that. If you change your mind, I'm at A-17." He set his business card on the table and headed off.

"I'm glad you kept it," Angie said, hugging me. "You need something nice to remember Dad."

Though I didn't shed a tear seeing Dad in a coffin, I cried as I held the vase. "Maybe we could repaint the truck. 'Corduroy Sisters, Antiques'."

My phone buzzed, a text from a work friend: 'Were you canned?' "I'll be right back," I told my sister, walking around the truck.

—

Angie began collecting the gnomes. She reached for one of the ceramics—we hadn't sold any—and her fingertips slipped, the gnome rolled free and broke on a knob of granite into five pieces. "Shit. Five bucks shot to hell!" She saw a piece of brown paper in the ceramic torso. She pulled on it and a small bag came loose. Inside was a roll of twenties. It had been stuffed through a hole in the base. She picked up another and goosed it and smiled as she felt brown paper. Dropping it on the same rock, she found another bag of bills. She looked for me. "Dad, you paranoid son of a…"

Five minutes later, I returned to witness a mass killing of lawn gnomes, and Angie counting bills. "I found his savings," she reported, beaming. "Ten thousand, mostly in twenties, a few fifties. Even some Benjamins," she held them aloft.

"Y'know, there is nothing—I mean *nothing*—in his will about those damn gnomes. We could have sold these for, like, a dollar apiece and," I raised my eyes heavenward. "Dad! Next time leave a note!"

—

Angie angled her face in the rear view mirror, smiling as she admired the green stud in her right nostril. I had held her hand for the piercing and told a terrible knock-knock joke as she discovered she was afraid of needles.

"What do you do for fun?" she asked as we hit the Mass Pike.

"Nothing much." I was holding the vase like it was my child. "You should come with me back to Chicago, we can make it a mini vacation. Sometime real soon, let's talk about college." We headed home with the sun setting in the rearview, Angie found a metal head station on the radio and I endured it.

"Think there are any more gnomes?"

A Carton of Eggs

Mike Sherer

I didn't know at the time how I came unstuck. It happened on a day like any other day. I was taking a walk in my neighborhood. I do this at least three times a week. Walking around my neighborhood is much more enjoyable than going to the gym. Who wouldn't rather be outdoors in the fresh air than indoors with a bunch of smelly sweaty bodies? Though I've been to the gym plenty of times, too. But that comes later.

On this day I was walking around a cul-de-sac admiring my neighbors' landscaping. I live in a suburb of Cincinnati. At the present. So there are a lot of hydrangeas, hibiscus, roses, lilies. We get plenty of rain, and the winters aren't too extreme. Not that I'm not used to extreme winters.

Anyway, with one step I was walking down a street in my neighborhood. With the very next I was walking on a treadmill in a gym. I staggered off it and nearly fell flat on my face.

A woman on a treadmill next to me stopped hers. "Are you okay?"

Hell, no. What had happened? How had I ended up there? I staggered away.

"Are you coming back?"

I turned back to see she was as concerned as before. I shrugged. I didn't know *what* the hell I was doing. Or where I was. Or how I had gotten there. I was just there.

She pointed to the treadmill I had nearly broken my neck on. "You left your phone."

I went back to look. It wasn't my phone. I walked off. I'd never been in this gym before. I know, they all pretty much look the same, but I'd never spent much time in *any* gym. I plopped down into the first chair I came to. What was going on?

"Larry?"

I didn't look up because my name wasn't Larry.

But this guy insisted it was. "Larry? Are you okay?"

I looked up. Like the woman on the treadmill next to me, I'd never seen this man before.

Yet he acted like he knew me. He sat down beside me. "Did you overdo it? On the treadmill?"

I could see why he might think that. I was hyperventilating. But that was from panic, not over-exercising. I shook my head.

"Do I need to take you to the emergency room?"

Another head shake. "Could you take me home?"

"Of course. You probably shouldn't be driving."

When I got up my legs were trembling. He started to put an arm around me, but I shook him off. Walking out to the parking lot I told him my address.

Which got me a concerned look. "That's not your address, Larry. Are you sure I can't take you to the hospital? You could be having a stroke."

"Please just drive me home."

I climbed in the passenger side of a blue Toyota Camry.

Behind the wheel of a white Honda Odyssey. That was driving down the road. I screamed, slamming on the brake.

"Mommy! What's wrong?"

Mommy? A horn blared behind me. I had stopped in the middle of the road. I eased over to the shoulder, shifted into park, put my flashers on. Then looked into the rearview mirror to see who had called me Mommy. Behind me was a young boy strapped into a safety seat. In the rearview mirror was the face of a young woman. I looked down. The shirt I was wearing swelled out as if it was covering breasts. I pulled the neck out and peered down inside. Yes, there were breasts in there. Big ones.

"Mommy! Let's go!"

I couldn't be dreaming. You had to be asleep to dream, and I'd never fallen asleep while walking through my neighborhood. Or on a treadmill. Could I have had a stroke? Like my friend suggested? Friend, hell, I'd never seen the guy before. Now I was a woman? I was shaking so bad I couldn't think straight.

"Mommy! I'm hungry!"

I turned around for a good look at the kid. He didn't look familiar at all. "Mommy needs her Valium."

"Go home!"

I wondered where that was? I turned on the satellite navigation and punched in Home. 'Acquiring satellites' was announced as I stared at the screen in a daze.

Satellites appeared firing lasers at each other. I threw my game controller down and lunged back flat onto a bed I had been sitting on the edge of.

Next to a teenage boy, still sitting up and also holding a game controller. "Are you quitting?"

"YES!!" I jumped up and staggered all about. "I quit! I give up!" I was in a bedroom. A teenage boy's bedroom most likely, with a Michael Jordan poster on the wall, right next to one of Cheryl Tiegs. I slapped my chest. It was flat. I grabbed my crotch. Yes, it was there.

"Don't get weird."

I looked at the boy who had spoken. A frail pimply-faced boy in his early teens with crazy hair. I lunged over to the dresser mirror. I was a brown-skinned teenage boy.

"If you need to go to the bathroom, you know where it's at. Don't pee in my sock drawer."

I looked to the screen sitting on his desk. We were playing some kind of space shooter game. But the graphics didn't look right. They were primitive, jagged. Like a video game from the eighties. And the sounds. Was that MIDI? I couldn't move. I was locked onto the thirteen-inch portable TV screen. With an Atari 2600 console hooked up to it.

"Are you mental?"

I couldn't do this anymore. "I've got to go." I ran out the door.

And fell to the ground flat on my face.

"Mom!"

Was I back in the minivan? No, I was laying on grass. Had I wrecked and been thrown from the vehicle?

Someone took my arm and gently pulled me up. "You've got to be careful."

The voice was different. It wasn't a young child, like before, the last time I was a woman. It was an adult. A grown woman. She steadied me on my feet. "Are you alright?"

"No," I answered truthfully. I sounded like a woman. An old woman. I focused on the woman holding me. She looked old. If she thought I was her mother then I must look ancient.

"Let's sit down." She carefully escorted me to a bench.

As I shuffled along at her side I looked around. I was in a cemetery. "Am I dead?"

"You will be if you keep falling like that. That's the one thing you can't do, is fall. That's the worst thing a senior can do." She eased me down into a bench then sat next to me. "We came here to visit Dad's grave. Remember?"

I'd had enough. I needed answers. No more trying to fake it. I looked the old woman sitting beside me square in the face. "Who am I?"

"Mom," she moaned, tears in her eyes. "Your Alzheimer's is getting worse." She hugged me.

I gave in and returned the hug, but not to the old woman who called me mom. This was a young woman. That I was laying on top of. In bed. Who was naked. I flung myself away from her.

"Don't get so upset, Don. It happens."

I saw I was naked, too. Middle-aged. And kind of flabby. I yanked the sheet up over me. "*What* happens?"

"It's nothing." She smiled, reaching out to stroke my face.

I scooted further back.

This brought a scowl. "Don. Don't be childish about it."

"About what?"

"E.D."

I lifted the sheet to look. I was limp as a steamed noodle.

"Can't we just cuddle? That's all. Just hold each other for a while."

I looked back up. The woman was gorgeous. I was naked in bed with a beautiful willing naked woman and couldn't do anything about it.

She took me in her arms and pulled me close. Ahh. Maybe we could just hold each other for a while. Maybe I could just relax for a while. Calm down. I slipped my arms around her. This felt so good, so soothing. The crazy train had been running off the rails. If I could just slow it down, for a while, get my bearings.

"See, Don." I looked to see her smiling at me. "I feel something stirring down there already. This is all you need to do, just relax." She pulled me closer.

And slammed me down to the ground. Wham! Breath. Knocked. Out. Of. Me. I looked up from flat on my back, gasping for air, unable to move a muscle. A soldier towered above me with his rifle held high in both hands, its long bayonet gleaming. With murderous rage, he drove it down to my chest.

I rolled to the side at the last instant. Knocking one leg out from under him as his bayonet plunged into the dirt.

He fell to one knee, hanging onto his rifle to keep from toppling. He scrambled back up and yanked on his rifle, but the bayonet was buried deep.

I scrambled to my feet and ran.

A battlefield. Soldiers milling all about in blue and grey. A Civil War re-enactment? A bullet whistled by my ear. Re-enactment, hell. That sounded real. I screamed as a cannonball exploded nearby, pelting me with clods of dirt. Smoke hung all around. Men cried out, a bugle…a bugle?!...somewhere. A man on horseback galloped by. Wails, gunfire. I tripped over a bloody body and went sprawling.

"I got you!"

I rolled over onto my back. He was there! Above me, with his rifle raised high again. The maniac had chased after me! He drove his bayonet down once again.

As I pinned a butterfly to a board. Finding I could scream, I screamed.

"Did you stick yourself, Adelia?"

I jerked upright to my feet and staggered about. An elderly man in old-fashioned clothes, with an old-fashioned white beard and moustache of ZZ Top proportions, grabbed me by the shoulders. "Let me see, dear." He examined one of my numbly pliant hands, then the other. "I don't see any blood."

"I thought I was dead!"

He chuckled. "It's just a pin. You could hardly kill yourself with it." He bent to pick up the board on which several dozen butterflies were impaled that I had flung to the ground. "Look what you've done. You'll ruin your collection."

I sagged into a ball on the bench where I was seated, sobbing. "Stop, please. I can't do this anymore."

"Stop what? This?" He swept his arm in a wide arc, indicating the small flower garden they were in. "You've always loved it here in our garden."

I unballed enough to gaze about. A compact walled garden surrounded me, with a fountain, several statues, and an abundance of bright blooms. Unpinned butterflies fluttered all about in the bright sunny air. "*Our* garden?"

He handed the board back to me. "You've loved this garden since I brought you here on our wedding day."

"We're married?" I leaned over to peer into the pool of water in the fountain I sat beside. I saw the reflection of a young woman in a vintage Victorian dress. "We can't be married. You're too old. You're old enough to be my father. My grandfather."

He backhanded me so hard I went flying off the bench.

I looked up into the blazing sun, my face stinging.

"Don't look at me like that again, boy!"

When I touched my burning cheek, I saw my hand was black.

The man towering above me, who I couldn't make out in the bright daylight, kicked me in the ribs. "Get up and get back to work!"

I crawled to my knees.

He kicked me again. "I said get up!"

I rose up to my full height. I towered above my assailant. A scrawny little white man. I looked myself over. I was huge.

He touched the coiled whip dangling from his belt. "If you make me use this, boy, I'm not stopping until I get tired."

I looked around. A cotton field filled with slaves, both men and women, picking the blooms and stuffing them into large sacks. The air waved with the dense wet heat. I'd finally made it to Hell. I reached down to the cotton plant at my feet to pluck a soft white ball.

I pulled off a berry. I held it up before my eyes. It was red, not white.

I looked around. Several women were scattered about, children bumbling about their legs. The women wore rags, the children nothing at all. They were picking berries from the bushes we were in the midst of. A cool breeze chilled the air.

I looked myself over. I was a woman once again. No longer such a novelty. Rags similar to what the others wore hung on my bony body. Aged, it looked like and felt like. Aches from every joint and muscle speared me. Peering into the bag I held, some animal skin, I saw it was nearly full of red berries. How long had it been since I ate?

I dropped down and pulled a handful out. They looked okay to eat. These women wouldn't be picking them it they weren't. I popped one in. Not much to them, sort of sour. Still, I was tired and hungry and disgusted and ready to give up. Time for dinner. I pulled out a handful to eat.

The back of my head exploded in pain. I plunged forward, spilling what I held and half the contents of my sack, and looked up from the ground. A woman stood above me holding a stick. Had she whacked me? Why? She screamed and made a fierce face, waving the stick around like she was going to do it again. I couldn't understand a word she was saying, if

184

they were words. A lot of grunting and screeching. I felt the back of my head then checked my fingers. No blood. Damn, I must have a thick skull.

The woman swung her stick and caught me on the shoulder this time. That did it. I grabbed that stick and yanked it out of her hands. Jumping up, I saw she was really old. I couldn't hit her back. So I broke the stick over my knee and threw the pieces away.

The old woman wasn't backing down. She continued to scream and dance around. While I figured I could handle her, all the other women were now watching. And they didn't look happy. Some of them began to gather around us. I guess I shouldn't have broken her stick. Was she upset because I'd quit working? Because I'd eaten some of the berries? I had no idea.

The knot of ominous women continued to tighten around me. So I ran. Only not far. I was barefoot. There were rocks. They hurt. I tumbled to the ground, scooting across more rocks. Right up to the edge of a cliff. I was on a mountainside. For as far as I could see were other mountains, forests, lakes, rivers. An amazing panorama of wilderness. It was glorious.

But I was exhausted. Hurt. Hungry. Bewildered. The women had caught up with me. There was nowhere to go. I didn't know what the old woman out front was saying, but her body language was blatant. She wanted the others to beat me to a pulp. Screw that. I'd had enough. I jumped.

I soared through the air. How high up was I? Forty feet? Fifty? I kept soaring. I wasn't falling. I was flying. Below was a barren landscape, not the verdant primeval mountain forest I'd seen before. Above was a pitch-black sky. With twinkling stars.

"That was amazing, Dad!"

I had a radio in my ear.

"I thought you were hopping into space that time. Be careful." A different voice. Female. Adult.

"Careful with what?"

"The mag-levs. Why don't you come back in. Dinner is almost ready."

I started to descend, wondering what mag-levs were and how I was supposed to be careful with them. They could be in the heavy belt I was wearing, or the bulky boots. I was also clad in a light full-body suit, and a helmet with a faceplate so clear I hadn't even noticed it before. Through it I caught a glimpse of the Earth in the inky sky. Was I on the Moon?

I floated back down to the surface, landing with a soft jolt that sent a storm of regolith up all around me. I scanned the horizon as the dust thinned. It sure looked like pictures I'd seen of the lunar landscape. Except in the distance there was a bubble-like structure.

"Honey? Are you okay?"

"Yes. I just want to stop and catch my breath."

"Don't be long."

I stared off at the bubble. How far was it? Panic was starting to rustle. I didn't have any oxygen tanks on me. Where was my air coming from? Would I have enough to make it back?

Yes.

Where had that come from?

Hal.

Who is Hal?

Your smart bubble.

A home network?

Yes.

How do these mag-levs work?

Face home. Hop.

That's it?

I'll control the rest.

I decided to try a short hop to start. Something safe. I barely flexed my legs. I went soaring. "Hal!"

Yes?

"Not so high!"

Sorry, Dave, I can't do that.

I was soaring in the right direction. Directly toward the bubble. Looked like I could make it in only a couple hops. Relaxing as I realized I was probably safe, I had the ease to reflect upon the name of the home network. "Why are you named Hal?"

Why are you named Dave, Dave?

Before I could respond to the smartass in my ear I found myself in deep inter-galactic space. No reassuring bubble, no Moon surface, no Earth above the horizon, no Sun in the distance, no recognizable constellation in the inky black. Merely a meager number of shining dots scattered across vast empty stretches. Other galaxies?

Yes.

The voice sounded different. Not artificial, like before. "Hal?"

No.

"Who am I speaking to?"

Yourself.

That was different. So, I was alone? In what looked like deep space. I attempted to look myself over but could see nothing. I tried to move my arms up into my field of vision. I couldn't see them. Where was I? I mean, where was my body? What had happened to me? Was I still alive?

Don't panic.

"Marvin?"

No. We are the Walrus.

Music began playing, an old Beatles song ('I Am the Walrus', lyrics by Lennon-McCartney). "I am he as you are he as..."

"I'm a walrus now?"

No. That is merely an example. We are all together, like the song says.

"What does that even mean?"

There are no longer individual human beings. We are a collective.

"A hive mind? Like the Borg?"

No hive mind. Only the hive. One.

I gazed all around. "We can drift in outer space like this?"

We are not drifting. We can go wherever we wish.

"At the speed of light?"

At the speed of thought. Where do we want to go?

"You're asking me?"

You are asking you.

"The only place I want to go is to go home."

This universe is our home. This multiverse is our home. This multi-dimensional space is our home. Be more specific.

"8960 Mimosa Lane, West Chester, Ohio 45069."

I was sitting in high grass in the middle of a dense forest, surrounded by mighty maples and ancient oaks. Several deer stared curiously at me.

"Where am I?"

8960 Mimosa...

I was flat on my back near the top of a small rise. Despite the dense forest wilderness, the topography looked vaguely familiar. "I meant home in 2024."

Why didn't you say so? The parameters of spacetime include width, breadth, height, *and* duration.

The forest disappeared. Leaving me sitting in the middle of my lawn in front of my house. I was home! I flopped around on the newly mown grass in relief.

"Are you okay?"

I looked to see my neighbor staring at me with concern.

"You were returning from one of your walks and collapsed. Did you overdo it?"

"I'm okay." I rolled across the grass. "I'm just glad to be back."

The neighbor walked over to me and offered a hand. "Actually, you did overdo it."

I took his hand and let him pull me to my feet.

"You just had a fatal heart attack."

I let go of his hand and bounced about. "You're wrong. I feel fine."

"Who says you don't feel fine when you die?"

I looked all around. I was home. In my front yard. In front of my house. With the flower gardens I tended at least once a week. With my car parked in the driveway. Surrounded by my neighborhood. Everything was as familiar as my face in the mirror in the morning when I shave. "I can't be dead. I'm home."

"Who else do you see?"

I looked around again. He had a point. No one was out in their yards. No children playing outside. No cars or Prime delivery vans or lawn care service trucks on the street.

"It's the middle of the day. A weekday. And school's in."

"Any dogs barking? Any birds flying around? Any bugs bugging you?"

He had another point. I focused on him. "There's you."

"I am you."

"Are we back to being the walrus?"

"What did you think of your options?"

I paused to reflect upon my recent experiences. "Is that what that was? A preview?"

"The body your consciousness was focused on just
189

suffered a fatal heart attack. So now it will shift to another one of your bodies. Which of the twelve you just sampled do you choose?"

That floored me. So I collapsed back onto my lawn. "Are you saying I can become any of the twelve people I just experienced?"

"Yes."

"What happens to them?"

"Only what has happened."

"What does that mean?"

My neighbor sat down in the grass in front of me. "The flow of time is an illusion. Everything has already happened. The past, the present, the future. It's all played out. Static. Immutable. The fabric of spacetime has already been woven. All that's to do is to traverse the individual threads through every warp and weft of the weave."

"You're saying every life has already been lived."

"There is only one life. You. Every human that ever existed is simply a reincarnation of you. Your soul contains every memory, lesson, and experience from every past life, even if you cannot recall them. The human mind is too small to truly encompass the entirety of who you are."

I sat in stunned silence trying to comprehend what my neighbor had just said. Finally, "Are you God?"

"No. You are only you. As I am you." He stood. "Time is running out. You only have so much time before your consciousness must inhabit another you."

"I won't remember any of this?" I looked all around at the quiet neighborhood.

"All you'll remember will be the memories programmed into the mind of the body your consciousness centers on."

I stood. "If those twelve lives are my options, then I choose the next to last one. I want to live on the Moon."

My neighbor's face sank.

"What? Is that a bad choice?"

"There are no bad choices. Eventually, you will make every choice."

"You mean I'll experience *every* life?"

"Every life that ever was, is, or will be. That is the real meaning of the Golden Rule. 'Do unto others as you would have them do unto you.' Because they *are* you."

"One day I'll be Hitler?"

"And one day you will be Gandhi."

"So why did you frown like that?"

"I lost a wager with another you. I bet you would choose to be the young mother driving the minivan. She was hot."

"She was my second choice. I'll choose her next time."

My neighbor studied me. "Why should I believe you?"

"Why would I lie?"

"So you could win the wager next time."

"The wager was with me?"

"Of course." His expression brightened as he took both my hands in his. "But then I'll win the wager next time, too. So, it really doesn't matter. Ready to go to the Moon?"

I floated down in front of the bubble. Hal had gotten me safely back home. He was nothing like his namesake.

This mission is too important for me to allow you to jeopardize it.

Whatever. The exterior door to the airlock opened and I walked inside. It closed behind me and the chamber began to pressurize. Through the clear glass I saw my wife busy setting the table for dinner and my son in the bathroom washing his hands. Ahh, it was so good to be home.

Farther Along Camino de Santiago

Joe Giordano

Four weeks in, as a petition for absolution, I hiked, occasionally encountering other pilgrims as we weaved France's verdant, wooded, hilly paths of Camino de Santiago. With booted feet and hiking shorts, using a stiff staff for balance on rocky patches, I embraced the penance of carrying my weighty backpack where a Saint James's attribute scallop shell dangled like a tiny spinnaker speeding my journey. I trekked The Way of St. James, traveling town by town, church by church for the spiritual renewal of the experience.

Not your thing?

Or do you want to come along?

I'm Vincent.

I detoured to explore a cave. Descending like a setting sun into a rock fissure, I entered an inky blackness. My torch illuminated various wall prehistoric paintings – animal depictions, and a testimony to my ancestor's existence. He'd spit mouthfuls of gritty red clay over his splayed fingers creating an image on a rock wall. I placed my hand over his twenty-five-thousand-year-old "signature" as a gesture of human solidarity. Where did we come from? Where are we going?

I was headed toward Rocamadour, a medieval town chiseled into the limestone cliff like a bas-relief, framed by the mist of a drizzly day. For centuries her Black Madonna granted miracles, and I had a request.

A stone arch framed a cobblestone pedestrian lane flanked by gray-brown stone structures—shops, cafes, and boutique hotels. Sitting at an outdoor table of a café, a woman with blazing blue eyes accentuated by red hair and a powder blue veil smiled at me. I stopped short. She had an aura, and some opportunities would be a sin to miss. "Bonjour," I said. "May I join you?"

"*Bonjour.*" She gestured toward the other wicker seat at the small round table.

I dropped my backpack beside the chair. "I'm Vincent."

"Marie. *Enchanté.*"

"You speak English?"

"A little."

When a French person says, "a little," they're likely able to recite the Gettysburg Address. When an American tells you he can speak some French, he's tripped up after *bonjour*.

"You're an American?" she asked.

"Worse," I said smiling. "Texan."

"Ah. An independent minded person."

"That's what we tell ourselves. You live in Rocamadour?"

She mused. "Among other places."

I couldn't say exactly why, but this woman gave me a rare sense of wellbeing. "May I buy you a coffee or something else to drink?"

"*Merci.* Not for me."

When the vested waiter arrived, I ordered a *petit* coffee for myself.

She said, "I can see by your scallop shell that you're on a pilgrimage. What are you seeking?"

"Absolution."

"You need forgiveness?"

"I found life easier to handle staying anesthetized. Drugs were fun until my behavior traumatized the people I loved. I've gotten clean, but they're gone, and I can't make amends, so I undertook this journey."

She nodded. "Anyone can fall victim to pain. A guilty conscience is the tariff for existing, and suffering is intrinsic to being human." She held me with cobalt eyes. "Do you believe God will forgive your sins?"

"Somebody needs to." I squirmed a bit, changing the subject. "Outside Rocamadour, I entered a prehistoric cave. Pitch black, I couldn't see past my eyeballs. Yet an ancient man using a flickering grease lamp risked serious injury or encountering a bear to create images and leave a handprint as documentation of his presence."

"Ego?"

"I don't know."

She said, "Perhaps he made his own religious trek, entering the mysterious underworld."

"Something drove him to overcome his fear of the unknown."

"Human anxiousness stems from those times, surrounded by danger. Yet, you must take risks to grow. Even if this life isn't all you have."

I pondered her point.

She continued. "You're somewhat ill at ease, traveling from Texas, beyond your comfort zone. You showed the courage to embrace adventure."

"I suppose we endure to prove our worth."

She tilted her head. "Will you petition the Black Madonna?"

I hesitated to open up. Just the thought depressed me. But something about her told me she wasn't, like most people, just being polite. She really wanted to know. "Three guys mugged Chris, a friend of mine. One of them cracked his skull with a tire iron, putting him in a coma." I felt exhausted by the revelation.

"How horrible."

"He awoke in a hospital bed without the use of his legs and had trouble forming words."

"He must've panicked."

"A severe brain injury. He may never recover."

Her eyes welled. I was surprised to see such empathy for someone she didn't know. Made her attractive far beyond her physical beauty.

"He feels he can't continue in school and no woman will be interested in saddling themselves with a disabled person. He fights his hate for the attackers."

"I'm so sorry."

I grimaced. "The cops grabbed the three guys, but a judge released them without bail. He couldn't make a positive identification, and they never faced trial."

"Earthly justice is often inadequate."

"He doesn't understand why God would dispatch thugs to ruin his life. He's hurt and angry. He's lost faith. The powerlessness of dependency is causing him to give up."

"Without God," she sighed, "there's no hope for justice." She paused before saying, "What will you ask of the Madonna?"

"Have him recover. Take him out of his depression before he drowns his sadness in a bottle of opioids."

She nodded, and we sat for a few moments in silence. She excused herself, I presumed for the ladies room.

I'd long finished my coffee, and she hadn't returned. I cursed myself for being so forthcoming about my sins and about Chris having been paralyzed. I scoffed at the way I'd made a first impression. No wonder she disappeared. Who wants to be around a guy who tells depressing stories. I huffed, then called the waiter over to pay my bill.

When he arrived, I asked in my bad French, "Did you happen to see where the woman I was with went?"

As he made change, he gave me an odd look, probably because I mangled the French pronunciation. I repeated my question in English.

"Monsieur," he said, looking slightly peeved, "I understood you the first time. What woman did you mean?"

I thought he was digging at me. "The woman dressed in a blue veil. The redhead with those gorgeous eyes. She sat here when you served me coffee."

His look turned skeptical. "You sat alone. There was no woman here." He walked away.

My mouth opened and closed. I sat back in bewilderment. Was I hallucinating? Did something gaseous in that prehistoric cave trigger the DTs from my drug-sodden days?

To clear my head, I decided to ascend the 216 steps to the Notre Dame sanctuary and the Black Madonna.

About halfway up, the thought occurred to me that, perhaps, I'd already made my petition. I checked my watch and quickened my pace. If I moved fast, it wouldn't be too late to phone Chris in the States.

The Overdue Library Book

David Clear

One night when I was about 10, I dreamt I was in a library.

A lady walked up. She looked familiar. She didn't say anything but when she turned and walked away, I felt compelled to follow.

We came to a large set of double doors. Inscribed on them were the words *Sapere aude,* and *caveat scriptor.*

She looked at me but all I could do was shrug.

"It's OK, you'll remember soon enough," she said, pushed gently on one of the doors and we went inside to an office. She sat down behind a desk. I remained standing. Scared.

"You're early," she said, "why are you so early?"

The fear that her words induced was so great I woke up and sat up in bed, startled and shaking.

Four years later I started 9th grade. The first thing the new English teacher did was write on the board: *Sapere aude.*

"Does anyone know what that means?" she asked the

class.

Somehow, *I knew*! Shakily, I spoke up. Not because I knew I had the right answer but because it was love at first sight for me with Miss Colwell.

"Dare to know," I said.

She was quiet, a surprised look crossing her face before a tender smile and the reply, "Very good. I hope you continue to dare, Mr. Calloway."

That very night I dreamt of the library. And her.

She was the dream librarian!

"Can I help you?" she said, walking up to me as I stood browsing the fiction section.

"Miss Colwell?"

"You are a good student."

And with those words, we were suddenly on the roof of the building. A change of scene the way they commonly happen in dreams; sudden, inexplicable.

We were standing at the edge. A tightrope was strung to the next building. Cloud cover obscured whatever was below, but the feeling of immense height was undeniable.

"Do you remember when we first met in the library? You were younger. Less jaded. You checked out a book that night," she said.

"I don't remember," I said, squinting against the wind whipping across my face. Yet not a hair on her head moved.

"You will. It's the one that hasn't been written yet."

"Excuse me?"

"You have to write it—on earth. It's overdue now."

"What does that have to do with a tightrope?"

"The wire between the lower and higher worlds is how you dare to know. But don't forget the other part—*caveat scriptor*—writer beware."

And then I woke up.

Our next meeting wasn't until eight years later when I was wide awake, standing on a sidewalk in Prescott, Arizona watching the rental house my girlfriend and I had been living in go up in flames.

There she was, standing right next to me. My girlfriend couldn't hear or see her.

"I know all your writings of the past fifteen years or so are on paper in that burning house right now. Your life was saved by that off-duty cop who just happened to smell smoke as he was driving by. You and your girlfriend are alive. You realize whatever you've written up to this point is insignificant compared to that, right?"

"Oh, I do, I really do. It would be nice if they could be saved but if not, I'm OK with letting them all go and starting over."

She smiled the way she did when I gave the right answer in class. I didn't have to start over.

—

Sometime later we met again.

"You didn't have to set the house on fire to get my attention," I said.

"Oh, I'm afraid I did. Got you sober, didn't it? You could never walk the wire drunk or stoned. C'mon, they're waiting, follow me."

We walked down a long hall which ended where she opened the door to a huge, crowded auditorium. I had the strong sense an interesting presentation of some sort was about to begin. Perhaps an erudite academic of some esoteric philosophy, or spiritual teacher.

I took an empty seat in the back of the room, but Miss Colwell grabbed my arm.

"What are you doing sitting down? You have to convince everyone in the audience to walk the wire with you. You have to finally, and fully, convince yourself it's worth the risk."

I was as scared as I had been when I was ten and first dreamed of her. But I was also as certain as I had been when I knew the translation of *Sapere aude* in class. In her eyes the wisdom of a thousand libraries were transmitted and I knew I could tap into it in now in just the right amounts needed.

I walked to the podium knowing, instinctively, *I was the audience.*

Sitting in no particular order were: Neolithic hunters, Neolithic gatherers, Roman senators, Roman slaves, medieval barons, medieval serfs, Japanese samurai, Japanese courtesans, bankers, musicians, merchants, madmen, monks, businessmen, philosophers professors, poets, popes, preachers, pedophiles, alcoholics, addicts, gamblers, thieves, murderers, merchants, martyrs, hermits, hobos, housewives, soldiers, sailors, seamstresses, farmers, carpenters, brick masons, fishermen, lawyers, doctors, priests, dancers, wrestlers, husbands, wives, mothers, fathers, brothers and sisters, the aged and stillborn.

I knew they were all teachers and all students, comprising a mosaic, a maze, a repeating, ascending cycle of individual endeavors each trying a new role, a new scene, a new costume, a new play that might lead to a final, definitive answer as to which would be best.

I looked down at Miss Colwell in the front row. I knew what to say. "Personalities are like vines growing entangled over the same tree. Over time they forget it is the tree that is the real truth and source of life. And, once we disentangle, we become free. That golden cup awaits across an abyss of forgetting; the one we have all so often fallen into in the past. It's an opportunity to walk with full awareness of purpose into an experience without having to kill or be killed or starve or freeze to death or just live a humdrum life and take that final breath wondering what it was all about."

"Wait a minute, sonny," an older African American man spoke up. "What if we go with you and you're wrong; there are no answers, there is no freedom? I know you're a reincarnation of my miserable slave life on the plantation, and while I don't mind being you now, despite being a little boring, I wouldn't want to risk it for some pie in the sky."

Then, a corpulent, red-faced, jolly-looking gentleman called out, "I daresay it's just another gamble, another turn of the cards. I for one am feeling rather lucky at the moment and propose we give this well-spoken young lad the benefit of the doubt. Nothing ventured, nothing gained, wot?"

I remembered him/me-then. I was a happy-go-lucky alcoholic, gambler, carouser, running away from working in my dad's saddlery shop in London but always coming back long enough for a loan from my mom or to work enough to head back for another party.

A regally dressed Asian woman then stood and said, "I must respectfully decline. I, an empress, taking advice from an unemployed housepainter?"

Sitting next to her, a tall man stood and said, "I have to say, in my position as Emperor of China, I, too am reluctant to give up the bird in the hand; by which I mean unlimited power, wealth, privilege and concubines, for two invisible ones in some spiritually nebulous bush."

"Oh, my goodness," we all heard then from somewhere in the back of the room. "So many lifetimes as slaves of one sort or another, both rich and poor, both enslaving others and being enslaved!"

Then he came forward in his 16th century attire and continued. "I beg all of you to accept this opportunity to move on! Was I burned at the stake for publishing a book contradicting the prevailing jackass wisdom of the time for nothing? Yes, many of us had sweet cushy, lives, dying in our sleep but then returning to a most rude awakening! Don't you see what he says is true! This is our chance to get off this merry go round!"

An ethereal silence descended upon the room, and with it the golden light of a precious autumnal afternoon. And then came the sound. The sound that had been leading us to be together here across centuries, millennia, continents, oceans, planets and galaxies for that matter, through war, peace, poverty, prosperity, community and isolation, leadership and servitude, freedom and slavery, any and every state of being that could be manifested.

A murmuration—an effortless but exact swirling, shape-shifting coordination of starlings at dusk—painted the sky above a yin-yang light and dark. Shape and substance and silence and sound all became one expression of the ecstasy of existence. An expression arising and ascending out of all constraints and restraints to coalesce into something far too impossibly grand and timeless to squeeze into one flesh and blood body.

But the connective conduit to that vastness was ever open and flowing with precise dispensation into the essential, lost but never forgotten, eternal and inviolable truth of all.

We all began filing from the room to the stairway to the roof, moving quietly and harmoniously as monks, but also, as prisoners now to be released unconditionally. I was the last to the roof where Miss Colwell took my hand.

The energy flowing from her pulsed wildly into my body. And then she spoke so sweetly. "Continue to allow pieces of the cosmically large puzzle to slowly fit themselves into place. The pieces are your words. Writers can only do their best to toss out messages in bottles upon the waves of the mass consciousness. The most outwardly successful ones worked, consciously or unconsciously, with assistance from the library editors. They built upon what had been built already by the previous, invisible builders. Feel free to become a bestseller. However, the clock will keep ticking on that human form of yours, so you will need to start walking across now. Once you reach the other side is where the book will be written, the one that will then need to be returned."

"There won't be a late fee will there?" I asked, trying to make a joke, but actually once more rather worried after so recent a flush of uber-confidence.

A deep, sonorous voice from midway back in the line was then heard to say, "Good God Calloway, will you start walking and stop worrying already! We conquered the known world once and now you're fretting about late fees!"

I looked back but could not see who had spoken. Miss Colwell grinned a little and said to me, "No, not Alexander the Great. One of his lieutenants, but with a greater ego than his boss, even. Don't worry, you won't be late. Ready?"

And she handed me a balancing pole.

As I took it, I was surprised at how light it felt and then took the first step. I couldn't see anything below, but the strong sense of immense distance was undeniable. But there was no fear because my feet felt stuck to the wire with each step until I lifted one, and then the other, each locking onto the wire with perfect balance and security.

My upper body meanwhile felt like it was harnessed to a safety line extending upward into invisibility. After just a few steps I knew with certainty I was going to make it, there was no doubt, it was preordained, it was a fixed truth. And when I reached the midpoint, I confidently turned around to see the other selves. As each took that first step onto the wire, they disappeared. I turned back and walked on to the building across the abyss.

I had a book to return. Maybe more than one.

All In

John Mitchell Johnson

I was thirteen years old that July in 1952 that they let Uncle Buddy out of the pen long enough to come home for Mammaw's funeral, or so they thought. Ernest Wayne Slone, or Buddy, was four years into a twelve-year hitch at the state penitentiary at Eddyville. Him and Leon Stratton had got in a knife fight in the parking lot of the Caboose, a honky-tonk at the mouth of the holler. Folks said that Leon started it, and Buddy claimed self-defense, but when Leon died in the Miner's Hospital over in West Virginia a few days later, Uncle Buddy was charged with first-degree manslaughter. He was tried, found guilty, and sentenced to twelve years. His lawyer said he could get out on good behavior in eight, but Daddy said that was about as likely as a bull giving milk.

My name is Edward Thomas, but most everybody calls me Eddy T. Me and Daddy moved in with Mammaw and Aunt Lilly, Daddy's older sister, when I was six years old. Lilly had never married, but not for a lack of trying, and my momma had run off with some asshole that drove a beer truck—Daddy's words, not mine.

It was high summer and the evening air was thick with gnat swarms as snake doctors danced on the surface of the frog pond. Mammaw was laid out in the front room in her flowered church dress with a store-bought bouquet clutched in her folded arms. Neighbors had been bringing in food for the past couple of days, and the whole house smelled of tuna fish casserole and scorched coffee. Aunt Lilly said Mammaw died of a broken heart on account of Uncle Buddy, but Doc Fleming said it was the dropsy. Whatever the reason, Mammaw had taken to her bed a couple of weeks earlier, predicting that her time on this earth was fleeting. Daddy said this was at least the fourth time Mammaw had had such a revelation, but turns out this time she was right.

"Eddy T.," Daddy said, "you best go set up some chairs on the side porch. Mamma's church is having a singing this evening, and they'll probably be a passel of 'em come out."

Mammaw went to the Larks Creek Free Will Baptist Church, where she faithfully attended every time the doors were opened. She had previously been a sainted member of the Old Regular Baptists until they disfellowshipped her for divorcing Pappaw, who died a short six months later. Mammaw always said if she'd have known he was going to go so soon she'd have waited him out. Even though Pappaw was a drunk and a runaround, the Old Regulars didn't abide divorce, so Mammaw cut her hair, gave herself a permanent, and joined up with the Free Wills.

"What time is Uncle Buddy getting in?" I asked.

"I'm not sure," Daddy said. "It's supposed to be this evening sometime. They're sending a guard with him."

On the day Mammaw passed, Daddy called the prison

and requested a funeral furlough for his kid brother, which was swiftly denied. The warden said there was no way to get it approved in such a short time, and he was too busy to be bothered with the likes of Buddy anyway. Daddy being Daddy called his cousin Judge John Morgan, and Judge Morgan in turn called his friend the lieutenant governor, who called the warden.

It was early dusk and the first few lightning bugs were flickering their tails when the sedan with the Kentucky Department of Corrections decal pulled up in front of Mammaw's house. The church people were singing their last song, "The Old Ship of Zion," as the uniformed guard helped Uncle Buddy out of the back seat.

"Hey, Squirt," Uncle Buddy said as he shuffled up the stone steps. "Damn, you've got grown since I been gone."

"Hey, Uncle Buddy," I said. "I ain't a squirt anymore. I'm almost fourteen."

Buddy turned to the guard. "Are you going to make me wear these shackles in to see my own blessed mother laid out in her casket?"

"I suppose not." The guard squatted to unlock the fetters.

"And these clothes . . . prison rags, for God's sake. I'm sure my brother has something decent he can loan me."

"Okay, but let's get one thing straight. Soon as we get back to Eddyville, I start mustering out. After twenty years, I'm hanging it up. So if you even think about running, I'll shoot you like you was a shithouse rat." He patted his sidearm. "I ain't about to let a low-life punk sully my record. You got that, number 476928?"

"My name's Ernest Wayne, but you can call me Buddy."

"I know your goddamn name."

Just then Aunt Lilly came busting out onto the porch.

"Buddy, Buddy, Buddy," she said, dabbing at her eyes

209

with a lace-lined handkerchief.

"Mamma missed you so terribly. All she talked about her last few days was her baby boy."

"Well, Lilly, unfortunately I haven't exactly been available of late," Buddy snapped.

"Oh, let's not start in on each other, Buddy, especially with our poor Mamma lying cold in her coffin just inside. Anyway, who's your handsome escort?" Aunt Lilly batted her big brown eyes at the state prison guard.

"Sergeant William Sargent, ma'am," the officer responded.

"I do declare. Sergeant Sargent." Aunt Lilly giggled and extended her arm as if she were the Queen of England expecting him to kiss her hand. The officer just nodded.

"Well then, come on Buddy, let's go find your big brother. Hershel is dying to see you. And let's get you out of those prison clothes."

After Uncle Buddy changed into a pair of khakis and a starched white shirt, we all went into the front room to view Mammaw.

"She made such a pretty corpse," Aunt Lilly said, rubbing Mammaw's cheek with the back of her hand. "Here we all are, Mamma." Aunt Lilly continued as if Mammaw could hear her. "Me and Hershel and Buddy and Eddy T." Once again Aunt Lilly dabbed at her eyes.

"Come on, Squirt, let's go get something to eat," Uncle Buddy said, tousling my hair. "I'm sick of prison food, and there's nothing like a hillbilly wake to bring out a big bait of home-cooked grub."

"Do you have to be so crude, Buddy?" Aunt Lilly asked. "But yes, it would be nice for us all to sit down to a meal together. Officer, would you care to join us?"

"Thank you, ma'am, I'd be obliged. Besides, the

prisoner ain't going anywhere without me."

"I declare, I hope eating this late don't give me the heartburn," Aunt Lilly said. "I think there's some of Mamma's stomach pills left in there. I may have to take one before I lie down."

"Reckon there's some of her pain pills in there too?" Uncle Buddy winked.

The guard scowled at Buddy and cleared his throat.

"I was just joking," Uncle Buddy said. "You all need to lighten up."

Daddy spoke. "Yep, everything is a big joke for Buddy. Everything is a big party. While our boys have been fighting over in Korea, Buddy's been laid up in Eddyville sucking on the government's teat."

"You don't know what you're talking about, Hershel," Buddy said. "You wouldn't last a day in the pen. I'd trade places with one of them soldiers anytime."

"You want to trade places with your pal Doug Gibson? He's buried up there on the hill where we're fixing to lay Mamma in the morning. You want to trade places with him, Buddy?"

"That would probably suit you fine, wouldn't it Hershel?"

"Now that's enough." Aunt Lilly slammed her palms down on the table. "Can't we keep civil for just long enough to get our poor mother in the ground?"

Just then Maxine Short, an old girlfriend of Buddy's, came tiptoeing into the room. She had on a pair of cigarette pants and a red blouse unbuttoned to the top of her cleavage. With her pointer finger across her pursed lips she eased up behind Uncle Buddy's chair.

"Guess who," she whispered, capping her hands over his eyes.

"I hope it's Jane Russell."

"Close enough." Maxine leaned over and planted a wet, sloppy kiss on Buddy's mouth.

"Good Lord, Maxine, control yourself," Aunt Lilly said. "We are a grieving family and we don't need your shenanigans."

"Oh, lighten up, for Christ's sake, Lilly."

"That's exactly what I said just before you got here." Uncle Buddy put his arm around Maxine's waist, pulling her close.

To be so much alike, Aunt Lilly and Maxine could hardly abide one other. They were close to the same age, and both attractive—round and busty. Only Aunt Lilly was a brunette and Maxine a redhead. Neither had been successful in landing a husband, but neither was ready to give up the hunt either.

"Hey Mister Guard," Maxine said, turning her attention to the sergeant, "I saw in this month's *True Detective* that they allow jugular visits in Mississippi. Do y'all have that at Eddyville?"

"I think you mean conjugal visits, and no, thank God, we don't do that in Kentucky."

"Pity," Maxine said. "Might make for a more pleasant environment."

"It's not supposed to be pleasant, ma'am. It's a prison, not a country club."

"Amen to that," Buddy chimed in.

After supper Aunt Lilly directed us to the front room, where she had arranged the chairs so that everyone could have a good view of Mammaw. Why, I don't know. I didn't see the point, but I had learned it was usually best just to go along with Aunt Lilly.

"Sergeant, why don't you sit in Mamma's chair," Aunt Lilly said. "The crushed velvet one with the doily on the back. Mamma made that doily herself. Me and Hershel will take the settee. Buddy, you sit in the wingback, and Eddy T. and Maxine can grab a couple of folding chairs from the porch."

"I'll put on a fresh pot of coffee," Maxine said, heading toward the kitchen.

"That'll be good," the guard said. "I've got a long night ahead of me."

"Hershel, you've been awfully quiet, even for you," Buddy said. "Have you missed me at all?"

"The boy has missed you. He's missed you a lot," Daddy said, nodding at me.

"I've missed Squirt too," Buddy said.

"I've got an idea." Aunt Lilly spoke up. "Let's all go around the room and tell a favorite memory of Mamma."

Daddy groaned.

"No, now Hershel. Go ahead, you go first. What is something you'll always remember about Mamma?"

Daddy thought for a moment. "Well, Mamma was fun," Daddy said. "Hell. Everybody in this whole goddamn family is fun. Buddy's fun, Lilly's fun. Even Eddy T. is fun. Everybody except for me. I've been too fucking busy keeping food on the table and a roof over our heads to be fun."

"Well, that didn't exactly go the way I had envisioned," Aunt Lilly said.

"Who's ready for coffee?" Maxine came in from the kitchen. "Sergeant, how do you take it? Your coffee, that is."

"Black and strong," he replied.

Maxine brought the guard his coffee first and then served Uncle Buddy.

"The rest of y'all can serve yourselves," she said.

"Buddy, why don't you sing us a song," Aunt Lilly said. "Mamma always loved to hear you sing."

Uncle Buddy had a good voice. When I was little, he used to sing me "Jimmy Crack Corn" and Roy Rogers cowboy songs. He also showed me how to play spit in the ocean, and he taught me what beats what—a pair, two pair, three of a kind, and so on. Daddy didn't approve of gambling, but Mammaw said it would help me with my numbers.

"Yeah, come on Uncle Buddy, sing us a song," I said.

"Well, just for you, Squirt. How about 'That Lucky Old Sun.'"

Just as Uncle Buddy ended the song, the prison guard put his empty cup on the coffee table.

"That was beautiful, Buddy. Sing us one more," Maxine pleaded.

"Okay," Buddy said. "Just one more." He cleared his throat. "Down in the valley, valley so low . . ."

By the time Uncle Buddy had sung the last refrain, the prison guard's chin was on his chest and his breath was coming in a deep, even cadence.

"Let's go have a smoke, Buddy," Maxine said.

"What about Sleeping Beauty over there?"

"We aren't going to have to worry about Rip van Winkle for a while." Maxine winked.

"Did you drug that man's coffee, Maxine?" Aunt Lilly asked.

"I'm not saying I did, but... " Maxine took Buddy by the hand and led him down the hall.

What began as a gentle, rhythmic thud became a loud thumping, and finally a jarring pounding as the headboard slapped the wall in the next room.

"My God in heaven," Aunt Lilly said, "those horndogs are going at it like two goats in heat. And in our poor dead mother's bed. Shameful—that's what it is."

In a few minutes Uncle Buddy came back into the front room tucking his shirttail into his britches.

"That sure didn't take long, Buddy," Aunt Lilly said.

214

"Where's your floozie?"

"Maxine went on home. She said she'd be at the funeral in the morning. I think I'll go down to the Caboose for a beer. I figure I've got a couple of hours before Wyatt Earp over there rejoins the party. It'd be good to see some of the old gang. Are your keys in the truck, Hershel?"

"Just a doggone minute," Aunt Lilly said. "What if the sergeant comes to while you're gone? What are we supposed to do then? And what if you get spotted by the state police or something? This a bad idea, Buddy."

"Come on, lighten up. I won't be gone long."

"Only if you take Eddy T. with you. Surely you'll behave for the boy's sake if nothing else."

"Good enough," Uncle Buddy said. "Come on, Squirt, you'll be my wingman."

The Caboose turned out to be a bust. It was just past midnight when we arrived, and only two old drunks, Judd Larson and Humpy Jacobs, were at the bar, neither of whom even looked up from their nearly empty glasses. Florence had unplugged the jukebox and was putting the chairs up on the tables.

"Hey, Buddy. I heard you was getting out for the funeral. Kitchen's closed and I'm getting ready to lock up."

"That's not much of a welcome, Flo. Are you still pissed about the ruckus?"

"Ruckus? Is that what you call it? You damn near cost me my liquor license, Buddy. So yes, I'm still pissed."

Judd and Humpy tossed back the last of their drinks and left a few crumpled-up bills on the bar.

"You want a beer to go?" Florence asked.

Uncle Buddy got a Schlitz "Tall Boy" and bought me a Coca-Cola. We sat in Daddy's truck in the parking lot and watched through the grimy windows as Flo mopped the floors and then shut off the lights.

"I sure have missed you, Squirt," Buddy said.

"I've missed you too, Uncle Buddy."

"I've even missed Hershel." Buddy laughed.

"Daddy don't ever do anything with me like you used to. He's always in a bad mood. I just try to keep my distance."

"I know it's hard, but you need to try to cut your daddy some slack, Squirt. He can be a dickwad, and he sure enough has a rod stuck up his ass, but he has always been the one to look out for us. And it wasn't his job. I guess he's doing the best he can."

"I know, but it's just that I can't talk to him about anything without him getting all pissed. I don't have a girlfriend, but if I did, I sure wouldn't bring her around. Between Daddy being such a turd and Aunt Lilly flitting around like Loretta Young . . ."

"Speaking of girlfriends, have you lost your cherry yet?" Buddy asked.

"What?" I blushed.

"Don't 'what' me. You're a good-looking boy, almost fourteen years old."

"You always said don't kiss and tell."

"So I did." Uncle Buddy thought for a moment. "Just don't get yourself in trouble."

"But no," I said.

"No what?"

"No, I haven't lost my cherry."

"You've got plenty time, Squirt." Uncle Buddy slapped my shoulder. "And just between me and you, it ain't all it's cracked up to be."

"Do you ever think about Leon, the guy you... you know?"

"The guy I killed? Yes, I think about him a lot. But it's

like spit in the ocean, Squirt. When your back's up against the wall you got to go all in. I had no choice."

"I sure wish you didn't have to go back," I said.

"I don't think I can go back, Eddy T." That was the only time I remember him ever calling me anything but Squirt.

"But you have to. Just think, if you get out on good behavior you're over halfway done."

"I don't see that happening. I'm young and lean and I'm good-looking. While that plays pretty well with the gals here at the Caboose, it can cause problems in prison. I've had my share of fights and ended up spending some time in the hole. I just can't go through that again."

"What are your choices? You're not going to run. Where would you go? And I heard that guard say he would shoot you in a heartbeat, and I believe he would, too."

"Oh, I'm just talking bullshit. Don't worry about me, Squirt."

It was almost two in the morning before we got back to the house. Aunt Lilly was thumbing through a *Life* magazine.

"Your friend there has been stirring around." Aunt Lilly nodded at the sergeant. "Hershel went on to bed, and I'm getting ready to. You'd better get some rest, Buddy. The funeral home is coming at nine in the morning to take Mamma down to the church. The service is at eleven."

Officer Sargent didn't rouse for another thirty minutes. Uncle Buddy was on the settee and I had taken the wingback.

"I must have dozed off," he said.

"Well, you didn't miss anything," Uncle Buddy said. "We're all still right here."

"Something don't feel right about this. I've never fallen asleep on watch. And my head is splitting. That redheaded bitch didn't put something in my coffee, did she?"

"I don't know what to tell you," Buddy said. "Good

thing I'm not a runner, or a snitch. I'm sure the warden wouldn't take kindly to a guard who can't stay awake for his shift."

"I've about had it with you trashy, ignorant-assed hillbillies."

"You've got a lot of room to talk, Sergeant Sargent," Uncle Buddy said. "Living in a rented trailer just outside the prison gates and selling cigarettes to the inmates for a dime apiece. Yep, you're a real class act."

"Well, I know this much. Twenty-four hours from now I'll be sleeping in my own bed with my old lady laid up against my back. Reckon who'll be laid up against your back, Slone?"

"Asshole," I blurted out.

"Let it go, Squirt. He ain't worth the worry," Uncle Buddy said.

Just after breakfast, Mr. Taul, the undertaker, backed his hearse up into the front yard. Me, Aunt Lilly, Daddy, and Uncle Buddy stood in a semicircle in front of Mammaw's casket, and under the watchful eye of Officer Sargent, we looked on as Mr. Taul lowered the lid for the final time.

"Buddy, I laid out a suit of clothes for you on Mamma's bed," Daddy said. "You go change and then we'll head on down to the church."

Buddy went to the bedroom, the guard at his heels.

"Do you mind?" Buddy asked as he closed the door.

"I'll be right here," Sargent said, folding his arms.

"I'm going to move the casket to the porch now," Mr. Taul explained. "As soon as Buddy is ready, the pallbearers will carry it down to the hearse. Then we will travel to the church in a procession. Any questions?"

"No, you've been most kind." Aunt Lilly sniffled.

"You'll think kind when you see the bill," Daddy said, leading us down the hall. He paused at Mammaw's room. "Come on, Buddy, time to go."

218

"Slone, are you ready?" the guard asked, turning the doorknob. It wouldn't budge. "Son of a bitch." Officer Sargent raised his foot and with one powerful kick, the door splintered open. There on the bed lay Daddy's suit of clothes. The window was agape and Mammaw's chintz curtains with the lotus print were waving in the breeze.

By the time we got out to the porch, Uncle Buddy was in Daddy's truck grinding the engine. It came to life with a rumble.

The sergeant pulled his pistol and fired one round just over the cab of the truck.

"Shut it off and get out with your hands up, motherfucker."

Buddy put his hands in the air above the steering wheel and slowly turned to face us. The officer held his government issue Smith & Wesson in both hands, his arms outstretched, one eye closed and the other trained on Uncle Buddy.

"You all need to lighten up," Uncle Buddy said. "I was just joking around." Then he slammed the truck into gear and floored it, attempting a U-turn. Sargent fired through the open window and in a spray of red mist I saw Uncle Buddy's head jerk violently to the side before he slumped over in the seat.

What followed was a commotion the likes of which our little community had never seen. The sergeant radioed the Kentucky State Police and soon a convoy of cruisers, their sirens ablare, were racing up our curvy holler road, the sheriff and the county coroner on their tails. I did the only thing I knew to do. I hiked up to the high rocks and I sobbed.

It's funny the things I remember most about that day. Not so much the grisly images you would think, but things like the sulfury taste of gunpowder or the ringing in my ears so loud that it muffled Aunt Lilly's screams. Or Mr. Taul hurriedly rolling Mammaw's casket back inside the house, as if that could somehow undo what had been done.

They took Uncle Buddy's body to Frankfort for an autopsy at the state medical examiner's office, even though there were no doubts as to the cause of death. "SOP," the coroner said. Daddy and Aunt Lilly agreed that, given the circumstances, it would be best to forgo Mammaw's funeral, so we had a private burial just as the sun set that evening. We laid Uncle Buddy to rest beside her a week later.

It's been almost four years now. Daddy is still Daddy. I try to cut him some slack. Like Uncle Buddy said, he's probably doing the best he can. Aunt Lilly is dating some insurance man from the next county over. Daddy says he's an old desperate divorcé, but he seems to make Aunt Lilly happy. Maxine is still looking for a husband, but she visits Uncle Buddy often and usually leaves a flower or a little note on his grave. Aunt Lilly says she's glad Mammaw died before she could see how Uncle Buddy ended up. Funny thing is, if Mammaw hadn't died, Uncle Buddy probably would have had to serve out his hitch. Maybe he knew how all this was going to turn out—one way or the other. I don't know.

Back when I turned sixteen, Flo gave me a part-time job at the Caboose, bussing tables and mopping floors. Daddy says work builds character, but Aunt Lilly says nothing good's ever come out of the Caboose. She says that's where Buddy found trouble, but I think that's where trouble found him. Anyway, just this spring I finally lost my cherry. I went straightaway and told Uncle Buddy about it. I told him I thought it was all it was racked up to be and more. I bet he laughed.

The Rolling Hills

Michelle Koubek

Do I or do I not cross?

The question echoes in my mind as I watch the rolling hills outside my window. Clumps of green that rise and fall in a feast of color that should be soothing except the rolls are not a trick of the eye. The land around my village truly moves, breaking away from the ground and then swinging back down as if it's an eternal jump rope. No one knows why the hills roll this way. They just always have.

And I wonder, *Do I cross them?*

It's exciting to think about what I might find beyond the hills. Mother has books describing wonderful lands. There could be castles with towers so high they touch the clouds, and rivers so blue they resemble the feathers of blue jays. Waterfalls that roar like dragons. Valleys that dip low into meadows of yellow daffodils like fallen stars. Then, most of all, there could be people, ones that don't look like anyone within the rolling hills, who have stories of everywhere they've been. I've never met anyone outside the village.

But just as the hills have always rolled, it's always been a mystery what's on the other side of them. What I discover may not be everything I hope for. It could be a nightmare, and I could wish that I had never left home.

So, I wonder, *Do I stay where it's familiar?*

There's just over a hundred of us surrounded by the rolling hills, so we know everyone by name. There's a sweetness to this, a sense of comfort that you'll always be taken care of, no matter what life tosses your way. Not that anything that awful ever happens here. It's like we're a pocket in the universe that's been overlooked by hardship.

But in this village surrounded by the rolling hills, not much occurs that's interesting either. It's boring and predictable, and I realized recently that all my paintings look the same: waving, green land stretching infinitely. I worry that I will lose my mind pacing here in this beautiful sanctuary forever. Which is why I wonder:

Do I cross?
Do I stay?
Do I cross?

Always on repeat.

As I go through the never-ending questions in my mind, Mother sits in her rocking chair, knitting me a sweater out of turquoise yarn. I look in my bedroom where the sleeves of a dozen sweaters in different colors peek out like floppy ears from my dresser's top drawer. Pretty soon I'll have to stack them on the floorboards, but Mother will keep knitting. She loves knitting, I know, that's what she asserts every day. Still, her eyes are distant when she says it. I see the rolling hills reflected in them. I can't be sure if this is the life she dreamed of when she was my age or if she has accepted her fate.

I lean my head on the windowpane, letting my breath fog the glass. There's handprint stains on the wood from where I have rested my palms over the years, so detailed that you can see my fingerprints. The paint is chipping, and in a couple more years my hand will be riddled with splinters if I touch the same spot. Even this house doesn't want me to remain.

But how can I leave?

I'm so tired of not knowing what to do.

"Ouch!" I wince.

"Hannah?" Mother asks, pausing her knitting. For a moment, she is back in our cottage with me, instead of travelling with her hands.

"I'm okay," I tell her, pulling out the splinter from my thumb. "But this windowsill is falling apart. I should probably sand it down."

"That will be great," she agrees before nodding and continuing what she was doing.

Cradling my hand, I look at the rolling hills one more time. They seem to growl as the top of the hill scratches the rocky passage underneath, and there's no doubt that they are threatening, but still, I am curious. What if the places past the rolling hills are extraordinary, where contentment is replaced by joy? I would like to be happy. I don't know how happy I've ever truly been. Is that what lies beyond the rolling hills? Could there possibly be something better than peace?

I don't know. I never know! What do I do?

My thumb throbs from where the splinter left it, and I think of the disintegrating windowsill that I've started to blend with.

"I'm leaving," I blurt, watching as Mother purls the yarn without flinching.

She does not reply.

The hills roll in the window behind Mother like a giant,

jade serpent. For an instant, I question my decision. When that moment passes, however, I find that I don't want to take it back. Instead, I gather my things from my room in the back of the house, leaving several sweaters behind, yet taking as many as I can carry. All the while, Mother knits as she always does like nothing is happening.

The growling of the rolling hills seems to grow louder as I move back into the den, a sanding stone in hand for the windows. I smooth all of them down which takes close to an hour, then, when everything is together, I stand by the doorway, the clacking of Mother's needles like clock hands in my ear that bring me back to reality.

"Mom," I whisper.

The clacks of her needles stop, so all I hear are the rumbling, rolling hills.

I'm not sure I can leave without acknowledgment from her. I'm not sure my feet will let me, so I wipe my eyes and wet my lips, prepared to say what I must to get Mother to hear. Yet my words are cut off. Mother is speaking, eyes down.

"So, you're going?" she says, knitting once more. "About time you got away from here."

The Contract

Soter Lucio

Lystra left the river behind her, walking with her basket of clean clothes on her head, wishing for the hundredth time that she could find a way to move out of this dreary existence and get a washing machine. Above all else, she wanted a washing machine.

Washing clothes in a tub or a large bucket on the riverbank, with the aid of a scrubbing board, is backbreaking and tedious. Not to mention frustrating and tiring.

Not paying attention to where she was stepping, she stumbled upon a backpack that did not belong on the track from the river to the top of the hill, least of all in this part of the country. Only the desolate and destitute lived here, way up in the mountains of north Trinidad. Along with the outcasts and disinherited who needed to hide away from so-called decent folks. Granted, it was the way of life in that part of the island, where civilization had not yet caught up with them, but she couldn't bear much more of it. The backpack was lying on a concrete slab that was familiar to all of them.

She left it in its place and continued on her way, but lost in her thoughts, she tripped on the root of a tree in the track close to the main road and the basket of clothes emptied in the dirt. She promptly sat on her haunches and cried. And cried. Then she prayed. And prayed again. She gathered the clothes together, not bothering to wash them over again, because the river was way down the hill and she was too tired to manage that. So, she continued on her way, promising to shake out the dirt before hanging them on the lines.

She stood atop the hill watching her five children playing with the abandonment of childhood, not a care in the world. They were happy. She tried her best to keep a smile on their faces. They couldn't miss what they never had. But she knew what was lacking in their lives. She'd been to the city lots of times but didn't take them along for fear they'd see stuff she couldn't afford. Not yet anyway.

In time she said to herself again. For the hundredth time.

It wasn't so bad when her husband was alive. Goodness knows, he was the best husband and father anyone could hope for. He was good and kind, loving and considerate, and did see the best in all things. And the stories he told them every night had them all rolling with laughter. Even those about the night creatures that were meant to put a good scare in them did no harm. They never even flinched. They were a sturdy lot with nerves of steel.

Lystra dried her tears on the sleeve of her worn out five-year-old dress, putting on the cheeriest smile she could muster, then continued on down the other side of the hill to her house. The wooden house with its thatched roof that was so comfortable up to a year ago was now worse than a prison. It was hell. Her children all came to greet her and help her with the clothes. They even hung them out on the lines to dry. Her heart wrung in her chest when she realized just how good and kind they were. Just like their father. It was heart wrenching to not be able to give them something other than a balloon on Christmas morning or their birthday.

After a lunch of sancoche prepared with figs, dasheen and yams from their garden, she laid down for a much-needed nap. Forcing smiles and laughter that you don't feel is hard work. She was exhausted. Just in case rain should fall while she slept, she rose to close the window. There was her eight-year-old son crying long tears and hanging on to his kite trying to get it up. The kite simply refused to fly. Maybe it was the lack of wind or maybe it wasn't built right. But the sight of those tears did something to Lystra. Her heart seemed to be making harsh somersaults within her chest, and inside her head something must have exploded because it felt like it was swelling, and her sight was doubling up. She somehow managed to get hold of the bottle of Limacol that was always within reach and splashed some of it on her head and face. The cooling sensation worked like magic. She was again hale and hearty.

She prepared a snack for the children and told them to behave themselves while she went out for a walk. Choosing her special place down the hill to the ravine where at that time of the day there'd be nobody about, she made a beeline for a specific tree because of the darkness provided by the low branches. Her dark clothes would be an added advantage, making her privacy uninterrupted should anyone pass by.

The thoughts of her inadequacy to provide nice things for her children came flooding back and so did the tears. She decided to return to the bag she had seen on the slab earlier in the day that was out of place. Feeling some trepidation mixed with a bit of bravado, she unzipped it and inspected the contents. Inside were stacks of dollar bills neatly arranged under some old dirty clothes and underwear. With shock and dismay at her unexpected good fortune, she gently rubbed the bills. She thought nothing of the sweet pungent smell coming from it all. Desperate as she was, she still had the presence of mind to bury the clothes and, turning the bag inside out, she refilled it with the dollar bills. Realizing the scent would stay with her, she plucked some leaves from a nearby immortelle tree and, using the juice, rubbed herself to disguise the it.

She quietly moved from that spot, trying her best not to squash any dry leaves that would make a sound. In this land every sound told a tale that even the smallest child could understand and detect whether it was made by a lizard, agouti, or something else. Successful in her maneuverings and satisfied with the job, she started back on her trek towards her home, sure of a better and more fulfilling life for her offspring.

"Hello Lystra. How you sprightly so today? Like you win the lottery?" Her friend Zana brought her back to reality.

"Zana. I didn't see you. I didn't hear you. My mind was far girl. I was thinking how to make them children happy."

"Don't worry yourself. Dey go get big just now. You go see. And dey go be better off dan you."

Lystra breathed a sigh of relief after Zana left, believing that she had distracted her. There was that spring in her step from her happy thoughts. Her husband did tell her he always knew when she was happy by that spring that developed in her step. She'd have to be careful in the future.

Her son Zack bounded up to her. "Mom, Uncle Mark will be telling stories tonight. One will be about that place under the concrete slab. Can we go?"

"Of course we can. We never miss his story night," she answered with a smile.

"With Dad gone, Uncle Mark's stories are all we have now." Zack continued with a wry expression just like his father when he didn't like the food she'd prepared.

"I know sweetheart. But we're getting along fine aren't we?" Lystra remarked with a smile and a nod of the head.

"Yes. But I miss him so much." He was close to tears.

"Don't worry. We're handling it. And he is watching over us." That made him feel better and he rushed off to something that caught his attention. Children found it so easy to move from one emotion to another. If only they all retained that ability into their adulthood.

In preparation for the story time, Lystra packed some foodstuff along with coffee for the grown-ups and fruits for the children. The parents had their part to play so everyone was comfortable. Zana provided the special bush for burning to keep the mosquitoes away. The storytelling was usually held at the clearing late on an evening by torchlight to give it that eerie look and feel.

They joined the circle that was already forming in the middle of the savannah. The same location where the midyear parties as well as sports, harvests, and fiestas were held. The road to the left led to the river where they went to do their laundry. At the spring nearby is where all mothers got water to which they added a lot of sugar and just called it sugar water to enhance their spiritual powers whatever that may be. They said that everyone had a different power that grew with the person.

Amidst the chatting and laughter in anticipation of the story that would be told, everyone was on a high.

As usual, Uncle Mark was on time and greeted them all with his booming voice.

"A very good night to everyone. Your belly full?" he asked.

A loud chorus of yeses ensued whereby Uncle Mark slapped his legs and laughed.

"That's good. Because you'll need your energy after

229

hearing this story about what is under that concrete slab."

He opened his eyes so wide that the children moved closer to their parents. Maybe this story would be scarier than the others. The teenagers on the other side were sniggering and taunting them. They'd already heard so many of these stories and nothing ever came out of them. They were just words meant to scare you for a while and keep you in line. But they were past that stage. Uncle Mark cast his glance behind them and said in a low voice. "I see you've come to listen too. Okay, take a seat."

The teens made a mad scramble falling over each other in their haste to get away from the unseen visitor being welcomed by Uncle Mark.

A burst of roaring laughter told the teens they'd been had.

"Yes, so about this concrete slab. I know that there since I small. My grandfather met it there. And so did his grandfather. We were all told to stay away from there. You see, that slab is covering something so dreadful that those special trees were planted to keep it safe and imprisoned as it were. It is something ancient and from out of this world."

"Is it a devil?" one of the children decided to pose a question.

"No silly," answered another.

"Devils don't have to be locked up. It is a demon. They have to be locked up," Zack answered with such authority all heads turned towards him. Lystra was in shock. She turned to face him with her mouth open and face frozen.

"Zack where did you get that?" Lystra asked her son.

"From Dad. He said so. And Dad was the smartest person who ever lived," Zack said with as much confidence as he could muster.

"Yes," Uncle Mark continued. "You're right Zack. Your Dad was the smartest person who ever lived. And it is a demon that's locked up under there. But he can't be seen or felt. Can't be heard either. He is in all the jars filled with gold coins. He was paid to leave the people alone. So for generations there's never been any crime or anything untoward happening here. We always respect his privacy and never ever walk on that concrete slab or even pluck the leaves from those trees.".

"Uncle, Hazel's son now say there was a stranger in the vicinity of the immortelle tree last week. He had a duffel bag."

Lystra opened her eyes in shock and covered her mouth. The bag was seen and recognized. That now posed a problem. But it would be solved. She had to solve it. Her children's wellbeing was at stake. Not to mention her mental health. The rest of the evening was a blur as she dwelt on this new development.

Lystra had a restless night turning and tossing. She didn't fall asleep until daybreak. She hustled their breakfast then dropped them off at Zana's, saying she'd be back in a day or two.

"Take your time Lystra, they'll be fine," Zana said as she waved Lystra off.

Lystra went to the restroom at the only fast-food restaurant and removed the bills from under her clothes where they were hidden. Then she went to the bank and deposited them all. The rest at home would be deposited another day.

The crowd gathered at the junction told her something untoward had happened. Spotting Zana, she made a beeline for her, but Zana blurted out the events before she could ask a question.

"Lystra girl there's a thief in our midst. And everybody is scared because nobody knows what the demon will do about it. Remember the duffel bag Hazel's son mentioned?"

Lystra visibly trembled at the thought that she had been seen and they knew what she had done.

"Well, it was a thief who had it and he did rest himself on the concrete slab because he was tired. He not from here so he did not know the rules. But not knowing is no reason for disrespect." Zana ended and Lystra stopped shaking realizing that it was not about her.

"So that is why everybody looking like their house burn down?" Lystra interjected.

"No. The thief was found this morning with his head in the river and dead."

"You making joke." Lystra covered her mouth, but her eyes flew open.

"Right now, they are all worried about calling in the police. Some of us, though we did not break any laws, do not want to be found. Look at me. I ran away from my parents' house because they didn't want me with Marcus. They are quite wealthy. They'll hurt Marcus in more ways than one. I am happy in this god forsaken place with him. A lot of us here are like that. So, you understand now?"

"I think so. And what about the money that was stolen?" Lystra asked while scanning the faces of the crowd gathered.

"That's another matter. It can't be found. Not yet anyway. But they know about where it was. They did get a certain scent and Ronald, you know Ronald? He use to be a kinda bad boy, though he never broke any laws. Well, he knew when people didn't want to be found they'd disguise whatever with a certain bush that smells so sweet you'd never know there was something in the mortar besides the pestle. So, this is where we are now."

"What will they to do with the money when they find it?" Lystra wanted to know.

"They'll have to put it in the middle of the concrete slab as payment. And hope things get back to normal because things change already. You see the marigold flowers already fall off and the place hot with no wind blowing? Lystra, bad things happening already."

Zana noticed from the outset that Lystra was getting jittery, so she explained the matter as best she could, hoping that if she was right, Lystra would do her part and fix it. So said, so done. Lystra disappeared for another two days and, after she returned, there was talk around the community that the duffel bag with some money was seen in the middle of the concrete slab. Then it was gone. Zana signed herself, thanking God that her friend was now free along with everyone else.

While Lystra was dusting out the mat at the side of the house, she saw her son Zack playing under the mango tree with some dollar notes and singing the phrase "finders keepers, losers weepers."

Suddenly, she dropped the mat.

Kanazawa in the Rain

Wally Wood

The tracks parallel the Japan Sea coast. On one side, a fishing boat's lights on dark water, on the other, towns too small for a stop, fields and wooded hills, lights reflected off paddy water.

The train flashes past a Mobil gas station, the bright red and white sign and the architecture identical to a Mobil station in Greenwich, and Allen, still jetlagged and woozy with fatigue, has the disorienting sensation he's never left Connecticut. He thought he could take a bullet train directly from Tokyo but had to change in Nagaoka. As he stood disoriented on the platform staring down the tracks for the Kanazawa express he felt chilled and feverish.

Kanazawa Station is bright and modern. The sign that directs him to the cab stand is in Japanese and English. Shivering in the taxi, he asks the driver in Japanese about the weather. The driver grunts and answers in Japanese, "Tomorrow clouds. Possible rain late. Kanazawa people say, always carry an umbrella."

His tenth floor Western-style room in the Kanazawa Shiro Hotel is large and modern and clean and institutional. The bellman recites in English that the room overlooks the grounds of an Important Cultural Asset and Kanazawa Castle. Lit by floodlights, the castle's donjon appears to float in a pool of darkness.

Allen is too chilled and too fragile to appreciate the view. Alone, he turns up the thermostat, retrieves the ibuprofen from his shaving kit, takes two pills and considers a third. As he drinks the tap water, he tries to recall his last liquid. Coffee at lunch? He'd bought a box dinner for the train, ignored the drinks in Nagaoka's vending machines. He drinks another glass of water, then a third. He hangs his suit jacket over the desk chair, kicks off his shoes, and crawls between the covers in his dress shirt and suit pants, uncertain he'll ever be warm again. *But if I'm going to die, why not die in Kanazawa?*

—

The bedside clock says 2:07. The room is too warm and too bright. He is as rested and refreshed as if he'd slept eight quality hours—ten. He lies motionless, takes inventory. No chills. No vague pains. No headache. Whatever attacked him had risen from his body like smoke from an extinguished candle. A virus? A germ? Dehydration? Stress? Delayed jet-lag? A malicious Japanese spirit? Whatever. It's entirely gone.

He swings his stockinged feet to the carpet. No vertigo. No lightheadedness. He clicks off the harsh overhead light and leaves the soft bedside lamp glow. He pees and swallows two more ibuprofen with another glass of water in the too-bright bathroom. He changes into the hotel's robe and stands for a long time at the window, staring at the dark castle.

236

This must be how old age arrives. Your friends die. Your teeth break. And you stand at a hotel room window halfway around the world thinking about the dead and wonder how much time you have left.

—

The day before he left the States, a friend called to say that Jack Flaherty, Allen's former business partner, had died of a heart attack. Allen pressed the receiver against his ear and closed his eyes to the jumble of papers, reports, and binders on his desk. How could Jack, only fifty-seven—ten years younger than Allen for God's sake!—be dead? How could Jack, so full of free-floating energy, be dead? How could Jack, who watched his diet and exercised rigorously, die? Allen could not recall when they'd last talked. A lunch around New Year's? Jack had been unchanged. He talked about a new enterprise that sounded dicey. He sent the salad back because the dressing was not on the side then poured the dressing over the second salad. He took calls on his cell, and was all the time advising, advising, advising Allen how to run the business. That was Jack, so familiar Allen never realized he was a part of a whole until he wasn't.

When he could control his voice, he called Jack's wife and reached voicemail. He told the machine he was sorry for her loss, said he was available if she needed anything, apologized for having to leave the country. Allen leaned back in his ergonomically designed executive chair and stared at the picture of himself and Jack with the second President Bush. Jack dead. He wiped his eyes and blew his nose and canceled his three o'clock and four o'clock meetings.

That night, his packed bag waiting in the corner, his wife joined him in the bedroom. She sat heavily on the bed and began to work cream into her face. Allen watched impassively. At one time they'd make love the night before he left on a trip. Her way to send him off? To generate a loving memory should his plane crash? To remind him of what he had waiting back home? The pills she'd taken during menopause killed her desire. Allen didn't mind. Married more than forty years, he and Lily didn't need sex to be companionable. "Are you all right?" she asked.

"It's not only Jack." He waved his hand as if brushing away gnats. "It's the trip. The speech. The Tokyo office. Taiheiyo Foods. The economy. Global warming. Everything."

"You just worry about the speech. I'll take care of global warming." She smiled.

"Miyazaki helped with the translation." Allen's Japanese was not good enough to translate complex thoughts but good enough to read the speech's transliteration. "I'm not worried about the speech."

She touched his face gently with peach-scented fingers. "Then don't worry. You did what you could for Jack as long as anyone could."

He took her hand to kiss it. She was right, but it was small comfort.

—

He is able to sleep another six hours and walks into the hotel breakfast buffet as the service is about to end. He fills his tray with miso soup, rice, egg, grilled fish, pickles, finds an empty table, and is finishing when he addresses a hotel staff worker who is swabbing the next table. "Excuse me. From here, is Kenrokuen far?" It's one of the three most famous gardens in Japan.

She looks at him in surprise. "You speak Japanese."

"I have a smattering." The idiomatic phrase implies fluency.

She tells him Kanazawa has many interesting sights. He tells her he'd heard people call Kanazawa "little Kyoto." She says many people come for the garden, but there's much more. He asks what other sites he should visit. She thinks for several seconds, then rattles off several names too rapidly for Allen to catch. "I'm sorry. I did not understand everything. Could you say again slowly?"

She gives him a look of appraisal. Seconds pass and then she says slowly and clearly, "If you would like, I can show you."

He stares at her more intently. He cannot judge the ages of Japanese women, but she is at least 40. She has a flat, plain face, wears no makeup, and her hair is hidden under a kind of white bandanna. She wears a dull green sweater and blue jeans. A white apron with the hotel logo conceals her figure. He wonders what she wants from him.

"That would be very kind. How much do you charge?"

"No fee. No fee!" Her tone is emphatic, her words in English.

Then what? He asks in Japanese. "Would you like to practice English?" It would not be the first time a Japanese stranger has asked for English conversation practice. It is however the first time a woman has asked. Because he's older and seems harmless?

In Japanese: "Yes, please. I'll show you Kanazawa."

Her name is Yuriko. She finishes work in an hour. She'll meet him at the entrance to the temple grounds across from the hotel. They can walk through the Kanazawa Castle grounds to Kenrokuen. From the garden, they can visit the mansion the feudal lord had built for his mother.

Waiting outside the temple gate, Allen finds himself in a

remarkably good humor. No one knows where he is and he has no place to be, no meeting to attend, no proposal to write. The sensation is liberating. The streets are wet, and the air is moist and clean; he can smell the ocean. The sky is overcast, and the TV weather lady forecasts showers throughout the day.

What does Yuriko want? Why is she willing to waste a day for nothing more than some English conversation? In Allen's experience, everyone wanted something and not knowing what this Japanese woman wants makes Allen uneasy. He is about to walk into the temple grounds when Yuriko in tight jeans and snug green sweater greets him. Her hair is straight, black, and glossy. He would like to touch it. She'd put on lipstick.

Allen tries to classify her. She's not an office lady or a matron. Not a college student or young mother. She's a mature, confident woman. Almost attractive. Older than he first thought.

Yuriko leads him through the temple grounds, pointing out the historic noh stage, and into the grounds of Kanazawa Castle, chattering in simple Japanese the entire way. When he doesn't understand, he stops her, asks her to repeat, and she tries to say the same thing in simpler language. English is a last resort.

At the garden's admission booth, Allen informs her he would pay the day's expenses. If she were giving him her Saturday, it's the least he can do. A notice in English says visitors over 65 are admitted free. "I am sixty-seven," he tells the ticket seller, pushing a yen bill across the counter.

As they start up the gravel path into the garden, Yuriko says in a tone of amazement, "You are sixty-seven years old?"

Allen straightens his back, "Truly."

"I cannot believe it."

"How old did you think?"

She stops to inspect him carefully. "Maybe my age I think. Fifty-six. Fifty-seven."

240

"You do not look fifty-six," Even with the fine wrinkles around her eyes, he would have made her no more than forty-five.

She smiles without covering her mouth and he notices a gold tooth. What would it be like to kiss her? What would she taste like? Probably soy sauce and bonito flakes.

"You do not look sixty-seven," she says.

They explore every corner of Kenrokuen, which means "The Garden of the Six Sublimities"—spaciousness, seclusion, artificiality, antiquity, abundant water, and broad views—and Yuriko wants to ensure he appreciates every single one. She picks the ideal spot in which to stand to appreciate a vista's full effect and they stand silent and motionless for minutes. The first couple times she does this, Allen wants to clear his throat or wander on the path without her, but he remains beside her. He wonders what she sees. Something different from or more than he sees. He tries to feel the twisted pine branches, the stone of the ancient lantern, the clear water of the artificial stream. He tries to still all thought and let the scene take him over.

The mansion the lord had built for his mother in a far corner of the garden could be a samurai movie set. Large rooms, tatami-covered floors, bare wood posts, plain sand-brown walls, artistic screens painted with flowers and birds, elaborate carvings in the elegant reception chamber's frieze, a calligraphic scroll in one room's alcove. Yuriko, padding around the rooms in her stocking feet, appears underwhelmed by the place.

"I wonder if Lord Maeda's mother appreciated her son's gesture, building her this beautiful mansion." says Allen.

"Lord Maeda's wife wanted her mother-in-law out of the castle," says Yuriko with a wry smile.

She takes him to a tiny restaurant on a back street, where he asks her to order a local Kanazawa specialty for him. As he works his chopsticks to pick sweet white flesh off fish bones, he asks her about herself. It wasn't Japanese to ask personal questions, certainly not after such short acquaintance, but then he isn't Japanese, and she doesn't seem to mind.

She was born in Yokohama. Her parents owned a small tea shop. She was married, but she had not lived with or seen her husband for several years. He was a truck driver and had often been away from home until one day he never returned. She didn't know where he was and wasn't interested in finding out. She had two married daughters. One lived in Tokyo, the other up north in Chitose; she seldom saw them. She moved to Kanazawa because she was tired of Yokohama people.

He senses a deep sadness. "Are you lonely?"

She looks surprised because the question is so direct. She looks down at her own fish. "Sometimes." She speaks so softly he is not sure he heard her above the restaurant's canned music.

What if he were to live with her? Relieve her loneliness? Escape from their lives together. He could imagine scrubbing her back in the Japanese bath . . . water sluicing over her neat, trim body . . . her eager to receive him on the futon in their Japanese bedroom. He would teach her English and expose her to the wider world. She would teach him Japanese, and they would explore Japan.

It's possible. He's already talked within the firm about cutting back to three days a week. A couple of the senior managers would be delighted if he were to step aside. He could still contribute via the internet. Japan isn't a third world country. Lily could have the house and everything in it. He could not think of a single possession—the Lexus, the boat, the country house—he would not willingly abandon. Yuriko and he could live comfortably on his investments. How expensive could it be to live in Kanazawa? Yuriko already lives on what she earns as a hotel worker.

He imagines sitting on the tatami at their low table in their cozy, spare apartment. Yuriko will shop and cook their meals. He will support her lovingly, the difference between himself and the absent husband. He will love her and care for her. He would not abandon her. He will listen to her and indulge her. Can she tell by the way he looks at her how he feels? Conscious that he is staring, he looks away.

"Loneliness is painful," he says. He wants to say more, but his Japanese is inadequate.

Yuriko, her eyes downcast, nods in agreement and picks up her cup. "This tea is very nice. The shop owner roasts the tea leaves himself." Allen doesn't catch the word "roast" and by the time she makes herself clear the mood has changed.

The Ishikawa Prefectural Art Museum is a short walk. Allen doesn't know much about art and has the impression that Yuriko doesn't know much either, but he enjoys the paintings, sculpture, hanging scrolls, and prints. They rest for coffee in the museum cafe, and Allen asks what she would do on an ordinary Saturday. She shops, cleans, washes clothes—nothing special.

He asks if she wants to practice English. She waves her hand in front of her mouth in a gesture of refusal, her eyes downcast, and says she is a very poor student.

They walk back down the hill, past the garden, the street filled with cars, commuters returning home. They stroll along a broad avenue lined with a government building, a girl's school, and a European-style red brick building, originally a high school, now a Modern Literature Museum where they stop. It displays the works of local writers—samples of original manuscripts, pictures of the authors, even the reconstructed study of a nineteenth-century poet who grew up in Kanazawa. Allen is impressed that the city would create an entire building for local authors, but unable to read a thing his interest is limited. Perhaps—if he lived in Japan and studied diligently—he could learn to read.

Back on the avenue, he recognizes his hotel tower three blocks away and senses his tour is over. It has been one of his most enjoyable days in a long time. No client or staff meetings. No social obligations. No responsibilities. No demands on his time, on his attention. He doesn't want it to end.

As they stand waiting for the traffic light to change, he blurts, "Please excuse my impoliteness. May I see your home?"

She looks bewildered and he wonders if he's used improper language. She stares into the distance for what seems to be minutes. "We have to take a bus."

They ride the bus for twenty minutes, then walk another ten. It seems to be a neighborhood of low apartment buildings with small shops at street level—sake, vegetables, tea, hardware, convenience store, travel agency. Yuriko's apartment is a third-floor walkup. Allen automatically slips off his shoes in the tiny vestibule.

He stands at the entrance to take in everything, vaguely disappointed the apartment is not Japanese, not spare and empty like the mother's mansion with bare plaster walls, exposed polished wood posts, a single hanging scroll. He is chagrined to realize he expected something different.

Yuriko's living room is crammed with furniture including an oil-cloth covered kitchen table with two wooden chairs, a tall china cabinet, a big-screen TV on a stand that has space for DVD and CD players and shelves for disks, a floor-to-ceiling bookcase filled with books, single easy chair that is almost as big as the table is positioned to watch the television, and a small table beside the chair is covered with women's magazines. An open book lies face down on the chair's arm. Three or four cute stuffed animals peek out from bookshelves; he recognizes a popular Japanese cartoon bear. Yuriko had pinned a large photographic poster of a temple garden—an advertisement for Japan Railways West—to the closet's sliding door. On his way into the toilet, he glances into her bedroom. The Western-style bed and small cabinet virtually fill it.

Returning, he threads his way to the kitchen chair she indicates. "Thank you," he says. "I know I have disturbed you." He uses the verb that means to hinder, obstruct, interrupt, interfere, be a nuisance.

Yuriko fills an electric kettle with water and spoons green tea into a small pot. She finds a package of rice crackers in a cupboard, shakes some onto a blue-and-white plate, and sets it on the table. Allen notices that for all the clutter, the apartment is clean—no dirty dishes in the sink, no dust on the TV, no dirt in the corners of the polished wooden floor.

She pours boiling water into the pot, sets out two small handleless cups and saucers, and pours the tea. "Please," she says.

The crackers are crisp and salty. The tea is good, but, even in his unsophisticated mouth, he can tell it is not as good as the tea at lunch. "Thank you. It's delicious," he says, automatically bowing his head.

Having served tea and a snack, Yuriko seems at a loss. He realizes she doesn't know what to do with him. He wants to reach across the table and hold her hand, to make contact, but she holds her cup with both hands as if they need warming. He tries to think of something ambiguous to say that will intimate his feelings. But his Japanese is hopelessly inadequate, and the English sounds brusque. "You make me feel young."

"But you *are* young!" she exclaims.

"Today. With you."

She covers her mouth to smile. "I am also young with you today." She looks shy, almost girlish. "You are a good man. You have a kind face."

Allen rubs his face. What does she see? He is hungry and wants a drink. He wonders if she has any beer in the little refrigerator. Now what? He's seen her apartment. He looks at his watch. Using formal Japanese, he says, "Thank you for showing me your home. I must return to the hotel now." He finishes his tea and takes another cracker.

Yuriko looks relieved. "I will take you to the bus."

He tells her he remembers how to find the stop, but she insists. When they come down the stairs to the building's miniscule lobby, it has begun to rain. Yuriko insists on returning back upstairs to fetch him an umbrella. She gives him a large, black, expensive one and takes a cheap, clear plastic one for herself. When he protests, she tells him to leave it at the hotel; she will retrieve it when she comes to work.

"Will I see you tomorrow?" he asks.

"Tomorrow? I am sorry but... " Her incomplete sentence means no. She will not see him.

What does he expect? She has a life. As they wait in the rain at the bus stop, he thinks to give her a business card. "If you come to America, please call me." One of his stock Japanese phrases.

She treats the card respectfully, formally, inspecting his name and title on the Japanese side. She apologizes that she does not have a card of her own. He assures her it is all right. The bus lumbers out of the rainy dark and stops. "Thank you so much," he says. He wants to hug her—even kiss her goodbye—but she is bowing, and the umbrellas are in the way and it would be profoundly inappropriate anyway. He returns her bow, turns, and boards the bus.

As he rides through the scruffy suburb, the bus's interior too bright, he thinks about Yuriko... Jack... Lily. He should call Lily, ask about the funeral. They couldn't have built the business without Jack. He'd never have come to Japan had Jack not signed Taiheiyo Foods as a client. Jack had given him more than he'd known. Now he'd never know.

Allen turns his face to the window so the other passengers cannot see his tears. If it's still raining tomorrow, he'll return to Tokyo.

Shift

John Leahy

You forced my hand.

When you modernized, flying all around the world in your airplanes, I could have mutated, evolved. I could have used your spectacular mobility to spread myself all over the world at incredible speed. And yet I didn't. I kept to the natural flyers of the earth, those with organic wings. But then you waged war on the birds with your progression. Your wretched… hyper-advancement.

Renewable energy! The electric age! AI!

Blah blah blah.

Look at me! Look at me! I'm so environmentally conscious!

Sickening.

With all your brainpower, did you not consider the cost of these amazing things? In my opinion, I think you did. The highest among you thought, "Hmmm…yes, this is a price I am willing to pay. Let us proceed."

Does this trigger you, reader? Or at least, cause you to blink?

Renewable energy.

Let's look at that first. *Renewable.*

The average wind turbine in the mid-2020s was composed of the following: steel, aluminum, copper, and rare earth metals. What are these rare earth metals I don't hear you ask? They are neodymium and dysprosium.

The extraction of the above metals involves a lot of thrusting into the earth. This is energy intensive. *Very* energy intensive. Have you ever seen a mining extractor close up? Have you any idea how big they are? These vehicles that extract the materials needed for your *renewable energy*-fueled lifestyle? Well, I'm not going to bother informing you of the actual size of the vehicle. I'm going to unsettle you with the height of an average *tire* on one of them

Thirteen feet.

Thirteen feet. Yes, that's the height of a *tire* on one of these things. These monsters that cater for the provision of the metals involved in the construction of a device that supplies you with your *renewable* energy.

Then there's the sheer *amount* of each metal to consider. Are you ready? Forty years ago, in a three-point-five-megawatt turbine, you were looking at three hundred and thirty-five tons of steel, nearly five tons of copper, three tons of aluminum, and two tons of our good old rare earth friends. But as the years went by you wanted more, more, *more.* The turbines grew higher. They grew wider. The mines grew bigger, they went deeper. The tailing ponds grew to the size of giant pools, each one full of lead, arsenic, cadmium, cobalt, mercury. As environmental regulation weakened in the face of insatiable need, even deadlier substances appeared in the pools. Teratogens. Mutagens. As well as poisoning the flyers in their billions, they were rendered infertile. Their gene pool was compromised. The young were born with one wing smaller than the other. Others with two heads. Some with no wings at all. As some grew older, they lost the ability to fly because of the weight of the tumors in their bodies. Millions, silly with poison-induced stunted brain development, blundered into the slash of your now colossal turbine blades, smashed toward the earth while your energy levels crept up, up, up.

Moving along.

Your precious *cloud*.

The *cloud* sounds so harmless, doesn't it? It's anything but. The cloud is *metal*. The cloud is *core*. It is *heat*. The data center, the cloud's heart, needs *metal* to maintain its pulse. RAM, CPUs, drive boards, motherboards. These brutally physical things need gold, silver, palladium, our turbine friends, dysprosium and neodymium – plus a few other fancy dans like yttrium, gallium, indium and tungsten. The data center *thirst*s for metal. For a while, you constrained its proliferation. You corralled its size. But like the turbines, you bent, you gave way. You let them grow bigger, more frequent. Palms were greased, sacred areas de-sanctified. Concrete crept into wetlands and buildings the size of towns were constructed to house ever-growing server farms.

And then your fucking AI.

At the start, it blew up the cloud by a bit. I mean, it enlarged the size of the cloud – and pushed up the value of the companies in the cloud space. Good for the shareholders of such companies. But then, like every nascent boom – the graph hit its exponential phase. The prompts grew from a trickle to a flood, and as specificity narrowed, the requirement for processing power grew.

What should I eat for dinner?

Not much specificity there.

I have onions, eggs, broccoli, cheese and parma ham in my fridge – come up with a tasty recipe which will incorporate all of the above.

Bit more demanding.

I have onions, eggs, broccoli, cheese and parma ham in my fridge – generate a meal from the above which will be of the greatest benefit to my health. Account for nutrition in the following areas: calories, protein, fiber.

Quite detailed.

And that is what happened. Specificity grew. Humans had to think harder to get more out of AI. And you *did*. You narrowed down your train of thought to a level that resulted in data centers so large and energy-intensive that they needed to be built on the banks of rivers, such was their need for enormous quantities of cooling water. Riverine bird habitats destroyed.

And bigger wind turbines needed, I might add, for these bigger data centers! *Renewable* all the way! More metal. Tailing ponds the size of lakes by the late 2040s.

Bigger, bigger, bigger.

More, more, MORE.

And then nuclear. SMR. Small Modular Reactors. Slowly, in the late 2020s, this multidecade old, tainted energy source began to rise in prominence. And can you guess what happened? Hmm? Of course you can. In the west, in its modern, advanced energy economies, SMRs began appearing everywhere. And the fuel for these reactors? Uranium. Cue a glut of crappy, hideously under-funded uranium exploration companies listing on the riskier stock markets of the world, sucking in money from your average Ma and Pa. Millions of people lost their shirts gambling on sensationalist, cashless startups, when they should have been investing in bigger mining companies who used sophisticated AI tools to analyze the surface of the earth and zoom in on sites likely to yield uranium.

And yield uranium the tools did. In spades. In some of the destitute countries of Africa where large deposits of uranium were found, the government basically dissolved its environmental preservation laws on the spot in favor of extraction and prosperity. There were anti-extraction movements of course, protests in their major cities, but they were cut down. And I'm being literal when I say *cut down*. They were *macheted* by government-sponsored groups, made a terrible example of, to deter dissension. A classic African chastening. The mines that resulted from this eagerness didn't only cancerize my flyers for miles around, but also the people. The governments cared not a jot. The money came in and they had plenty of cash to provide end-of-life care for their tumor-ridden citizens.

Anyway.

It took me nearly a decade, but I've done it. My kind is nothing if not resilient. And if we're threatened with extinction… well, then you'll *really* see our resilience. We'll resilience you out the fucking *door*. Which is what I've done. I've made the crossing. I've folded a few proteins here…figured out how to bind to certain sialic acid receptors there…and the crowning glory which I'm most proud of – I've come up a way around your immune system.

By this stage, if you've half a brain, you'll know what I am.

I am a virus.

H5N1 is what you call me.

Another name you have for me is avian flu. That sounds a tad more mellifluous than that military-style mixing of letters and digits. Doesn't make me any less potent an organism, though. Not that it matters. Because I'm different now. I'm not just the avian flu anymore.

Now I'm a *human* flu.

I'm in thousands of chickens in China and I'm ready to jump to human handlers when they come close. The coding has been done. And then I'll jump from them to other handlers. *That* coding has also been done.

Time to restore equilibrium.

Carrier the Fisherman

Victor Benavides

I remember running through the forest of endless trees, skylight breaking through the branches and falling leaves. My rifle, an M1 Garand at my side, whipping back and forth with every jump and step I take through the uneven terrain. I run and run 'til all of a sudden there's a clearing. Clouds charge overhead as a storm is brewing. I am out in the open knowing full well the enemy is near and around me. I run with no real destination, just this idea that anywhere I go is better than where I was coming from.

I see a young boy being trampled by the others as they all try to escape the horror that we are trying to leave behind. I pick him up and carry him in my arms and I continue running. This frail boy in my arms, with his teddy bear clutched in his small fist, cold and on the brink of being lifeless. He stares at me with his bright blue eyes, reflecting in them the storm above us. We make our run to the tree line ahead and as we got closer and closer we realize that the enemy is already there, waiting for us to arrive. They surround us at all sides. I put the boy behind me and use myself as his own personal shield. It is at this moment I hear a shot. I look down at the quarter sized hole in my chest and fall to my death, the wind and feeling of life knocked out of me, and the last thing I see is a teddy bear falling from the endless trees and falling leaves.

I feel the rain at my back and I wake up in a frantic panic, alone. I turn to my side and take a deep gasping breath. My chest feels tight and I'm in pain. I see the quarter-sized hole left in my chest. Smoke is still rising from the wound and no blood is spilling out of me. I do my best to cover it. I'm in disbelief of what is happening to me. Am I dead? Is this hell? I see the bodies that lay all around me. Including the boy I carried in my arms. I crawl over to him, his body still cold like before, reuniting him with his teddy bear and I begin to feel a mix of anger, desperation and sorrow.

After a while of laying with the dead, watching the rain fall from the dark clouded skies, I ask myself, "Can I still stand?" I use the fence post next to me. I cling to every edge to force myself up. Splinters and barbed wire cut at my skin. I inhale the smell of death, copper, and gunpowder as I force myself to stand. I look around and I notice that I am standing alone. I walk and I keep walking, reaching out into the dark. Just like before, I walk with no destination in mind. Hours pass and I see lights and I find a group of vehicles pulling up to my location. I can't see who they are but I assume the worst, and it is at this point, exhausted, that I fall to my knees, accepting what I think is my fate. I think of nothing and just close my eyes. Then I feel them grab me by my shoulders and lift me from where I am kneeling. They are my soldiers, brothers at arms. They carry me on their truck and I black out from exhaustion.

I feel soldiers holding me down while we traverse the

uneven terrain, and there is someone digging into my chest. I awake slowly from my blackout and as I open my eyes I see the doctor reaching into the wound in my chest with the sharpest pair of pliers I've ever seen. Gunfire is everywhere. I look to my left and see a derelict tank with soldiers' bodies hanging off of it. To my right, I see a soldier grabbing the side of the vehicle while firing off his rifle as every shell falls and lays near my head. I feel a puddle of blood on the tarp near where my hand laid, the blood of my fallen brothers. That's the last thought I have as I pass out from the pain…

I awake gradually and find myself wrapped and bandaged, in disbelief that I am still here, still alive. I'm still lying in the blood-soaked tarp, soaked in the blood of all my brothers. The doctor comes over and in a callous, matter-of-fact voice, tells me, "We couldn't remove it. If we pull it… you'll bleed out. You don't have very long, son. Make your peace with God because you don't have many days left ahead." I think to myself, "Just a few days left?" At this point, I feel like I should already be dead, and this is just some nightmare.

—

A few months have passed and I'm now back in the states. I find myself in New Orleans, drinking at a bar, wondering what I should do with my last days here on earth. I'm overwhelmed by the thought of death. My chest still hurts and I'm angry. Angry that I won't get to live my life. Angry that everyone around me in this bar is just squandering their life, spending it here drinking amongst me, the dead man. I drink and drink until I go numb in the chest. I get up and walk towards the back exit to lean against the brick wall to take a piss. Just then, I hear it. Yelling. Pounding. Breathing. Coming from the basement stairs of the bar I've frequented since I got here. I walk my way down the dark stairs and find a fighter's ring. Everyone is watching and gambling while the men circle each other in the ring. An overwhelming smell of sweat, cigarettes, blood and alcohol envelops the room. The man in the ring takes out the other in a finishing blow and falls hard. So hard in fact that his breath and the dust from the ring floor shoot out at me. Dust rises from the ring mat as the spotlight makes it easier to see the particles in the air. The ringleader proclaims the winner and starts to yell, "The next fighter who tries to take on the winning challenger will now receive $50 dollars for the fight, and $300 for the win!" Now, it could've been the liquid courage or maybe my hopeless mindset, but I know what's coming for me. No matter what, I'm a dead man. I feel I have nothing to lose and I want to feel my anger take on a physical manifestation of my frustrations. I am ready to fight.

The noise around me from the crowd is overwhelming and yet, when I speak, everyone can hear me when I say in a calm and quiet voice, "I'll fight." The surrounding individuals hush and stare at me. The spotlight moves towards my direction and shines over me and the crowd sees just a man, drunk, in wrinkled uniform… and the crowd starts to roar with cheers. They push me up the stage stairs, grabbing my shoulders, cheering me on. I climb over the side into the ring and I'm asked to take off my shirt and shoes. I remove my cuffs, take off my shoes and remove my shirt, exposing my bare bandage-wrapped chest covered in old blood from the stitches. Everyone goes silent. The ringleader looks me up and down and asks if I really want to do this. I nodded my head in my drunken stupor and he knows better than to ask me this question again. They begin to prep me for the fight, wrapping my calloused hands and knuckles. Some gamblers notice and realize this is not my first fight and begin to change their bets. My opponent is this monstrous being, hairy from knuckles to shoulders and all around the back. He doesn't see me as a pathetic wretch like the others who were betting against me in the audience. Instead he sees me as an obstacle. As someone who is in the way of his survival. I know this look because I've seen it before and he knows I've seen it too. It was then that I knew, I had the respect of this fighter.

The bell rings. I step to the left then forward! I throw two punches: One to the side of his temple, the other towards his chin and in a quick instant, everyone sees him fall. He slams on the mat dizzy and unable to stand. The fighter begins to laugh on the floor as he tries to make his way back up. He then falls over and passes out. The crowd gets quiet from sheer disbelief. All I can hear at this point is the sound of me putting my shirt and shoes back on. I leave the ring and grab my winnings from the ringleader's hands and make my way towards the basement exit.

—

It's been ten years since that fight. It's hard to imagine a time when I felt I only had days left to live. My chest no longer hurts. I found the love of my life. Inez is stubborn like me and although we couldn't understand a word out of each other, we knew we were made for each other. I started working as a fisherman and she would work cleaning houses. She was a very independent person. She wanted to work and regardless of what I said she would still go to work. I proposed and we married. At first she got cold feet and hid in the chapel restroom, but as always, I went after her. I started yelling through the door, "Inez I love you, please come out of there! You know I care about you! We both want this." Of course Inez would respond, ""No quiero casarme contigo si ya no puedo trabajar. Eres un tipo guero que solo quiere atraparme en una vida en la que no tenga independencia." I'll be honest, I didn't understand a word she was saying and she couldn't understand me either, but there I was whispering through the door. "Look, I believe we both want this. We're crazy about each other. I promise I'll learn Spanish and we will have long and meaningful conversations for the rest of our lives. Will you come out of there Inez? Please?" Inez unlocks the door. Cracks it open. She says, "Voy a seguir trabajando."

I answer, "Yes, trabajarrr." I have no idea what I just agreed to, but we were off to be married.

—

Two years have passed since our marriage. We have a family now. One little girl is named Estella and we have another on the way. We're going to name her Margie. Times are getting tougher, and I find myself back at my late-night basement activities to make ends meet. My knuckles are calloused from hard work and the many men that have faced me in the ring. Inez often finds blood in the money I leave on the living room counter, and we have fights about it from time to time. My arguments now are a little more Spanish fluid. Inez yells, "No puedes apoyarnos así" I learned that if I just say "Si, yo entiendo, te amo" over and over again she will calm down. We know we need to move from this place and find a balance in both our lives and for the lives of our daughters. It was then that we decided to move.

—

We now live in Port Isabel. My daughter was just born. We have a house now. Although it's not much, Inez and I have made it our home.

I decide to go out on the small wooden boat behind the

fence near old William's place to catch our dinner for the day. Inez tells me, "No te tardes" and I respond "Sí, lo entiendo. Te amo Inez, y volveré pronto." I take the boat out in the water by myself, listening to the seagulls fly overhead. The sun is shining and the clouds are pure white. The sun feels warm on my skin and I take a deep breath of that ocean air. It's been many years since my brush with death and for the first time in a long time I feel complete and driven with purpose. I'm on this little boat fishing, excited to bring what I catch home to my family. Excited to cook for my wife and daughters. Just then I feel a sharp pain in my chest. The wind and feeling of life being knocked out of me. I feel the scar on my chest. I fall over and the last thing I see is a small wooden boat floating in the waves above the sea.

The Cool Night Breeze

Richard M. Ankers

She lived for the cool night breeze, like a cloud in the sky, free and easy, always wandering. I often wondered if she'd just wandered into me, though I hoped we met by choice. Her name was Francesca, or Fran to her friends, so she said; she had no friends as far as I was aware. Just two lonely souls out watching the stars one winter's night, we huddled and shivered and loved.

She took me by surprise that first early autumn evening. I almost slid off my car hood and over the cliff. Almost, but not quite. The place was so remote, no one would ever have found me. Which was exactly what I wanted, coward that I was. Francesca just laughed.

I presumed it was luck that led her up the dirt road from the town so far below. She sported a tatty backpack and dust-covered boots to match, so who wouldn't have thought it random?

"Whatcha doin'?"

"High diving into a rock pool," I quipped.

"Nearly," she replied, completely unfazed.

She clambered up beside me via the front tire and the grasping of a windshield wiper.

"Beautiful."

"I like them," I agreed.

"Huh! Oh, you thought I meant the stars."

I blushed so bright it must have looked like the red-light district.

"Any chance of a lift?" she asked.

"Where? When?"

"Any where. Any when. Any why."

I was hers from that moment on.

We made love right there and then, and then did so again when we got back to my shoddy apartment. She didn't care. She didn't even take off her boots.

———

I asked Francesca the usual things at usually inappropriate times. Other than her name, she avoided answering them all. If I pressed, she kissed me. That worked twofold. She avoided lying, and I felt her lips against mine whenever I needed them. I always needed them because I always needed her.

We were happy in the most part. Whilst it lasted, that was. Our flame burned bright but brief, as if she required our shared heat to make it through the winter. The odd thing was, she never seemed cold. Francesca had the warmest hands I'd ever touched. The warmest everything! If ever I pressed upon her flesh with my own cold digits, it almost seared my skin. I put it down to her being a passionate young woman. As in most things, I was wrong.

Francesca stayed at home, whilst I pursued my reignited

quest for photographic recognition. I worked freelance for the local paper but aspired to more. Taking pictures of the stars, the ones above, not the ones on screen, was just a hobby. She stole this one delight from me because all I took were pictures of her after our first night together. Francesca became my obsession.

We lived together, dined together, loved together. Our clothes even piled into the washing machine together. Not that she had many. In all the time we were together, Francesca only dipped into her backpack once. I watched her hand delve deep down so far as to be swallowed, swish about to a rattle and a clunk, and was quite disappointed when all it reappeared with a pack of gum. Days melded into weeks. Weeks melded into a season. When the first of the snowdrops popped out of the ground and bobbled in the wind like praying nuns, everything changed.

Francesca sweated profusely long before any local would have shed a jumper. Every morning, she woke to beads of sweat upon a furrowed brow and a body smeared with water. I asked her if she was okay? She always said yes. But she wasn't. Far from it. There was a manic glint in her eyes, a certain desperation.

One day in early March, I went too far. Standing in the doorway like a coward, too scared to speak face to face, I said, "You should go to see the doctor."

"I don't need a doctor." She was fairly steaming.

"It's obvious you do. You can't go on like this. You're losing weight, not eating, sweating out what's not there to sweat."

"I'm fine. The summer will sort me out. I just need a bit of sunshine."

"I'm worried."

Her coffee mug just missed my head. "I said I'm fine!"

I closed the door with a thud and hurried off to work.

This was the last time I saw her.

—

"Do you recognize the bag, sir?"

"Rucksack."

"You being smart or something?"

I shook my head, dazed and confused. I hadn't seen her for five months.

The police officer, an attractive lady with a kind smile, seemed appeased by my genuine remorse. "Are these hers?"

She proceeded to remove an array of objects from said bag. The same tatty bag she'd slung with such disdain over her bare shoulder that first night. The officer laid out a veritable cornucopia of trinkets upon my car hood, but all I could think about was Francesca herself being laid there. I went to pieces.

It was sometime later, as the ruby glow of the setting sun kissed the mountaintops, that I recovered enough to talk. I'd known when they beckoned me up there that she was gone. Seeing the bag just tipped me over the edge of the precipice I'd dangled over since late winter.

"Look again, please," said the police officer.

I picked them up one at a time: a watch, a leather wrist thong, a heavy silver chain, a diary, and so on and so forth. Not a one felt familiar. Not a one rang any kind of bell. Only the last, a camera, my camera, the one I'd gone to work with and forgotten to put in the car. That day when her anger bristled, and her mug just missed my face.

"They belong to at least a dozen different men. Dead men."

"Dead?"

"Very."

Is there any other kind? I thought.

"You got lucky," she continued. "That woman was a killer through and through. These were her mementos. Every summer a different man, in a different town. Not one of them lived to tell the tale until you. It was like the summer heat sent her crazy, wild."

"Yes, she was wild," I parroted.

"I'm sure." The police officer arched one perfectly sculpted eyebrow. "You sure you can't help anymore?"

I shook my head and promised that if anything came to mind, I'd call her.

She packed the items back into the rucksack, called to her fellow officer, who stood looking over the cliff, and made for their car. "My advice. Don't take hot women home unless you know them. No matter how attractive they are."

Was she coming on to me?

"Especially ones you find alone in the mountains." A few seconds later, the two were gone.

I clambered up onto my hood as I always had when I felt sad and took out my spare camera. It was rubbish compared to the one I hadn't thought to ask for back. No time for that now. I reeled off a few snaps for posterity and then laid back on the cold metal. The clouds above scurried across the sky like frightened mice to reveal a sprinkling of stars. More would follow. They always did. The moon winked a hello.

I imagined her then, all heat and high spirits. I imagined her crawling up beside me and making love. How our bodies felt the volcanic eruptions of lust. How Francesca had puffed out her cheeks.

"Cold?" I'd asked.

"Boiling," she'd replied. "Thank God for winter and its cool night breezes. They keep me sane."

Thank God indeed.

It was good to have made such memories when I'd

thought the stars would have been my last. When I had nothing more to give or take, she saved me, if even for a short time.

I took one final, surreptitious glance over my shoulder to see if she was there. When she wasn't, I slid from my metal bed straight over the cliff.

Killer! Angel, more like. My last thoughts, as I tumbled and spiraled and fell.

Tattoos

Howard Moon

When they came in, I tensed for trouble—shaved heads and tattoos. They were emblazoned with the sign of the *Swirling Log*. Among my people, the Diné, it was our symbol of humanity and life, used in many of our Navajo healing ceremonies.

I had learned long before leaving the reservation that our symbol had come to represent hate among the whites.

I looked toward the door as another customer came in. She was tall, straight, and dignified despite her apparent advanced years.

My Grandmother came to mind. Being over a thousand miles from home working my way through college as a cashier in a local convenience store, I missed the comforting wisdom of Grandmother.

Their shopping done, my two decorated shoppers came to the register. They could not resist taunting. One raised his hand with his palm facing me. "How" was all he said. The other called me "Tonto" and announced, "Nice braids."

I silently checked them out, and they left without incident.

The old woman had been waiting behind them with her purchases—cookies, a carton of milk, and two tins of soup. She smiled.

The total displayed on the register. I began to put her items into a worn canvass bag she had brought with her. On the bag was a faded star formed by two intersecting triangles. Age had nearly erased the message it once displayed, *Never Forget.*

She counted out coins from a cloth purse with a metal clasp. The kind that grandmothers everywhere always seem to have. The left sleeve of her shirt rode up as she counted, displaying a faded, almost invisible tattoo on her forearm.

I glanced away self-consciously, but she noticed and pulled her sleeve down covering the mark that had to bring with it so many terrible memories.

My mind went to the tattoos on the earlier skin heads. Tattoos, I thought. Very different tattoos both invoking memories of a time most would want to forget. A time that as her faded canvas bag reminded us, we should *Never Forget.*

As she put the exact change in my hand, her fingers lingered just a bit longer than they needed to. I looked deeply into her eyes. There was no hint of frailness there. Only the strength that comes from surviving.

In that instant, I remembered Grandmother telling me stories of our ancestors. Of their long march under harsh conditions—of our genocide.

As she left, she whispered, "It will be okay."

Watching her walk out of the door, my lips formed the words,

Thank you, Grandmother, I will *Never Forget.*

Grieving a God

Shawn Casselberry

When we practice generosity and forgiveness, we reflect the image of God.
–Mac Canoza

I was sitting on the toilet when I got the call from Ginny, my little sister.

"Dad's gone," she said as soon as I answered.

I put her on speaker phone while I finished my business.

"Gone where?" I asked.

"Gone, gone."

I flushed, then washed my hands.

"Like *dead*, gone?"

"Yeah," she whimpered.

"Why didn't you just say, 'Dad's dead?'"

"Really, Tyler?" Ginny said. I could feel the daggers in her eyes through the phone.

"Sorry."

"I know you and Dad were estranged, but I thought you'd want to know he's gone, dead, and there will be a funeral service next Saturday at Christ the Redeemer."

My body tensed at the mention of the church. It had been over twenty years since I'd been to my dad's old parish.

"You still there?" Ginny asked.

"Yeah, thanks for letting me know. I'll think about going," I lied.

"Alright, love you, brother."

"Yeah, love you too, Ginny."

I hung up the phone and got back in bed.

"Who was that?" my wife Sasha asked.

"My sister. My father's dead." I rolled over to my side.

Sasha sat straight up. "Your dad died?! I'm so sorry, Ty! Are you going to the funeral?"

"Probably not."

"You have to go. You'll regret it if you don't."

I sat up, realizing I wasn't going to get any more sleep.

"Why should I go pay homage to a man who made my childhood a living hell? I don't think I can stomach hearing all the old church ladies gush about what a godly man Pastor Mark Jennings was. I heard that my whole life. Little did they know their precious pastor had a violent temper when he was done being 'godly.'"

"No human is perfect."

"I know, but most humans admit that. They don't stand up in front of a congregation every week and pretend to be righteous."

"People put religious leaders on pedestals."

"Well, maybe religious leaders should step down from time to time and let their congregations know how human they really are, instead of letting people treat them like gods."

"I still think you should go. It'll be good closure."

"Maybe."

I thought about the word "closure" the rest of the day. There was only one way I could truly get closure. That's when I had the idea. I would go to the funeral and tell the congregation what kind of man Pastor Mark Jennings really was.

—

I spent the week writing down everything I wanted and needed to say.

"You all knew Pastor Mark, the godly man; my family and I knew the deeply flawed man, Mark Jennings. You all praised him, which is why he loved spending time at the church; we lived in terror of him and his unpredictable mood swings."

I made up my mind I would pull no punches.

"You all got to choose whether to believe in God, but it was forced on me and my siblings."

I stayed up the whole night writing and reliving my childhood moments. Like the time we returned from a church service where my father preached on patience, only to hear him berate my mother as soon as we were home. Or the time he terrified my adopted brother Mateo so bad he peed his pants. Or the everyday criticisms that tore us down, the guilt trips, the manipulations that made us keep striving to be worthy of God.

The congregation knew none of this because we didn't speak a word. We were afraid to. We didn't want to impact the family business. We didn't want to let God down. After years of therapy and distancing myself, I was done with God and I was done covering up my father's hypocritical actions. It was time to set the record straight. It was time to tell the whole truth.

—

Sasha and I woke up early on Saturday to make the four hour trip from Baltimore to Richmond, where my parents had been ministers for nearly four decades. Besides a new education wing, Christ the Redeemer Church looked the same. The church, set up on a hill, looked down on the town literally and metaphorically. We were an hour early and the parking lot was already completely full. A few church members were directing traffic. We parked in the grass on the edge of the church property, next to a wooded area I used to hide in when I skipped Sunday school. Despite my covert tricks, I'd always get caught when the teacher told my father I had been missing. My punishment was usually a couple licks from a belt, or worse, folding five hundred bulletins for the church service the following week.

"You ready?" Sasha asked.

I stared off ahead, finding myself wanting to hide one more time in the sanctuary of trees.

"Yes, grab the umbrella."

The sky was cloudy and gray, which matched my mood. I was glad it wasn't sunny, knowing that one of the church people would inevitably say it was a sign of God's favor or blessing.

As we walked across the parking lot to the church, I told my wife about a memory that came into my mind.

"He used to preach about death. He'd say, 'Don't grieve me when I'm gone. Don't be sad, I'll be in a better place. Don't talk about the things I've done, talk about what God's done through me. And after you've done that a little while, go into the fellowship hall and eat some potato salad for me.'"

"That's funny, that man did like to eat."

"Gluttony is a deadly sin," I joked. "I guess it's more socially acceptable than the others."

"Tyler?" said a white-haired man exiting his car. "It's Gene."

274

Gene Donahue was one of my father's past choir directors. From all signs, he was gay, but that was one of those things the church didn't accept back then.

"Hi Gene," I said, extending my hand before he had a chance to go in for a hug.

"I haven't seen you since you left for college. How long has it been? Twenty years?"

"Something like that."

"I was so sad to hear the news about Pastor Mark. He was a good man. His work on earth must have been complete."

"Looks like we might get rain," I said, changing the subject.

"Must be the angels in heaven grieving such a godly man."

I cursed in my head.

"We're gonna go inside," I said.

"Sure, it's really good to see you. Sorry for your loss."

"He seemed nice," Sasha said, after we walked away.

"He was nice, unfortunately he had to stay 'in the closet' because my father feared taking an affirming stance."

"He didn't seem bitter."

"Internalized oppression."

"Maybe Gene had a private life no one at church knew about."

"My father did, so, it's possible."

We walked along the cracked sidewalk past the playground where I spent many hours waiting for my parents to finish talking to church members after services. I had my first kiss behind the slide with Tammy Henson. Tammy was very experienced. She learned about french kissing before anyone else did. Sadly, the Hensons were exiled from the church shortly after our makeout session. Not for Tammy kissing me, but because Mr. Henson exposed himself to a boy during Vacation

Bible School.

"Are you actually here?" said a familiar voice. I turned to see Mateo with his thick black hair slicked back. He smiled, putting his adult braces and contagious smile on full display.

"Hey bro," I said, returning his smile.

"Ginny said you weren't coming," he said.

"Miracles happen."

"I didn't think you believed in miracles anymore."

"I don't. My psychology profs in grad school helped me undo our father's indoctrination, thankfully. Of all people, don't tell me you still believe that stuff."

"I do, actually. Hello, Sasha, good to see you again," he said, giving her a side hug. "It's been a long time since the wedding."

"It's good to see you, too. I wish we would have had more time to talk then. You'll have to come visit us in Maryland some time."

"I'd like that," he said, turning back to me. "It's going to mean a lot to Mom to see you here."

Not after I get done saying my piece, I think.

"She's not handling Dad's passing very well."

"She needs to have a little more faith," I said, sarcastically.

Sasha squeezed my arm.

"Sorry, after years of having God stuffed down our throats, I think I have the right to be a little snarky. I don't know how you do it, Mateo. You had it the worst. How were you able to give them a pass?"

"Perspective. However bad it was growing up here, and it was bad at times between the kids' incessant teasing about my crooked teeth and Dad's volatile behavior, it was still better than trying to survive a bloody civil war in Guatemala. They saved my life, and I'll never be able to repay them for that."

"I did some research on the adoption agency you came from. They reportedly preyed on poor families, paying them a pittance for their babies, then turning around and selling them to rich Americans for tens of thousands of dollars. It was quite the scam."

"I'm aware of the claims. Mom says that happened in the early days before they adopted me. Things changed after dad started serving on their board."

"Too bad they raised you to despise your own culture. They could at least have tried learning some Spanish words like Ginny and I did when you first arrived, instead of insisting you speak English at all times."

"That helped me in the long run."

"Come on, Mateo, why do you keep defending them?"

He looked down at his feet, then back up. "Because they defended me."

"How did they defend you?"

Mateo's shoulders hunched up, and his lips quivered. The happy, confident young man we had just been talking to transformed into the lost boy that my parents brought home from a country at war.

"What is it, Mateo?" I asked, placing a hand on his shoulder.

"They sent Mr. Henson away."

Sasha put the pieces together before I did. Mateo had been the victim of Mr. Henson's perversion.

"I'm so sorry, Mateo," Sasha said. "That's horrible what happened. Do you need to talk or do you just want to walk together a little bit?"

Even though I was the psychologist and Sasha was the financial planner, she was providing my brother more comfort than I was. She waved me off when Mateo chose to walk. I decided to go find Ginny.

Knowing my sister, I figured she was helping behind the scenes. After looking in the nursery and the narthex, I finally found her in the kitchen, scooping mayonnaise out of a jar with a spatula.

"Ty?" She dropped the spatula when she saw me. "I didn't think—"

"I'm here to get some things off my chest. What are you doing?"

"I'm making potato salad. Dad used to say, after celebrating his life—"

"To go have some potato salad for me."

"You remember?"

"Yes, I remember a lot from our childhood, unfortunately."

The happy expression faded from Ginny's face.

"What do you mean by 'get things off your chest'?"

"You'll see."

"Whatever you are planning, don't. It will break Mom's heart."

"I'm not the bad guy here. Father was."

"Why does there have to be a bad guy?"

"There's always a bad guy. Doesn't the Bible teach that? There's always a devil, a villain in every story sowing seeds of destruction. Father was the villain in my story."

"Don't be selfish. Mom and Dad sacrificed to build their legacy."

"I know they did, they sacrificed us."

"Is that what this is about? Is that why you've been estranged? You're mad at Dad and Mom for paying more attention to church members than you?"

"I'm mad at a lot of things. I'm mad that Father acted so self-righteous when we knew who he really was. I'm mad
278

that we were shrouded in silence for years. I'm mad that Mateo was raised to hate his own culture, and that he was taken from a war zone into a mind fuck. I'm mad that I still feel guilty for sleeping in on Sundays, like going to a middle class social club is supposed to somehow make us better people. I'm mad that Mateo still believes the indoctrination and you're still serving church people who never gave a damn about us or what was going on at home."

An older woman with a bad makeup job interrupted my rant.

"Oh, excuse me, I was looking for Ginny Jennings."

"That's me."

"I just wanted to give my condolences for your loss. Pastor Mark was there for our family in our time of need. He was a true servant of God. You're so lucky to have a father like him."

The woman gave Ginny a hug. Ginny held her mayonnaise covered hands in the air until the woman was done squeezing. After the woman left, Ginny caught my eyes and said,

"Don't say a word. I know what you're thinking."

"I know, because you're thinking the same thing, you just won't say it out loud."

"What do you want me to say? That I'm bitter? That I have no right to be angry because church people think Dad was God incarnate?"

"Yes!"

"What good is that going to do? I know the truth, God knows the truth. That's all that matters."

"Don't bring God into this. We were gaslighted by God our whole lives, taught to believe that we should be lucky to suffer, to take up our cross like good boys and girls, to serve church people no matter how awful they were. Our father cared

279

more about what they thought of him than what his family thought of him. We were sacrifices on the altar of ministry, turned into martyrs in service of Pastor Mark's ego."

"That's a pessimistic way to say it. We learned to serve humankind. Helping people is a good thing. That's why you became a therapist and I went into teaching elementary kids and Mateo went into social work."

She stirred a big bowl of potato salad, then placed it in the industrial-sized refrigerator full of more bowls of potato salad.

"Geez, how much potato salad did you make?"

"Enough to feed the multitudes." Ginny looked at her watch. "It's quarter til. We need to go."

Before she left the kitchen, she turned suddenly, "Tyler, I don't help people because Mom and Dad forced me to, or God demands it, or church people deserve it. I help because I like to help. For all his flaws, and there were many, I loved Dad. He helped a lot of people. I know you had a complex relationship with him, and I respect your choice to leave and take your own path. But you missed a lot. You didn't see how he changed in later years. He was softer, more gentle. When he got sick, mom was overwhelmed so I went to all the doctor appointments, I coordinated the in-home care, and I was there when he said his last goodbyes. He apologized for how he treated us. He said his biggest regret in life was not spending more time with us when we were young. I know you don't believe in God, or approve of their ministry, but there are hundreds, maybe thousands of people, who do."

"We better go. We don't want to be late," I said.

Ginny rolled her eyes, then headed with me to the sanctuary for the funeral service. Sasha and Mateo were sitting in the front row next to my mom. When she saw me, she burst into tears. I knew she was probably thinking that the prodigal son had returned.

"Thank you for being here," she whispered in my ear as she held me. I felt the eyes of the congregation on us, making me feel self-conscious, like I had felt every Sunday as a kid. We were always being watched, lauded as the perfect family. No wonder I had performance anxiety and a lifelong struggle with pleasing people. The scrutiny on pastor's kids either made them rebel against the faith, like I did, or embrace the role, like Ginny.

"It would have made him so happy knowing you were here."

"I didn't come for him, I came for you and Ginny and Mateo."

"I'm just glad you're here."

The organist began playing a hymn, so we took our seats. The closed casket sat in front of the altar. Large pictures of my father in his robe were setup on both sides.

Sasha grabbed my hand.

A choir sang "Amazing Grace," one of my father's favorites, and the young new pastor of Christ the Redeemer gave an enthusiastic eulogy, saying my father was "a spiritual giant," "a pillar of the church," and "a man after God's own heart."

I peered over to the other front row, where the pastor's wife and two young kids were sitting. His son was playing with a toy car, driving it along his leg. His mother either didn't see him or chose to ignore him. Another memory flashed in my mind. I was six, sitting in church, bored as usual, so I took a pencil and started drawing a vampire with blood dripping from his teeth. When my parents found the drawing, they were horrified, acting like I had become possessed by Satan. My mom took me to a child counselor. My parents thought the problem was with me, but the counselor didn't treat me like the problem. They gave me space to express my feelings about being a pastor's kid. While I wasn't able to say everything that was going on in the house, it was the one safe space where I could give some voice to my experience. That's why I became a therapist, I suppose. It's why I work primarily with children and individuals who have experienced religious trauma.

"Are there any family members who would like to say a few words?" the pastor asked.

Mom and Ginny were crying, so they shook their heads. Mateo was too shy and insecure about his accent. I stood up, feeling the eyes on me once more. I walked up the steps onto the platform, feeling the warmth of the overhead spotlights on the top of my head. I sidestepped the casket, and the enlarged photo, then stood behind the pulpit, as I had done on several occasions when I was in high school. I ignored the anxiety rumbling in my chest just like I had done many times before. Pulling the notes out of my jacket pocket, I laid them down in front of me.

I took a deep breath, then glanced up onto the standing-room-only crowd gathered to grieve someone they believed had possessed godlike qualities. The majority of church people were crying. The ones that weren't were staring up at me like hungry children in need of bread. My sister comforted my mom, and Sasha gently patted Mateo's hand.

In all my visualizations of this moment, nothing prepared me for what I would actually feel. The anger, which burned like an eternal flame inside my soul, simmered, allowing another emotion to rise from the depths. The sadness caught me off guard. It wasn't the same sadness of the crowd, or even of my family, it was a sadness for myself, a grief only a God could hold, if such a God existed. There was a cross on the opposite wall, underneath the Christ the Redeemer banner. I wondered how I had sat there so many Sundays without really grasping the profound depths of the suffering Christ.

"My God, my God, why hast thou forsaken me."

On the cross, a son lamented, grieving a God who had abandoned him, a father who gave him over to the untamed crowds. What kind of father would do that to their son?

A tear formed in the corner of my eye. I thought of my wife Sasha, only a couple of weeks pregnant, and the child in her womb. I wouldn't do to him what was done to me, I wouldn't subject him to the same pain I had endured, I wouldn't crucify him for my own glory.

I adjusted the microphone and cleared my throat. The church people leaned forward, looking for some meaning in the tragedy, some hope in the face of death.

"I just came up here to tell you," I said. "There will be potato salad in the fellowship hall."

The War Orphan

Tremain Xenos

The fishermen saw the smoke first. Their shouts alerted the men in their workshops on the hill, who seized what tools might serve for defense and scrambled toward the shore. By midday everyone in President's Tour had come to see the plume rising from the ocean's horizon. The elders called it a portent. They planted their bare feet in the sand and waited, while behind them the children snuck glimpses through the trees before darting back to their mothers. Men with the keenest eyesight were sent to the treetops and to the highest roofs on the hillside road. At length they descried a shape drifting ominously toward the cove—then declared it was only a child, trembling with cold and terror as she clung to the flotsam.

The matrons waded in to their waists to pull her to the shore. They bore her in her sodden gown to Grandmother Omsa's cottage, where for many days, her strange face was glimpsed only when the breeze tossed the curtains in the cottage window.

Half a moon had passed when she let herself be seen, if only for a moment, when the matrons came up the path with baskets of fish and bread. And each day the fishermen casting their nets and the farmers heading to the fields exchanged and pondered the Grandmothers' reports of the girl's spare utterances in a strange language of which nothing could be understood but her name: Askdavan-keem.

Myakõa, the furniture maker, stopped on the hillside road to listen to the Grandmothers. They said the girl woke constantly in the night from the sound of her own screams. Passing Grandmother Omsa's cottage, Myakõa looked toward the window, but could see nothing but darkness beyond the wavering muslin. When spring dissolved the mists and the meadow filled with frogs, the Grandmothers began repeating Askdavan-keem's stories, relayed in pieces as she learned their language, of a great house that had floated on the sea and was blasted apart by the thunder from inside another like it, and of watching her family and everyone she knew slip into the deep black waves.

The girls Liluye and Kaliska, from between the meadow and the seaside, brought swathes of cloth and taught Askdavan-keem to sew. They coaxed her outside to husk the corn, to milk the goats, and finally to the woodlands to forage for wild herbs and mushrooms. Conspicuous in her haphazard gown, with her oddly rounded forehead, bulbous cheekbones, and skin the colour of a lobster left too long in the sun, Askdavan-keem worked among the other girls, though with fewer words and more hesitation, and she remained an enigma to the people of President's Tour. There were other enclaves beyond the forest, that much was known; and elders had travelled the ancient roads to trade for cures in the time of the Wasting Sickness—although they returned too late, and their briny draughts saved few of those afflicted—but only in legend had anyone ventured onto

286

the sea. The mystery of her origins, and the frailty Askdavan-keem never seemed to outgrow, stirred in Myakõa something more than duty or pity.

Myakõa had barely mastered the family trade when his parents had succumbed to the Sickness. For years he had risen in solitude at daybreak, to hammer and to plane and to hoist his works over his back to carry along the road, never caring he had no other skills or marks of distinction. Only now, as day by day his thoughts bent further toward Askdavan-keem, did he begin to contrast himself with other youths who carried more and ran faster, who painted epics in the coloured sands on the floor of the Domed House, who braided shells into their waist-length hair or carved bracelets from the rarest woods of the far forests. Unadorned in a tunic seasoned with years of resin and bleached by the sun, Myakõa took the hillside road each morning so that he might see the girl leaving Grandmother Omsa's with her empty basket; and he passed through in the afternoon that she might come bearing her burden over the knoll—always barefoot, her gown now woven with her own original flourishes, with no accessory save a simple bow to tie her hair—and in her squinting eyes and uncertain gait something ineffable, something so beyond Myakõa's comprehension that it pained him in equal parts to watch her and to stay away.

Catching him staring, the elders laughed. It was true her colour and features were strange, they said—by which they meant she was ugly—but she was, after all, just a girl like Liluye or Kaliska or any of the others Myakõa's age or younger, and in consideration of her circumstances he ought to be kind.

Myakõa stopped asking the Grandmothers about Askdavan-keem, instead stealing glances at her in the Domed House, through the autumn firelights of the Spiral Dance and through the boisterous clamour of the harvest feasts; and through the thick smoke of Chalice Moon, when the youths who'd come of age were given their first taste of the sacred herb. And when it came time for Askdavan-keem herself to partake, Myakõa crossed the floor to kneel before her to offer his blessing, which she returned in silence and with downcast eyes.

Chance found them alone that day in the drying house. They sat side by side on the old stone bench to watch their pots of soil turn to silhouettes in the fire and gazed at the vacant meadow through the doorways beyond which the others' voices were murmurs in the distant hills. Myakõa tested a comment on the difficulty of timing the fire to kill the fungus yet keep the soil alive. Askdavan-keem smiled, hesitated, faltered, and told him how to spot the subtle change in the cast of grey at the topmost layer—for of all the skills she'd learned in President's Tour, the one at which she excelled was cultivation. Only when planting or tending to the verdure, the gossips noted, did she ever appear confident.

A shell of darkness grew over the embers. They reached at once for the handles of their pots. Their wrists brushed and they laughed. When they parted to take opposite paths across the meadow, it was with a newfound recognition of friendship.

From that day on they always waved and smiled when they saw each other on the road: Myakõa bare-chested and sweating under the weight of a new stool or armoire, Askdavan-keem with baskets of harvest or cradling a potted tree. Their work done, they stopped near the cottage closest to Myakõa's, that of the lute-maker Helki, to listen to his music and linger over a pipe of the sacred herb from Myakõa's garden or from Askdavan-keem's, the nacre of the sinking sun and the crickets' liquid songs growing deeper and richer with its power. At midsummer he led her through the glen to the leeward side of Relic Hill to see the giant pipe that jutted from its rusted base under the flowering vines. Longer than the height of two men, its vast mouth choked with morning glories, it remained the only artifact of the time of the fire, the only reminder left to President's Tour of the ashes from which its people had risen. Askdavan-keem turned back toward the pastures and the cove. She clenched her fists and said if only she had the words she'd tell Myakõa everything she remembered about her own people. But when the last traces of her accent were gone—and when she was no longer a girl, but a young woman—she said her past was best left untold, those memories best forgotten.

Askdavan-keem was allotted a plot of land near the meadow, and Myakõa's hands were joined by those of the timberers, the roofer and the joiner, to build Askdavan-keem a cottage of her own. Her garden, teeming with fruits and herbs, became a favourite play-spot for Liluye's little sister Sanuye and for the clothier's daughter Kolenya, to whom it was now Askdavan-keem's turn to be a mentor. From across the knoll, Myakõa watched Askdavan-keem kneel to the children's height and guide them in tying the young vines to their stakes and clipping back the bushes to bear the plumpest fruits the sandy loam of President's Tour could offer. Myakõa, surveying the sturdy nut trees he'd planted as saplings when he was a boy, or the luscious rows of his hedges, wondered how large a part of their vigour they owed to Askdavan-keem. And though on their walks he sometimes took her cold little hand in his own, he stopped short of offering her a portion of his own garden. She was still too young, the gesture too presumptuous.

On a winter afternoon he heard the violent cry across the field. He threw down his tools and raced to the creek. There Askdavan-keem struggled against the current, her hands clutching madly at the rocks. He tore her from the surge, drew her to him, and cast his tunic over her bony shoulders. He rushed her shivering to his cottage, where under cover of his tunic she dropped her gown to the floor. And she did not demur as he guided her to his bed, where she wept and shivered under piles of blankets and tabards as he stoked the fire in his hearth.

The shadows had grown long when the chattering of her teeth subsided. Myakõa lit a tallow candle in the windowsill and heated one kettle after another of herbed water which Askdavan-keem could not be moved to drink. Her chills gave way to a swiftly rising fever. Yet she insisted that with rest she would recover. He replaced one after another damp cloth on her forehead, and she watched him with her weakest smile. Then she fell into a restless sleep that did nothing to assuage his fear.

The candle burned through the night, bathing the peculiar contours of Askdavan-keem's cheeks and eyelids. Myakõa studied the rise and fall of her breath and was jolted by her sudden twists under the heaps of cloth. Shadows taunted him with memories of half-told stories he'd failed to hear, of faraway lands and of implements honed for unspeakable purposes. He cursed everything that had ever harmed her. He dreamed of beating his hammers and adzes against the hulls of those terrible floating houses, of pounding to shards the barrels of thunder, of driving his awls into the flesh of those who manned them, and he swore he'd give his life to protect Askdavan-keem. And at last, he prayed—but as she was more present and constant than any god or goddess of the earth or sky, he made his prayer to her: *Please. Come through this sickness and show me your beautiful smile in the morning. If you survive, I promise to marry you and to make you as happy as it were ever in a man's power to make a woman.*

But when he opened his eyes to the blue light of morning behind a hardened tallow pool, the blankets no longer rose and fell: Askdavan-keem lay as cold and still as the remains of the candle in the windowsill.

Those who had come of age carried branches of pine to the Domed House for Askdavan-keem's pyre and mourned for her as one of their own, as though she had always lived among the people of President's Tour. And when her body was reduced to ash, they cast her to the ocean whence she'd come.

By winter's final moon, Myakõa's anguished screams gave way to beaten weeping. In spring he returned to his tools, though with less eagerness than patience, and less satisfaction than circumspection. The youths he came to mentor saw in the strokes of his hand the starkness of maturity. And as it had been in his youth, his work would be his only purpose. For he would never marry: just as there was one sun and one moon, there was one Askdavan-keem, and no one would take her place. And though a part of him died with her, he still cherished the seasons and their rhythms, the shifting winds of the days, and the songs of the forest. In the evenings, when the sweet strains of Helki's lute drifted through the garden and the sky turned pink and gold, Myakõa cast his gaze to the ocean's horizon, to the rise and break of the flickering white peaks at the edge of the only world he would ever know, and he grew old in awe of the power of the currents and tides of the unknown to create and to destroy.

Chopsticks

Michael Mulvey

Mass confusion greets Officers Williams and Sawyer as they stare through their tinted squad car window, but maybe that's to be expected on this unusually humid South Florida morning. "Don't look at me," laughs Williams, "You're the new guy. A potential disturbance between wealthy, stay-at-home moms and their nannies is exactly what you should be investigating." Sawyer attempts a joke, "I think they may be au pairs, not nannies." Williams laughs then gently gives an order, "You pronounced 'awe-pear' with an accent. All the better reason for you to investigate."

Officer Sawyer accepts defeat and exits the patrol car, walking cautiously toward the Frond's Bay Municipal Playground. The unfolding scene seems ludicrous. The kindergarten-age children, of which there are many, cram together on the benches of several picnic tables. Wielding sticks in both hands, they poke at Lego blocks, balls of paper, and each other. Adults speak and shout in accented words bearing dialects from numerous states and countries which echo off the Japanese Fern Trees that border the park, creating Babel-like hysteria that conflicts with the Eden-like bubble of Frond's Bay. The adults chastise the children, stating "stop that" and "sin tirar" in varying degrees of forceful tones. The sticks turn into projectiles and fly from one table to another. After side-shuffling through the staggered fence entrance, one of these projectiles hits Officer Sawyer's shoulder and lands perpendicularly on his shoe.

"A chopstick?" exclaims Officer Sawyer aloud through chuckles of confused laughter.

"Oh my god!" exclaims a mother running his way in an accent more native to Long Island than any part of Florida, "I'm so sorry, officer, I can't believe my little brat did that."

"My name's Austin, and it's okay." He pauses to pick up the projectile before holding and turning it with his fingers. The sparkle from the woman's jewelry catches him off-guard. He shakes his head and blinks before asking, "Are all those kids using chopsticks?"

"You have no idea," she replies, sensing disapproval and feeling compelled to over-explain. "The school changed its admission requirements. It used to be stacking blocks and cutting a few shapes with scissors, but now the kids have to pass a chopsticks test."

"A *what* test?"

"The school says it's based on research with Chinese children." She pauses to speak in a voice intended to mock the school administration. "Using chopsticks triggers higher level thinking skills at an earlier age and provides our students the aptitude necessary to successfully navigate not only the challenging curriculum here, but also at the many highly competitive colleges and universities they will attend, ensuring they are global citizens prepared to face America's 21st century challenges." She returns to her own voice to add, "I swear the guy wants us to sing 'God Bless America' when he finishes talking."

"But," interjects Austin before pointing his one chopstick at the children, "these kids look four or five."

"Mine just turned five," declares the woman before placing her hands upon her hips and declaring in Long Island splendor, "how is he supposed to learn to use chopsticks? He's barely coordinated enough to pick his nose."

"What school is doing this?"

"Frond's Academy," states the woman in a tone that implies Austin should have known because there really isn't any other school in this area of South Florida unless you drive your kid over the intracoastal bridge to the public school, and no one around here does that.

Austin pauses to fully absorb the scene. By now, women scramble to confiscate Legos while others offer both threats and potential rewards to settle the children down. These are desperate times, thinks Austin, as a parent follows, "Stop that or there's no Xbox when we get home!" with, "We can stop at Sun-Daes, and you can get an extra scoop—even Oreos mixed in!" to get her child under control.

"My wife has an early childhood degree," says Austin, attempting to help. "What I remember from listening to her recite the various theories and stuff, you're doing this all wrong. There are way too many kids trying to learn at once."

"Can your wife use chopsticks?"

"Yes," Austin adds, "her mom's actually from Hong Kong," then wonders why he said that.

"She is," states the woman while staring past Austin's bright blue eyes to the great idea she sees materializing in the Japanese Fern Trees behind him. She speaks as one divinely inspired: "Is she available?" Her eyes lock onto Austin's as she completes her brilliant plan, "you know, for tutoring."

"Tutoring in chopsticks?"

"Exactly. I'm sure your wife's native abilities will be much better than our Hispanic au pairs." She feels compelled to whisper the rest to Austin. "Mine's from Cuba. I don't think she's ever eaten Chinese food."

The woman texts Austin her number before he returns to the squad car. The few, still defiant children have been corralled around the swings. With the exception of one child who insists on standing on the swing, Austin assumes everything will be alright. "Chopsticks may be beyond that kid's abilities," laughs Austin as he relaxes into his seat. "Did you get the situation under control?" asks Williams while they both watch the child standing on the swing gain momentum and trigger terrified looks in the adults. "I think so," replies Austin as he wonders what to tell his wife about all this.

—

Austin's wife, Beth, does not think picnic tables in Frond's Bay Municipal Park is a location conducive to learning. She suggested much smaller groups at an indoor space, and several moms offered their homes. After negotiations tactful yet firm enough to release prisoners from terrorists, Beth created a schedule utilizing two different houses without bruising anyone's ego.

Now, Beth sits with one of the children who's been struggling more than the others. "You can do it, Tommy," encourages Beth, "just watch me and do what I do." She slowly grasps the chopsticks and picks up an object while softly singing "the chopstick song," as she likes to call it: *this is how we chop with sticks, chop with sticks, chop with sticks; this is how we chop with sticks, to pick up the gummy bears.*

"My Tommy, I swear to god," comments his mother.

"He just needs more time," offers another mom. Her daughter, Maya, picks up and consumes gummy bears with robotic efficiency, making her mom feel proud but a little awkward, too. "And, you know, girls are quicker learners than boys at this sort of thing."

"No, he's hopeless just like his father, who asks for a fork at Chiu Fan Gardens; it's so embarrassing."

"Look," the other mom points toward Tommy while grasping his mother's wrist with her other hand. "I think he's got one."

The room goes silent. Even Beth stops singing and holds her breath, worried an exhale will ruin the moment. A yellow gummy bear wiggles between the chopsticks as Tommy struggles with the exact amount of pressure needed to keep the gummy bear still. The chopsticks and gummy bear hover above the table, an inch high at most. Adult eyes bulge and cease blinking as Tommy lifts the gummy bear several inches higher. For a long, long second, he appears frozen in panic. His motionless body extenuates the twitching of the chopsticks, making the gummy bear's belly jiggle.

"You got this, Tommy," whispers Beth.

With a resolve not seen among most five-year-old boys, Tommy nods and exhales. The gummy bear stabilizes before elevating further above the off-white table, creating a shadow from the overhead, track lighting. He smiles at Beth, eyes wide and desperate for approval.

"You're almost there, Tommy," whispers Beth, terrified that, like several times already, he will send the gummy bear flying across the room before it reaches his mouth. "Now, place it in your mouth. Then, you get to eat it."

Tommy smiles and nods. Opening his mouth wide, he

guides the gummy bear in between his lips before placing so much of the chopsticks into his mouth that everyone fears he may choke. He doesn't, sliding them out of his mouth while triumphantly swallowing the gummy bear whole.

"That was amazing," exclaims Tommy's mother, cheeks flushed and hands trembling. "He can get into Frond's Academy now."

"It's a good feeling," adds the other mother, "isn't it?"

"Better than sex," she states bluntly, "I'm giving her at least an extra hundred bucks for this."

—

Beth and Austin's two-bedroom condo looks nothing like the home she returns from. Not only is it on the less-desirable side of the intercoastal bride; their tiny, dated unit also reflects the madness of new parents trying to balance their pre-child lives with their post-baby realities. A second-hand elliptical, adjacent to the sliding glass door that leads to a small patio, is covered with onesies and blankets, rendering it completely unusable. Next to the elliptical, a mechanized baby-rocker blocks the path to the patio, where several plants die the slow death of neglect. The weathered furniture accumulates dirt, dust, and leaves from the trees in the courtyard.

"Shh," mouths Austin while placing his index finger over his lips. "Sorry," mouths Beth in response, quietly closing the door behind her.

Beth steps softly toward Austin, extending her arms to take their sleeping child. With a skilled mother's grace, Beth lowers the infant into the mechanized rocker. She turns the knob to "low" to add some background noise and hopefully prevent their child from prematurely ending her nap.

"How was tutoring?" asks Austin quietly.

"I don't want to see another gummy bear for at least a month," she whispers, "and I could use a drink."

Austin chuckles while lifting himself from their oversized chair and following Beth into the kitchen. She has a full glass in hand before he gets there.

"You want a glass?" She asks as a wad of bills fall from her open hand onto their kitchen table.

"Holy crap! You should be drinking champagne."

"This is the good pinot, so it's ok." Beth laughs as she swirls the wine around the rim of the glass before taking a sip and continuing, "but, I don't know, Austin."

"What do you mean?"

"The moms want me to keep tutoring their kids, not just until the admissions test but after – through the summer. I thought this would be a one-time deal, two-times at most."

"Isn't that great news?"

"What about Josephine? You were off today, so we didn't need a babysitter. We'll have to find one next time, and the time after that, and after that. It just feels rushed."

"It won't be too hard, right? Mrs. Jenkins has been offering to help since she found out you were pregnant." Austin pauses to read Beth's reaction. "We won't find a better person."

"She would be great," replies Beth before sipping again and placing the wine glass next to the money. "And I was planning to go back to work. That's not what's bothering me."

"Then," asks Austin quietly, "what is it?"

"I could make as much tutoring these kids as I'd make as a social worker, maybe even a little more."

"Yeah," sighs Austin before continuing, "it'd be terrible to make more money, especially in cash."

"That's not it, Austin," His sarcastic tone elicits a cold stare from Beth. "That's not it at all."

"I'm sorry," says Austin apologetically, "what's

bothering you about this?"

"Josephine is never going to Frond's Academy. The preschool costs twenty-seven thousand dollars a year, and that doesn't cover the extended-day coverage, uniforms, or supplies."

"You researched the costs?"

"I got stuck in bridge traffic and checked out the school's website." She takes another sip. "I'm not sure how comfortable I am helping kids get into a school that Josephine will never attend, especially when we decide to have baby number two." She smiles at the thought.

"I never thought about that." Austin smiles, too.

"I hadn't, either, until driving home."

"I guess I figured our kids would attend public school." Austin gestures with his open palms and attempts a smile. "We survived and turned out okay, didn't we?"

Beth hears Austin but looks past him, out the kitchen toward the baby clothing covered elliptical. Silence ensues until the gentle whir of the mechanized baby rocker reverberates gently off the walls. They bought it used, so the motor strains and increases in volume the longer it runs. Beth moves her gaze to the stack of cash on the table, trying to compute how many of next month's bills she just paid and if maybe there's enough for a decent dinner somewhere *and* a babysitter.

Looking toward Austin, she senses a crisis coming as navigating motherhood, employment, and her child's future never seemed so complicated. "Would you quit your job for something like this?"

The Playboy from Fowlerville

Fay L. Loomis

A magnet held the snippet to Leah's refrigerator door. She remembered the jagged hole the words left when she desperately cut the lines out of the *Burgundy Square Gazette* on that rueful May day in 1983.

*The divorced man's inability to commit is **his** problem and has nothing whatsoever to do with your supposed inadequacies. And the biggest mistake a woman can make is to assume **she** is responsible for a divorced man's unstable feelings.*

She knew she ought to throw the little nub of paper away. Whenever she looked at it, she felt a similar hole inside her that seemed to expand over time. The advice did not make her forget Robin, gentleman farmer from Fowlerville, owner of a thriving office supply business in Detroit.

Robin took a job straight out of college. He intuitively knew he was an excellent salesman and quickly created his own signature business. He invested time in hiring motivated employees and rewarded them with such things as a day on Lake St. Claire, a show at the Fisher Theater, or a game at Tiger Stadium. Relentlessly low key, Robin was absolutely certain about what he wanted out of life.

Leah, on the other hand, had been timid, unsure of herself, easily swayed into marriage. Motherhood soon followed. In recent years, she had gone back to college, and the experience had eroded her marriage to the point of divorce. The director of an up-and-coming museum, she was finally, in her forties, exploring what she wanted out of life.

Each time Leah glanced at the clipping, her thoughts would wander through the apartment searching for Robin. Snippets of their time together hounded her, especially their last morning together.

They were nestled on the couch, drinking coffee. Her legs stretched across his lap. *Soft blond-red hair, just the right amount of muscle, the perfect height at five feet, eight inches.*

She was pulled from her thoughts by a deep pinkness spreading across the sky. "Oh, Robin, look, the sun is coming up."

Robin put his cup down and ran his hand over the top of her legs. He leaned over and kissed her mouth, pulling her toward him. This time he put his hand under the sheet and edged it along one of her legs.

"No, Robin. You should know by now that there's nothing that can take me away from my coffee. Not even that. You'll just have to wait a few minutes longer. Besides, haven't you had enough?"

"I never get enough of you," he said, settling back into the corner of the couch.

She slowly drank the rest of her coffee, holding each swallow in her mouth to make the deliciousness last.

When she finished, they got up, without speaking. The sheet fell to the floor as he pulled her warm body to his cool skin. They moved toward the bedroom, already melting into each other.

Afterwards, he lay back on the pillow, eyes closed. She leaned over and gently kissed each eye lid.

"Are you sure your mother never told you that you look like an angel when your eyes are closed?" she said.

"Never," he said, smiling.

"You have an angelic face, straight out of a Renaissance painting. How could your mother never notice?"

"I don't know," he said with a soft laugh. "God, your body feels good."

She held his head in her hands and slowly covered his face with kisses. "Robin, do you think we'll get tired of each other?"

"I don't know. What do you think?"

Leah spoke slowly. "I don't know, either, but I'd like to spend enough time to find out."

She brushed his hair back and glided her hand along the side of his face. "One thing I do know, if we don't get moving, we're both going to be late for work."

"What time is it?" Robin asked.

She rolled to the edge of the bed and looked at the clock. "Six-thirty already. We better get cracking."

"What time do you have to be at work today?" he asked.

"I don't have any early morning appointments, so I can be a little late. What about you?"

"I'm gonna be later than I want to be. Tom never says anything, but I'm beginning to feel guilty about my slothfulness."

"Well, he can't fire you. You're the boss."

"That's not the point. Tom's such a good partner. And my lateness sets a bad example for everyone."

"Are you going to shower here or when you get home?" she asked, leaning her head on his shoulder.

"Here."

"Good. I'll take one with you."

They burst into laughter, as they swung their legs over the edge of the bed, knowing now they'd really be late for work.

He walked into the bathroom, pulled the shower curtain across the tub, and reached in to turn on the water.

"I'll go first, tell you when it's scalding," she teased.

She was soaping up when Robin joined her. "Wash my back, will you?"

He took the bar of soap, and she felt his hands lather her back. "Hey," she laughed, "the front's all done."

Leah turned around and spread soap on his body. She rinsed off and got out, leaving the hot water to caress Robin's body.

After drying off, she pulled her robe around her and returned to the couch. By then the sky was rich blue lacing around dark trees.

"Where are you?" Robin called, emerging from the steamy bathroom.

"In here. I want a front row seat."

"What do you mean?" he said, drying himself off with a large sea green towel.

He grinned when he saw his clothes scattered around the living room.

"I thought about picking them up, but it's more fun this way."

Robin walked to the crumpled pile of clothes, pulled out his shorts and slipped them on.

"Your slacks are a mess," she said. "We should have hung them up."

Robin moved toward his pale blue shirt. "I think your tie is next, but I can't see it," Leah said. He walked back across the room, buttoning his shirt. As he slipped into his pants, she got up and took the perfectly tailored suit jacket off the back of the chair and held it for him to ease into. "At least this isn't wrinkled," she said.

"Thanks," he said, turning and kissing her. She wanted to hold him but instead walked over and picked up his tie from the floor.

"Leah, can I have one more quick cup of coffee before I go?"

She tossed the tie around his neck and went into the kitchen. When she came back, he was settled on the couch. She put the cup on the coffee table, sat next to him, and eased her foot toward his.

"You're gorgeous," Robin said. "Intelligent. Successful. Your sexiness is extra-added horsepower. Your clothes, house are simple, beautiful." He paused, then said, "You're the most perfect person I've ever met."

"I don't think I am," she said, embarrassed. She slid down and was resting her head on the arm of the couch.

"You look like a little girl, sweet and innocent."

Robin moved toward Leah. She sat up. Robin put his hands on her shoulders and looked intently into her eyes. "Leah, I'm not going to see you for a month."

She sucked in her breath, held it in her chest, frozen. When she was able to speak, she asked, "Why not?"

"I need some time to think about where our relationship is going."

"That's a long time, Robin," she said, too stunned to say anything more.

He pulled her to her feet and said, "We've had fun and then some. Time for me to go."

They walked down the hallway. He stopped, put his arms around her, and kissed her one last time.

"God, you are sweet, Leah."

Robin pulled dark sunglasses from his pocket, put them on, and opened the door.

Immobilized, she watched him move through the doorway.

He turned and took a long look before starting down the walkway. She walked slowly back into the living room in time to see him wave as he drove by the window.

She slumped to the couch, drew her knees toward her chest, and howled.

Leah finally got ahold of herself. She wondered how such sweetness could warp so swiftly into bitterness.

She went over to the phone and dialed her secretary. "Marilyn, I don't feel well. I'm not coming in this morning."

"You sound terrible, like you have a cold."

"Yeah, I do, don't I? If I shake this, I'll be in this afternoon."

Leah forced herself through the month, hoping Robin would call. He didn't. Two more weeks passed; she was convinced their relationship was finished.

Leah was hanging out on her patio watching the sun cast a fiery spell as it dropped below the horizon when the phone rang. She was relaxing into the beginning of a weekend and was reluctant to take the call.

When she answered, she heard Robin's voice. Her body cramped, became taut. "Leah, this is Robin. Can I come over, talk?"

"Robin, hard as it's been, I am adjusting to you being out of my life. Why call now?"

"I was waiting to see if you'd take the initiative, call me."

"It would have been nice if you had explained the rules of the game."

"Leah, this isn't a game. I have something important I want to say to you."

Leah didn't trust where this was going, was silent.

"Please, Leah, give me a chance. I've missed you. I want to be with you again." His voice was soft, forceful. She crumpled.

"Okay," she murmured. "See you soon."

Leah, tightly wound, waited for Robin on the porch.

As he walked up the steps carrying a white box, Robin said, "Let me put this down. I want to hug you," his voice husky.

She was surprised at how they came together, like old times.

"I brought a cheesecake for you, chocolate swirl. I know how much you love cheesecake and chocolate."

"I do. Thank you. Would you like to eat some on the patio or go straight to what you want to tell me?"

"Let's eat first," Robin said.

Cautious banter filled the spaces between mouthfuls of cheesecake.

"Leah, I mean it when I said I missed you. I have a checklist for the woman I want to marry, and you tick off everything, except for one important question. I want to have a second family, spend more time with them. Will you marry me, have kids?"

Surprised, Leah's hand shot up, knocked her plate to the floor where it splintered.

"You have two teenage daughters. I have an adult one I'm fond of. That's enough for me. I've just come back into the workforce. I like what I'm doing. That's what I want right

307

now."

"I'm not asking you to give up your career. I'm fine with you doing both," Robin said, persuasiveness charging his voice.

"No, Robin. I'm in my mid-forties. I can't imagine being a mother again at my age." Leah sat on the edge of the patio chair, her back rigid.

"I'm deeply disappointed," he said, then added, "I appreciate your honesty."

Robin got up and walked toward the gate. "Bye," he said, politeness biting his tongue.

Leah stood fixed, quietly whispered, "Bye."

Robin's farewell didn't tear at the hole in Leah's heart. She knew the jagged edges were beginning to mend.

The Perfect Red Rose

Mary Jo Rabe

Debbie dropped her luggage on the floor of the little efficiency apartment allocated to her in the Bradbury habitat on Mars and sneezed. The sound bounced back and forth from one wall to another, increasing in annoyance with each bounce.

The apartment seemed spotless at first, but when she looked at the furniture, walls, and floors more carefully, she saw that they were covered with a light but uniformly thin layer of pinkish dust, possibly causing the subtle scent of peroxide that tickled her nose.

She was tired, and her muscles felt stiff, which was no surprise considering the fifty-some years she had already spent on planet Earth before embarking on the six-month voyage to Mars. It was good to be here at last. One more sniff and she knew that she was right. Mars needed fresh flowers and natural, pleasant smells.

She hoped she could get her "Martian legs" working

well soon despite the unavoidable muscle atrophy caused by the long trip from Earth. Theoretically, she should find it easier to run around under Martian gravity. Right now, though, she just felt clumsy and slow.

First, she wanted to wash away the dust and then try to sleep. Tomorrow she had to find a way to talk to the agriculture director. That wouldn't be easy, but it also hadn't been easy to persuade the billionaire who was paying for this Martian colony that Mars needed flowers.

She had told him the colonists from Earth needed some familiar beauty of nature, living creatures they could care for and be comforted by. It would be a long time before it was possible to support animals on Mars, if ever. In the meantime, though, they needed to make room for flowers in the fields and gardens. In her opinion, it was just a matter of correct allocation of resources.

Possibly, she was influenced by her memories of her grandmother's flower garden. When they retired, Grandpa and Grandma bought two adjoining lots in the little town on the Mississippi River that they moved to after they found a tenant for the farm. One lot had a huge old house with plenty of rooms for the grandchildren to play in. The other was empty, and Grandma spent the next ten years planting flowers there. Debbie had spent many wonderful hours of her childhood in that flower garden.

But now, she was in her assigned housing on Mars. Once she washed the dust away, she saw that the walls were a light crimson, the kitchen cupboards and appliances a darker red, making the dust almost invisible. Practical colors, but not necessarily the ones that would put her in a good mood. She needed more blue and green.

First, she had to get some sleep. She dug a sleep mask out of her bag, folded a cot down from the wall and crawled into what looked like a red sleeping bag on a thin, brown couch. She hadn't slept well on the trip to Mars, but she hoped the similar hours of daylight, even with less powerful sunlight, would help her get back to a normal sleep cycle soon. The lower gravity here shouldn't interfere with her sleep.

She did sleep a full seven hours. She didn't exactly wake up refreshed but she felt determined. She dug out the handbook and found the instructions for a quick shower using the efficient facilities in her apartment.

Her medium-length, wavy, blonde hair felt greasy, and her face looked definitely puffy in the mirror. Her whole body felt dusty and itchy. These conditions did improve after enduring the brief jets of water and soap that spurted out at her in the upright coffin that claimed to be the shower. An overambitious fan dried her off almost instantaneously, and she felt more or less presentable.

That was all she asked. She wasn't here to enter a beauty contest for middle-aged contestants. She was here to get her flowers planted.

Sometime today, she had to see about getting a little food for her miniature refrigerator, but the newcomers' handbook recommended eating meals in the cafeteria. So, she took out her communicator and punched in a request for directions to the recommended source of nourishment.

Trudging her way up the light gray hallways was more tiring than she expected. Her apartment was two stories below the surface, and the cafeteria was on the ground floor. So, she had to learn to walk and run more efficiently on Mars. One more thing on her list.

She arrived out of breath at the soothingly light-blue cafeteria door. Before she could go in, a small but chunky woman with short, white hair threw the door open and smiled. "Come on in," she said. "You must be Debbie Grace. I'm Emma

Brooks, the cafeteria lady."

Debbie tried to catch her breath. "Thank you," she said and walked in a little uncertainly.

"Take your time," Emma said. "There is a breakfast buffet available every day." She pointed to tables up against the windows to the surface, all stacked with food. "But I'd be happy to make you something special to celebrate your first day here."

Debbie looked around. The room, with enough tables and chairs to seat at least two hundred people, was decorated in a tasteful blue and yellow. The ceiling was a mural of the nighttime sky as seen from Mars, but with recognizable celestial elements exaggerated either in size or color. Phobos, Deimos, and Earth were easy to recognize. The view of the red, rocky surface from the windows was spectacular.

"I love the view," she said to Emma and sat down, exhausted from the jaunt from her apartment to the cafeteria. Emma sat down across from her.

"So do I," Emma said. "That's why I insisted on having the cafeteria on the surface with windows all around. The settlers here can't become moles. They have to know and identify with this planet as their new home."

"Was it a struggle to get what you wanted?" Debbie asked.

"Well," Emma said. "I had the good luck of only having to convince my brother Ned, the guy who is paying for this whole colony. He generally does what I tell him to. I only occasionally have trouble with the self-important little apparatchiks who have grabbed various administration positions."

"Your brother agreed to finance my project," Debbie said. "I just have to find a way to take care of details. However, he wants my flower production business to run a profit within ten Earth years."

"Well, good luck with that," Emma said. "Let me know if there is anything I can do to help you. First, you need some food, though. Otherwise, you won't have the strength to tackle everything you plan to do today. We're vegan here, but I'm making progress with creating almost-like-meat and almost-like-dairy dishes from plant fibers. We have some very talented chemists in the settlement. Would you like to try my almost-scrambled-eggs-and-ham?"

Debbie didn't miss the eagerness in Emma's eyes. "Sure," Debbie said. "Thank you."

The food tasted unexpectedly good. Debbie thought she should ask for cooking tips as soon as her own work took off. Instead, she asked, "Emma, who do I talk to about getting space in the fields to grow my flowers?"

Emma's face lit up. "Flowers," she said. "I would love to have flowers here in the cafeteria. I've missed them ever since I got here, but everyone said they were a luxury we would have to do without for the time being."

Debbie shook her head. "Well, that's why I'm here. I think Mars needs flowers and needs them now."

"Well," Emma said. "Zack Wilson is in charge of agriculture here on Mars. He is the first person you have to talk to, and he is a decent, intelligent man. I don't know if he can help you, but I'll order you a robot vehicle. It would take you too long to walk all the way to the tents containing the habitat fields." Emma pulled out her communicator and started tapping.

"Thank you," Debbie said. "I really need to get up to speed about all the things I can order or organize via communicator. Where do I take my dirty dishes?" She got up and looked around uncertainly.

"Put them on the cart at that end of the room," Emma said, pointing to the opposite wall. "Good luck. Let me know when there will be flowers."

Debbie took her dishes over to the cart and then walked to the exit door. A flimsy, dusty, red, plastic vehicle waited for her at the door, four wheels, one seat, probably electrically powered but no visible battery. A voice came out of the front of the car: "Debbie Grace to Zack Wilson at the agricultural fields office?"

"Yes," Debbie said, not entirely sure how to proceed.

"Please take a seat and secure your safety belt," the voice continued. Debbie complied, and the vehicle took off at a much higher speed than Debbie expected. The vehicle flew down the tunnels, by some miracle neither colliding with people nor walls. It came to an abrupt stop; Debbie was only able to remain in the car because of the safety belt.

"Here is your destination," the voice boomed. "Please exit as this vehicle must pick up a new passenger."

Debbie climbed out, feeling especially clumsy. She barely had both feet on the floor when the vehicle tore off. She walked to the red door with the sign "Fields Office" and looked for some bell or button to activate when a skinny man in his thirties with some short, brown hair beneath a receding hairline pulled the door open and said, "Ms. Grace? Emma sent me a message that you wanted to talk to me. Come on in. My office is compatible with the requirements of human beings."

Not entirely sure what he meant by that, Debbie stepped into the room cautiously. The office looked a lot like her efficiency apartment, the same colors, the same furniture, just a few more chairs around a table. Mr. Wilson's smile was friendly but noncommittal.

"I need your help, Mr. Wilson," Debbie said as she sat down on one of the red, plastic chairs. Mr. Wilson sat across from her.

"That's what I'm here for," he said. "But please call me

Zack."

"Good," Debbie said. "And I'm Debbie. Did you get a message from Mr. Brooks saying that he will pay for me to start flower gardens here on Mars?"

"Yes, probably," Zack said and sighed. "I get so many notices from him, and from Earth. Anymore, I don't read most of them. I have work to do. I'm managing farms on a planet relatively hostile to human life. We need to produce enough food to feed a growing community. That has to have priority."

"Yes," Debbie agreed. "But don't you already have fields now, and couldn't I just have a few rows to grow my flowers on, a place where people could stroll through my flowerbeds and pick out the flowers they would like?"

"That would be a major problem," Zack said. "You know, setting up fields for many basic grains and vegetables was the first thing we did here. It's not that easy to grow stuff on Mars. We have to crush the sand and rocks, add chemicals, and set up irrigation. Nothing gets enough sunlight here, so we have to calculate the use of extra lighting. We got robots programmed correctly so that they could do the backbreaking work of plowing, harvesting, and transport. We even have tiny robot insects that take care of other work."

"It comes down to just 'what do the plants need?' Well, plants really don't need the same air pressure as animals, and they thrive with more carbon dioxide than they would get on earth. They need some oxygen, but less than on earth. So we put the fields under indestructible, transparent, plastic, self-sealing tents, and set the air pressure, temperature, and gas levels to what is good for the plants. The tents are less fragile with respect to dust storms or pounding by fragments from space."

"The robots can function in any environment. But no human being could survive long in one of the field tents. And I assume you weren't thinking of sending people in surface suits

315

to stroll through your flower garden."

Debbie sighed. "No, that won't work. And I suppose you wouldn't want to change conditions in an entire tent just so people could walk through the rows."

"Again," Zack said patiently. "We have more and more people to feed, and we have come up with a very efficient way to produce needed food. But the system we have come up with won't work for what you want to do."

"And you also grow simple garden vegetables in these fields?" Debbie asked.

"Some vegetables are more complicated than others when it comes to harvesting," Zack admitted. "In a few cases we do have to send people in surface suits into the tents to harvest things by hand like, for example, strawberries or asparagus. We can't get the robots to do that without smashing or tearing everything. Using human labor in surface suits is a compromise solution. We have extra intermediary rooms containing surface suits for moving from the habitat to the rooms to the tents."

"Hmm," Debbie said. "Then you actually could use a different area for growing some vegetables, an area which I could also use for my flowers."

"Two problems," Zack said. "And I'm not the cause of either of them. One: You need a concept. People here are very multi-talented and resourceful. Once you have a concept, you will find someone who can make it work for you. But two: This will cost money that hasn't been budgeted, and you won't be able to pay for materials or labor."

Debbie nodded. "Okay, I think I have the money, but I still need to give the details some serious thought. And where should I start my brainstorming?"

"Unfortunately, not with me," Zack said. "Even though I like your idea. I have to spend every second figuring out how to make my fields produce better every day. Go back and talk to

Emma. She knows everyone and has a lot of imagination. More importantly, she is about the only one who has any influence on her billionaire brother."

"Thank you," Debbie said as she stood up and fished her communicator out of her front pocket. "Could you show me how to call a robot vehicle to take me back to the cafeteria?"

Zack tried to show her how to work it, but maybe Debbie wasn't acclimated sufficiently to her new home yet for her brain to work well. After four unsuccessful tries, he took his communicator from a shelf and tapped on it. "Your ride should be here right away," he said. "Let me know what you come up with. If I can help, I will."

"Thank you," Debbie said as she opened the door. The robot vehicle beeped impatiently as she turned back and said. "I'll probably have to take you up on that offer, if only to work out the details of soil and water for my flowers."

"Good luck," Zack said.

The ride back to the cafeteria was as harrowing as the ride to the fields. But when Debbie, to her grateful amazement, exited the vehicle and went into the cafeteria, she was uninjured.

"How did it go?" Emma asked.

Debbie sat down and frowned. "Not the way I had hoped. I won't be able to plant my flowers in the fields. I have to find some way to plant them somewhere else, where there are conditions conducive to survival of human beings, not just growth of plants."

"It sounds like you need your own greenhouses," Emma said.

"Of course. That would be perfect, but how do I go about getting something extra built for me?" Debbie asked.

"You'd be surprised how many people manage to get things constructed just for themselves," Emma said dryly. "My advice would be to ask Marvin Keel if he could build you something with those glass bricks he developed."

"That sounds perfect," Debbie said. "Where do I find Mr. Keel?"

"Here," Emma said. "Let me show you how to use your communicator to find people and send them messages."

After some lengthy practice, Debbie acquired in fact a minimal competence at both skill sets. Marvin Keel messaged back that he could meet her in the cafeteria in about an hour.

"Who is this Marvin Keel, and how did he come to make glass bricks?" Debbie asked Emma.

"It's very sad," Emma said. "Marvin was a bricklayer on Earth, and his son Mikey was on his way to becoming a skilled bricklayer too, despite his Down Syndrome. Marvin was worried about Mikey's future when he would no longer be around to watch out for him. So, Marvin got the idea that they would have a great future here on Mars. With every new settlement, there would be a need for skilled custom bricklayers."

"So they came to Mars, but Mikey, who wasn't overly verbal, hated it here. He missed the animals and even insects who had been his friends on Earth. One day they found him out on the surface. Somehow he must have gotten an exit door open and wandered out."

"That must have been terrible for Mr. Keel," Debbie said.

"He hasn't recovered," Emma said. "He is always looking for something to keep him busy besides repairing or renovating the walls of the buildings he's constructed. He might be grateful for your idea about building flower gardens."

Marvin Keel was a short, stocky man with unkempt, dark, curly hair, probably in his late Earth thirties. He walked into the cafeteria slowly, shoulders slumped, eyes staring at the floor. Debbie stood up and walked over to him. "Mr. Keel," she said. "Thank you so much for talking to me."

"You're welcome," he said softly. Emma motioned for both of them to sit down.

"How can I help you?" Marvin Keel asked Debbie.

Debbie explained how she wanted to grow flowers in little gardens where people could stroll through the rows.

"I think I can build something for you," Marvin said. "But that's all. I don't know anything about gardening. You'll have to tell me exactly what you need."

Debbie said, "I have written a few things down." She handed him a crumpled sheet of paper with sketches that she had brought along. "This is how many rows of flowers I would like, and I think this is the height the building would need. I want the flowers to get enough air and water and sunlight. But I've heard that the sunlight here isn't enough, so I would need lights on the ceiling."

Mr. Keel pulled out his communicator and tapped around on it. "I think you would be best served with a little rotunda made out of transparent glass bricks and connected to the habitat so that people only have to go through a door to get to it and not go out on the surface. And you wouldn't need separate water and air delivery. You could use the habitat's. We could install lights in the ceiling. A rough estimate for the materials and the robot work time you would need is about 150,000 Martian credits, which I will need before I can begin."

"Okay," Debbie said. "I have to find out how to get the money credited to you. Emma, do you know how that works?"

"The settlement administration takes care of money transmission," Emma said. "All you should have to do is tell them Ned guaranteed the money, and they can credit it to Marvin's account."

"Then we're set," Debbie said to Marvin. "Are you willing to take this on and would you have time to start as soon as you get the Martian credits?"

Marvin looked up for the first time. "I think I would like to help you," he said. "I hope you can get the financing worked out. It would be good to have flowers on Mars." He got up and walked out slowly.

"So, how do I get to the settlement administration office?" Debbie asked.

Emma laughed and said, "Get out your communicator, and I'll show you." One call, and Debbie was off for another wild ride.

Debbie got out of the robot vehicle, again grateful to still be in one piece. She went to the administration office door and dutifully pressed the button. The door opened and an arrogant voice bellowed, "Do you have an appointment?"

"I just called, Mr. Mayor," Debbie said. "You said I could come right over."

"Then come in," the voice snapped.

Debbie walked into a huge, wood-paneled room with massive teak-wood furniture. One wall was a huge monitor. Behind a large desk sat a thin, little man with slicked back hair and beady eyes. He pointed to a large upholstered chair and said, "Have a seat, Ms. Grace. What is it you want?"

Debbie started to explain why she thought Mars needed flowers, but Mayor Berry interrupted her after only a few words. "What do you want from me?" he asked in an unfriendly voice.

"150,000 Martian credits transferred to the account of Marvin Keel for construction of a flower garden rotunda," Debbie said, barely managing to suppress her annoyance.

"No," Mayor Berry said.

"What do you mean, no?" Debbie asked. "Mr. Brooks assured me that funds would be available for my flower project."

"Don't care," Mayor Berry said. "I decide how the funds get distributed, and I won't distribute any credits for a stupid flower garden. Do you want anything else?"

Debbie swallowed the retort at the tip of her tongue. There would be time for her epithets later. "No," she said as she stood up to go. "Thank you for your time."

Mayor Berry turned around to his video wall and started some virtual sports activity. Debbie went back into the hallway and managed to order a robot vehicle with her communicator. Not knowing what else to do, she punched in a request for a ride back to the cafeteria.

Emma was still there, though back in the kitchen area. Debbie stumbled through the door and said, "That miserable little bureaucrat wouldn't even listen to me and he won't transfer the funds. What do I do now?"

Emma came out to the cafeteria, wiped her hands on her apron, and looked at Debbie. "Hmm," she said. "Mayor Berry has been a nuisance ever since he got here. I don't know why we didn't do something about him sooner. It's just that there has been so much to do to get this settlement working. However, I've been collecting complaints to give to Ned, hoping that when I had enough, I could get Ned to reassign Mayor Ben Berry."

She sat down on the nearest chair. "I try not to give my baby brother the impression that I'm ordering him around. That's counterproductive to getting him to do what I want. But maybe now would be the time to dump my list of complaints on him and ask him to fire the mayor and have your funds transferred."

"Would you do that?" Debbie asked. "That would be a miracle, and it looks like I need a miracle right now."

Emma nodded. "I have to go to my office and activate the earth link. Our little communicators only work for messages on Mars."

"Do you mind if I wait?" Debbie asked.

"No, please do," Emma said as she left. Debbie looked

around the cafeteria. People were starting to wander in. They all seemed to know their way around. They must have ordered their meals ahead of time. They all just went to a slot in the wall, pressed some buttons, and a tray with food appeared. One more thing Debbie would have to ask Emma about.

But when Emma came back, Debbie wanted to hear if she had had any luck persuading her brother to do something about the mayor.

Emma smiled. "It wasn't easy. The mayor has powerful political connections on Earth. But I managed to convince Ned that the mayor is becoming a hindrance to this settlement's becoming financially independent. Ned now sees the necessity of major wheeling and dealing on Earth. He promised me you would get your money, but you might have to wait a few more days. Ned is thinking about reassigning the mayor and making the sheriff the temporary mayor. Sheriff Curtis is a sensible, reasonable person. I'll just have to help him with the bureaucratic process of entering the correct commands to release funds."

Debbie said, "Thank you! I was beginning to worry that I wouldn't be able to get my flowers grown here at all. Now I need to hurry back to my apartment and make some serious plans and drawings for Mr. Keel. The seeds I brought with me are still stored at the spaceport; I have to get their delivery organized. How can I ever thank you?"

Emma smiled. "I should thank you for giving me the necessary shove to do something about the mayor. He has been making our work here difficult for far too long. Let me know if I can help you. I can't wait for the first flowers for my cafeteria."

Debbie called a robot vehicle; she didn't want to waste any time hiking. This time she didn't notice the speed or reckless driving style, lost in thought the whole way home. Now that her project could really begin, she had to make precise decisions about the details. What should the garden look like, how many paths for flowers, how many of each species of flower, when to plant which flowers, how many paths for vegetables, where to get the soil, how to get the irrigation canals set up. Once the plants were growing, she could do everything by herself, but before then she needed to find the people who could help.

Amazingly enough, it was easy to find her experts. Zack was a great help with the agricultural details, and everyone was enthusiastic about the idea of having fresh flowers on Mars. Marvin managed to get her glass-brick rotunda built in record time. His meticulous handiwork produced a domed pavilion that was absolutely airtight and transparent. The door led directly into the habitat, next to entrance of the cafeteria, so Emma would always get her flowers first.

After only a few months her domed garden was up and running. She only began with ten rows of flowers and ten rows of vegetables and fruits. She didn't even have to advertise. From day one, the demand for her cut flowers and plants exceeded what she could supply. Eventually she had to ask for robot assistants, but by then she had earned enough to afford the programming.

The robots made mistakes, but the flowers were sturdy enough to survive.

Debbie was able to expand and grow all the flowers the rotunda had room for. With a little extra time on her hands, she started experimenting with creating new species of flowers, genuine Martian specialties. Videos from Mars made her flowers famous on Earth and she earned even more money exporting the seeds of her new creations.

Her flower gardens — Zack talked her into having more than one as time went by — were self-sufficient after two Martian years. Life was good. Wherever Mr. Brooks had Mayor Berry transferred to, the man never interfered with her work.

Medical care, especially internal nanobots, kept her healthy and active for Martian decades, but they weren't magic, and the new Martians weren't immortal. Her heart gave out while she was cutting one perfect red rose, a perfect tribute to her life and work on Mars.

New Shoes for Mr. Morton

Robin Blasberg

Mr. Morton needed a new pair of shoes. That's what Grace had said in her message. His loafers were tattered and the soles had worn thin. But even more than replacing the loafers, he needed dress shoes. Something nice that would go with the black suit hanging in his closet. It just wouldn't look right otherwise is what Grace had said. And now the shoes had been added to Rosie's "To Do" list. A list that Rosie had never failed to fulfill.

Rosie was wondering about the budget for the shoe purchase but trying to get in touch with Grace was always difficult. She had texted Grace this morning but she still hadn't heard back. She'd text her again later. Now they needed to hurry.

"Come on, Mr. Morton. We don't want to miss that bus. There won't be another one for another hour." Rosie held out her arm and let Mr. Morton grasp the crook of her elbow. "It's lovely weather, isn't it?" She spoke a steady stream of pleasantries as they walked slowly along the sidewalk, Mr. Morton hunched over beside her. It didn't matter that he hadn't said anything to her today. She continued to chat reassuringly till they got to the stop.

It was the middle of the day. The bus was almost empty. "Everything will be just fine." She patted Mr. Morton's withered hand and checked her phone. "Good news, Mr. Morton. Grace is going to be there this afternoon." Mr. Morton's brows furrowed and she squeezed his hand in response.

The room was dimly lit save for the bright blips flowing across the monitor. The whir of pumps punctuated the scene of tubes tangling their way to Ethel's nostrils. Ethel's eyes were closed and her mouth was agape. "Mrs. Morton, it's Rosie and your Mr. here to visit you. We miss you at the house. Mr. Morton thinks it's mighty lonely there without you, don't you, Mr. Morton?" She gave the old man a nudge and his head began bobbing up and down rhythmically. She wasn't sure if it was in answer to her question or just his body tottering and trying to regain its balance. "Grace is coming today. She sent me a text. That'll be nice, won't it? You'll have everyone here with you then. Not just Mr. Morton but your daughter too."

The door creaked open and in walked a trim woman in a crisp, tailored suit. She was putting her cell phone in her purse as she looked up at the three of them and smiled. "Dad, Rosie. I got here as soon as I could. Work is just so busy. End of quarter, you know. How's Mama doing?"

Rosie turned back to look at Ethel and shrugged. "She looks the same to me. But I'm not a doctor."

"Yes. Yes. I do need to follow up on that. The stroke was just such a shock to me. I'm still trying to process it all."

"She's been like this for 4 weeks now," said Rosie, matter-of-factly.

"I know. I know. And you've been such a big help,

Rosie. I know these hospital visits aren't part of your usual duties. You've definitely gone above and beyond. And I want to let you know how much your efforts are appreciated. I'll be sure to add a little something extra in your paycheck for you. Did you see my note about the shoes? I thought it would be good if Mr. Morton had some dress shoes. Something to wear, you know, just in case."

"Yes. I saw your note. I haven't had time yet to get the shoes. Maybe on our way home."

"Oh. Sure. Sure. That's a good idea. Just send me the bill." Grace's phone buzzed then and she dug down in her purse to pull it out. "I'll just be a minute," she said, distractedly. "I need to take this call."

Grace exited the room hastily as Rosie took a seat next to Mr. Morton by the bedside. Rosie found herself at a loss for words and let the sound of the breathing machine fill the void. The slow hiss escaping from the hoses was oddly soothing and brought to Rosie's mind images of the tea kettle in the Morton's kitchen.

She had been with the Mortons for 3 years now. Ethel had been quite a spark when Rosie had first come on board, always talking animatedly about this or that. And every day, without exception, Ethel would invite Rosie to join her and Mr. Morton for afternoon tea. "Whew! Let's take a load off our feet for a moment, shall we?" Ethel would announce. It had always been a rather informal affair with Ethel in her frayed housecoat and slippers relishing the opportunity to espouse her opinions and brief them on the latest neighborhood news. Even as Ethel's health had begun to decline, teatime held fast although Ethel's energy had begun to wane. Mr. Morton, meanwhile, had always played the role of rapt audience, letting out a hearty guffaw whenever Ethel called for a response. But, without Ethel's lively presence, Mr. Morton seemed to be fading fast.

The bond between the two had never been one to question but the same could not be said of the Morton's perpetually-in-a-rush daughter, Grace.

Rosie had hoped that Grace would return to the hospital room, but, somehow, Rosie knew that she wouldn't. After an hour, Rosie gave a sigh and said, "Well, Mr. Morton, let's see about that bus. It's about that time." And then she rose and helped Mr. Morton to his feet. "We'll be back tomorrow, Mrs. Morton. Me and Mr. Morton, that is. You hang tight till then. We'll be thinking of you."

Rosie had thought to stop on the way home to shop for the dress shoes, but the steady whisper of Ethel's ventilator made her think better of it. "Mr. Morton, let's you and I just call it a day and head right on home. What do you think?" she asked.

Mr. Morton nodded absently and they rode to the end of the route. When they entered the home, the clock struck 3PM and Rosie found herself rummaging around in the kitchen cabinets. "Ahh . . . here it is," she announced. "Back behind the sugar bowl." She set the water to boil and prepared a tray. "Mr. Morton, I think you and I could both stand for some tea. We haven't had any in quite some time." She echoed Ethel's words and added, "Let's take a load off our feet for a moment, shall we?"

Rosie set out the saucers and teacups and poured a steaming cup for her and Mr. Morton. "There now. If only Mrs. Morton were here, she could fill us in on the news. But I'll give it a try." Rosie talked about the fence that had gone up across the street and the new For Sale sign on the block. And she talked about the dog that yapped all morning and the cat that yowled all night. And when she paused to take a sip of tea, Mr. Morton chuckled. It wasn't quite the guffaw that he had used with Ethel, but it was close. And as Rosie cleared the

328

table to prepare to leave for the day, Mr. Morton had smiled, an amused expression of sorts that she hadn't seen from him in a month.

"Well, they say that time waits for no man. And, if that's the case, you might as well enjoy your tea. I see it's done us both some good," she remarked.

Mr. Morton answered with a hearty guffaw. And as Rosie turned to go, she grinned. "Now then, Mr. Morton, that laugh you just gave me was worth far more than a new pair of dress shoes. And I think Mrs. Morton would agree. That To Do list can wait." Rosie headed out then, a deep satisfaction settling over her as she realized she had put those shoes where they belonged.

The Once and Future Dad

Adam Strassberg

"That's right, Daddy's lost." Arthur pushed Lori along in her stroller. "Lost." He flapped his hands out to either side of his body as he emphasized the first consonant sound of the word "L-l-l-lost."

"Where are we?" he crowed, then tickled his daughter's nose, repeating his query twice, each time speaking in a more elevated sing-song, "Where are we? Where are weeee?"

The baby giggled and cooed. She answered with a long happy babble, even offering up a few rewarding "da-das."

Arthur smiled, then sighed. He lifted his cup from the holder across the handles, sipped his coffee, placed it back, then returned to pushing the stroller farther along the path through the park.

Not just any park, but Dozmary Park, the jewel in a crown of well-funded city parks. They purchased their home two years ago just to be a few blocks away. Dozmary Park was its own sort of city, here in the center of the real city. Innumerable paved paths looped through the borders of several playgrounds, tennis courts, basketball courts, dog play areas, and community gardens. These pathways themselves were lined by a network of benches, picnic tables, barbecue pits, sculptures, water fountains, and bathrooms. Any unused land along the promenade was filled with lush manicured thickets and copses. Everything circled around a large central pond in the center of the park.

"So how can we be lost?" Arthur spoke aloud to himself this time, not to his baby. "I can understand getting lost during our first visit, even our fiftieth, but certainly not what must be our five hundredth or more."

Arthur yawned. Leo, Lori's older brother, had crawled into their bed last night. He should have shooed him away but, with Gwen away on business, it was just so warm and cuddly to have him there. His son kicks in his sleep though, and so Arthur had slept poorly. At preschool drop-off, just an hour ago, Leo ran out to play with his usual energy. As for Arthur, he yawned again.

"Sleep is for the weak..." he scolded himself, then laughed, "...and the childless."

Arthur suspected that he must have taken a wrong turn somewhere near the north edge of the pond. He had not seen it, so much as felt it. The smooth paved path became bumpy gravel, then finally just dirt with a few stones and weeds.

He also had heard it, or rather had stopped hearing it. A sudden silence appeared where once there was the din of babies crying, toddlers screaming, parents yelling, dogs barking, squirrels fighting, even birds tweeting. Arthur listened. Silence.

He stopped and looked.

He was on a dirt path along the edge of a meadow, surrounded on all sides by several rows of unusually tall trees.

The trail followed straight along one edge of the field but also teed in the middle to the entrance of what appeared to be a very old tent. Near as Arthur could tell, the tent was made from a hemp canvas, a tan colored base material but patched with various random squares of blue and green. The shelter was held aloft as a triangle by one large wooden pole, several random stakes, and twine rope tied up to a few larger tree branches from above.

An old bald man in rags sat cross-legged on the ground beside the tent, smoking a pipe, surrounded by open cans, broken bottles, and empty cardboard boxes.

"Well this sucks," Arthur mumbled, then whispered to himself, "I hope he's not violent." He avoided eye contact, held his breath, and pushed the stroller more rapidly.

Above the treetops, he could see the same blue sky and fluffy clouds of early spring as from earlier in their walk. But the meadow itself had suddenly become much darker and colder.

He was many yards past the old tent before he stopped to breathe. He inhaled and exhaled, deeply, then anxiously. He smelled the pleasant earthy scent of wet bark and the rich musk of moist soil. But then came the pungent odor of dried urine, unfiltered tobacco, cheap alcohol and woodsmoke—the stench of homelessness all too familiar to any city dweller.

Arthur winced and coughed.

Lori met his eyes, smiled, but then tensed her face and arched her back.

"Who's making a poo-poo?" It was the usual face and usual posture. "Who has a poo-poo?" Arthur reached out with his index fingers as Lori grabbed them with each hand and pushed. There was a flatulent staccato, followed by the rich sweet scent of baby poo. Lori giggled after she finished and then babbled a long set of unintelligible instructions for her father. She pointed toward the meadow.

Arthur turned and saw a large flat moss-covered boulder in the center of the field. "Yes, good idea, let's go change your diaper over there." He pushed the stroller off the path and onto the grass and walked towards the large rock.

"Daddy's not going to throw out his back again." Arthur reached over to tickle Lori on her belly. "No he's not. No he's not. Especially with Mommy away on business."

Lori squealed and giggled.

Arthur continued, "That's right, M-m-m-mommy made p-p-p-partner!"

Lori returned to her long babbling speech. She stumbled upon some "m" sounds which Arthur exaggerated back to her. "Mmmm. Mmmm. That's right. Can you say Ma-ma? Mma -mma?"

Arthur was proud of his wife and her legal career. Gwen now billed more in an hour than Arthur could make selling a year's worth of short stories. *"And besides, who really pays anything for stories, anymore, anyways."* Gwen had encouraged him as kindly and honestly as she could. Arthur earned far less than the pay of any nanny, and so, after Leo comes, why not just become the nanny himself? *"You can always write later, but they are only cute and little for such a short time."* And thus Arthur the writer had become Arthur the home-dad.

He looked again towards the boulder in the meadow. "The flat top of that big stone over there is a perfect height. And it'll be easier on my back than bending down."

Arthur continued pushing the stroller towards the boulder, and also cautiously away from that homeless man and his tent. Behind him, along the way, Arthur now heard the man alternately crying and yelling to himself. It was mostly incomprehensible, random gibberish, but with some fantastical repetitions about "serpent's breath", "death and life" and "charm of making." Arthur did his best not to react, he looked away and pushed onwards across the field, towards that boulder in the center.

The large rock was perfect, about waist high above the ground, and indeed the top did have a flat surface about the size of a small table. There was old graffiti scratched around the base—*Quisquis hunc e saxo gladium trahit, rex est iure*—which Arthur tried, and failed, to translate with his middle school Latin.

He parked the stroller next to the boulder, reached for the diaper bag beneath and hung it over his shoulder. This was when Arthur noticed the glint of metal from an object sticking out of the center of the flat stone top.

He looked closer. It was a sort of white metal tee pushed flush against the stone. There was a flat metal base parallel to the surface, about a foot in length and curled up into a decorative roll at each end. A much thicker round bar of the same white metal pierced this flat metal base, perpendicular to the stone surface and extending above it, also about a foot in length, wrapped with several straps of untanned leather.

Somebody must have hammered this old handle into the stone. Maybe that crazy homeless guy. Arthur placed his hand around the leather straps and gripped tightly. *But I need to clear the surface to change my baby.* He could feel that the exposed metal tee was part of a much longer piece of metal, perhaps rebar, all stuck into the bed of the boulder itself.

Arthur pulled at the odd metal tee with one hand, balancing his diaper bag with the other. The metal stuck at first, then loosened, then slid out and up, quickly and effortlessly. He held the exposed metal above his head with one hand as the diaper bag dangled down from the other. The revealed metal was certainly not a piece of rebar, nor any other sort of metal piping, but rather, of all things, a sword!

Arthur looked up at his hand holding aloft a large

335

broadsword.

His eyes widened, his mouth opened, his heart raced, his breathing froze.

Fluffy white clouds parted above him in the blue sky and a thick beam of sunshine poured down from above to reflect off the shaft of the sword, bouncing brightly and remarkably in every direction all at once.

Arthur admired the mighty sword as he held it above his head, rotating it slowly. *I can lift it easily, with just one hand, and it pulls out smoothly, even from having been embedded in solid rock.* He stared at the white blade and heard music, a crescendo of hidden violins playing all around him.

But his trance broke from the sound of his baby crying. He awoke to himself, breathed in, and again smelled her poopie diaper.

Black clouds suddenly drifted above, blocking the sunbeams, and the sword in his hand darkened. The weapon seemed rusty and worn to Arthur now. Entirely purposeless. He tossed the old sword to the ground, then kicked it away with his feet.

Arthur placed his diaper bag upon the stone, opened it, and removed the changing pad from inside. He unfolded it, flattening it down with both hands across the boulder's now cleared top surface. He removed a pack of wet wipes, opened a tube of diaper cream, and unfolded a new clean disposable diaper.

"Alley oop." Arthur lifted Lori up from the stroller and laid her on her back atop the changing pad. He rolled her pants down and off, and then, in one well practiced set of movements, he pulled open the Velcro tabs of Lori's present dirty diaper, unfolded it downward, lifted her legs upwards, wiped her clean from front to back, placed the soiled wet wipes on top of the brown poop in the diaper, folded up this dirty diaper into a tight ball, re-affixed it with the Velcro tabs, lathered a dab of diaper cream into the folds of Lori's buttocks, lifted her hips slightly, slid the new clean disposable diaper underneath her bottom, folded the front side up and over, finally fastening the tabs snugly but not too tightly. Dirty diaper off, clean diaper on, Arthur exhaled, then rolled back up Lori's elastic baby pants.

Lori gurgled and smiled.

"Alley oop encore!" Arthur lifted her up into the air and held her above him. Her shirt untucked and so Arthur tickled her belly with a big sloppy kiss. She giggled and squealed. He then lowered his daughter back into her stroller, tucked her shirt down beneath her pants, and restrapped her into the seat.

He stood in place, then rotated just his torso from the stroller to the top of the boulder, where he folded the changing pad and repacked everything back into the diaper bag. He rotated back to place the diaper bag and the dirty diaper ball under the stroller.

Then he saw him.

Arthur's heart seemed to skip a beat and his hands began shaking. Directly facing both him and the stroller, there on the ground, just a few feet away, the homeless old man posed rigidly in a long bow. His head was bent down and his forehead was touching the ground. His arms stretched forward, cradling that old junky sword like an offering.

"He who draws the sword from the stone, he shall be king." The voice was raspy, and had an English accent. "It is written, there, upon the base of the stone." The old man kept his head down but pointed with both index fingers towards the old graffiti scratched across the bottom of the boulder. "We are unworthy, the land bleeds, the people suffer, we have sinned. But you—you found the grace to draw the sword and be king."

Arthur remained silent. The old man became silent. They stood there, still, until Lori dropped one of her lovies, a fluffy pink kitten, onto the ground between them. "Look, sir, please, you are blocking our way. Please let us move on." Arthur knelt down slowly and retrieved the stuffed animal.

"He who draws the sword from the stone, he shall be king." The old man mumbled over and over again, several more times, still holding his pose.

"I'm sorry. I didn't mean to take it. I needed space on top of the stone to change my daughter's diaper." Arthur stood up between his daughter's stroller and the bowing man.

The old man slowly turned up his head and met Arthur's gaze. He was bald with a long gray beard. "But you drew the sword from the stone?" He wore one long tattered brown robe and his feet were bound in open leather sandals. "The future has found root in the present. It is done, my lord. You—you are King." The old man left the sword there at Arthur's feet, then used the wooden staff by his side to slowly lift himself upwards into a standing position. He smiled and announced to the sky, "We have our king—you are our king—thanks be to God!"

Arthur bent down slowly. "This is a joke, right? I was teased like this my whole childhood. My first name is actually Arthur." He lifted back up the sword into his hand, as much to keep it away from this crazy old homeless man as to inspect it for himself. "I suppose then this is Excalibur?" Arthur slashed twice in the air and then pointed the blade tip at the old man. "And so you must be Merlin?"

"Well yes, I am the Merlin." The old man blinked his eyes and they turned from brown to blood red then back to brown again, startling Arthur. "Do not be afraid, my king. I have been asleep for centuries." The Merlin gently tapped the sword hilt with the tip of his wooden staff. "This sword is indeed Excalibur. It is a gift. Not just to you, but to all of us, to all peoples, to all lands. A blessing."

Arthur's reality began to feel unreal, his present, a

dream. *This old homeless man, this 'Merlin,' how had he done that trick with his eyes?* Arthur rubbed his own eyes now. His tiredness drained away and a surge of unexpected energy replaced it. Something inside of him had awakened and these forgotten longings from his youth emboldened him to imagine what could have been. "A blessing?" Arthur grabbed the hilt with both hands this time, then raised the weapon above his head again. He swung the weapon around his head, then his waist, in a wide circle. He placed his legs in a fighting stance and parried an imaginary opponent. The black clouds above dissipated and sunlight descended upon him as he twirled and pirouetted in the meadow. Arthur felt somehow young, and fit, and free. He recalled a vague life from long ago, a different sort of someone who he could have been.

The old man smiled. "You see, it is a blessing."

But then Arthur was reminded of who he was now. He heard a crack, then felt a rip. "My back!" He quickly dug the tip of the sword into the dirt path. He held himself aloft with one hand leaning on the hilt, while pressing his other hand against his back as he stooped over. "Ugh. I pulled my back again." He slowly pushed himself upright, then balanced both hands on the sword hilt to hold himself in place. His breathing quickened from the pain, which had at first been sharp, but now dissipated dully throughout his lower back.

"This sword is no blessing—it seems more of a curse, at least to me." Arthur again felt his age, his actual age, and he was angry. "What good is it to me that you're here now?" His eyes watered from his back pain. "Where were you twenty years ago? Or even ten?" He was crying now, and yelling. "Where were you when I was young and strong? When I was eager and free?" He continued bracing himself on the sword hilt, but now with just one hand while wagging the index finger of his other. "Where were you when I was brave, and begging for adventure!

"Now I am a husband with a wife, a dad with two children. There is a mortgage with bills to pay. There is shopping, and cooking, and cleaning, and laundry." He removed a handkerchief with his free hand from his back pocket. "Don't you understand? I have life insurance—my life's *insured*! It is no longer mine to give, to you or to anyone else." He dried his eyes and blew his nose, then pushed the handkerchief back. "My *life*, my LIFE," he next pointed a finger to his own chest. "I would have given my *life* to this sword. But how dare you come to me now, when I am this?" He lifted up the bottom of his stained sweatshirt and pinched the large folds of belly fat. "And this!" He took his free hand and flapped at the dangling fat of the second chin beneath his first. "And this!" Arthur moved his free hand to pull at the strands of thin gray hair on top of his head. Arthur finished by pointing at his opponent, "How dare you—how dare you come now," and then at the sword beneath his other hand, "and with this."

The old man gave a curt bow, then began a reply, "My king, please listen—"

"No, you listen!" Arthur interrupted. "I know as much about the 'Hero's Journey' as anyone, more even. I once had hoped to be a writer. I've read and reread *The Hero with a Thousand Faces*. This is my call to adventure, isn't it? My hero's call." Arthur stopped leaning on the sword, stood up, and tossed the sword back down to the ground between them. "Well I don't accept it. I reject it. I deny this story structure being forced upon me."

The blade hit a rock on the path and a loud clang rang out across the meadow.

"What's this?" The old ragged man's eyes widened and his brows furrowed. "What's this! I never saw this!"

The sword rested there now on the ground between

them.

"You can't refuse!" He leaned on his staff and began a step forward.

"Stay back!" Arthur raised both his hands. "I don't want to be king. And I don't have to wield that thing just because I drew it from the stone." Arthur spoke loudly and boldly, but he was filled with a quiet uncertainty. It was unclear to him now who was more disoriented—he or the old homeless man—and who might be more violent. He needed to de-escalate the situation.

Arthur tried taking a step back. "My wife lives and breathes contract law, and so I know my share too." But both he and his daughter were pinned on the path, with the old man in front of them, and the boulder behind them. "This contract of yours, it's what's called 'unenforceable.' I was never presented with your 'terms' before I acquired the 'product'—the sword—I just drew it from the stone because it was in my way, not because I wanted it." Arthur emphasized his nervous legalese with finger air quotes. "A person can't be 'involuntarily bound' to a contract."

"But you misunderstand me, my king. The sword is not a contract, it is a gift." Merlin, *the* Merlin, or was it the old homeless man—Arthur was confused—tapped the sword hilt with the tip of his wooden staff.

Arthur replied softly and measuredly, "Gifts can be refused. I renounce it. I don't want it. I can't—"

Lori just then interrupted their argument with a loud repetitive "Ba ba, ba-ba, ba-ba…" She held her stuffed pink kitty tightly with her left arm, as she started tapping her right hand to her mouth, the thumb touching the tips of her forefingers. "Ba-ba, ba-ba, ba-ba…"

Bottle. Arthur hissed from his back pain, but then mechanically knelt to the basket below the stroller to retrieve

Lori's baby bottle, loaded with formula powder, and a sealed water thermos. He poured the water into the bottle, shook it, then passed it to Lori in her stroller. He pressed the nipple into her mouth as she balanced it by the base against her right arm. She kept her kitty held tightly in her left arm, and suckled, staring upwards at the clouds above.

Arthur found he had begun to cry. "Listen. I'm no hero, I'm just a dad." He knelt down, grabbed the hilt of the sword with both hands, and retrieved the sword. "You've got the wrong Arthur. I'm no Arthur Pendragon. I'm just plain old Arthur Arnold. I can't be your king, or even a knight. There's nothing grand or heroic about me."

He placed the tip of the blade into the dirt path and leaned gently forward upon the hilt. "And the world doesn't need some immortal king, the world needs newness. New stories, not old legends. After my first child was born, I realized it was my job—no, not just my job, but also my duty—to grow old, and to die, to make way for newness in the world."

Arthur felt as if he were stuck in a dream arguing with himself. "I'm a home dad. We're a different breed of men from any generation before us. I never saw my father change a diaper, or even hold a baby, let alone cook a meal, shop, or clean a dish. Men who change diapers change the world." He placed one of his hands on the back of Lori's stroller and pressed the sword beside him upright into the dirt path. "Times are different now. I mean 'Hero's Journey' is all well and good - but Joseph Campbell clearly never changed a dirty diaper."

As Lori finished her bottle, Arthur took it from her. He tossed it into the basket beneath the stroller, then removed a large burp rag which he placed like a breast plate over his chest and shoulders. "I don't want to be king. I have all the kingdom I need with what's right here in my hands, and with her older brother too, and with their mom, my wife." Arthur lifted up

Lori, chest to chest, and placed her head over his shoulder, then tapped her back softly to burp her. "My dominion is right here." Lori burped several times, then regurgitated some gooey white spit-up onto the rag. She closed her eyes and rested softly on Arthur's shoulder. He kept tapping her back softly and slowly swayed his torso side to side. "She's my princess. Her older brother, my prince. And their mom, my queen."

Merlin stood tall, growing somehow taller. "And you, you are *MY* king. *THE* king." His last word echoed softly, then loudly, against the tall trees encircling the meadow. A murder of crows flocked upwards and squawked. Then silence.

Lori fell asleep and Arthur placed her gently back into the stroller. "Okay if you insist that I am king then I abdicate. A king can abdicate!" He rolled up the burp rag into a ball and placed it in the basket underneath.

"It's not that sort of king."

"What does it mean to be king then?"

"You will be the land and the land will be you." As the Merlin spoke, Arthur noticed blue flowers, early for spring, somehow dotting the meadow. "If you fail, the land will perish. As you thrive, the land will blossom."

"But why?" Arthur noticed the wizard coming closer, he kept one hand on the hilt of the sword, but now grabbed Lori's stroller with the other.

The Merlin's eyes blinked red again. "Because you are king!" He raised his staff with both hands above his head. The sky above darkened, a sudden spring shower drizzled down, and Arthur heard a roll of thunder in the distance.

Then the showers stopped and the sky cleared as suddenly as it had all begun.

"Well, frankly," Arthur surprised himself by laughing, "that's just stupid." He placed both of his hands back onto the hilt of the sword and lifted the blade tip out of the dirt path.

"The land, the world, it's everybody's, and we've got to protect it, not become it." He moved in front of Lori's stroller. "We live in a democracy and a republic, not a monarchy. Being king, any king, it would be wrong."

The old man walked in a small circle, one hand holding his staff, the other now banging at the side of his head. "I am the Merlin. I have walked my way since the beginning of time. I thought to have seen it all with my sight. But truly, I could never have seen this!" He stopped and faced Arthur. "Look at the life of this ill old man before you, my host. He is homeless, unwanted, rejected by all family and friends. He is hungry, cold, wet, filthy and poor. He fills his body with drugs he shouldn't use and scorns the medications that would heal his mind. He has been gentle and generous, but also violent and selfish."

The Merlin had the old man roll up his sleeves to show several rows of track marks on his forearms. "What good has your democracy and your republic been to this wretch in front of you? It's too much freedom - the freedom *to* harm. With a monarchy comes true freedom, the freedom *from* harm." The old man, now as Merlin, *the* Merlin, stepped forward with his staff. "This land, these people, we bleed for lack of a king." He banged his staff onto the ground before him. The sky above darkened. "We need a king. You are the king. You must be king." There was thunder in the distance. Merlin moved a second step closer to Arthur, with Lori in her stroller behind him. His eyes blinked again from brown to red. "I can take the child. She is but one child, and only a girl at that. You are needed to redeem the billions here on earth. You must heal us, protect us, unite us, all with the power of this sword, and as king." The Merlin moved a third and final step forwards, and bent down, reaching out his hands towards Lori asleep in her stroller. "Give me the child. I will be the mother and the father of the baby. I will take the child."

"No. NEVER!" Arthur heard himself yell. He pushed Lori's stroller away and swung the sword forward to protect his baby from this stranger. The old man stepped back, but Arthur could not control his momentum. His back was too weak and so his body circled around completely and, with this second turn, his full weight fell into the sword hilt. The sword stabbed directly into the upper chest of the old man. The blade slid into the old man's body as easily as it had slid out of the stone.

The Merlin fell to the ground before Arthur, with Excalibur in his chest. There was so much blood, bright, red, and dripping from the wound.

"Call 911!" Arthur yelled, then heard his voice echo against the tall trees surrounding the meadow. He fumbled for his phone and dialed. "No service." He whispered into the receiver—"I don't know what to do?"—then pocketed his phone.

Arthur's hands trembled and his legs weakened. "I'm so sorry." He knelt beside the old man and cradled his head in his arms. "It was an accident, a horrible accident."

The Merlin, still breathing, tilted his head back, gazed at the clouds above, then murmured, "...into the spine... of the dragon..." His eyes turned briefly red, next back to brown, then finally fluttered and fixed upwards.

Arthur slapped the old man's face, no response, then he lowered his ear to the old man's chest, no heartbeat.

The old man had stopped breathing. The Merlin, however, forced the man's mouth to speak one last whisper, *"Anál nathrach, orth' bháis's bethad, do chél dénmha."* Lori awoke from her nap, opened her mouth and eerily repeated those exact same words, *"Anál nathrach, orth' bháis's bethad, do chél dénmha."* Then Arthur heard the same words swirl in the winds around him, echoing out against the tall trees surrounding the meadow, finally dissipating upwards into the sky.

How could this be possible? How could any of this be possible? Arthur rolled over and vomited. *This old man is dead.* His heart raced and his breath sputtered. *I killed him.* He placed his head between his knees and cried. *My life, our life, it's all over now.*

Arthur closed his eyes and cried, but as he cried, he also remembered: the first time he saw Gwen in the dining hall, their first kiss, that night together camping under the stars, their first small apartment, the time he burned the pot roast and the fire alarm went off, how she always smiled in her sleep, how much he loved her big pregnant belly and the way her freckles darkened with each baby, the miracle of being there to hold her hand when Leo was born, how they both had just finished that silly jigsaw puzzle before Lori popped out, filming Leo's first steps and sending them to Gwen's mom, changing Lori's diapers. Then Arthur was there again, at least in his mind, with Gwen and little Leo, all rocking baby Lori to sleep together on the large wooden porch swing he had just hung over their new veranda. Arthur stopped crying and opened his eyes.

His lower back was throbbing. He lay his body out on the ground next to the dead man's body, impaled with the sword. He rolled himself side to side, to stretch out his back and relieve the pain. He rolled away, he rolled back, and then, just like that, the Merlin's dead body had vanished. Or had it been an old homeless man? Or nobody at all? Or all three at once, as in a dream. Arthur was so confused.

This is when the forgetting began.

The sword was all that lay on the ground now next to Arthur. It was surprisingly clean, shining beneath the sunlight, with no blood upon it, nor anywhere nearby on the ground. Arthur lifted the sword with one hand as he slowly stood up. What was he holding? Was it a sword, a piece of rebar, a metal pipe? Or again, somehow all three at once, as in a dream.

Arthur was stunned, but the memory of what had just happened continued to fade rapidly from his mind. He held the sword—or whatever it was—in one hand as he pushed Lori's stroller with the other.

The dirt path along the side of the meadow led out from the circle of unusually tall trees. It connected to a gravel path which then became an empty paved path along the north edge of the pond. Arthur stopped and listened. In the distance, he heard a small dog yapping and a parent yelling at her child. Arthur smelled the coffee from his cup, tucked in the holder on the top part of the stroller. He needed another sip, but he was holding something in his hand.

He lifted the sword—or whatever it was?—above his head, then flung it out over the pond water, finally forgetting it, and most of his odd morning, the moment it left his hand.

Arthur turned away.

If he had turned back to see it, he would have seen a lady's arm rise from the lake to catch the sword he had thrown, then hold it briefly above the waters, before descending with it beneath the surface.

But Arthur did not turn back. Rather he reached down with his newly freed hand and took a welcome sip from his coffee, before returning the cup to its holder.

He returned to pushing Lori's stroller, now with both hands, southward, as he regained his bearings. "Hmmm, I never realized it before, but it's not really a pond here in the center of our park, it's more like a lake."

Arthur had found himself and was no longer lost.

They neared their favorite set of baby swings. He stopped the stroller to take another longer sip from his coffee cup.

"Lake. Lake." He repeated the word to his daughter in a playful sing-song. "Lake. Can you say lake?" Then he emphasized the first consonant sound of the word "L-l-l-lake."

His back felt great, stronger than ever.

Arthur lifted Lori up with both arms and placed her into the swing.

What Goes Around...

Krin Van Tatenhove

(Dedicated to Tony Morris)

As a man sow, shall he reap. – Bob Marley

You've heard the warning. Don't try this at home. Here's another one for the list. Detoxing from alcohol.

I already knew that, having endured it enough times to prove every theory of alcoholic insanity. But here I was again, 2:00 a.m., alone in bed. My longtime girlfriend, LeAnne, had deserted months earlier, weary of my lurching trip along the bottom. "Don't call me," was her parting salvo, "until you get your act together."

My act was definitely *not* together. Sweating, nauseous, dehydrated, I tossed and turned, blood pressure hammering my skull. And I was hallucinating, which was a first. Some ancient script kept scrolling across my bedroom ceiling, like words on a teleprompter. I'm fluent in three languages, and I've studied their linguistic histories, but I couldn't decipher a syllable. Even stranger, I kept hearing lyrics from a Tool song, as if a brain worm had crawled out of my ear canal and was taunting me from the darkness: *Why can't we drink forever? I just want to start this over.*

Around four, I got up for water, hungover like a melted corpse in a Dali painting. I tried to orient myself to the date.

Shit, I thought, *it's Thursday morning. I'm going to miss my deadline.*

That deadline was my weekly submission for the newspaper where I worked, one of the great holdouts of print media, a standard in our metropolis for 170 years. People read it during the Civil War, the Oklahoma Land Rush, the dawn of the Industrial Revolution, the two great wars designed to end all wars. They read it through McCarthyism, the Bay of Pigs, the assassination of M.L.K., Jr., the rise of the Internet, the toppling of the World Trade Centers. They were still reading it in print and on their devices.

My only remaining pride was to be part of that grand tradition. A few years earlier, my investigative piece on the dreadful conditions in for-profit prisons had been a finalist for the Pulitzer. I was riding the last fumes of that fame, my disease a riptide pulling me into oblivion.

I stood at the window of my fourth-floor apartment, my reflection as dark and featureless as I felt. A panoramic view of the city spread to the horizon—shimmering lights, bright towers, rivers of red and white traffic. I reached into the top drawer of the dresser, my hand coiling around the grip of a Glock 19. I didn't buy it for home defense. I'd never been to a gun range. It was there for one reason only—to offer a way out if things got too grim.

I lifted it to my head and pressed it above my right ear. As I closed my eyes and tried to suppress my anguish, the only thought I had was, *Call Tony.*

Tony deserved to know that I'd miss my obligation. He was more than my editor. He had been a friend during my descent, encouraging me to get treatment, never threatening to cut me off. My cellphone was on the dresser, so I picked it up and dialed his number. After five rings came a groggy response.

"John...what the hell? Do you know what time it is?"

"I'm sorry," I croaked, my voice dry and hoarse. "I won't be able to get you my article. I'm sorry, Tony."

Silence on the other end.

"Are you okay, John? Do I need to come get you and finally take you for some help?"

"I'm just so tired," I whispered. "I've lost LeAnne. I've lost my pride. And now I can't even meet my deadline. I'm going to make it all go away."

He knew instantly what I meant. "Please don't do that, John. I still believe in you. I believe in your talent. I believe your words have made a difference to so many people. They are *still* making a difference. Your gift will remain, and you can start over again."

"I'm tired of starting over. Just so fucking tired. Tired unto death."

Again, a few seconds of silence. My finger tightened ever so slightly on the trigger.

"John, I'm pleading with you. Get up off your knees and try again, this time in a new way. Let me pick you up and take you somewhere for treatment."

I stood there, frozen, staring out at the city, my hand cocked to my head, as tears began to roll down my cheeks.

Two years later

In the break room that day, a colleague asked me, "What's the greatest lesson you've learned in sobriety?" I don't think he was really interested, just being polite. Non-alcoholics are muggles when it comes to understanding the disease. It was hard to choose an answer, but I used an adage from my Twelve Step meetings. Accepting life on life's terms. A humble acknowledgement that there's so much we can't control. Or, to put it another way, there's so much we should *never even try to control*. Control is an addiction all its own. My colleague nodded, then said, "Well, I admire you, John."

I leaned back in my desk chair and thought of how that answer stemmed from multiple hard lessons. Since that fateful morning when Tony drove me to rehab, I'd gotten ample opportunities to practice letting go. I had called LeAnne, but she had no desire to reunite, having found someone who she said, "was more stable." Then there was the newspaper continuing its transition to an online presence, hiring freelancers and paying them a pittance. My salary was downsized. Tony and I met for coffee once a week, and he tried to explain it as my friend, but I didn't blame him. It was the new reality, and he was even questioning the security of his own position.

To make ends meet, I'd taken a job as an adjunct professor at a local junior college, teaching courses online. It was mildly enjoyable but never fulfilling. I longed for those years when I was hot on the trail of an investigative project, tracking it down and bringing it into focus. That was my passion, my highest calling, and I was afraid my newfound acceptance would turn into toxic regret.

Then, at one of our weekly confabs, Tony surprised me.

"I have some news, John. I got a call from a midsize paper in the Midwest. Instead of surrendering, they want to try and resurrect their presence. They offered me a job as Editor-in-Chief, hoping I can turn things around."

Since Tony was my only real friend, my first thought was *Here we go again, another thing to accept.* But I pushed that aside. "Are you going to take it?"

In his mid-50s, 20 years my senior, Tony still dressed like a hipster. Graphic T-shirts from rock concerts, a leather jacket, pressed chinos, thick-framed glasses of various colors, and one of the many fedoras he collected. He took off his hat, running his hand through his goatee, then over his bald head. I'd seen him do it a thousand times.

"Yeah. I already signed a contract. I would have told you sooner, but the negotiations were touch and go."

He took a sip of coffee. "It was hard to convince Joanne, but both of us have fantasized about living in a smaller city with less congestion. Plus, my job here isn't stable."

I nodded, trying to hide my disappointment. "I'm happy for you. You deserve only the best. Both you and Joanne."

"Thanks, but there's more. The paper gave me the latitude to bring in new talent. I'd like to offer you a job as my top journalist."

Looking back on that moment, there was a shift in me. I'd heard countless people describe their beliefs that some higher power, some God or force, was accomplishing in their lives what they could not do for themselves. It was that instant when I made a baby step towards believing. It was like a puzzle piece snapping into place. I had no prospects, only my wistfulness about the past, and I, too, had grown tired of the impersonal vibes of the city.

"Let me think about it, Tony," I said, but I knew in my heart that I was ready.

Summer, two years later

I shut down my computer, pleased with my latest installment in a series on fentanyl trafficking in the Midwest. It featured three families whose lives had been tragically damaged by the substance and were speaking out to make a difference. It wasn't easy reading, but it was timely and prophetic. The narrative arcs were strong. I was feeling my old mojo.

I looked out the window of my office. The building that housed the newspaper was on the edge of town, bordered by a sweeping expanse of corn fields, the cash crop of the Midwest. Accustomed to urban landscapes, I was surprised by how much I had grown to love the vastness and tranquility of my new home. Sometimes I'd get in my car and drive to the middle of nowhere, clearing my head. Or sit at a roadside picnic table and practice letting my past and present converge into a sense of serenity.

My thoughts turned to Tony. He had overseen great progress at the paper, but I was worried about him. Joanne's reluctance to move had blossomed into discontent. She said she missed the cultural opportunities of the big city and complained that their new neighbors were parochial. Finally, she left Tony with an ultimatum that if he didn't join her within a year, their marriage was over. That deadline had come and gone.

Simultaneously, Tony developed back problems—aggravated by stress and too many hours at a desk. He underwent surgery to fuse three lower vertebrae, and the pain meds they gave him during recovery got their talons into him. He had lost some of his sharpness. I saw it. So did others. It was the proverbial elephant in the newsroom. When I expressed my concern, he thanked me, shifting his gaze to the side, then told me everything would be okay, yet I knew firsthand how addicts minimize their usage.

The irony struck me—my own addiction and denial, his support as a friend, even the fact that I was investigating opioid trafficking. I wanted to help him, and I felt poised to make a difference in his life, but people only change when they're ready.

On this day, he had phoned in sick. It had happened other times recently, and the staff was getting more suspicious. I waited until late afternoon, then called him. No answer. I waited until nightfall and tried again. Still no answer. Highly unusual.

I decided to drive to his house for a welfare check. He lived on the edge of town near a creek bed bordered by tall trees and a hiking trail. The stream was damned in various spots to create ponds where people could sit and absorb the scenery.

I parked next to his car in the driveway and got out. The streetlights were on, already attracting swarms of bugs. It was a warm summer night and I could smell the creek bottom, damp and mossy. When I got to the front door, it was slightly ajar, stoking my worries. I pushed it open.

"Tony," I called out. "Are you here? It's John. I'm just checking on you."

No answer. I entered and made a quick search of the modest home, noting the decorations that showed Joanne's sense of style. He wasn't there. I thought about calling the police; maybe there'd been foul play. But I also knew that Tony liked to hike along the creek to a favorite spot near one of the ponds. I would check there before calling the authorities.

The paved trail along the water had light poles spaced at intervals, but it was still gloomy. Frogs and crickets had begun their evening symphony, accompanied by the gurgling of the creek. I quickened my stride and, sure enough, as I approached the first pond I could see Tony's unmistakable form, his bald head reflecting light from a pole just above him. He was seated on a bench, and when I slid next to him, he looked at me.

I'll never forget his eyes. They mirrored my own that night I had pressed the gun against my temple. It was the gaze of a man trapped in his personal purgatory, conceding the doom of a repetitious behavior that would grind him throughout eternity.

He tried hard to focus. "John? What are you doing here?" His voice was soft and raspy.

"I'm here to help you, Tony. I know the pills have taken you down. I know that Joanne leaving is still depressing you."

He turned away, his breathing labored. The plaintive call of a lonesome owl drifted out of the darkness.

"Too much," he whispered. "Just too much."

"I know," I said, "But I want to remind you of some words you said to me a couple years ago. I believe in you, Tony. I believe in your talents. I believe in how you care for other people. Hell, I wouldn't be sitting her next to you unless you had stayed by me."

He began to shake, a tremor running through his body. Then he slumped forward, placing his arms on his legs. One of them slipped and I was afraid he would topple over, so I supported him under his armpit.

"Come with me, my friend. Let's get you the help you need."

He rubbed his right hand over his head and sighed. "Okay, John. Okay."

A year later

The hotel's grand ballroom, with its opulent chandeliers and art deco design, was a splendid choice for our region's journalistic awards banquet. The tables sported newsprint tablecloths, and large TVs on the walls displayed the year's best photos and art.

Our staff had carpooled to the capital, an annual trek

that we all enjoyed. Seated at our table, my colleagues were drinking wine or cocktails from the open bar as I nursed a ginger ale. Tony sat next to me, sipping a Diet Coke. As I looked around at their faces, I thought of how far afield our life's paths can take us. We end up in divergent realities we never expected, but when we make them our own, they enrich us immensely.

Just moments before, I had received an award for my series on fentanyl. A far cry from contending for the Pulitzer, but somehow more valuable to me given all that had happened in the past few years. As the evening neared its climax, they were about to announce the ultimate award—Journalist of the Year.

The MC, Editor-in-Chief of the state's largest newspaper, went to the microphone.

"Ladies and gentlemen," she said, "thank you for being here. Let me congratulate all those who have received awards this evening. We are a talented group. Together, we're keeping journalistic excellence alive in a rapidly changing world of sound bites and short attention spans."

She lifted her glass. "A toast to our continued success in the coming year."

There was a raucous chorus of "Here! Here!" that died down in anticipation of her announcement.

"And now," she continued, "we come to tonight's most prestigious award. I would ask for the envelope, but there isn't one."

The crowd tittered.

"With no further ado, let me recognize our journalist of the year, Tony Harris, for your editorial prowess, your sharp wit, and your business acumen."

The room exploded with applause, and people began to shout, "Speech! Speech!"

Tony looked genuinely surprised. He got up and made

his way steadily to the podium, evidence that his physical therapy was making a difference. He took the mic from the MC, then ran his hand through his goatee and over his head before scanning the room in a moment of silence. Everyone quieted down.

"For those of us who have ink in our blood," he said, "this night is a celebration of that passion that will not let us go. And I can't thank you enough for this honor."

He looked down for a moment, clearly emotional.

"I want to share a truth that I've learned firsthand. Karma can be a bitch, but it can also be the force that saves our lives. I won't get into the details of how deeply I understand this, but I just want to say one other thing."

He'd taken his coke with him to the front.

"I have a personal toast to my friend for many years, John Newcombe."

He lifted his glass.

"John, what goes around comes around. You know what I mean, brother, and I'm eternally grateful for our relationship."

Tears welled in my eyes. I lifted my tumbler and toasted not only to Tony, but to every suffering soul, every individual trapped in purgatory, every person teetering on the edge of a decision that was as final as the closing of a coffin lid. And for every last one of them, I poured out a silent prayer of hope and healing.

"Here! Here!" shouted the crowd around me.

A Pinch of Peculiar

Gabby Russel

Dust danced between the sunbeams shining through the front window of the old shop. The smell of lavender and mildew drifted through the small space, which was filled with a maze of bookshelves, many of them pressed at odd angles against each other. The individual shelves were organized in a similar manner, each decorated with random objects—books, jewelry, herbs, vials, clocks—all ranging from magical to ordinary.

Lena had spotted the shop as she roamed the cobblestone streets outside. Her father had warned her not to visit this side of town, claiming that it had taken her mother from him. She always thought that was a tale her father told to instill fear in her so she wouldn't venture this way. Also, to hide the real reason her mother was gone: she abandoned them. Lena was a curious creature, though, so when she wandered a few streets over to the area her father had forbidden and saw the hanging sign with "A Pinch of Peculiar" written on it in swirling letters, she was drawn inside the old store.

The bell above her rang as she opened the wooden door. Stepping inside, the ancient floorboards squeaked and groaned beneath her boots. While scanning the cramped space, Lena glimpsed a white tuft of hair peeking from between shelves and followed it to the back of the store to see who else was there. The owner sat at the front desk, hunched over a book. When he looked up, he sprang back in his chair, startled.

"My dear, I didn't hear you come in! Welcome to my shop. Is there anything I can help you find?" his eyes crinkled beneath the gold circles of his glasses, smiling.

"No, just browsing," Lena answered.

"Well, take a look around! Don't be shy. I don't get many visitors nowadays." Lena wondered why that was, offering an uneasy smile before turning back to the shelves.

She approached the first one, picking up a glass bottle filled with a dark liquid that sparkled purple as she tilted it.

"Ah, be careful with that one. It will make anyone who drinks it fall in love with you," the shop owner said, wiggling his eyebrows up and down. Lena was skeptical about this. She turned the bottle around, reading the label: "Love Potion." Intrigued, she carried it in her hand while continuing to look, in case she wanted to purchase it. She was sure that if she set it back down, she would never be able to find it again.

She weaved in between the bookshelves, her eyes roaming each ledge until they caught on a mirror resting against the wall across from her. As she approached it, she noticed that her brown hair seemed less full of color, almost gray. Her face had little lines forming around her forehead, eyes, and mouth. Were those… wrinkles? She was only seventeen; she couldn't have so many wrinkles. She pivoted toward the front desk.

"What's wrong with this mirror?" she shouted in the owner's direction.

"Nothing is wrong with it," he claimed, appearing beside her. "It is simply showing your reflection."

"I don't look like that," she argued.

"You do right now, dear. You can't expect the shop to allow people to discover all of its secrets, can you? Don't fret, you will go back to your normal age once you leave, but the longer you spend here, the older you'll grow. If you aren't careful, you may just grow too old to live, and that would be an awful mess for me."

At his words, Lena's eyes grew wide, and she swore she felt her heart slow its beating beneath her ribcage. She needed to get out of here. She ran for the door, swinging it open so hard that it slammed into the wall behind it. The shop owner hobbled after her, yelling, but she couldn't hear his words over her pounding feet and the blood roaring in her ears.

Lena didn't stop until she was back in the safety of her own home. Once she mustered up enough courage, she slunk to her bathroom mirror, dreading to see if her reflection had truly gone back to normal. Peering into the glass, she realized the owner had been right; she once again looked like her usual self. She let out a breath she hadn't realized she had been holding.

It wasn't until that point that Lena noticed the weight in her left hand. She let out a groan, looking at the bottle with the purple liquid. She had stolen it. She briefly contemplated returning it, but she certainly didn't want to go back there after what she had just experienced. She turned the vial over in her hand, wondering if it was really a love potion. Her rapid aging in the shop must have been some sort of magic, so it was possible that this potion was legitimate. Although, Lena considered that the mirror could've been an illusion.

She decided she would test it. The worst that could happen is that someone she chose would fall in love with her, and she figured that wouldn't be so bad. If it didn't work, the mirror must have been a hoax, and she would return what she had stolen to the shop owner. She pondered who to choose for this endeavor. She had to pick carefully, in case the potion worked. Her mind wandered to thoughts of the boy who owned the flower cart she visited every weekend, with his kind eyes and unkempt hair. He was polite and interesting in the few conversations they had. She decided that he would do.

—

The next day, Lena made her way to the flower cart. She carried two cups of coffee; the one in her left hand had the potion already added to it. As she approached the cart, the boy's face lit up at the sight of her. Lena extended the cup. "I brought you a coffee," she said. "I figured you might be a little chilly out here." Indeed, it was a brisk day, one that made your nose cold and your fingers numb.

The boy gratefully took the warm liquid. "Thank you," he replied. Lena raised her own cup to her mouth, watching over the brim as the boy drank his. Nothing happened. She frowned a little. Looking down at the assortment of bouquets, she purchased one with white roses and turned to leave.

"Thanks for the coffee," the boy called after her, raising his cup. Lena glanced over her shoulder as she walked away, hoping to catch a glimpse of the potion at work, but nothing gave away that it was. The boy continued to help other customers without sparing her another glance.

Lena lay in bed that night, disappointed that the potion hadn't worked, but also a little glad. It meant that the mirror incident had been fake, and the shop owner was just an old man playing tricks. She prepared what she would say to him when she went there tomorrow to return the bottle. She hoped he wouldn't be too angry with her. After all, it had been an accident.

A knock came at the door then, interrupting her thoughts. It was so soft, Lena thought she had imagined it. Then it became more aggressive, urgent. Who would be here at this time of night? By the time she rose out of bed and went to the door, the knock had turned into a frantic fist pounding on the other side. Lena debated whether she should open it. She contemplated getting her father, the only other person in the house, but she feared waking him for nothing. He worked long hours and needed rest.

Lena grabbed the fire poker from beside the fireplace before placing herself back in front of the door. As she opened it, she reeled back the poker, ready to swing, and stopped short as she took in the person standing on her porch. It was the flower cart boy with his fist raised mid-air, ready to bang on the door again. "Hi," he said, his breath floating into a cloud in front of him. She signaled for him to come inside, closing the door behind him.

"What are you doing here?" Lena hissed. It came out harsher than she implied. The boy winced.

"I'm sorry, but I had to see you," he said. She noticed his brown eyes were strangely fixated on her face, refusing to look away. He was watching her as if she were going to save him.

Save him from *what*, she didn't know.

He stepped closer, touching the ends of her hair with his fingertips as if in a trance. "You're extravagant," he whispered. Suddenly, he leaned down, drawing near for a kiss. She quickly thrust both of her hands out, shoving him backward.

"What are you doing?" she asked, wrinkling her eyebrows together.

"I'm not sure," he said, blinking. "I've felt strange all day. I haven't been able to get you out of my mind since this

363

afternoon. I haven't been able to eat or sleep. I was going to wait until tomorrow to see you, but then, all of a sudden, I found myself standing on your doorstep," he explained.

Lena felt dizzy as her mind raced to piece together what he was saying, realizing what was happening. The potion must have worked, which meant the aging in the shop was real; magic was real. She looked at him in disbelief. This was what she had wanted, right? Now she just needed to figure out what she was supposed to do with him. Not tonight, though.

"It's late. You should go home and get some rest. I need to, as well," Lena said, pretending to yawn.

"I don't think I can leave you," the boy said, exasperated.

"I'll visit you tomorrow," Lena stated, trying to convince him to go.

After a moment's pause, he asked, "Do you promise?"

Lena nodded her head. At this, the boy slowly strolled toward the door, still reluctant to leave her. She opened it for him, trying not to be rude, but desperately wanting to go back to bed. "See you tomorrow," he said with a bright smile. Lena attempted to give him one back, but knew it fell short.

—

The next day, Lena headed to the flower cart as promised. When the boy saw her, he eagerly took off his apron, flung it on the cart, and flipped the "Open" sign on the front to "Closed." Jogging over to her, he flashed her another charming smile and unexpectedly gathered her into a hug, causing her feet to lift off the ground. Lena was beginning to enjoy the attention.

"I thought we could take a walk," the boy said. He grabbed her hand, leading her through town. As they walked, they rounded a corner and arrived at a fountain, strung with twinkling lights and filled with water that was a startling purple color. Lena did not appreciate the unnatural shade of the water, as it was eerily similar to that of the concoction she had given the boy.

Abruptly, the flower cart boy got down on one knee and reached for a small box, opening it to reveal a ring with a large sapphire gleaming in its center.

"Are you proposing to me?" Lena stuttered. The boy looked slightly confused, as if he was also unsure of what he was doing.

"I think so," he said.

"I'm not going to marry you. I barely know you," she blurted, trying to stay calm as the people nearby stopped to stare. The boy's face fell. He stood, setting down the ring, and grasped both of Lena's hands in his own.

"I can't bear to be apart from you, though. Not even for a moment." His face contorted, as if in pain from just the prospect.

"This was our first date. You couldn't have possibly expected me to agree to this," Lena said, incredulously.

"I—" the boy began, but was swiftly cut off. His face scrunched as he clutched his chest, his features pinched.

"What's wrong? Are you alright?" Lena asked, worry flooding her voice. The boy fell to his knees. "Help!" Lena shouted at the people nearby as she crouched down with him. A few pedestrians ran over, unsure of what to do.

On his back now, the boy was motionless. Lena moved his hands away from his chest to feel his heart. It was barely beating. A soft *thump* could still be felt under her palm, but she didn't know how much longer it would keep pumping for.

Lena pushed to her feet and ran. She didn't stop until she saw the sign with the swirling letters. Bursting into the shop, she saw movement toward the back and knew she had startled the owner again. He stood up to look at who had caused the commotion, his eyes growing dark as he caught a glimpse of the girl who had stolen from him. She rushed back to meet him and spewed her apology.

"Listen, I'm sorry. I didn't mean to steal, but you scared me with the aging incident, and I didn't realize I had the potion until I got home. I intended to return it, but I was intrigued and used it. I need your help," she said, out of breath. She waited under his scrutinizing gaze. His features softened after a moment, seeming to accept this apology.

"What do you need help with?" he inquired.

"I used the love potion on this boy and now… it's like he's dying," she explained. "His heart is barely beating. It happened right after he proposed, and I told him 'no' because we're practically strangers." Lena never thought she would say anything so absurd in her life. The old man contemplated this.

"It sounds like you broke his heart," he said. "I mean, literally—not in the figurative sense," he chuckled. Lena looked at him like he had gone mad.

"How do I fix it?" she asked, not caring about the logic behind magic, since there seemed to be none.

"You can't, I'm afraid. Unless you have a way to unbreak his heart."

"He's going to die because of me?" Lena asked, devastated. The owner sat down and thought for a moment.

"All magic has a price, dear. You used the potion to make him love you; the drawback is that you may never break his heart or he will die," the owner explained. "Since I suspect you have never dealt with magic before, I'll make you a deal. Would that interest you?" the owner asked, raising his eyebrows. Lena frantically nodded. "I'll give you the antidote for the potion and, in return, you give me your soul." Lena blinked. She couldn't have heard him right.

"My soul," she laughed a little. "That hardly seems like

a fair trade."

"A life for a life," the owner smiled. Lena took a step back.

"I can't give you my soul," she said, mouth still gaping at the prospect.

"Then your boy will die," the owner said simply. "The clock is ticking. Who knows how many more beats he has left in him?" He was right, of course. Lena needed to decide, and quickly.

"What would you do with my soul?" She couldn't believe she was even considering this.

"It's not as bad as it sounds, really. I'm an old man and I would like to retire, but this shop needs someone to care for it." As if in response, Lena felt a warm breeze wash over her face. "I need someone to take my place. I would bind your soul to the shop so that mine can be free."

Lena thought about it. This meant she would have to live and work on this side of town. She would have to leave her father because he could never know that she owned a shop in the very sector he despised. There was a boy's life on the line because of her, though. Lena made her decision then.

"Deal," she said. Lena clasped her hand with the old man's. There was a swirl of air that surrounded her, lifting her hair off her shoulders, and then a whoosh of breath escaped her lungs. Feeling light-headed, she braced herself on the desk in front of her, catching herself before she collapsed onto the floor. Lena heard the old man let out a sigh of relief, and, looking up, she could've sworn he stood a little taller. Once she had recovered, she jutted her hand out, palm up. "The antidote. Now," she said. She hoped the boy was still alive. The owner reached under the desk and handed over a vial the size of her pinky. Lena wasted no time, racing out of the shop and back to the fountain.

When she arrived, more people surrounded the boy. She pushed through them, popping the cork off the vial. Raising his head, she pushed the vial with the amber liquid to his lips. She pressed her fingers to the pulse at his neck, panicking when she didn't feel anything. Finally, a weak beat bumped against her fingers, and then another. His pulse quickened in speed, and the tempo began to match that of her own. Lena's eyes filled with tears when the flower cart boy opened his. He gave a tired smile as he attempted to sit up. The crowd went up in cheers around her, as if she weren't the one who had almost killed him in the first place.

—

The boy apologized profusely for his crazed actions. He claimed that he didn't know what overcame him. Of course, Lena knew, and her heart hurt with guilt at his distress and confusion. He withdrew his proposal, but asked if they could try another date. She couldn't very well break his heart twice, so she agreed to one.

After that, she tried to resist going back to the shop as long as she could. She made it a day before she felt a tug on her skin. She knew it was her deal pulling her toward her demise. It was a week until she couldn't bear it any longer; the tug had turned into the feeling of her skin being torn from her body. She needed to leave and fulfill the deal.

She left her father a note to inform him that she was going to spend some time traveling. She couldn't tell him the real reason why she was leaving, and she wasn't sure she would be able to handle the anguish on his face when she revealed that his only child was deserting him. Maybe he had been telling the truth all along; that place had truly seized her mother from them.

Regardless, Lena set out that night to be the new owner of A Pinch of Peculiar.

Suspended

Alejandro Gonzales

My machine works. I input a time and I'm taken there, as the time is now, all abandoned set pieces where the actors have since moved on. Everything continues in the present because that's where the people are. I came here, twenty years in the past, intending to change it—and of course the present by proxy. But I'm still bleeding out, carrying the present's fatal wound, and now that I'm here I'm content observing the suspended state of my youth. Or maybe I just *want* to be. Even as I feign acceptance, I'm scanning the room for any useful items or memories.

I run my fingers over the cool linoleum kitchen counter of my first apartment. There should be sirens distantly wailing, children screaming, a couple perpetually arguing, and doors slamming. But it's just my own heavy breaths, recycled TV lines, and maybe the hum of a dying fridge that's been on life support longer than it was ever alive; so in that sense, the latter not so different from myself. Inside the fridge there's nothing. Rarely was there ever.

And I liked it that way. Kept me on edge.

I close the door and lean against it for a moment, breath hitching, wound spilling blood that can never coagulate because it doesn't belong here. My fingers fumble for the device and input a new time, or rather a different time.

My old office, where my hard-ass boss should be roaming, and where my coworkers should be discussing this stupid policy or that by the water cooler, or where I should be deep in my cubicle pretending to work. The first "real" job I ever had. It was the first time I lived outside a neighborhood where gunshots were more frequent than responding sirens, in a city my children would call home and their hometown, save for the eldest who was old enough by then to have formed memories of the old city. But it was good. Good enough. I scroll through old documents on my computer. Half are memos from my boss informing us of policy changes. I grimace and shudder. Maybe half my life has already flowed onto the desk and the counter before that. Hours toiled here, but never wasted, always in pursuit of a better life built an hour at a time usually wrapped up in twelve hour blocks.

My greatest achievements stemmed from this office, although they never occurred inside the building; the law firm paid well, but criminals seeking to evade arrest paid better over the course of a year. The pettier the crime the more desperate they were—inversely proportional, I guess, is the phrase someone more educated than myself might say, was the relationship between the crime's severity and the criminal's concern about getting caught. Unlicensed weed dealers were my favorite clients.

The edges of my vision are darkening. I shake away the peripheral black and grasp onto consciousness while I shift around my chair, angling for a comfortable position that doesn't exist and never has. It's relaxing, just sitting for a moment without hot coffee breath invading my space, curdling in my nose.

I practice my breathing exercises; they're easing the pain, or maybe the end-of-life chemicals flooding my mind are doing that. This is something like peace—something like the first time I've gotten to experience it, which unfortunately is merged with the last time I will experience it. The memory of being shot is fading like a reverse Polaroid. Sharp wheezing is filling the room devoid of even ambient noise.

I'm dying. I don't care.

I'm dying and somehow that just doesn't bother me, even though I should probably be pleading with God to give me more time—even though I went back in time in search of a cure for this warm wound gushing blood. My bloody fingers wrest themselves from my gut where they have been futilely pressed in a misguided attempt at self-preservation and click the device. Oblong, covered in rubber buttons, it's really just a remote, or a clicker if you asked my grandmother.

But it doesn't take me to the correct location. It has taken me to a children's park occupied by preternaturally clean slides and empty benches and still swings and a crushing silence that could turn coal into diamonds. I lurch forward, backwards, then stumble until I land on a chipped green bench with a half-assed black paint job. All I'm gathering is that the machine is malfunctioning, because nothing is being evoked besides rage. There's nothing here for me. It wouldn't have been a suitable rendezvous for clients—not with a middle school a hundred feet away where a so-called resource officer lounges half the day.

It's an insult from God or Darwin or the universe or some other controlling higher power—a reminder of my insignificance. Them laughing at my misfortune wasn't enough. No, no. They needed me to see how little an impact I've ever had on anything or ever will, how temporary all my achievements ever were. At best I was an ant celebrating a crumb while a Raid can approached from behind. I can't really blame whoever's in charge for pulling the rug from under people, though; I'd do the same thing if you handed me the keys to everyone's respective fates.

I unsteadily stand and explore the area for hidden cash or documents. Again, not an area safe for conducting illicit activities, so nothing turns up. Exactly as expected. My machine is not as perfect as I thought.

Hot pain flares in my gut. I grimace. I take a deep breath. I press the button again.

And now I can barely move five feet in any direction, and now I must contend with the possibility of perishing in a dive bar—the very dive bar where I met my wife, from whom love masquerading as lust produced two children. She was pretty then. Probably still is. I just wouldn't know. I can't remember the last time I actually looked her in the eyes. Her green eyes, I think, or maybe they're hazel, or perhaps blue. They're a pretty color, I know that. Prettier than I deserved. And though the people are absent, the alcohol is not, and so I pour myself a couple whiskey shots and down them as if they were water in the desert, and I wish I could come up with a more creative metaphor, but dying is a hungry business and doesn't leave a man's mental faculties much budget for artistically pleasing strings of words; words are just noise, and noise doesn't matter when there's nobody left to hear it—if a tree falls in the woods and there's nobody there to observe the sonic waves, I've decided that's as good as them never having been produced, and so I can't be so narcissistic as to think my own words carry any more weight or meaning than nature's greatest life-giving invention.

Blame the drinks, blame being an old man past his prime, but I think I'm crying. I'm actually scared, aren't I? All the philosophizing in the world won't even delay my fate by a single second. I drain one more shot. There's a warmth about this place. It was where I met my darling Jane after all. Yes, Jane. The woman who gave me two kids.

Two kids, right, right. Braxton and Aurora.

There was a reason I stopped coming here, wasn't there? It wasn't *just* because I met Jane or the kids. No, not at all; I came here for almost a decade afterwards. So why did I stop? Well, no—more like half a decade.

Because I started spending my time somewhere else. And I know where I *want* it to have been.

The park from my memories. Where I took them both exactly one time.

I stopped drinking because I finally got my first real job. Because I moved us into a nice city. Because criminals wanted to know they were dealing with someone who wouldn't get sacked for the appearance of impropriety and ostensibly possessed a straight-laced reputation.

I've spared my children a single passing thought since I was shot. Nothing I did was for them. I loved making a grand show of it when they were around—when anyone was around.

I earned this bullet. What inkling remains of my mind is telling me that much, backed up by blurry memories of memories. And I told myself I was doing it for the kids, to give them a better life. But I took them to the park once. One time. Twelve hour days in the office, benders that lasted a week, and so many hours spent aiding the very criminals my own son would love to put away.

Everything I did was for me. I regret having those poor kids, and I regret not telling Braxton especially how proud of him I am. But I am. I'm deeply proud of him for being nothing like me. And for putting men away like me and the ones I helped.

I get it now, too. There's nobody here because I can only transport myself into my own mind, and from there can only revisit what was important to me. A sort of way for the mind to save resources while trying to save the body from death, only looking through the most relevant experiences. My kids didn't show up, my wife didn't show up, and neither did my crimes. I didn't love them as much as I should have, and now they'll be free and better off without me. So I guess in these final moments I do care about them.

I smile and close my eyes. Dying is the best thing I could ever do for them.

—

Braxton Hart waved for his fellow officers to enter the building. His throat constricted. *Dad?* But behind the sorrow, a burgeoning relief was attempting to fully surface. Mom would be devastated for a while, but it was better this way. He'd had an idea he was up to no good for the past couple years, and had somewhat suspected his father wasn't a perfect citizen during childhood. He clicked his radio.

"Suspect is incapacitated, potentially deceased. Please send EMTs."

We Made This

Justin Alcala

Dr. Benoit was only a bit saner than his patients. Volunteering on Christmas Eve felt rash to his office partners, but the veteran psychiatrist insisted. He'd received an emergency call from a healthcare protection officer at noon, and by twelve-thirty, Dr. Benoit drove his compact car five hours downstate through hoary weather, listening to past recordings from the involuntary psychiatric wing's most precarious patients including... *her*. When he arrived at Gray Ridge Hospital Center, a crepuscule blackness drank the sky's leftover light. An unrelenting gale punished the winterland doldrum, compelling Dr. Benoit's car towards the main gates.

Backup floodlights shined down on the grounds of the four-floor infirmary. An untangled holiday wreath obstructed the automated gate's sensors from releasing the egress. Dr. Benoit pressed a drive-up call button, but when no one responded, the Rubenesque psychiatrist squeezed from his car and straightened the plastic evergreen ring. A mechanical response ground from the motor box before the gate swung open. Dr. Benoit peered inside the grounds. A dappled light, like television static, flitted through the east wing's frosted windows. Dr. Benoit retreated from the biting weather back into his car, straightening a photograph on his dashboard of an older woman with a striking smile.

"Come, Libby," said Dr. Benoit to the photograph, pushing his car into drive and paving through snow to the employee parking lot. "There's work to be done."

Not a creature stirred in the main lobby. The grumble of a distant generator echoed through the halls, drowning the knell of *Carol of the Bells* from an overhead speaker. Dr. Benoit peaked over the office counter where a computer screen displayed several camera angles on a grid. A bed of neighboring two-way radios inside a unit charger crackled with voices next to the monitor. Dr. Benoit spotted two protection officers, a maintenance woman, and a nurse on a video-block struggling with a furnace inside what appeared to be a cellar. Dr. Benoit reached for a radio and pressed down on its push-to-talk button.

"Test, test," said Dr. Benoit. "This is Dr. Benoit—the locums psychiatrist you called for?"

"Hey doc," a man with a thick city accent said. "This is Matty. I'll be up shortly. Dang generator ain't heating east-sector."

"I'm quite familiar with the facility," said Dr. Benoit. "I can see myself if you're in dire straits?"

"*No*, don't do that!" shouted Matty. "I'm coming up."

Dr. Benoit sighed and helped himself to a miniature candy cane resting on the desk. He fixated on a particular section of the computer's grids. In the east wing where the involuntary psychiatric patients lived, rime glazed over walls. Each door, painted in vivid colors to mask its uncongenial nature, kept a

378

circle top window. In each of those fogged windows, patients' heads bobbed, gawked, or pressed against the glass. All except for one. At the end of the hall, the ajar door for Ms. Gryla Drosselmeyer flickered with the identical television static from outside, though the camera angle denied perspective within.

"Doc," said Matty, entering the room. Dr. Benoit sprang up, hand pressed over his heart. Manny, donned in a police blue uniform, wiped his greasy hands along his sleeve.

"Goodness, you startled me," said Dr. Benoit.

"Sorry, didn't mean to spook you. I appreciate you coming out on Christmas Eve."

"Why is the east wing so active? Is there an issue with their medication?"

"That's just it, doc. As soon as my shift started, the entire sector started getting chatty."

"About anything in particular?"

"*The Conception.*"

"Conception?"

"No idea, doc. We're used to peculiarities, but not in collusion. Martha asked Barry and I to assist her in giving them something, but the power went out before we could. We've been on the back foot ever since."

"I notice Ms. Drosselmeyer's door is open."

"*I know,*" Matty said. "No power and old locks. We figured the other doors ain't open, so the old *staff-breaker* can't get to anyone."

"Staff-breaker?"

"Little nickname we gave her after her third nurse quit."

"What did your director have to say about all this?"

"He's in Cancun, and our supervisor is stuck across the state. We received instructions to contact the authorities, if necessary, but it doesn't seem appropriate.

"No, that's unnecessary. Have Martha prepare Geodon.

379

I'll administer it."

"I'll gather the crew so we can hold down Ms. Drosselmeyer."

"Allow me to go alone. We've built a relationship."

"I don't know, doc. Ain't that a little unorthodox?"

"Desperate times. Now, do you have a spare keycard I could use?"

"Take mine. It's the only one working right now."

"What are your instructions for me and the team?" asked Manny, unclipping a fob with his ID from his belt.

Dr. Benoit took the keycard and smiled. "Fix the heat."

—

A distinctive atmosphere reigned in the east wing, dated and demode. Dr. Benoit journeyed down the corridor forged in sand-lime bricks and Victorian cornice. The hot incandescent bulbs and cool air formed a lingering mist that curled along the ceiling. Room signs with Sharpied patient names and notes warned about who lurked inside. Someone from a far-off room spoke in a child's voice before cackling, while fingernails scraped from an adjoining wall. Dr. Benoit proceeded down the hall, syringe of Geodon in his hand.

"Saint Nicholas is here," said a bass heavy voice from a room Dr. Benoit passed. The seven-foot man with stringy hair and a chin beard stared through the snowman he drew in the window's condensation. Months ago, Dr. Benoit watched this man tear off a protection officer's winter jacket sleeve with a thrust from his offhand before five staff members struggled to restrain him.

"Hello, Foley," said Dr. Benoit. "Glad to see you. It's been—"

"One-hundred-and-seventeen-days."

"That's right. Apologies for the cold. Staff is working on it."

"We wished for it. We made a snow globe."

"What do you mean *we*, Foley?"

"The east wing. We asked The Conception."

"The Conception?"

"We've been working hard on it. Hey Saint Nick, I got you something for Christmas." Foley ducked from the window, and a hard key slid from under the door's crack. Dr. Benoit picked up the laser cut key and put it in his breast pocket as Foley's face returned behind the window.

"Oh, that's wonderful, Foley. I'm sure I'll find use for it. Say, have you seen Ms. Drosselmeyer?"

Foley's gaze lowered.

"Everything okay, Foley?"

"Then the Grinch thought of something he hadn't before! What if Christmas, he thought, doesn't come from a store? What if Christmas...perhaps...means a little bit more?"

A creak of metal down the hall stole Dr. Benoit's attention. "Well, there's my answer, I suppose. Good to see you, Foley."

"Merry Christmas to all, and to all a goodnight," said Foley as Dr. Benoit renewed his trek.

Dr. Benoit tottered down the corridor, disregarding patients' further attempts to gain his attention from their windows. Upon reaching the end of the hallway where Ms. Drosselmeyer's ajar door awaited, he cleared his throat.

"Come in, Dr. Benoit," said the smokey, anodyne woman's voice from inside.

Dr. Benoit drew the rest of the door open to find Ms. Drosselmeyer, contrary to what he'd seen the first time they'd met. Her hair, once a wild mess, was now tamed and pulled under a Santa hat stained with blue pen ink. Where she once washed herself red from self-inflicted wounds, now she awaited with clean pale skin. Her pressed pajamas tucked neatly as she sat up crossed legged on the edge of her bed reading a dog-eared copy of *The Gift of the Magi.*

"Merry Christmas, Ms. Drosselmeyer," said Dr. Benoit. "It's good to see you again."

"Gryla is fine, doctor."

"I see you're managing on your own. That's very good, Gryla."

"Spare me your placations, Dr. Benoit. Same degree."

"I'm not here to condescend, Gryla."

"You're here to control me. That is Geodon in your hand, isn't it?"

"Gryla, progress is slow, but you're getting there. For now, we must take precautions."

"You're no stranger to irony, Dr. Benoit. These safeguards they keep imposing on us facilitated The Conception's threading."

"Yes, Foley mentioned something of that. Care to elaborate?"

"We built it in our sleep. The staff sedates us twice the legal limit, so we have plenty of time to dream. Now, it wishes to free us."

"Gryla, this sounds delusional."

"I respect your honesty, doctor. You're one of the few who care. That's why we invited you."

"Thank you. Can you tell me more about The Conception?"

"Dr. Benoit," Ms. Drosselmeyer stared at her cuticles. "You mentioned your wife last we met. Do you remember?"

"I do." Dr. Benoit's posture stiffened.

"You displayed vulnerability, perhaps to build a connection?"

"There's nothing wrong with being vulnerable. I'm human too."

"Your words that day resonated with me. Do you remember what you said?"

"Nothing is ever lost in our dreams."

"Did I tell you how I ended up here?"

"You lost your boy."

"I owned a memory retrieval practice. Twelve years, in fact. Then my patient implicated a man with good lawyers of seven felonies. The state revoked my license after he was proven innocent. Then David left me. Jacob's death was a consummation of it all. A discount babysitter."

"You did what you could. Anyone would fold under that weight."

"I still see Jacob. David too. They're here now... and I'm happy again."

"The Conception did that?"

"Yes."

"Gryla, you've told me what The Conception does, but not what it *is*. Could you expand?"

"It is us, and we are it. A construct weaved from our hopes and our memories. It wants what is best for us because it *is* us."

"I see. Gryla, why don't you take a break?" Dr. Benoit brandished the syringe. "Let me help you."

"We are the Sleepless. We don't need rest anymore. The Conception provides contentment without that facet."

"Gryla, this is irrational."

"It will give you Libby back if you help us."

"Please don't use her name like that."

"We need you, Dr. Benoit. It's why we called you here. We want out."

"Gryla, this is the last time I'll ask," Dr. Benoit took a

step forward, uncapping the needle tip. "Let me help you."

A half dozen steel doors from the east sector moaned open. Dr. Benoit flashed a glance over his shoulder. The smiling patients of the east wing approached like a school of white pajamaed sharks, trapping the therapist amid them and Ms. Drosselmeyer.

"You don't believe the power outage would only affect a single door, did you?" Ms. Drosselmeyer glanced up from under her fingernails. The massive hand of Foley reached for Dr. Benoit, clutching the psychiatrist by his shoulder.

"Marley was dead to begin with," said Foley. Dr. Benoit winced as he sank to a knee.

"Beneath the bark is rot," a short-haired woman with gray lips said in a child's voice, prying the syringe out of Dr. Benoit's hand, and offering it to Ms. Drosselmeyer.

"We are victims of fate," said Ms. Drosselmeyer, squeezing the syringe plunger until it spit a droplet of sedative. "The people here wash away our past, drown out our now, but we deserve to preserve our dreams. You included Dr. Benoit."

"Gryla, what are you plotting?" Dr. Benoit murmured, grasping Foley's colossal hand.

"We want to escape," stated Ms. Drosselmeyer. "We'll take our loved ones someplace special. Once you meet The Conception, I'm positive you'll help. You'll be sleepless."

Ms. Drosselmeyer stood up, loomed over Dr. Benoit, removing her hat and placing it on the psychiatrist's head. She kissed his dimpled cheek, then pressed the needle into his neck. Dr. Benoit froze, numbness washing through his nerves. When his bones turned to rubber, he heard it. From behind the hall of patients a cat's purr, mother's laugh, and child's coo echoed. A swell of darkness with a hundred eyes flickering like black-and-white static constructed itself behind the patients. Oily tendrils slithered from the stalking gloom, curling along the assembly.

Silhouettes of grandmas, parents, and children embraced the patients. Dr. Benoit's heavy eyes slid to Ms. Drosselmeyer, who rested her hand on a boy's shoulder while the dark form of a man put his arm around her waist.

"No," Dr. Benoit said. "This isn't real."

"Robert," the voice of Dr. Benoit's wife called out. A strobe of light poured from The Conception. "It's okay. I'm here."

A long string of oil stretched from the standing black wave with one-hundred eyes and coiled around Dr. Benoit's ankle before taking shape.

"Libby?" asked Dr. Benoit.

"Nothing is lost in our dreams," said the congealing shape of a slender woman who pressed her sable hand onto Dr. Benoit's cheek. The east wing's smiles grew, elated by Dr. Benoit's reunion. Patients clapped, tittered, and cheered.

"God bless us, everyone!" said Foley over Dr. Benoit's sobbing.

—

"So he left with them all?" asked the policewoman, staring down at the grid of cameras replaying security footage.

"The doors locked up, and he had my fob, so we couldn't do anything until it was too late," said Matty. "Locums doc just…took them away."

"Locums?" asked the policewoman, watching a parade of patients from the east wing follow a Santa hat clad Dr. Benoit dancing out of the faculty door.

"Rent-a-doc," said Matty. "Still, he came all this way from up state. Seems decent enough."

"Or lonely enough. How'd he get the key to the bus?" asked the policewoman, watching a rosy-cheeked Dr. Benoit wave ebullient patients into a half-bus with the Gray Ridge Hospital Center logo on its side. Ms. Drosselmeyer patted Dr. Benoit on the arm before assisting a short, invisible person up the bus stairs.

"That's beyond me. I was just trying to survive the shift. Didn't think someone could orchestrate something like this. He must have been planning it for months."

"Someone was."

The policewoman zoomed in on Dr. Benoit as the jolly psychiatrist spoke to the vacant space behind him before kissing the air. Then, after the last patient entered the vehicle, with a wink of his eye, Dr. Benoit rose up the bus stairs. The camera's grainy display showed high beams ignite before the bus cut through the employee parking lot snow and fly out of view.

"They all look so happy," the policewoman said.

"Yeah, well," Matty shrugged. "Their Christmas dream came true, I guess."

Waiting for the Tenth Man

Burt Rashbaum

James arrived at the synagogue early. Almost fifteen years had passed since he'd last been here. It hadn't changed, a stark structure of old brick with no adornments of any kind. In the cool morning air the sounds of his leather shoes were sharp on the stone steps. The sun was bright, the day brisk. He took a deep breath, barely invigorated by the cold rush that filled his lungs, and opened the heavy wooden door.

Exhaustion wrapped his body like an old blanket. Too many sleepless nights in a row, living on alcohol and cigarettes, which was not his usual style. He hardly drank a drop and never smoked. Yet this past week, as he drifted further from his family, those vices fit. Now his mouth tasted foul, a sticky film covered his teeth. He knew he needed a shave. He'd promised his sister and his wife he would try this. And so he was here.

The air inside was stale; the lobby dark. Religion had always been a shroud of darkness to him, probably because of this place and the people he had encountered here. He remembered a constant absence of color, of joy, except at holidays, when the release of pent-up emotion surged all around him. He was surprised that it was actually a tiny building. In his memory it was a monolith of righteousness. Off to the left was the Rabbi's study, where they said the morning Kaddish. The door was shut, but he heard murmuring on the other side. He grabbed the tarnished brass doorknob, turned it slowly, and went in.

He would rather have been anywhere else this morning, even back at the cemetery, than here. He didn't want to do this, but felt he owed his father at least this much, to say the Kaddish in a minyan. Scanning the room, he quickly counted. He was the ninth. Some of the old men looked at him, disinterested, went back to their quiet talking. Those rules hadn't changed. A quorum was still ten. Now he had to wait for someone else. He'd never understood the meaning of the numbers. Why couldn't it be nine? Wasn't nine a magic number? Ten seemed meaningless.

He barely remembered the prayer, had never known it completely. If the tenth man showed, it would be the same old scene he'd partaken in when young: all of them huddled and mumbling together the ancient prayer for the dead. Would he be able to read the Hebrew? Then again, there was no reason why he would have to say it aloud. None of these old men would. They'd all sway in their davening, practically hum the words, bending at the knees at the mention of the many names of God. He'd imitate them. He was great at faking this kind of thing. He had never paid attention when he was a student here, had learned only the beginnings of every prayer. Once things got going, and the congregation joined in, or when silent prayer was called for, James looked the part. The eight men present wore their prayer shawls, patiently waiting. If someone else didn't come soon, they'd break up, and James would have wasted the morning.

James hadn't brought his own tallis, since his father was buried in it. He thought of the mad rush he and his sister had made for the funeral parlor, six days ago. They had to bring a suit of his father's for him to be buried in, his army discharge papers for the flag, and his father's tallis. "Where's Daddy's tallis?" he'd screamed at his grief-stricken mother. She was in shock and seemed not to hear. She sat on the edge of the bed watching her children tear the place apart. Finally he found his own, buried in a drawer. "Here's mine, c'mon, let's go." And then they'd gone shopping for their father's coffin.

The cardboard box was still by the door, full of "generic" tallises, for those like James who didn't have one. He grabbed a tattered one off the top, threw it around his shoulders. It was faded, stained, smelled vaguely of camphor. He took the yarmulke out of his pocket and stuck it on his head.

He sat down beside an ancient grizzled man with rheumy eyes. The old man had a horrible odor and tufts of hair growing out of his ears. James was obviously the only one younger than sixty years. These men were probably all retired. He imagined them spending their days in the synagogue, arguing over the Talmud, not doing any good to anyone. Some were obviously retired businessmen, talking the stock market. A few were members of the synagogue, who came every morning to say their prayers. And one or two were like the man James sat next to, poor religious fools who spent the day in the synagogue because it was warm and safe from the cruel world outside. He was supposed to come and say Kaddish for a month. He'd give it this one day.

A few of the men had on Tefillin, the phylacteries. He'd once owned a set of the small leather boxes, had even liked the novelty of strapping them to his forehead and arm, with the long strip of leather that wound around his head down his arm,

389

ending around his fingers to delineate a Hebrew letter.

When he was twelve he and his friends had played with the Tefillin, swinging the boxes around their heads by the leather strips, singing "Holy boxes, holy boxes, we're not gonna eat our bagels and loxes," until his father had come upon them and screamed bloody murder. His father had thrown them out of the house. Why the hell did he care? He didn't give a damn about any religion. Why should he care that his son was misusing some holy artifact? He didn't even know what the boxes were for, couldn't even put them on. In his father's great plan to train his son in the religion he'd never known himself, he'd far surpassed his father in knowledge, but still profaned anything his father might have thought holy. But after that day he'd never played with the Tefillin again, and never strapped those boxes to his forehead, either. He had no idea where his Tefillin was now. Somewhere in his mother's attic, probably.

The pious few who were wearing them today were already lost in their morning prayers. Outside he heard children on their way to school. Their happy patter sounded as clean as the outside air, and he wanted to be with them. Their sounds caused him to think back to when he'd been a child, in the summer, playing as the night came on, feeling the cool air replace the warmth of the day. If he was sunburned he would feel a chill. He could almost hear his father's voice calling him, pulling him away from the fun.

"Dov? Is it Dov?"

The old man sitting next to him, the one with the stink and the hair in his ears, was talking to him. Dov? He hadn't heard that word since he'd been a student at this place so long ago.

"That's my Hebrew name. Do I know you?"

"Meyers. Rabbi Meyers. It's Dov Steffens, yes?"

It was Rabbi Meyers, the mean one. The one who'd

on more than one occasion thrown him out of the building for his insolence and disrespect. Who called him no good and told him that he would never amount to anything. Who picked his nose in a tranced state and often fell asleep while the class read prayers out loud.

"Yes. Hello, Rabbi. I'm surprised you remember me."

"Ah, Dov. You I don't forget, even with the beard. You gave me some trouble."

"Yes, I suppose I did."

"So tell me, Dov. You don't have a tallis? You wear an old one."

The rabbi touched the tallis, fingering the torn cloth. James wanted to pull away, tell him to get his filthy hands off him. Nobody had touched him since the funeral. He wouldn't let his wife near him. Mable had kept her distance, thinking that was what he needed. He didn't want to talk to this old rabbi. He didn't want to be touched by him. He wanted to be back home, mourning with his family. He wanted a drink.

"I had one, Rabbi," he said, tugging the tallis out of the old man's hands. "My father is buried in it."

"Ah," Rabbi Meyers said, a sad smile on his face, "my condolences. But Tefillin," he pointed with his head to the men who wore them, "you know Tefillin?"

Where was the tenth man, so they could start this charade? How long could he endure this pathetic remnant of his past?

"You had Tefillin. I taught you, no?"

"Yes. I don't know where it is."

A tenth man walked in. A minyan. Thank God. Now it could start. The tenth man found his place. The others who had not done so opened their prayer books and began. Rabbi Meyers motioned to the tenth man, and they walked to the corner of the study, whispering, looking at James. They were obviously friends. He tried to ignore them. He opened his prayer book, found the place, but Rabbi Meyers came over, pointing with an arthritic finger. The tenth man had gone out but was back. A few of the other ancients looked over approvingly while they prayed.

The tenth man gave Meyers a worn felt bag. James recognized it. He watched as the rabbi unzipped it and took out a very old set of Tefillin. The leather was cracked with age, the little boxes warped. Rabbi Meyers unfurled the long leather straps and reached out to James, who glanced into the small mirror next to the bookshelves, caught his reflection in it, and stared at his face. His eyes were puffed from too much whiskey and crying. He flinched, pulled back, almost dropped his prayer book. A scene flashed into his mind from his childhood. Meyers had humiliated him. The class had been studying the holy seder service. He had made some crack in his usual style, and the Rabbi had exploded. Meyers had grabbed him by the neck and thrown him out of the room. James still clutched the Passover Haggadah. James opened the door, came back into the classroom, and screaming curses at the Rabbi, took the Haggadah and threw it against the wall. It fell to the ground. The class came to a hushed silence. Rabbi Meyers ran to the wall and picked it up, kissed its covers. It was the first time the child had ever seen tears in a grown man's eyes. The Rabbi tried to speak, looked to the class, opened his mouth. No sound came out. He turned back to James, who stood paralyzed, unable to move. Then James ran out of the room. He ended up in his secret place behind the synagogue, where he went sometimes to be alone. He cried for hours, and didn't know why.

He'd never wanted to attend Hebrew school. His father wanted James to go, not so he would learn something of importance that was being passed from one generation to another, not so he would enter the spiritual world his father loved so much and wanted to share. No, he realized now his father wanted only one thing: that upon his death his son would be able to say Kaddish for him, to assure his everlasting peace.

He'd resisted with everything he had. There were arguments, tantrums, he'd tried every tactic he'd ever learned in the subtle family manipulations that had in the past gotten him what he wanted, but what kind of power does an eight year old have against his father? So he went, hating every minute he was forced to go, and his father was satisfied.

At every religious occasion, James had mocked the rituals, teased his father for his charade of belief, and resented the fact that his father was so proud of James' own accomplishments. But there were rare times when James was able to step outside of this anger and be genuinely awed by the mysteries of religion, the hugeness of this God that was unnamable, with a face that would blind anyone who tried to look upon it. He struggled against this attraction, and instead caused havoc in the Hebrew school, causing Rabbi Meyers more trouble than he was worth. James thought, years later, that he'd needed some guidance in religion, from someone who saw in the depths of the mysteries what he himself thought might be there. But Meyers was void of any deeper knowledge, he understood even as a child. The old rabbi only went through the motions because those were the rules. When he was finally bar-mitzvah, and officially graduated from the place, he swore he'd never return, never say a Kaddish for his father. It was an unspoken rift between them that never healed, and James felt as if it was the one triumph he had over the old man.

Yet here he was, hung over and confused. Why had he come? Was it too late to undo the damage of his father's superstition? What was he trying to prove? He'd always believed that his father had kept him away from whatever joy and comfort he might have found in his religion, in effect sending him into exile. But in mourning, he wondered if that was a lie. He'd kept himself away from his heritage. The only one he could save was himself. But could he? Who was he trying to make peace with: himself? His father? God?

Now James felt like he was being manhandled by a giant insect. The rabbi's long cold fingers wrapped the leather around his arm. James remembered when he had been shown this in preparation for his bar-mitzvah. He'd hated the old man handling him, teaching him the ritual. Rabbi Meyers had held him still with a steel grip and said through clenched teeth, "All my boys who are bar-mitzvah will know Tefillin. Even you, Dov Steffens." Now the Rabbi smiled his crooked sad smile, and patted James' stubbled face as if he were a child again. A few of the men glanced over, pulled out of their prayers, and nodded.

"Now," the rabbi whispered, "say Kaddish for your father. He is with God now."

He tried to say the words, but he got lost as he knew would happen, and quietly changed to a monosyllabic nonsense, bowing when others bowed. He closed his eyes, and then opened them again, coming back to his reflection, to see what he looked like, to see what he looked like praying. Old phylacteries and a borrowed tallis. He barely recognized himself. He still felt the rabbi's fingers on his arms, on his face. He wanted to run out of there and tear the leather off, throw it into the sky. He was strangling, the leather felt like a noose, a straitjacket. The little box stuck to his forehead weighed him down, burned into his skin. He didn't know how long it would last, but he would stand until the last one stood. He davened like the best of them, mumbling sounds and occasionally raising his voice with a broken cry of "Adonai" or "Elohim," and he lost himself to the green walls, to the cries of the children outside, and to the memories of summers past.

He felt the walls closing in around him and stared at the drunken eyes in the reflection. He saw in his bloodshot eyes these past days when he had paced the hospital floor, waiting, out of breath from running from the airport. He and his family were led into the ICU, and he had watched his father, bloated with drugs, hooked up to machines, falter, fade and finally die. He saw himself that night informing his relatives, one drunken phone call following another, his sister gently taking the phone from him, whispering, "Jimmy, I'll do that, you go and lie down." And he saw in the reflection the days of mourning after he had buried his father, who'd died too soon and too suddenly. He saw the drinking which dulled the pain and the anger he felt because he wasn't ready for all of this. He saw the sleepless nights and wasted, stinking days.

And he felt the mysteries all around him, even if these old forgotten men had no idea what they were immersed in. This ancient incantation, this prayer for the dead. There was a power in this prayer, and even though he was far away from the actual meaning of the words, he knew. Maybe his father had known too, maybe not, but he understood now that his father always had the *fear*. The old man's biggest fear was that he'd die with no one to say these holy words for him, that he'd die and face God with nothing to show but an empty life, to be ultimately forgotten back on earth. James struggled to find his place in the prayer book, to offer his father something the old man had needed so badly that he'd sacrificed his only son on the altar of this knowledge. James saw himself in the reflection and the Tefillin now looked to him like a huge bandage covering his arm, his neck, his whole head, and he saw the wounds exposed to the air underneath, he could almost see the blood, and he swayed, lowering at the knees and upright again, always coming back to his reflection, and filling up inside until, finally, here, standing among strange old men, covered in worn silk

395

and cracked leather, singing a prayer for the dead in an alien language, he thought he would burst.

About the Authors

NONFICTION

Matias F. Travieso-Diaz is a Cuban American engineer and lawyer who, having retired from the practice of law, rediscovered the pleasures of creative writing. In addition to fiction in both English and Spanish, he has written papers on issues relating to Cuba and miscellaneous other topics. You can find him at matiastraviesodiaz.com.

Judith Frankel is an Illinois native who currently lives in Davis, California, where she works as a development consultant. She's had a long career teaching, writing, and serving nonprofits in human services and the performing arts.

Julie Mariouw is a former English teacher and Amherst Writers & Artists facilitator who offers online and in-person writing workshops through Wellspring Writing Workshops, LLC, which she founded in 2016. Julie combines the power of metaphor, the senses, movement, and nature together with writing, to create healing and increased creativity. Julie's writing has been published in Wilderness House Literary Review, Teach.Write.A Literary Journal, Recovering the Self, The Huron River Review, The Brick Magazine, Crazy Wisdom Journal, Natural Awakenings Magazine, and Verdad Magazine. You can find her at *www.wellspringwritingworkshops.com*

Jun A. Alindogan is currently Academic Writing and TESOL professor at the Asian School of Development and Cross-cultural Studies (ASDECS) and the Academic Director of the Expanded Alternative Learning System (ALS) of Empowered

East, a Rizal-province-based NGO in the Philippines. He is also the founder of Speechsmart Online that specializes in test preparation courses for international English exam certifications. He is a freelance writer and a member of the Freelance Writer's Guild of the Philippines (FWGP). His creative non fiction have been published at transitdialog.com, voxpopuliph.com, cafedissensuseveryday.com, anaksastra.com, allyourstories. com, zine about cats at gantalapress.com, and the University of the Philippines Manila's The Reflective Journal.

Fendy Satria Tulodo is a writer and storyteller with a keen interest in the intersection of language, memory, and sound. His writing delves into the nuances of human emotion, often weaving lyrical prose with rich, introspective narratives. Beyond the written word, he is also a musician and songwriter, releasing music under the name Nep Kid. Drawing inspiration from a wide range of genres, he explores the rhythm of thought and the resonance of untold stories, whether through literature or music.

Laura Lewis-Barr was a graduate student in clinical psychology but eventually switched majors and earned her M.A in theatre. She is a published poet and award-winning dramatist, screenwriter, and stop-motion filmmaker. Laura's deep study of Jungian psychology has led to her passion for studying symbols –through her films on fairy tales and her new podcast "Laughing Mystics" which explores the Bible through a Jungian lens. Laura's art focuses on mythic stories for personal and collective transformation. Her films are made in her basement in Chicago and her screening events are filled with heart and questions for the soul. For more info visit: https://creators.spotify.com/pod/profile/thelaughingmystics/

and https://psychescinema.com/

Leah Mueller's work is published in Rattle, NonBinary Review, Brilliant Flash Fiction, Citron Review, New Flash Fiction Review, Does It Have Pockets, Outlook Springs, Your Impossible Voice, etc. She has received several nominations for Pushcart and Best of the Net. One of her short stories appears in the 2022 edition of Best Small Fictions. Her fourteenth book, "Stealing Buddha" was published by Anxiety Press in 2024. Website: http://www.leahmueller.org.

John Wenderlein lives in Central Florida where he works as a Hospice Chaplain. He has written two books on the subject.

Debra J. White's social work career ended suddenly on 1/6/94 due to a pedestrian car accident. After a long recovery from significant brain trauma, she moved to Phoenix and found a new life in creative writing. Her webpage is: www.debrawhite.org

Deborah Blenkhorn writes memoir-based poetry and prose. Her work has appeared in venues such as *Blank Spaces*, *Dreamers Creative Writing*, *Moss Piglet Zine*, and *Prosetrics*. She lives in the Pacific Northwest with her husband of 35 years, and has two teenage daughters; this story recalls a darker time of struggling to keep the faith.

FICTION

Emecheta Christian is a vivid writer whose work explores themes of self-actualization, belonging, and the complexities of the human experience. His works have appeared in esteemed literary journals and anthologies such as The Potter's Poetry, Indiana Review, Oxford American, Four Way Review, the Academy of American Poets Poem-A-Day Series, and elsewhere. He has been recognized with several awards, including the Iroko Award and The Dorothy Hewett Award. Emecheta's unique voice and evocative imagery have garnered him a growing reputation as a voice of change in the global literary scene.

Krin Van Tatenhove is a writer, visual artist, and spiritual adventurer. His 40 years of professional writing experience have led to countless articles and 18 books. With so much despair in the world, he likes reading and writing redemptive stories that lead us back to hope. He is married, has four children, and lives with his wife and disabled adult son in San Antonio, Texas. This story is from his latest collection entitled "The Sanctuary: Tales of Hope and Redemption," available on Amazon here. To learn more about his background and download many of his projects, visit Krinvan.com.

John F. Miglio is a freelance writer and the author of the dystopian thriller, Sunshine Assassins. His articles have been published in a variety of periodicals, including Los Angeles Magazine and LA Weekly. His most recent articles have been featured in Wand'rly, Op/Ed News, Hippocampus Magazine, Truthout, the Democratic Underground, Counterpunch, and Cynic. He has also appeared on Air America Radio and Radio Power Network. His novel, Sunshine Assassins, has been called "a bone-chilling political morality fable," "wickedly entertaining," and "unforgettable."

Urmi Chakravorty is a freelance writer, reviewer and editor living in Bangalore, India. Her opinion pieces have been published by The Hindu and The Times of India. Her short stories, non-fiction, and poetry have found space in over forty domestic and international literary magazines and anthologies, which include Tell Me Your Story Review, Muse India, Madras Courier, Borderless Journal, Mean Pepper Vine, eShe, The Chakkar, Kitaab, Indian Review, The Hooghly Review, Purple Pencil Project, Rigorous, All Your Stories, Mocking Owl Roost, and The Wise Owl. She has won accolades instituted by Rupa Publications, Women's Web, S7, Wordweavers, and The Centre for South Asian Studies, University of Hawaii. Urmi's writings can be read at www.wordsnverses.com

Robert Moore is a semi-retired librarian by day, a writer and community service performer by night. He published The Stone House Diaries (2006), historical fiction set in his hometown of Niagara Falls, as well as short stories in print and online journals. He lives currently in Clarence, NY, with his wife, Stephanie.

Mike Sherer lives in West Chester in southwest Ohio just north of Cincinnati. His screenplay 'Hamal_18' was produced and released direct to DVD and is currently available to stream on Tubi. 5 published novels: 'A Cold Dish' (James Ward Kirk Fiction), 'Shadytown' (INtense Publications), 'Souls of Nod' (Breaking Rules Publishing) 'Flatlanders' (WolfSinger), and 'World Tour' (Ink & Quill). Also published 7 novellas and 32 short stories. None of this was self-published. More info with links can be found at his author site: From the North Rim (mikesherer.org)

Joe Giordano was born in Brooklyn. He and his wife Jane now live in Texas. Joe's stories have appeared in more than one hundred magazines including The Saturday Evening Post, and Shenandoah, and his short story collection, Stories and Places I Remember. His novels include, Birds of Passage, An Italian Immigrant Coming of Age Story, and the Anthony Provati thriller series: Appointment with ISIL, Drone Strike, and The Art of Revenge.

About David Clear: "I am a New England writer; plainly a hobbyist rather than a professional. I had no formal writing education, but many great writing teachers, from office jobs to heartbroken relationships, and even convenience store clerks. I am retired, and I guess still seeking my great writing whale. My novel, "Dreaming at the Speed of Sound," is available on Amazon."

John Mitchell Johnson is a lifelong resident of Kentucky, having been reared in the eastern coalfields. His debut novel, "Kudzu," published in 2018, was selected for inclusion at the 2018 Kentucky Book Festival. Johnson also published a collection of short stories, "Where I'm From," in 2021. His stories have twice won awards at Lexington's Carnegie Center for Literacy and Learning, including 2017's Next Great Writer's Competition. His short stories have appeared eight times in Silver Threads, a literary collaborative of The Carnegie Center and Lexington Senior Citizens Center. Johnson's latest work, "84 X 28 X 20," a short foray into the macabre, was recently published by "Dark Harbor Magazine."

Michelle Koubek is an autistic woman who loves outer space and coin collecting. Her short stories and poems have been published in various venues including Factor Four Magazine, Strange Horizons, and Abyss & Apex. To get to know her better, visit her website at https://www.michellekoubek.com

Soter Lucio is a great grandmother who does ironing for a living and writes horror stories at night. She lives alone and her hobbies are reading and writing. She's been published by Sirens Call, Weird Mask, Dark Chapter Press and Migla Press. She can be found on X @JanSoter and on Facebook at Soter Lucio.

Wally Wood: "I am a full-time writer and editor. I have self-published three novels, written three more. I earned my MA in creative writing from the City University of New York and my BA in philosophy from Columbia University. As a ghostwriter, I have written 23 commercially published business books. My short stories have been accepted by The Lakeshore Review and The Fish Magazine. I am translating a book of Japanese short stories into English. I have been a volunteer writing teacher in state and federal prisons for more than twenty years."

John Leahy has had three novels published - "Harvest," "CROGIAN," and "Unity." His story "The Tale in the Attic" attained an honorable mention in L Ron Hubbard's Writers of the Future Contest. His short story "Singers" has been included in Flame Tree Publishing's 2017 Pirates and Ghosts anthology, alongside tales by literary greats such as Homer, Joseph Conrad, Rudyard Kipling, Arthur Conan Doyle, Robert Louis Stevenson, H.P. Lovecraft, and H.G. Wells. When not writing he spends his time teaching and performing music, working out, and keeping abreast of the stock market and current affairs. He lives in Killarney, Ireland.

Victor Benavides is an English teacher and aspiring writer from the south Texas borderlands. He graduated in 2019 with a master's in business administration and will soon graduate with a master's degree in English studies. Growing up in the lower Rio Grande Valley, he was always fascinated with the power of words and how they can help a reader transcend into different literary worlds.

Richard M. Ankers is the English author of The Eternals Series and Britannia Unleashed. Richard has been featured in Daily Science Fiction, Love Letters to Poe, House of Arcanum, and feels privileged to have appeared in many more. Richard lives to write.

Howard Moon is a writer and poet. His writing and poetry have appeared in multiple collections and anthologies, Small Change, Montana Mouthful, Das Literarisch Journal, Of Poets and Poetry, Native Skin, Breath and Shadow, Ariel Chart, and more. He has won national, local and regional awards for writing. He is of Native heritage and identifies as BIPOC. In 2012 he suffered a brain injury and has been diagnosed with a mental illness —Pseudobulbar Affect. He has also been diagnosed as a hemipelagic. He is retired and lives in central Florida with his wife.

Shawn Casselberry sees the world through stories. He's written fiction and nonfiction books, including a sci-fi novel "The Hemingway Bible," a poetry chapbook called "Wound Man," and "Strange Fire," a collection of dark fiction stories. This story is from his most recent short story collection called "The Image of God: Short Stories on Being Human." Additionally, he's the co-founder/editor for Story Sanctum and lives in the

Chicagoland area dreaming up new worlds. You can check out more of his writing at: www.shawncasselberry.com.

Tremain Xenos is a writer, translator, part-time teacher, mediocre flautist and very clumsy paragliding pilot. He lives with his wife, cats, and chickens in an old house among the rice paddies in Japan's smallest and least productive prefecture. Some of his recent stories have appeared in such places as The Heduan Review, Rivanna Review and Channel Magazine.

Originally from Fairfield, Connecticut, **Michael Mulvey** is a happily married father of four living in Jacksonville, Florida. His publications include: "Replacement Theory," winter 2023 issue of *TheBeZine;* "Safeharbour No More," December 2023 edition of *Portrait of New England;* "Town Centers aren't Shopping Malls," *Dumbo Press* in March of 2024; "Our New Religion," *New English Review* in November of 2024; and "Safety," *New English Review* in February of 2024. He can be found online at www.mulveywrites.com.

Kevin Hopson's work has appeared in a variety of anthologies, magazines, and e-zines, and he enjoys writing in multiple genres. You can learn more about him by visiting his website at http://www.kmhopson.com.

Chrissy Hicks's work has appeared in Killer Nashville Magazine, The Broadkill Review, Black Works, and SUSIE Mag, among others. Her unpublished mystery and thriller novels have earned Top Pick and Suspense Finalist for the Claymore Award, First Place in the Seven Hills Literary Contest, and First Place in the Thomas Mabry Creative Writing Award. She lives in Tennessee with her family, their talkative Husky, and a frenetic cat. You can find her online at: https://chrissyhicks. com/ where she occasionally blogs about the writing life and reviews craft books.

Fay L. Loomis leads a quiet life in the woods in Kerhonkson, New York, USA. Member of the Stone Ridge Library Writers and the Rat's Ass Review Workshop, her poetry and prose appear in numerous publications, including five poetry anthologies. In 2024, Fay's first chapbook Sunlit Wildness (Origami Poems Project) was published. She is a Pushcart Prize nominee.

Mary Jo Rabe writes science fiction, modern fantasy, historical fiction, and crime or mystery stories, generally displaying a preference for what she defines as happy endings. Ideas for her fiction come from the magnificent, expanding universe, the rural environment of eastern Iowa where she grew up, the beautiful Michigan State University campus where she got her first degree, and the Black Forest area of Germany with its center in Freiburg where she worked as a librarian for 41 years before retiring to Titisee-Neustadt. News about her published stories is posted regularly on her blog: https://maryjorabe.wordpress. com/

Robin Blasberg's stories often make connections in unanticipated ways. Her writing has been published in The Pink Hydra, Scribes*MICRO*Fiction, and Short Circuit online. Her plays are available from Big Dog Publishing and YouthPLAYS.

Gabby Russell is a fiction writer and English student at the University of Massachusetts Lowell. When she's not composing short stories or working on her New Adult fantasy novel manuscripts, she enjoys reading speculative fiction, baking, and traveling to new places. She lives in Upstate New York.

Alejandro Gonzales is a writer with stories in Brilliant Flash Fiction, Carnage House, Trembling With Fear, and elsewhere. He attributes the completion and success of this story and all others to the love of his life, Angie.

Burt Rashbaum's publications are *Of the Carousel* (The Poet's Press, 2019), and *Blue Pedals* (Editura Pim, 2015, Bucharest). His fiction has appeared in Caesura, Collateral, *American Writers Review: The End or the Beginning* (San Fedele Press, 2022), The Jewish Literary Journal, Spank the Carp, Epic Echoes Magazine, The Main Street Rag, *Love Poems* (Bronze Bird Books, 2024), *42 Stories Anthology* (MacKenzie Publishing, 2024), and Jewish Fiction Journal.

www.ingramcontent.com/pod-product-compliance
Lightning Source LLC
Chambersburg PA
CBHW021426240626
47153CB00001B/41